ALEX WOLF

& THE BLACK FIRE BOOK

ALASTAIR WOODGATE

ALASTAIR **WOODGATE**

OTHER WORKS

Alex Wolf & The First Prelude

CONTACT

W: www.alastairwoodgate.com

FB: www.facebook.com/alitheauthor

T: www.twitter.com/AliTheAuthor

T: www.twitter.com/SirHenryWolf

Dedicated to all those who have helped.
You know who you are.

BY ALEX WOLF

Many years have passed since the dreadful events recorded in my books took place, but the memories haven't faded. No, the memories today are as strong as they ever were; but only *now* do I feel able to give a true account of what befell me and my family those long years ago.

If you look through the annals of history you will see the name of Wolf appear on many an occasion. Often said to be one of the richest families in Europe, which I must say was always overstated, we were always destined to make headlines. And my god, the headlines we made.

I will admit that when I was growing up I didn't understand the privileged position I held in the world and that I took many, many things for granted; none more so than the love of my family and the love of my friends whom, I am ashamed to say, I treated despicably.

It is only now, with their consent, and of course with the help of my dear friend, that I am able to bring these stories to you.

This is not an easy story to tell, as I'm sure you will understand once you have read it. I did many things that I wasn't proud of and that I shall have to live with for the rest of my life. I did, however, do many things that I *am* proud of; which for me, at that time in my life, is a reason to celebrate. I am now an old man, but with the help of others I will begin to recount to you the strange story of the Wolf family and our fight for humanity.

My name is Alexander Gunnar Wolf and I always thought I was different. As it turns out, I was right.

IT BEGINS

Why did it have to rain today of all days? ·

Alex walked to the open window on the other side of his bedroom. It had been completely unremarkable weather during the last week; dull overcast days followed by dull overcast nights; but that day looked like it would have nothing unremarkable about it whatsoever. If there was going to be a storm, as Alex suspected, it was going to be a big one.

He supposed that he should have seen this coming. Wolf family history being as it was, no family event would be complete without a storm of epic proportions, metaphorical or meteorological.

Alex pushed the heavy oak-framed windowpane away from him. Rotating on its smooth brass hinges it locked into its frame with a loud, satisfying *clunk*. The sound of falling rain outside silenced in an instant. Golden or not, the sudden quiet was a relief. Alex let out a resigned sigh, walked back across his bedroom and fell onto his bed, not even bothering to take off his slippers.

Before the thunder had woken him moments ago, Alex had been truly, genuinely, gloriously happy. The reason being that he had been fast asleep. Nestled under his thick, heavy duvet, head sunk into his sumptuous goose down pillows and sleep surrounding him like the reassuring comfort blanket he once coveted as a child, his head had been clear and he had dreamt of nothing.

Well, nothing dark, terrifying or miserable, that is. And for Alex, that was good news. It was only during these rare hours of sleep that Alex seemed to find any happiness.

As he lay on his bed, no longer able to hear the thundering groans of the sky above, he watched the silent rain hammer against the windows. Staring out across the well-kept grounds, he saw the ever-growing winds shake and bend the huge oak trees on the edge of the Silver Forest. Knowing what lay in store for him today, and having nothing better to do at 2:30am, he felt the only option was the path of least resistance. He slid down under the duvet, closed his eyes and drifted off to sleep.

"Alex?" A muffled voice said from somewhere above his head. "Alex, it's time to get up."

No, not again! Pretend to be asleep, perhaps he'll go away. Alex desperately tried to hold on to the last remnants of sleep as it slipped away from him.

"Alex! For God's sake, get up! What the hell do you think you're doing? It's four o'clock and your father wants you downstairs. *Now.*"

It was no good. Tempting as it was to wind up the man who had ruined that glorious slumber, it would only end with Alex losing out in some way. Pushing the duvet away from his head, Alex instantly screwed up his eyes to the bright light coming from all around. As they slowly adjusted, he could just make out the shape of a very tall, broad-shouldered figure looming over him. It was Archer, the family driver.

Alex had known, the minute he'd entered the room; the slight whiff of stale alcohol was always a giveaway. He also knew exactly what was going to happen next. Right on cue, and with a sudden rush of cold air, the duvet was pulled off him in one swift movement, leaving him suddenly exposed like an insect under a swiftly displaced rock.

"Why do you *always* do that?" Hissed Alex through gritted teeth, his eyes still squinting against the light. "Do you think it's going to make me get up any quicker? I could have you sacked you know! And can you *please* not call him my 'father'. I hate that!"

"Firstly, young man, the reason I do it is because, despite what you say, it *will* get you up faster. Expensive though this duvet no doubt is," he brandished it aloft in his clenched fist like Jason with his mythical golden fleece, "it seems to me to be the one thing that you're permanently attached to. So wherever it goes, you go. Secondly," he continued with a slightly twisted grin on his face, "you've been trying to get me sacked ever since you could talk. *But* as you don't pay my wages you don't have that luxury. And finally," Alex rolled onto his front and pressed his face into his pillow, trying to block out the voice. "I call him your '*father*' because it's a damned sight better than some of the names you've been coming out with lately."

Alex stifled a yawn. He hated it when Archer was in that kind of mood. No doubt he was hungover from a heavy night's drinking and yet, unlike most people would be, incredibly buoyant and ready to extol his opinions to all that would listen–as well as many that wouldn't.

Alex rolled over to give his bedroom intruder another mouthful, but as they stared at each other an unspoken understanding seemed to pass between them.

"Look," Archer went on, his gruff voice softening slightly, "I know this isn't an easy day for you but... well, it's the same for all of us isn't it? So... so will you just get up and sort yourself out? *Quickly*, please. The service starts in *one* hour, and I know how long it takes you to get ready."

Archer turned on his heels and strode to the bedroom door, "Lights on or off?"

"Off." Alex mumbled sulkily.

Archer flicked the switch on the wall and strode out of the door; pulling it closed behind him, leaving Alex in the dark, duvetless and deflated.

He was right, of course. It wasn't going to be an easy day for anyone, but Alex still didn't see why he had to be so involved in proceedings. He didn't want to be involved.

Feeling cold, he grabbed two big handfuls of duvet and pulled it back over him, sinking into his soft pillows to ponder the day ahead. He lay for several minutes, staring at the ceiling, thinking about who might be attending that day.

He imagined there would be lots of so-called friends coming. People who, he knew, were only interested in his family due to their vast wealth and social standing. There would be immediate family of course, but more than likely the extended members of the family that they didn't see very often would be there too.

Lots of false concern and snooping around the grounds then. Everything this family does has to be a big production, a big show. Why can't it just be a small affair? Something personal?

With a roar of pent-up frustration, Alex threw the thick duvet off him again and rolled to the other side of his enormous bed. Squinting in the dark, he reached for the three stainless steel buttons that were set into the wall next to his bedside table. The first button was to turn on the lights. They burst into life as though the sun had just come crashing through the ceiling.

Idiot. Ignoring the shapes that were swimming in front of his eyes, he pressed the second button, turning on the heating. Keeping his finger firmly pressed against the metal switch, he waited until he could feel the hot air push against his body like an invisible, all-covering blanket. For some reason Alex had always liked a room to be hot enough to bake bread in, and besides, he wasn't paying the bills.

The last button was to turn on Alex's music, loudly. As the first refrains of *Lacrimosa* thundered from the huge, free-standing speakers in front of the enormous north facing window, Alex swung his legs out of bed and stood very slowly. Not bothering to put his slippers back on–which must have come off during the night–he walked, almost ceremonially, across the room to take his shower.

Entering the cavernous bathroom, he felt a calmness descend over him. The room was covered from floor to ceiling in three foot square dark slate tiles, which gave the space a sombre air and the feeling of being underground. The minimal lighting, recessed in various alcoves, lit the room with a soft golden glow. Alex had chosen this particularly flattering type of light with the sole purpose of making him look good in the mornings when he first looked in the mirror.

The mirror in question was three feet high and ran in a single strip from one side of the vast room to the other. Again, Alex had chosen this himself as it allowed him to walk across the bathroom while keeping an eye on how he looked. Standing just inside the doorway, he lazily swung the thick, heavy bathroom door shut with a measured kick.

Silence would have reigned in the almost tomb-like room, had it not been for the magisterial music still reaching Alex's ears through the speakers set discreetly into the ceiling. As the score grew in energy and intensity, Alex looked at himself in the mirror and was rather pleased with what he saw.

He had never been the best-looking boy at school, but he was raffishly handsome and carried himself with confidence–or at least he thought so. His slightly elongated face and overly pronounced nose were offset by startlingly blue eyes, a strong chin and a head of thick blonde hair (Alex had always preferred 'golden') that always seemed to look good no matter what he did with it. Today was a case in point; after a rough night's sleep it stood up awkwardly at various angles, but nevertheless it had an effortless, tousled charm about it.

For a nineteen year old, Alex was a respectable 5'11" and three quarters (he was sure that he would break the six foot barrier any day). While he was quite broad-shouldered, he was not as well-built as he'd have liked to be. Not surprising really, considering the complete lack of strenuous activity Alex engaged in. Still, there would be time for bulking up later on. At the moment he was pleased with the way he looked and he stood silently for a further couple of minutes, simply admiring himself.

When he finally managed to pull himself away from the mirror, he walked several steps further into the long bathroom, and at the same time, gently ran his hand over a smooth brushed metal panel set into the slate wall just before the shower. There was barely a second's delay before the heavens opened. A cascade of water poured from above as if by magic; hot steaming water gushed from the ceiling like monsoon rain.

Alex stepped under the torrent and let the water wash over him for several minutes before he even thought about expending any energy to clean himself. As he stood there, head tilted up to the ceiling, his mind wandered again to the day's proceedings.

He'd been trying to block it out for the two weeks since the accident, desperately trying to hide any emotion and feeling from the outside world, trying to deny what had really happened. But as he stood in the darkened room, engulfed in water, steam and the powerful music, he could picture the scene all too clearly. It was too vivid, too much.

There was no denying it anymore. In the next hour, what he had been dreading for two whole weeks was going to happen. Before he knew it, he was crying; tears of fear and despair streamed down his face. Though instantly washed away by the thundering water of the cleansing waterfall, the tears were there and they were real. His body shook violently as from nowhere, the waves of realisation and incredible pain of loss coursed through his body.

A life had been taken. A life was over and he still couldn't believe it. He didn't want to believe it.

He leant forward, hands above his head and pressed his face against the hard, warm tiles and slowly the tears subsided. The moment, like so many others before it, had passed.

He couldn't let anyone see him like that; it wasn't the done thing in his family. Despite not being particularly bothered about etiquette, this was one rule he wasn't going to break.

Not today, get a grip.

Realising he really needed to hurry, Alex quickly washed his hair, ran his hand back along the wall to stop the cascading water and stood for a moment, dripping water onto the dark bathroom floor.

Standing once again in front of the mirror he noticed how red his eyes were. He blinked quickly, willing them to return to normal before towelling himself down and returning to the bedroom.

Suddenly and without warning there was a tremendous *boom* from outside. Startled, Alex ran to the huge folding windows that looked out onto the estate. Thinking that some other terrible thing must have happened, he looked out across the grounds, but all he could see was a thick grey mist that sat above the ground blocking his view of anything beyond the balcony below. Panicked, Alex turned to run to the other window but stopped mid-step. This wasn't another disaster; this was something much, much worse.

Boom. Spinning round, his focus snapped to the clock sat on his desk. *4:58am.* He was supposed to be outside, playing a pretty major role in the day's proceedings, and he only had two minutes to get there. He quickly yanked the damp towel from around his waist–grateful that he was three floors up and away from prying eyes–pulled on some clean underwear and ran to the walnut clothes rail in the corner, where a crisp white shirt and pressed black suit hung ready for him.

Within seconds he was dressed and trying desperately to find his shoes while tying his tie with his free hand–a useful trick he'd learnt from his granddad. He dashed from one side of the room to the other hunting for the shoes then–remembering where he'd seen them–grabbed the damp towel on the floor and whipped it up over his head like an overly zealous magician, revealing a pair of very smart, if slightly damp, black brogues. Quickly slipping them on, he heard a third *boom* from across the grounds.

Finally he was ready. Fully dressed, he took another look at himself in his bedroom mirror. He was sweating from all the rushing around and it seemed to be getting worse. Wiping his forehead with his jacket sleeve, he suddenly remembered the heating.

No wonder! He hadn't remembered to turn it down since he came out of the shower. Dashing around the bed, he flicked the heating off and picked up his watch and cufflinks from the bedside table, dropping them into his jacket pocket to put on later. He triple-checked himself in the mirror, paused for a second to think if he'd forgotten anything, and dashed from his bedroom into a wall of cool air.

That the whole house was kept barely above freezing was, for once, going to pay off. Alex could feel himself cooling down immediately; the sweat cleared from his brow, and the chilled air wrapped him in a sense of peace and calm.

He set off smartly down the hallway, his feet barely making a sound in the thick lambswool carpet. Resisting the urge to run in case he began to overheat again, he opted for a strange trotting jog. Thankful again that nobody could see him, he desperately counted in his head–working out how long he had left before he was in serious trouble.

Picking up the pace, Alex reached the end of the hallway and jumped down the narrow stairway four steps at a time. As he reached the bottom of the stairs, the fourth *boom* broke the silence of the house.

Giving up all pretence, Alex sprinted the length of the lower landing, down the main set of stairs, across the entrance hall and reached the tall double oak front doors. He quickly tapped a code into the metal keypad in the wall. There was a high pitched *beep* and very slowly the doors began to swing inwards. As the gap between them widened, a strange vision opened up before him, like the curtain rising on a macabre play.

Across the gravelled driveway, and some way into the grounds, was a steep grass bank. He dashed towards it, seeing a crowd of maybe two hundred people standing halfway up, all of them facing away from him and all wearing black, their number disappearing into the grey mist. He stepped quickly through the ghostly crowd without stopping, hoping not to draw too much attention. After some gentle jostling and a few muttered apologies, he was through the other side and climbing the rest of the way.

At the top he could make out five dark figures, silhouetted in the early morning mist, and knew exactly who they were. Despite the chill air he felt hot again and his legs weakened.

Three of them stood shoulder to shoulder, facing him on the far side of a large, dark hole cut deep into the earth. On Alex's side, the other two figures had their backs to him. Wordlessly, he took his place beside them.

A final fifth *boom* broke the silence. As the sun's first rays broke through the misty haze above the Silver Forest, a frail and cracked voice somewhere to Alex's left spoke the words he had been dreading to hear for the last two weeks.

"Dearly beloved, we are gathered here today to mourn the passing of Rebekka Elina Wolf; daughter of Sofia and Henry, wife of Morten and mother to Lewis and Alex. Her life, though cut short, should be celebrated and honoured and remembered for all that was good. Let us pray."

CHAPTER 1

A TROUBLED MIND

Although the book had come into his possession many years ago, he still had no idea how to unlock its incredible powers–let alone harness them.

In all those long years, it had not shown even a hint of being any different to all the other books in his library. But over the last few days, all that had changed; the book itself had begun to change.

To most it would have been imperceptible, but then he knew every detail of the book so intimately that even the tiniest alteration didn't go unnoticed. As he sat in his private study at the top of his tower, he gazed at it with renewed interest.

The book was usually kept in a secure, temperature-controlled cabinet, set into the curved limestone wall of his office. Twice in the last two days though, he had taken it from its safe place and sat silently studying it on his lap.

The first change had happened two nights previously; the night of the thunderstorm. He had never slept during thunderstorms, afraid of them ever since he was a young boy. Caught outside during one of the worst ever recorded, he had become so terrified that he had cowered under a rocky outcrop for three days until it had passed.

This time, however, he had been sitting quietly in his study in complete darkness, watching the storm rage outside. It was around 4:00am when he had sensed something behind him and turned to see the book–set in its cabinet– glowing a bright, brilliant blue. It had only been for a few seconds, but in all the years in his possession he had never seen it happen; not even a flicker. That same night he had taken it out of its case and immediately noticed that it had not only altered its colour but it had also grown in size, thickness and weight.

Opening it with shaking hands, he had been disappointed to see that the pages themselves revealed nothing. There were still no words, no pictures, nothing to see, nothing to go on. For a man used to success, this had been his most frustrating moment of all. He *knew* there were secrets hidden in the pages of the book; he just couldn't get to them.

The following morning, he had made the decision to go and visit his oldest friend. As expected, she had not been pleased to see him at all. Although she didn't seem to have any knowledge of the things he had told her, he had still remained tight-lipped about his ownership of this book.

Many years ago he had loved the woman more than anyone, or anything, on earth, but he also knew that she was tough, cunning and ruthless when she needed to be; if she ever found out that he possessed the book, it wouldn't be long before it went missing from its secure, resting place.

Soon after the book had glowed blue, Zephyr had returned to make his report, confirming his suspicions that Frederik was indeed still alive. Zephyr had actually fought with him in the grounds of Wolf Manor and even sustained injury. That was extremely worrying, as it proved not only that Frederik was alive, he was also strong.

But how could Frederik be alive? He had been so certain that Frederik was dead he would have bet his reputation, company, fortune and family on it. If indeed he had returned, it would at least begin to explain the strange changes to the book.

He had instructed Zephyr to keep an eye on things—not only around his estate, but around Wolf Manor as well—and to track Frederik no matter what happened. He was only to report back if absolutely necessary.

Worryingly, it wasn't long before Zephyr returned. He had observed Frederik following the ageing Henry Wolf, first to the library and then to the lake. Henry had crossed by boat to his remote lake house with Frederik following through the woods that lined the shore. As Zephyr had waited in the water, silently watching for any sign of movement, the lake house had actually moved; only a fraction, but Zephyr had observed it nonetheless. Soon afterwards, the door to the lake house had opened and the boat made its way back to Wolf Manor; only, Zephyr had been certain there was nobody at the helm. As for Frederik, he had vanished.

There were a great many troubling things about Zephyr's report; he needed time to think and decide on his next move.

He thought about the second unexpected thing to happen to the mysterious book. If Zephyr's report was accurate—and they always were—at around the same time that the lake house had somehow shifted, the book had burst into flames. Black, writhing flames. He didn't know what this meant either, but he suspected that it wasn't good.

He had received Zephyr's second report only the previous night. As a result, he had spent that whole day deep in thought, the book clutched firmly on his knees. With Frederik back, things were likely to get difficult very soon. But what connection did that have to the book, and how could he finally reveal the words that were hidden in its pages?

He thought of the woman, too. What was *her* role in all this? She could become a problem, particularly if she was using her family or any other *outside* help. *No, not likely. Not now.*

There was a knock at the door and he looked up suddenly. "Enter." The door opened, revealing his butler like a statue in the doorway. "Ah, Bryson. What can I do for you?" He said, returning his gaze to the book.

"I was just going to suggest to Sir that he really should think about getting ready for the dinner tonight."

"Yes, of course. I shall be down shortly, Bryson. Oh, if you could bring the car round as well, please. I think I'll drive tonight."

"Would there be any particular car Sir had in mind?" said Bryson.

He thought for a second, "Yes, in fact there is. As it's a special occasion, I think I should take the new one, don't you?"

"Very good, Sir." Bryson replied stiffly, but he remained in the doorway.

"Was there anything else?"

"I was just wondering if Sir wanted me to telephone ahead, to let the hosts know that you would be attending this evening. After all, I don't think they are expecting you, are they, Sir?"

A fleeting smile flashed across his face. "No, that's quite alright, Bryson thank you. I'd rather it be a surprise. It's not often that a granddad gets to surprise his grandchildren is it. That'll be all Bryson."

"Thank you, Sir." Bryson closed the door.

He closed his eyes for a few moments, then very gently placed the book on the table in front of him, pushed himself to his feet and stretched out. Sitting in a chair all day was not good for a man of his age. He walked across to his desk and picked up a red book, thumbing through its various lists, notes and diagrams. It was a book of all his thoughts and ideas, his dreams and hopes, his fears and disappointments.

He thought it probably best not to leave it out on display, no matter how secure the room. Scribbling a few final thoughts in the first clean page he could find, he shut it tight and wrapped the thin leather strap back around it.

"*Hemmeligheter*," he whispered.

A huge circular section of the stone floor, twelve feet in diameter, slowly began to rise. It came to a stop just above his own substantial height. Inside, holding up the slab of circular floor, was a matte black square pillar of metal with a clear glass panel on the front and a polished metal plate on either side. He moved as if to embrace the metal structure but placed his hands onto the two metal plates. After a pause there was a quiet *beep* and the glass panel moved slowly outwards, allowing him to slide it gently to one side.

There were no jewels, money or other riches in this hidden safe. Instead, the whole space was occupied by twenty short black shelves, each containing twenty neatly stacked red books; all except the top shelf. This only had nineteen, with space for one more.

With great care, he slid the red notebook into the space. He stood back and admired the view of the pristine red books' spines all standing in line, as if they were saluting him. One book for each year that he had been alive.

CHAPTER 2

COMING HOME

On a beautifully sunny day at the start of June, Alex Wolf was inside, packing up his school bag for the last time. He had just finished the last exam he would ever sit, immediately followed by the last detention he would ever have to endure. Well, unless he failed all of his exams, of course, but even then there was no way his parents would pay for his re-sits. Not at this school anyway.

He was alone in the main school building, in front of a wall of polished wooden lockers that ran the length of the hallway. Due to his unplanned detention, his locker–number 802–would be the last to be emptied that school year. As a matter of fact, his detention had been about the state of his locker. Before leaving, he had been ordered to make sure it was properly cleared out, otherwise his parents would be receiving the bill for the clean up.

Having removed most of the food packaging–some empty, some not–certain choice magazine publications and a roll of fake banknotes he had used to purchase items from first years, he was doing a second sweep for any other items he might have forgotten.

As he peered into the depths of the locker that had been his only private haven during his time at school, Alex felt his whole body begin to tense. Occasional embarrassment was one thing, but the systematic humiliation he'd suffered as his personal items were paraded around the whole school was something he never wanted to experience ever again.

Realising that he was now just staring blankly ahead, Alex blinked hard several times before wiping his eyes on his jacket sleeve.

Clearing out two very crumpled shirts that had been covering a larger pile, Alex now noticed several items pushed right to the back of his locker: a pristine copy of *Basic Physics and the Laws of Mechanical Actions* that had never been used (a point that was highlighted to great effect with his GCSE results two years ago), a very tired but comfortable-looking pair of headphones, a fairly substantial pile of pink slips, and there–the thing he had been looking for. His most prized school memento; a perfectly preserved and one-of-a-kind photo of the gorgeous Miss Green; Deputy Head of English.

To this day, Alex was still baffled as to how the older student had stumbled across Miss Green in that particular situation–let alone taken a photo–but he carefully placed it into a hard-backed notebook for protection, before sliding it into his shoulder bag.

He bundled the books, pink slips and headphones into his arms and flicked the locker door shut with a single extended finger. With a small *snick,* the last trace of his school life was gone, along with the slightly tannic smell of rotting food that the headmaster had been complaining about for several weeks.

Agitated and feeling the years of frustration and boredom rise inside him, Alex turned from his locker and walked quickly down the wide empty hallway, only stopping halfway down to cram his armful of locker leftovers into the large, cast-iron dustbin that was set into the wall.

A feeling of great relief swept over him as he purged himself of the last material remnants of this school. He pushed his way through the double doors at the end of the hallway and stepped out into the glorious sunshine and sweet fresh air.

The usual milling crowds of doe-eyed students meeting their parents after a long term away from home were nowhere to be seen; and the only sound remaining was the distant hum of the groundskeeper, mowing the acres of well-tended grass ready for next year's students.

Walking out across the expansive gravel driveway at the front of the old school buildings, Alex considered pausing a moment to take one last look at the place that had been his home for the last seven years; a home where he had never felt comfortable; a home where he had not had any friends; a home where he had been miserable. But he simply carried on without turning back.

This is a good day; a day to look forward and not back; a day to embrace the new wonders that are about to unfold before me in the vast unknown that is my life; a day to– Alex froze.

In the distance, parked near the school gates and bathed in a golden, sunlit haze was the unmistakable silhouette of the car that had been sent to pick him up. This wasn't just any car, however. It was a very large, very expensive, black Rolls Royce. It seemed Alex's great day was about to take a turn for the worse.

The car itself wasn't a cause for particular concern, it was more the person that was likely sitting inside it that was worrying him. A jet black, long wheelbase Rolls Royce Phantom flying the Wolf family flag on its bonnet meant only one thing. His grandmother.

She'd obviously decided to make the long trip down from Wolf Manor to pick him up and, in the process, ruin his first day of new-found freedom. Alex squinted into the sun.

Maybe if I wait here a few minutes she might get out of the car to greet me. Then I can judge what kind of mood she's in. No, stupid idea. If she has to get out of the car that's only going to annoy her, and why bother riling the old witch?

Realising he had come to a complete stop, he steeled himself, yanked his bag further up onto his shoulder and strode towards the car, determined to look as confident and as impressive as he possibly could. As he walked the last few feet towards the car, his mind wandered to the last and only other time his grandmother had picked him up from school.

Halfway through his third year he'd been falsely accused of spying on the girls' hockey team via a number of conveniently placed holes in the wall of their shower room. As it turned out it had been a case of mistaken identity. Unfortunately for Alex, that revelation had come too late to stop the three hour tirade from his livid grandmother that he had had to endure on the drive home.

The hot topics of that particular one-way conversation had been Alex's moral code, the treatment of his female classmates and, most embarrassingly, his personal hygiene; or implied lack of.

Cringing at the memory of having to discuss these topics with his formidable grandmother, he found himself standing in front of the enormous rear passenger door of her car. He reached for the long silver handle, but just as he was about to grasp it, there was a soft mechanical clunk, the hiss of tight rubber seals coming apart, and the heavy door slowly swung open in front of him. With a roll of his eyes and a sigh of resignation, Alex slid his bag off his shoulder, flung it into the dark cavernous interior of the car and ducked inside.

As he looked up though, his dread turned to relief, which in turn dissolved into the awkward realisation that it wasn't his grandmother sitting there in her usual haughty way. It was his grandfather Henry, bent forward, face screwed up in pain, clutching Alex's heavy leather bag.

"Alexander, for goodness' sake, will you watch where you're putting your satchel," came the angry, yet slightly broken, high pitched voice from the man sitting on the other side of the car.

"Oh–sorry. Didn't realise it was you!" Alex replied, trying to stifle the sudden desire to laugh.

Still taken aback at this sudden upturn in his fortunes, he quickly pulled off his school jacket, roughly scrunched it into a ball and threw it onto the seat in front of him. It slid off the soft leather and onto the thick carpeted floor.

"You mean you usually throw your belongings at your grandma, do you? No wonder she comes back in such a foul mood every time she sees you." Although his eyes were still watering, Henry Wolf's moustache twitched at the corners.

"No, I don't actually," replied Alex, grinning. "Not that I wouldn't like to occasionally." Henry's moustache twitched for a second time before he burst into laughter.

Suddenly feeling rather upbeat again, Alex pulled the heavy door closed and sank comfortably into the soft, contoured leather seat. He stretched his legs straight out in front of him, gave a huge yawn and then stretched out even further.

Filling his lungs with air, he couldn't help noticing that as well as the strong overtones of high quality leather, there was the more subtle combination of sweet pipe tobacco and peppermint. This could only mean one thing; his granddad had been smoking and he didn't want his grandmother to know about it.

It suddenly dawned on Alex that this was probably the reason his granddad had come to pick him up in the first place; six gloriously uninterrupted hours of smoking time, without the risk of Alex's grandmother catching him and dealing out one of her notorious tongue lashings.

As Alex looked across at his granddad, he couldn't help but notice that he looked a lot older than the last time he'd seen him. Granted, this was over six months ago. Even so, he seemed to have aged more heavily than Alex had expected. His thick, wavy mass of light grey hair was now bookended by inch-wide streaks of white on either side of his head; beginning at his temples and growing just past his ears. It gave him the slightly comical look of an old badger. For most people this would be quite unfortunate, but for Henry, it sort of worked.

His long, tanned face was broken by two of his trademark features. The first was what he liked to call his *strong, proud nose*, although most people would just say it was big. This, Henry had always said, was a classic Wolf family feature; one which Alex liked to remind him no-one else in the family shared. Disconcertingly, Alex had noticed that his own nose was starting to show signs of joining the ranks of the strong and proud too; something his brother Lewis's friends were always keen to point out.

Henry's second distinguishing feature was a very large, very bushy, but perfectly trimmed moustache. This too was showing signs of age, the occasional white hair running through the lighter grey. Although his permanently tanned skin and thick grey hair made him look much older, he still retained his large, dark brown eyes that always had a spark of youth in them.

In his time, Alex's granddad had been something of a ladies man, although Alex only had Henry's word on this. As a younger man he had also been very well built and always kept himself in shape. This was something that Alex could believe; even at his age, Henry gave the impression of someone you wouldn't mess with for fear of a good, sound thrashing.

Henry was also what some might call *old school English*. When Alex would watch television and see some comedian doing a sketch about an aristocratic old man that lived in the country, it almost always matched his granddad's description.

At just under six foot four inches, Henry was tall for a man of 75. This was helped further by the fact that he never stooped and always carried himself extremely upright; which in turn was probably due to the fact that as far as Alex could work out, he had never done a hard day's work in his life.

He did, however, walk with a slight limp in his left leg. The general assumption was that this was an old war wound from a heroic battle of yesteryear, but Alex knew it was from the time Henry had tried to start a pig-running festival in the 60's and had come second place to a pretty substantial Gloucester Old Spot.

Despite all this, Henry was someone who Alex definitely aspired to be more like. *Yes, I will definitely work on my Henry-ness over the summer.* Alex grinned as he pictured himself in a range of different silk cravats and smoking jackets.

Leaning forward, Henry tapped the partition glass. As the car began to move, crunching on the gravelled school driveway, Alex leant back into his seat, closed his eyes and prepared himself for a peaceful and stress-free journey back to Wolf Manor.

"Alex," came a deep, gruff voice to his right, "We need to talk."

Alex's left eye opened slightly. His granddad wasn't looking at him but was still looking out the window at the scenery, so Alex closed his eye again.

"Alex? Are you listening to me?"

"Yes, yes, yes. I'm listening," said Alex impatiently, "What about exactly? Would you like to talk about the fact that you were pretending to be Grandma just to wind me up? Or would you like to talk about the fact you've been smoking your pipe in the car *again*? You tell me—choice is yours."

Henry chuckled silently to himself, "Firstly, if I *had* been pretending to be your grandmother, dear boy, then *surely* I would be wearing some of her ghastly jewellery and look like I was sucking on a lemon."

Alex opened both eyes to see his granddad, squinty-eyed and fish-lipped, and tried to stifle a laugh. "That didn't stop you from flying *her* little flag on the car bonnet though, did it? Or turning on the tinted windows so I couldn't see who was in the car. Or were they both just coincidences?"

"Actually, dear boy, they were necessary hangovers from some business function that she attended last night. I just forgot to ask Archer to change them back, that's all."

A likely story.

"Secondly, regarding the pipe, I can assure you that I haven't been smoking any such thing. You can ask Archer, I'm sure he'll tell you exactly the same." Alex glanced at the rear view mirror and saw Archer looking back at them, clearly smirking even though he couldn't see his mouth. "Although, probably best not to mention anything to your grandmother about this. You know how ah... *concerned* she is about my health."

Both granddad and grandson exchanged a knowing look and the deal was done. "Anyway, enough about all that. The point is, I need to talk to you as there are plans afoot!"

Alex didn't like the sound of that one bit. *Plans afoot* usually meant he would end up having to do something he didn't want to do.

"What *kind* of plans?" he asked, now wide awake.

"Oh the usual dark forces convening to try and stop you from having any fun," said Henry with a flourish of his hands as if to suggest black magic. "It's your grandmother and your father, I'm afraid. They seem to think that letting you have *any* time off at all this summer is a bad idea, which of course I wholeheartedly disagree with... *and* that you should perhaps be thinking about getting some sort of ah... job... with the company." By the time Henry had finished his sentence he was almost whispering, predicting Alex's reaction.

"What?" shouted Alex, sitting forward so quickly his seatbelt locked up. "What do you mean, *get a job*? I've just finished school! I've been slogging my guts out for the last seven years! Have they forgotten that?"

Alex knew that he hadn't exactly had it tough at school, but a touch of righteous indignation always added nicely to the effect.

"Just because that brother of mine is so desperate to leap into the family firm, it doesn't mean that the rest of us wouldn't enjoy a bit of rest and relaxation!" He sat quietly for a second before realising he may have missed something fairly crucial. "Actually, that's a point. Where *is* Lewis? Wasn't he supposed to be coming home with me?"

"I'm glad to see you're so observant when it comes to your brother," said Henry with a grin. "You know, it's a good job *I* know what he's up to otherwise he'd still be stranded at that school of yours."

"OK so where is he then?" said Alex, feeling rather stupid.

"I'm afraid," started Henry quietly, pre-empting another outburst "that your brother is currently halfway across the Atlantic, on his way to New York."

Alex sprang forward once more. Again the seatbelt locked, flinging him back into his seat. "What the *hell* has he gone there for? He's not started working for the company *already* has he?"

Henry looked slightly pained, "I'm afraid he has my boy. He's off to finalise a deal he's been working on for some time with your grandmother. By all accounts it's going to make the company a *lot* of money."

That's typical of Lewis. Always sucking up to Grandma, making out he's interested in the family business and flying around all over the place, having meetings… and in school time! Henry put his hand down the side of his seat and pulled out a crumpled newspaper. Folding it in half and flattening it down, he tossed it to Alex. He stared at the front page:

WOLFWOOD TECHNOLOGIES SEALS
MULTI-BILLION POUND DEAL

The UK stock-market reacted today to rumours of another multi-billion pound deal between Wolfwood Technologies and US company XIF International. Details are scarce but it is believed that the deal was secured by the youngest member of the Wolf family.

Lewis Wolf (19), who many believe will take over as CEO when Sofia Wolf steps down from the post, is currently in New York. Morten Wolf, Lewis' father, was unavailable for comment but a spokesman for the company released this statement…

He didn't need to read any more. "I suppose Dad's gone too, has he?"

"Ah yes… yes he has," said Henry quietly.

"Well that's a great *welcome home* for me then, isn't it?" He muttered to himself.

"Come on, old chap, don't let it get you down!" said Henry, "Just think, you'll have plenty of time to settle back in without anyone bothering you. What could be better?"

Alex could think of a whole list of things that would be better, but he was too angry to get into that. Ignoring the fact that the papers always seemed to forget that he and Lewis were twins, and therefore the exact same age, he was returning home to a more or less empty house *and* with the news that he was going to have start work immediately without any sort of summer break. It was then he had a sudden brainwave.

"Granddad, I was thinking that maybe I *should* start getting more involved in the business. Maybe I should go on a meeting somewhere for a couple of–"

Henry laughed. "Before you think about flying to New York for a two month long *meeting*," he said, "I've already had a better idea about how to get you out of work for a little while."

He pressed a small chrome button set into the armrest between them. With a click, a hiss and a sudden puff of what looked like dry ice, a hatch in the armrest glided open, followed by two diamond cut crystal champagne glasses and a chilled bottle of Veuve Clicquot champagne. Henry looked at Alex and with a wink, said, "A small token of my congratulations for finally finishing your scholastic endeavours. Now, if you wouldn't mind doing the honours, dear boy..."

Momentarily forgetting his bad mood, Alex took the bottle from the icy plinth, peeled off the soft foil wrapper and unwound the wire cage. Grasping the bottle between his knees, he wedged two thumbs hard beneath the ridge of the cork and pushed. With a loud *pop* and a whoop of delight from Alex, the cork flew out of the bottle and slammed hard into the glass partition. The car swerved ever so slightly and Alex caught Archer's glaring eyes staring back at him in the rear view mirror. The stream of bubbling liquid that had followed the cork had unfortunately sprayed all over Henry's lap.

"How many times do I have to tell you," started Henry indignantly, trying to mop his trousers with his jacket sleeve, "*hold* the cork and *twist* the bottle! If you ever do that in public, I shall disown you."

"Yes, yes, yes," said Alex now laughing at his granddad's wet trousers, "Do you want a drink or not?"

Henry, who had leapt forward in surprise at the sudden dousing, slowly leant back in his seat. As if to show Alex how it should be done, he gently took one of the crystal glasses, held it out in front of him and gave half a nod in Alex's direction. Scowling as Alex poured him barely half a glass, Henry reached into his tweed jacket pocket and pulled out a long black pipe.

"Er..." started Alex, shooting Henry a look of mock disbelief.

Responding with a wry smile, tempered only by the long pipe hanging out the corner of his mouth, Henry lit his pipe with a long thin match that he seemed to have hidden up his sleeve.

"You ah... won't say anything to your grandma, will you, young Alex?"

"Well that depends," said Alex, taking a long slug from his very full

Champagne glass.

"First class, dear boy," said Henry, ignoring the ambiguity, "Then in that case, I shall tell you my plan, so listen carefully." Henry pressed another small chrome button beside him and the glass partition flicked from clear to opaque in a split-second, blocking Archer from view.

As Alex once again sank back into his seat, chilled champagne in hand and the sweet smell of tobacco beginning to fill his nostrils, Henry laid out his plan of how he was going to get Alex a two month vacation.

The countryside silently rushed by and Alex found himself feeling more relaxed by the minute. It seemed like it might not be such a bad summer after all.

CHAPTER 3

WOLF MANOR

Alex woke with a start. He hadn't even realised he'd fallen asleep and now that he was awake, he felt disorientated and groggy. The smell of tobacco still lingered in the air, and he had the same odd taste in his mouth he always got when he slept with his mouth open. Sleepy eyed, he peered out of the window and tried to focus at the scenery passing by.

They were still moving at least. The silence of the cabin and smoothness of the ride often meant you had to rely on your sense of sight if you wanted to know if any progress was being made.

Alex wiped away the sleep from his eyes with the balls of his hands and then yawned. Eyes finally managing to focus, he saw they were deep in the rich, green countryside only a few miles from the estate, just passing the enormous oak tree that stood singularly in the middle of a field, not far from Wolf Manor. That tree had always been his 'nearly there' marker when he was growing up. It was the one thing he looked forward to seeing on the way to his grandparents' house when he would come and visit, but now it would be the marker for *his* house.

Home.

It seemed odd to call the place that after all these years, but after his dad's architecture firm had gone bankrupt nearly two years ago, Alex's parents had made the decision that they were going to move into the family estate to consolidate.

Morten, Alex's dad, had joined the family company–as would Lewis when he finished school–and Rebekka, Alex's mother, would continue her charity work. Alex had been sold the idea that they would be living under one roof as *one big happy family*. He still didn't understand why they hadn't just borrowed some money and bought somewhere else. Henry had told him it was something to do with his father's pride.

Initially, Alex had been dead against the idea, feeling that the more distance he could keep from his grandmother the better. Eventually though he had been talked round by his mum and granddad, who had both promised him his own space, exactly as he wanted it. This did sway him somewhat.

Although technically they'd been living at Wolf Manor for two years, Alex had hardly been back at all. Now that he had finished school, however, this would be his first chance to really get to know the place as his own home. And he was going to make the most of it.

He remembered visiting when he was younger, and how all his attempts at exploring had been thwarted by either his all-seeing grandmother or Archer. In fact, he only really had strong memories of the entrance hall and one of the front rooms. Everywhere else had seemed to be off limits back then.

Not now though. Now it was his home and he would be able to go where he liked, whether his grandmother wanted him to or not.

Alex sat up straight and coughed hard, trying to remove some of the fug from his mouth. Running his fingers through his hair to make sure it was still nicely tousled, he looked across at his granddad. Henry had drifted off to sleep as well. His crystal champagne glass was held loosely in one of his large hands and was dangling precariously above the floor. Remembering his own drink, Alex looked round to see his champagne glass on the tray table in front of him. Henry must have put it there after he fell asleep.

Oh well. May as well have another little drinkie before we get back Steady the nerves and all that. Pressing the same small chrome button in the armrest, he waited for the cloud of chilled air to disperse before taking the frosted bottle with both hands. It was empty. *Brilliant! No wonder he fell asleep, he's had nearly the whole bottle!*

He slammed the empty bottle back on the still-smoking plinth but just as he was about to close the hatch, something caught his eye. His granddad's pipe was protruding from the top pocket of his tweed jacket–and it was still smoking.

Amazed that the whole car hadn't already gone up in flames, Alex reached out and ever-so-gently pulled the pipe out of its silk-lined pouch, being careful not to spill any hot ash. He took one long sniff over the top of the pipe bulb, closing his eyes as the sweet aroma wound smoky curls up his nose, and then gently placed the pipe on the tray next to the empty champagne bottle. Double checking his granddad was still asleep, Alex slowly pushed the armrest cover back down and, with the telltale *snick*, both bottle and pipe were gone. Suddenly feeling a lot perkier, he looked out of the window again to see that they were now close to the outer gates of Wolf Manor.

To anyone else it would look like they were simply driving round the outside of a very large and very densely populated forest, but Alex knew that at any second a pair of vast wooden doors would come into view, set deep into the thick foliage of the surrounding trees.

Unlike most families of extreme wealth, who liked to shout about the size of their estates, it seemed the forefathers of the Wolf family had decided that discretion was more in keeping with their values. According to family legend, they had spent many years planting a thick ring of trees around the entire perimeter of their land to provide a natural barrier, even before they started the building work within; no mean feat, considering that the perimeter of the estate measured just over forty miles. Henry had once told Alex that there were over two hundred and fifty thousand trees planted in the perimeter rim, and Alex had never doubted it.

The car drove round the next bend and Alex spotted the small break in the tall trees coming up on the left; he was finally home. As the car slowed to a stop, he craned his neck and saw it for the first time in what seemed like an age; the entrance to Wolf Manor.

The car pulled to a stop and they sat for a few moments while Archer programmed the security code into the dashboard. Alex stared at the entrance. For an estate the size of Wolf Manor—well over 12,000 acres—the gates were remarkably modest. Hand-carved from solid oak, the thick, heavy gates were over thirty feet tall, but were also surprisingly narrow. Fully open, they looked like they would only just fit a normal car through, let alone any of the very wide, very low sports cars he was planning on buying in the near future. Musing that these types of cars probably weren't on the agenda several hundred years ago, he mentally added it to the list of changes he would make when he inherited the place.

The gates themselves were such a deep, rich brown they were almost black. As the bright afternoon sun shone directly on them though, Alex noticed lighter reds and browns sparkling in the light, giving the wood a richer, more lustrous appearance. At that point, the main feature of the gates shone out, brighter than ever; a huge silver 'W' embedded into the wood that spanned both gates. Alex marvelled at how bright and striking it was against the dark wood.

Finally the gates began to open and the car moved off, crossing the threshold of Wolf Manor.

Alex gave a deep sigh of relief. He didn't know why, but the whole area surrounding the estate entrance had always made him nervous. It was so secluded and thick-set with trees. He always had the feeling that there was something lurking in the undergrowth, just waiting to jump out and get him.

Putting it down to his over-active imagination, he told himself to relax and just concentrate on enjoying his summer break. As the car began to pick up speed however, he couldn't resist one last look over his shoulder.

The gates had begun to close at their usual leisurely pace, but as he stared back at them he thought he saw something moving out on the road. A large, dark shadow swept across the entrance outside the gates, stopped, then somehow moved inside and across the grass verge. It was only there for a split second but Alex was sure he'd seen something.

His heart beating faster, he unclipped his seatbelt and spun around completely, his knees up on the leather seat, looking straight back out of the wide rear window. He stared hard at the point where he thought he'd seen the shadow move, but the car was now too far away to see anything clearly, other than the last sliver of sunlight narrowing to nothing between the tall closed gates. Alex's heart was pounding in his chest and his hands were sweating.

Was it a person? Or maybe a large animal? The area was so secluded that it would be very odd for someone to be outside. Not unless they had a prior appointment and even then, they wouldn't be on foot.

Maybe it was just… But he couldn't think of anything.

He felt a shudder run through his whole body as he slid back round in his seat and sat for a moment. Deciding there was only one thing for it, he reached out his hand, placed it on his granddad's shoulder and shook. Nothing.

He shook a bit harder. Nothing. Even harder. Still nothing. Annoyed, Alex leaned over, raised both hands and brought his palms together inches from Henry's face. *Crack!*

With a sudden jolt and cry of "Rumpy!" Henry sat bolt upright, dazed and confused, his eyes darting round the car, searching for the source of his disturbance.

"What is it? What's happened?"

Alex couldn't help laughing at his granddad's startled expression, "And *who* is Rumpy?" he said, not even bothering to pretend he hadn't heard.

"What?" said Henry gruffly, "What do you mean Rumpy? Rumpy who? What are you talking about?"

That's what I'm asking you," Said Alex, enjoying the growing look of embarrassment on his granddad's face.

Henry gave a huge yawn and started rubbing his face with his hands, "I don't know *what* you mean, my lad," he said through thick fingers, "but if you wake me up like that again…" They sat in silence for a few seconds before Henry, holding a hand to his head said, "Damn Champagne. Stuff gives me a headache you know."

"Well I'm not surprised," said Alex, "considering you drank the whole bloody bottle." He stared at his granddad, waiting to see how he'd get out of this one.

"Ah... yes," started Henry, looking like a small boy being caught doing something he shouldn't. "well I didn't want it losing its fizz, you see... and you'd, ah... well, you'd fallen asleep... and it seemed such a shame to wake you." The excuse tailed off rather lamely in Alex's opinion, but Henry added his trademark wink and roguish smile to good effect. "Probably best not to tell your grandmother though, eh, old boy? Ah, don't want her getting the wrong idea." Henry continued winking but began to look like he was having some sort of seizure.

"Well, let's see how well your little plan works out before we make any promises, shall we?" said Alex slyly, turning his head away to look out the side window. The winking stopped.

Suddenly remembering the reason he had woken his granddad in the first place Alex spun back round. Henry had already closed his eyes again. "Erm, this might sound a bit odd," he said, not sure how he was going to phrase it, "but I thought I saw something a bit... strange, when we came through the gates."

Henry opened one eye, "It wasn't your grandmother, was it?"

"No..." said Alex quietly, "it was... it was like a shadow, moving around the gates. But a big shadow."

Henry opened both eyes and turned in his chair. Alex couldn't help notice that he looked worried. "Big shadow, you say?" he whispered holding Alex's gaze, moustache twitching.

"Yes." Said Alex, wide eyed in surprise.

"Moving... quite quickly, was it?" Henry's eyes searched Alex's face.

"Yes," he could feel his heart beating faster again, "very quickly!"

"Alex, I think I know what it was," Henry continued, his voice grave. "It was..."

"What?"

"It was..."

"What? What was it?"

"That *bloody* Vicar in his hot air balloon!" Henry burst out laughing.

"The *what*?"

"Yes," started Henry, yawning again, "he's finally been given permission to fly his ridiculous contraptions over those fields at the edge of our estate. Been hovering round all week taking people for rides. Trying to raise money for the Church or some such nonsense. Half a mind to take a pot shot at him, truth be told." Henry raised his arms as if he was holding a shotgun and mimicked taking aim. "*Boom!*"

Alex was not amused. He slumped back into his seat and sat there listening to his granddad still chuckling and making shooting noises out of the window. *Idiot. Letting your imagination run away with you again.* He sat in grumpy silence and stared out the window and eventually the shooting noises stopped.

The car was moving with practiced pace. Even though they were inside the estate, it was so huge that you could drive at absurd speeds and still take several minutes to reach the first of the family buildings. The long road through the estate was paved with small grey oblong bricks. Either side was a ten foot border of neatly mown grass, but beyond the grass were tens of feet of tightly packed trees; oak, ash, beech and birch all mixed together to form a dense leafy green wall, held up on thick wooden stilts stretching high into the sky.

Due to the closeness of the trees either side, the thick green canopies met high overhead, forming a natural ceiling, but the bright sunshine still punched its way through, creating a sparkling emerald light show. As Alex sat back, he pressed another small button on his armrest and the whole roof of the car changed from opaque black to clear transparent glass. He leaned back and watched the natural light show overhead. But as he gazed at the sky, the sun slid behind a heavy, dark cloud. The light show dimmed and the previously shimmering tunnel instantly felt dark and sinister.

The car travelled on for a few minutes and then, without warning, it broke free from the tunnel, just as the sun revealed itself once more. Light flooded the car again as the trees were sucked away towards the edges of a vast oval clearing; leaving just clear sky above.

The car began to slow as the long straight section of road they had been travelling on began to snake and weave into the distance, down towards the main residence.

As they drove at what seemed snail-pace in comparison, they approached the newest building on the Wolf estate, the glass lake house. Alex had heard about it, but he had never seen it. It was a truly stunning building, designed by his dad as a present for Henry's 75th birthday the previous year.

Apparently, Henry had recently bought himself a speedboat for motoring up and down the lake; Rebekka had suggested it would be nice for him to have somewhere special to moor it. This lake house was the result. As they passed by, with the sun shining brightly on its mirror-flat surfaces, Alex could only marvel at its beauty.

To all intents and purposes it was a glass cube, but one that measured thirty feet in each direction. The glass was completely transparent, so the one foot thick oak platform suspended halfway up the structure inside, forming the first floor, appeared to be floating in mid air. The platform extended beyond the cube on the far lake side to form a balcony, matching the oak platform base of the building. This too extended onto the water, forming a deck and mooring platform. Alex could just make out the canary yellow speedboat sitting idly in the water.

As exciting as the speedboat looked, Alex had never much cared for messing about on the water. Sitting on a sun lounger on a cruise boat was one thing, but racing around on a small speedboat was something else entirely. Far too high a risk of actually ending up *in* the water, and that would be one of his worst nightmares. It didn't matter how deep the water was, or if it was totally enclosed like a swimming pool, Alex could never get out of his head that there was always something lurking in the depths, waiting to drag him under. It gave him shivers just thinking about it.

As they drove on, the sun drifted behind clouds once more and the light that had previously danced on the corners of the lake house glass disappeared. The road started to widen and Alex felt his stomach lurch as the car started its gradual descent towards their final destination. It was an odd feature of the estate that the main residence was built in an enormous basin. Even though the house itself was very tall, its highest roof was still far below the level of the treetops that lined the entrance driveway.

Another odd, and perhaps more worrying, feature of the estate was that, less than a mile away and set much higher up at the forest level, was the main part of the lake. Over four billion gallons of water were held back only by the natural barriers of soil and rocks. Trying to ignore his imagination again, Alex just had to hope that it never flooded.

After travelling a little way further Alex spotted the fork in the driveway that branched left and back up into the forest. At the end of that road, hidden from view, were the company offices. Although both his dad and grandmother had their own private studies, it was in these offices that they spent most of their time; hatching their plans. Alex assumed that since Lewis had finished school he would also be spending a lot more time up there as well. *So, not all bad then.*

As they drove past the fork, Alex glanced up the road. He only just caught a glimpse of a low stone-clad building way off in the distance. No doubt there would soon be further discussions taking place in there about the best way to add even *more* wealth to the Wolf vaults.

Ominous dark clouds were rolling in, seemingly following Alex to his final destination. It was still bright enough to see Wolf Manor in the distance though and, as they descended further into the basin, the road straightened up, pointing directly towards the house. It was magnificent. Alex had loved the house from the very first time he'd been to visit as a young boy. Maybe it was the size; maybe it was how imposing and impressively old it was; he wasn't sure. But he loved it and was incredibly proud that he could finally call it his home. The car began to slow down and Alex took in the sight before him.

Set over six floors, the house was tall and wide; stretching out either side of the main doorway, giving it perfect proportions. The building itself was made from huge blocks of sandstone. Although light in colour, their size gave Wolf Manor the feeling of impenetrable strength, as if it would stand forever.

The canopied front doorway was arched in the same manner as the gates to the estate and the same dark wood had been used to create a single tall and imposing front door. Unlike the estate gates with their large silver 'W', the front door was fairly plain, except for a pinstripe of silver that ran from the top of the door to the bottom. Either side of the front door, two thick rectangular oak pillars stretched all the way up to the grey slate roof. Standing guard over the front door like two monolithic sentinels, they had apparently been cut from a huge oak tree that had grown in the middle of the grounds; that was, until the tree had been blown down during an enormous storm, some four hundred years ago.

Looking at the rest of the house, Alex noticed that all the windows had been changed since his last visit. Where before the windows had been small and numerous, a serious fire in the northwest corner the previous year had damaged enough of them to make minor repairs all but impossible. It had been suggested that it would be a good opportunity to replace and enlarge them. Solid oak frames had been used throughout, but many of the windows had been joined to form much larger ones, which presumably let in a lot more light. Alex felt a sudden urge to get inside and start exploring as soon as possible.

The car swung in a tight arc and came to a stop in front of the main entrance. The sky was a miserable grey and Alex knew it was going to rain at any second, but at least he was home. Finally home.

"Ready for our little plan then, Alexander?" said Henry, surprising Alex out of his thoughts.

Alex looked at his granddad, who was in the process of flattening down his waistcoat that had become crumpled during the drive. "Of course," he said, grinning. "I was born ready."

Henry chuckled and rolled his eyes, knowing full well that the one thing Alex was not, was born ready. "Into the breach then, dear boy. Into the breach."

The door opened on Henry's side of the car. He pushed himself up out of his seat and into the fresh air. Alex heard the old man's knees click, followed by a sharp intake of breath, before he began the slow walk up the steps towards the front doors.

Without warning, Archer's face appeared in the doorway. He grinned at Alex, but it wasn't a pleasant grin; more like a cat eyeing a wounded mouse that it was about to start playing with. Alex had known Archer long enough to know what this meant, though. Today it meant *If you think I'm going to come round there and open the door for you, you've got another thing coming.*

Sure enough, Archer stood up, swung the door closed, turned and practically skipped up the five stone steps after Henry. He followed the old man through the front door and it swung closed behind them with a loud thud.

Alex sat there fuming. *If there's one other thing I'm going to do this summer, it's get that idiot the sack.* He knew, of course that he never would be able to. Archer had been with the family far too long, but it didn't mean he couldn't try.

He sat in the car a bit longer; on the off chance that someone else might come and attend to him, but after several minutes no one had appeared. He got out, dragging his shoulder bag and crumpled jacket with him, and trudged moodily up the stairs.

As he reached the top step he heard the patter of rain on the car roof, before an almighty bellow of thunder opened the heavens. He ran the last few feet to the main door but even in those few seconds he was drenched, such was the ferocity of the downpour.

Reaching the stone-canopied doorway he looked back out over the vast expanse of the Wolf estate. He had to admit it was a magnificent sight. An inky grey sky, mottled with silver-black clouds and the blurring mist of rain hammering down across the forest boundary. As he stood admiring the view a flash of lightning lit up the sky, highlighting the top of the trees exquisitely against the horizon.

That was what he had wanted to see. Alex turned, pushed open the heavy oak door and walked into the warmth of Wolf Manor.

CHAPTER 4

WATCHING

Peering from his hiding place, the hooded figure scowled, and slowly retreated to shelter in the thick-canopy of tall trees. He continued to watch as the boy first climbed the stairs, then turned and looked out into the grounds.

The boy. Alexander. The boy saw me at the gates.

Two powerful hands slowly clenched and unclenched, before adjusting his rain-sodden hood against the growing wind. The storm was coming closer and, as if in answer to this thought, a flash of lightning pulsed across the darkening grey horizon.

The hooded figure smiled. It wouldn't be long before he could make his first move.

CHAPTER 5

SARA

Alex stood dripping in the open doorway. By then, the rain outside was bordering on torrential. He squelched inside and used a very wet foot to slam the door behind him, shutting out the noise in an instant.

Dropping his sodden bag and jacket to the floor, he tried to shake himself off like a dog, but his shirt was so wet it just clung to his body. The water from his hair dripped into his eyes, making him blink, but he was suddenly distracted by the smell of freshly cooked bacon.

He wiped his face with a sodden sleeve and noticed that there was no sign of his granddad or Archer anywhere. *Typical. Never mind me getting soaked in the rain, they can't even be bothered to bring me a towel either!*

The rainclouds were so heavy in the sky, they had almost completely blocked out any sunlight. The vast space in which he was standing, while warm, felt very dark and gloomy. He spotted a panel of big brass switches on the wall and flicked one upwards, flooding the room with light.

The reception hall of Wolf Manor was enormous. It had clearly been designed to both impress and intimidate guests; despite the house's light-coloured sandstone construction, the vast room had been lined with dark slate panels, stretching from floor to ceiling. Visitors often commented that it made the room feel dark and oppressive, but Alex had always felt it warm and comforting, like an underground bunker protecting him from the elements.

Something that had always struck Alex about the space was the lack of any personal items. There were no family portraits on the walls, no obscure pieces of old furniture dotted around, not even a coat rack. When he had mentioned this to his granddad, Henry had said it was because Alex's grandmother didn't like clutter. For once, Alex actually agreed with her. Although the room was bare, it didn't feel it; probably due to the hall's three overpowering features.

First was the colossal oak staircase. Starting from symmetrical points at either side of the hall it curved upwards and inwards towards the centre of the room where the two separate stairways met halfway up the height of the hall. This formed a mezzanine floor that lead off in both directions to the rest of the house.

The staircase itself was incredibly intricate. Themed around trees, the four newel posts were shaped like thick trunks with the balusters as their thinner saplings. The long, snaking banisters were covered in small, individually carved leaves; and each of the wide, uncarpeted steps was embossed with thin silver details that resembled tree roots.

Alex loved this staircase. As a child he would run up and down it, pretending that he was in a forest. Only once did he try sliding down the banister; the pointed leaves had left his best pair of Sunday trousers in tatters.

Leaving a puddle of water on the floor behind him, Alex strolled over to the staircase and up the first few steps, running his hand over the textured banister. As he made his way up, he looked towards the ceiling, and the second of the three features.

A huge glass chandelier hung high above the floor. It was a magnificent piece, but it was giving out so much light that Alex could only glance at it for a second before having to look away. According to Henry, the resident historian, the chandelier had been commissioned by Alex's great grandmother in the early 1900's and was one of a kind.

It measured over twenty feet in diameter and weighed close to eight tonnes. The chandelier itself was made up of thousands of tiny glass leaves that matched those on the stairway banisters; each one was etched with a small *W*. It was impossible to see them of course, due to the brightness, but Alex had often stared at them when the lights were off, staggered by the patience it must have taken to create them all.

He reached the top of the stairs and looked down over the banister at the third, and most impressive, feature of the room.

Cut into the stone floor was a large circle containing an enormous *W*, the peaks of which formed into sprouting trees that wrapped around and entwined the circle. Within the circle of trees stood a lone wolf, howling into the wind. It was the family crest and it looked magnificent.

The crest had been carved directly into the stone floor when the house had been built and matched the diameter of the chandelier, directly above it. In the late 1800s, however, the occupants of the house had made a drastic change. After many years of wear–and more than a few unfortunate trips on the deep carved ridges–they had decided to fill in the grooves with metal. Much like the gates at the entrance to the estate, the family crest shone out bright and clear from the dark stone floor, almost glowing beneath the chandelier.

Alex gazed at the resplendent crest and imagined hosting parties for all of his glamorous friends and having a thoroughly good time.

"Alex!" A voice from below pulled him from his reverie.

He looked down to see his mum standing at the bottom of the stairs. She was beaming up at him, arms outstretched with a bacon sandwich in one hand and a glass of milk in the other. Alex smiled back.

"Hi Mum," he said quietly, before starting back down the staircase, squelching with every step.

Rebekka Wolf was very tall, very slim and very attractive. Her usually wavy dark auburn hair was curled in a tight bun, revealing a slender face, narrow chin and high cheekbones. These somewhat chiselled features were offset by her soft, almond-shaped, dark brown eyes that matched Henry's. Although she had the look of someone who spent a lot of time and money on her appearance–every part of her was perfectly manicured, plucked or preened–she wasn't a vain woman by any stretch. In reality she was incredibly kind and generous to a fault.

It was her looks, however, that were always the focus of the media. Even when she was launching yet another charitable project, the stories would somehow work around to the clothes or jewellery she was wearing; usually followed by an ever-hopeful game of *spot the wrinkle*.

It wasn't just the media that focused on his mum's looks though. Most of Alex's detentions from his final year were the result of his Machiavellian retaliations to comments he'd overheard from his classmates. Even the annual parent/teacher day had ended disastrously when Alex spotted his science tutor Dr. Wallis gawping where he shouldn't have as Rebekka left the room. If putting laxatives in Wallis' coffee had been a slight overreaction, the 12 weeks of detention he received *certainly* was.

Alex reached the bottom step and his mum pulled him into a tight hug that sent some of the milk splashing to the floor as well as down Alex's back. She held him there for several seconds before letting him go.

"Darling, how are you?" she said, releasing him. Her eyes scanned his face, seemingly trying to take in every possible minute change in his features. "Apart from being wet... Alex, why on *earth* are you so wet?"

Alex nodded his head towards the window, "Rain, Mum. It's raining outside if you hadn't noticed?"

"Well why haven't you dried yourself then? Didn't Archer bring you a towel?" said Rebekka, sounding more than a little annoyed.

"Well," said Alex, sensing an opportunity, "I did ask him but… he said he didn't have time for all that" He added a mournful, downcast look at his wet feet.

"Archer!" Rebekka shouted over her shoulder into the silence. "Archer, where are you?"

"Here Madam," came Archer's voice through a doorway on the other side of the room.

He was pacing towards them and on hearing his voice, Rebekka spun round. "Archer," she started, voice raised "Alex is soaking wet. Can you *please* go and get him a towel like he asked you to. And clean up this milk, please. I wish you'd do as you're told sometimes. I mean really, what do we pay you for?"

Archer shot an angry look over Rebekka's shoulder at Alex. Alex was smirking and giving Archer the finger with both hands behind his mum's back. Archer started forward but then seemed to think better of it.

"Yes Madam… of course." He tilted his head, turned on his heel and strode back out of the room.

Tutting, Rebekka turned back around to face Alex who had just dropped his hands into his pockets in time.

"Those for me then?" said Alex eyeing up the sandwich and milk in his mum's hands.

"Oh, of course! Sorry, Dear." Rebekka said, her face and voice softening.

Alex took the sandwich and the remaining milk, barely managing a "Thanks" before tucking into both at high speed.

"So how was your trip back with Granddad then? Did you two have a good catch up? He was desperate to come and pick you up you know, he even wanted to know how to turn on the tinted windows so he could surprise you."

Alex paused momentarily in his eating. His eyes narrowed.

"Oh it was fairly uneventful to be honest," he said, wiping his mouth on his forearm. "We didn't even really talk much in the car. Granddad kept falling asleep. You know how old he's getting these days."

"He kept falling asleep?" Rebekka sounded concerned. "I'll have to get Dr. Marshall to come over and take a look at him again. I'm sure he should be more active, you know. But he just sits in his study all day, looking through his old books. That's why I was so surprised he offered to come and pick you up from school." Rebekka seemed lost in thought for a moment, then added suspiciously, "He wasn't smoking, was he?"

Alex was in two minds whether to say anything or not. On the one hand he would quite like to pay his granddad back for the tinted windows. On the other hand, he had given Alex an iron-clad plan for getting out of work for a couple of months, and he could easily make it very difficult for Alex if he didn't play along.

"Oh no, of course not. Couldn't even smell anything on him either. You know how I usually pick up on these things."

Rebekka still looked suspicious but then her face broke in a gasp of shocked realisation. "Your present!"

"Present?" said Alex. "What present? What for?"

Immediately, his mind was racing. He was going to get his hands on his trust fund early, and as a *welcome home* gift he'd been bought something from the long wish list that he always left lying around. Rebekka had already disappeared and Alex was left imagining which of the items on his list he might be getting.

The first eight items were cars, all of which were pretty pricey. He couldn't really see his parents going for any of those, especially not after borrowing–and subsequently crashing–his dad's McLaren three years ago.

Places nine and ten were both buildings, but Alex knew for a fact that one of them wasn't for sale. As his granddad had rightly said, "Where the devil would HRH live?"

There was a chance it was item number eleven. But what would be the point of owning a racetrack when he didn't have a car to drive on it? Then it struck him. What about a racetrack *and* a car? That would definitely make more sense. But no, he was getting ahead of himself and there was no point doing that. He would just have to wait and see.

Within a few moments he heard the staccato clicking of his mum's shoes on the wooden hallway floor. Before she even entered the room, she called out, "Now close your eyes."

Alex thought it best to play along; he closed his eyes and instinctively held out his hands. Forming a cup that he imagined would be perfect for a set of car keys, he listened as his mum's footsteps grew closer and closer.

"Ready?" she sounded like she was standing directly in front of him.

Alex nodded and immediately felt the cold touch of something metal and key-shaped in his hands. Tensing in excitement he slowly opened his eyes, hardly daring to imagine which car it was going to be. However, it wasn't quite the key that he'd been expecting. It was long and silver, with a large W pressed into its end.

This isn't right, what kind of a car has a key like this?

His mum was beaming at him, "Well don't stand there looking gormless. Come and have a look."

She turned and started walking back the way she had just come. Feeling more confused than ever, Alex stood for a few seconds staring down at the key.

It wasn't a car key; that much was for sure. Unless it was one of those awful old cars that needed a handle to start the engine.

Finding himself alone, he picked up his bag and jacket and ran after his mum. But by the time he reached the start of the long corridor, Rebekka was just rounding the corner at the far end. She must have been walking at great speed; clearly excited. Realising where he was, Alex slowed slightly.

He had never liked that part of the house when he was younger as it led to the private study where his grandmother sometimes worked; *The Lair*, as he used to call it. The corridor had a low ceiling and was painted a dingy grey-blue colour. Combined with the dark wood flooring that ran throughout the house and the lack of windows, it felt claustrophobic and unwelcoming. There was a single wall light at the far end of the corridor but it was switched off, and on such an overcast day there was hardly any light at all. It gave Alex the creeps.

Trying not to surrender to his vivid imagination again, he closed his eyes and walked quickly to the other end, avoiding bumping into anything by running his fingers along the walls. Feeling them eventually disappear, he opened his eyes; he was through.

Instead of turning right; which would take him down an even darker corridor–and even closer to the lair– he turned left. There was more natural light that way and as he walked on, he saw a battered green door. With no memory of what was behind it, he slowed down as he passed.

The door was suddenly wrenched open; Alex shrieked like a little girl and leapt back against the wall. Archer was standing in the doorway, sour-faced with his eyes fixed firmly on Alex. The smell of stale alcohol drifted from his tiny office. They stared at each other for a second, then Archer moved like lightening, so that they were within an inch of each other.

"Towel." He said in a low gravelly voice.

"What?" Alex said.

"The towel you *asked for*, Master Wolf."

Alex felt the breath rush out of him as something hard hit him in the stomach. Bent double, coughing and spluttering, he saw a rolled-up white towel acting as a very solid cushion between Archer's fist and his own stomach.

"Thanks," he coughed, still trying to catch his breath.

He managed to give Archer a pathetic, wheezy smile. Archer glared at him, dropped the towel on the floor and strode back into his office, slamming the door behind him. Alex knew he had deserved that, although the punch was a bit below the belt.

He slowly straightened up and took a deep breath, resting for a minute against the wall. He caught the sound of footsteps from behind him. Fearing that it might be his grandmother coming to find him, he grabbed the towel from the floor and moved away from Archer's door as quickly as he could. He turned the corner and found himself faced with a well-lit stairway.

Gingerly taking one step at a time, he began to descend into the passage which, he assumed, must run under the grounds of the estate. It was lined with sandstone blocks and beautifully lit all the way down its considerable length. At the far end, some 300 feet away, he could just make out a set of steps ascending back to ground level and bathed in natural daylight.

Convinced he could hear heeled footsteps approaching again he quickened his pace, then a little more, finally abandoning all pretence and breaking into a full sprint for the stairs. Before he knew it he had leapt up them, two at a time, and come to a dead halt in front of a large white door. Rebekka was waiting for him.

"Where have you been? I thought you were right behind me?" said Rebekka.

"Just getting a towel from Archer." Panted Alex. He screwed up his eyes and sucked in big lungfuls of air, imagining the near miss he'd just had.

"Well dry your hair and compose yourself a minute," said Rebekka, a little of the excitement gone from her voice.

Alex rubbed his hair thoroughly with the towel and slung it over his shoulder. Looking around, he couldn't for the life of him work out where they were. Either side and above him the walls and ceiling were bare stone. The door was painted a bright gloss white and was pretty unremarkable. The only points of interest were a small silver circle with a keyhole and a long silver door handle above it.

Alex had certainly never been through this door before. Remembering why he was there, and ever the optimist, he was still convinced there was going to be a shiny new car on the other side. He looked at his mum expectantly.

"Well, open it then," he said eagerly.

"I can't," she replied, rolling her eyes. "I don't have the key, do I?"

"Eh? Oh—yes, of course."

Alex stood apprehensively in front of the door for a moment, before trying his key in the lock. There was a small *snick* and the door moved forward slightly with a creak.

"Right, now close your eyes again," said Rebekka with barely-contained excitement in her voice, "and I'll lead you in."

Alex did as he was told. He heard his mother turn the handle and swing the door open. She took his hand and led him carefully into the room.

As soon as he passed through the doorway he heard the sound of heavy rain all around them, as though they had just stepped back outside into the downpour. He could even smell wet grass and damp stone. *But we can't be outside, surely?* He wasn't getting any wetter than he already was and there hadn't been any change underfoot. It still felt like he was walking on a wooden floor. He let himself be led for another few seconds before his mum let go of his hand. Instinctively he stopped right where he was.

"Ok," said Rebekka, an exhilarated nervousness in her voice; Alex could tell she was smiling. "Open your eyes!"

Intrigued by his new surroundings but ready to face his motoring destiny, he slowly opened his eyes. It took a second for him to realise what he was seeing.

"What the..."

He was standing deep within the grounds of Wolf Manor, on a circular wooden platform over eighty feet in diameter. He could hear the rain, he could see the rain, he could even smell the rain, but he couldn't feel it. He gazed around. *This doesn't make any sense!* Then he looked more closely.

They weren't outside at all. He was standing in the middle of a huge circular room, only one that didn't appear to have any walls.

But the room did have a wall; it was just one enormous sheet of perfectly-clear glass, wrapping around the entire circumference of the floor. It was so clear that it made the room seem as if it were open to the elements. All Alex could see were the grounds of Wolf Manor, stretching out in a wide panorama for hundreds of acres all around him.

Scarcely believing his eyes, he looked for the ceiling. This too was glass and appeared to blend seamlessly with the walls. Unless you were intentionally looking, the room appeared to be one huge open space. Despite the optical illusion, Alex estimated the room must still have been forty feet high, but it was so hard to tell. As he gazed up, all he could see clearly were the dark clouds rolling overhead.

The floor of the room was the same polished dark wood that was used throughout the house, but set into it were four enormous concentric rings, picked out in silver metal. Alex imagined from above it might resemble a posh dartboard.

He stood gazing around for several seconds then he closed his eyes, basking in the sound of the heavy rain on the glass. He felt calm and at peace. He glanced across at his mum who was bouncing on her toes and clutching her hands to her mouth, desperately trying to contain her excitement.

"So you like it then?" She asked expectantly. "Your father's been working on the design for months now. In fact, we only just got it finished in time for you and Lewis coming home!"

"Like it?" Alex said quietly. "It... it's amazing! But what's it for?"

He realised that there wasn't anything actually in the room. It was an incredible space, that was for sure, but apart from the small section of wall that housed the door, there wasn't really much else to look at.

"Ah," said Rebekka, raising her hands above her head, "that's the best bit."

She clapped her hands together, with an enormous *crack*! There was silence for a split second and then music; loud, glorious music crashed over Alex like a wave. He swung around, head spinning, desperately trying to work out where the sound was coming from. It was the most beautiful choral music, floating all around him, and above him, and below him. He felt goosebumps rise on his arms as he simply stared at his mum, open mouthed. Rebecca was laughing at his shocked expression, but he couldn't hear her above the music. Then, once again, she raised her hands above her head. *Crack!*

While the music continued, the outermost ring of floor began to move. Inch by inch, it rose from the ground. At first, Alex couldn't work out what it was. But as the first foot of ring became exposed, he realised; the section that was rising from the floor was actually a huge circular bookshelf that swept the nearly the entire circumference of the room.

One foot... three feet... six feet... it kept rising. Hundreds and hundreds of books were being lifted from the depths of the earth. Alex stood mesmerised. As the shelves reached almost twice his height, the music began to fade. There was a mechanical hiss and the magical circular bookcase came to a stop.

The room had taken on a completely different character; it was suddenly a library, filled with shelf upon shelf of books. It even smelt like a library; the dusty tomes had brought with them their distinctive centuries-old scent.

Alex looked at his mother, lost for words. She was smiling at him, clearly pleased with his reaction.

"The library was your granddad's idea, Alex. They're all from his private collection too you know. I think he thought that once you'd finished school, you'd perhaps like to do a little more reading?"

Alex noted the tone in his mother's voice. He knew that his parents had always worried about his lack of interest in reading. Lewis had consumed books like they were a food substitute, whereas Alex had preferred to play with building blocks and draw pictures with his crayons.

He walked to the bookcase and ran his finger along the spines of the books. Some were rough, flaking card; some were smooth, well-nourished leather. Many of them had dust on the spines but some looked brand new; although judging from the dates printed on them he could see that they were over two hundred years old.

Suddenly there was a loud hacking cough from behind him and he turned around. Rebekka closed her eyes but her eyebrows were raised and she looked slightly pained.

"Are you feeling ok?" said Alex, concerned at how hoarse his mother's cough had sounded.

"That wasn't *me*," she said, sighing, "it was… oh, well. Your granddad also had another idea. Well, more of a surprise really. But one for which I take no credit for whatsoever!"

Rebekka walked over to join him by the bookcase and, without raising her hands above her head, gave a long-suffering sigh and clapped again. *Crack!*

This time, the mechanical hiss came from the centre of the room. Alex saw the large wooden circle in centre of the floor lower a couple of inches, split in two, part slowly, and disappear beneath the floor. The instant the floor began to separate, smoke began to billow from the hole below. Alex watched in wonder as the hole widened and still more smoke poured out. Then there was another hacking cough, followed by the sound of a piano being played; badly.

Alex stared at the hole with a sneaking suspicion what was going to happen next. Sure enough, as the floor reached its final position, there was a new sound of hydraulics and from out of the smoky darkness, a tweedy figure began to rise from the depths. Alex began to laugh. First, thick grey hair, then a watery-eyed face sucking on a long pipe appeared from the smoke. As his granddad rose higher and the awful music grew louder, Alex saw that he was sitting on a black wooden stool, hammering away on the keys of an enormous grand piano. Unlike the playing, the piano was magnificent. Even in the dulled light of the room its gloss black body gleamed and reflected every spark of light that touched it. There was a heavy *clunk* as both piano and rider reached their final destination and the floor was whole once more.

"What do you think of my playing so far, young man?" said Henry loudly out of the corner of his mouth, winking at Alex. He was still hammering away at the keys and Alex was still laughing.

"Rubbish!" shouted Alex over the din.

"I must say, I'm all for a bit of hotboxing, my dear," Henry went on to his daughter, "but you didn't have to leave me down there quite so long, did you? Man could have choked to death."

Rebekka, who had been watching the proceedings with a look of exasperation on her face, strode forward, snatched the pipe out of Henry's mouth and put it on top of the piano.

"Well it wouldn't have been a problem if you hadn't been smoking down there, would it? What's Mother going to say?" said Rebekka.

"All part of the theatrics, darling!" said Henry and winked at Alex again. "Couldn't find any dry ice in my pocket, so I had to improvise. And as for your mother, well she can–"

There was a knock on the door. All three turned to see Archer standing in the doorway with a very grim look on his face. "Mrs. Wolf, I'm afraid Mrs. Wolf Senior wants to see you in her office. It sounds urgent."

Rebekka's face turned from frustration to worry. "Oh dear. That doesn't sound good, does it." She turned to Alex. "Don't worry. Give me two minutes and I'll be back," and then, turning to Henry and pointing at the piano, "and put that pipe out. Now!"

Henry was about to respond, but Rebekka was already walking swiftly across the room, her heels clacking on the polished wooden floor as she went. "I won't be long Alex and when I get back I can show you the rest of your presents!"

Alex only caught the first part of this sentence as Rebekka was already halfway down the steps with Archer following close behind her. He turned back to his granddad, who had finally stopped playing.

"So, the master plan begins." he said, grinning.

"Quite so, young man! As I said in the car, you help me with a spot of historical bookworming, throw in a bit of 'oh I so want to learn the piano again' and we're away. *Easily* string it out for a couple of months giving you a well-deserved rest, what do you say?"

Alex didn't have to think twice, "I'm in!"

On the journey from school, Henry had explained to Alex how over Christmas, certain members of the Wolf family–mainly his grandmother and father–had been discussing what he and Lewis would do when they finished school. The conversation about Lewis had been very short, by all accounts, as his path had all but been decided years ago; he would enter the family business and act as third lieutenant behind his grandmother and father. Alex, however, was a different matter.

Concerns had been raised from said parties that he had never been very academic. Nor did he possess much of a business brain. The words *lazy, idle* and *dreamer* had been mentioned. Alex resented the first two, but still didn't see what the problem was with being a dreamer. Fearing that a plan of hard labour and business training would be put into place over the summer–no doubt as soon as Alex returned home–Henry had sprung into action.

Pointing out to his daughter that Alex really did need some sort of break after his schooling, he had quietly suggested that with a little guidance over the summer months, he might be able to convince Alex to pick up his music again. Of course, he would need to spend a lot of time with the boy and not have him distracted by some *job*. Rebekka, who had always felt Alex received a rough deal at the hands of her mother and husband and would have loved to see Alex back at the piano, had agreed at once.

Henry then put forward the idea of adapting the design of Morten's conservatory so that it could become an artistic haven, of sorts. This would allow both of them to pursue their deepest creative thoughts, both musical and literary, in peace and relative seclusion. He did insist, however, that it be kept very *hush hush* so it could be a surprise for everyone. Rebekka agreed not to breathe a word. With that, the battle was won and Alex's summer was secure.

"That's the spirit," said Henry, popping his pipe back in his mouth. There was a long silence as they both stood there looking around the room.

"You didn't tell me I was going to get a whole new room to myself though," said Alex, still struggling to take it all in.

"Well, as I said before, I will be dropping in from time to time, doing my teacher duties, checking out any new arrivals that might find their way in here." Henry winked again, but Alex didn't quite understand. Henry took a few more puffs of his pipe.

The rain seemed to be subsiding, reduced to a steady pitter patter. After a few moments' deep thought, Henry pulled out a small silver fob watch from his waistcoat pocket

"Good grief, look at the time! I'd better be off. Leave you to it for a bit?"

"Er… ok?" said Alex.

Henry stuffed the watch back into his pocket and then went to leave, but after a few steps, stopped. He turned back to Alex and said in a gruffer voice than usual, "It is good to have you back, Alex. It's… well, it's been all too quiet around here lately. Good to have you back." He gave a small sniff, turned, and limped slowly from the room, closing the door behind him.

The rain had all but stopped and a peaceful calm descended. The sun was finally breaking through the trees in a last blaze before sunset and light was pouring into the glass room.

Alex walked over to the piano, his footsteps echoing slightly on the polished wooden floor. He took a seat on the soft leather-topped stool. Lightly placing his fingers on the keys, he felt their smooth, cold touch. As he sat there, poised to play, his mind wandered back to earlier days.

Alex had been forced into piano lessons from a very early age by his grandmother, who insisted he needed to learn about the finer things in life. Although he'd initially hated his weekly sessions with the aged Ms. Crease he soon realised he had a natural talent that he could use to his advantage.

The chore of being asked to play regularly at family events by his grandmother was always offset with serious financial gain. And of course, being an accomplished pianist always came in handy when trying to impress the sixth form girls at school. Sixth form boys, it seemed, were only interested in sports and drinking. At the age of 13, these two things held no interest for Alex whatsoever.

However it was on his 16th birthday that his enjoyment of piano took a definite upswing. At the age of 83, Ms. Crease sadly met her demise. Alex had never asked the cause, supposing it was probably some sort of very nasty knitting accident. Ms. Crease's passing left her flock of budgies without an owner and Alex, most inconveniently, without a piano tutor.

Fearing that he would abandon *the noblest of Arts* if he didn't receive swift and proper guidance, his grandmother insisted that a replacement tutor be found immediately. The deal his grandmother proposed—everything was some sort of deal in the Wolf family—was that if Alex agreed to continue with his lessons, she would continue to pay for a new piano tutor. Alex countered, saying that he would be happy to continue with his lessons, providing this time *he* could choose the tutor.

Of the five potential piano tutors, all of whom were at the very top of their fields and had studied and taught at the finest academies, conservatoires and institutions in the world, Alex considered the first four merely passable. But the moment Sara Harris walked into the room, Alex knew that she was the one.

Unfortunately for Alex he hadn't realised that Miss Harris was, in fact, a plant by his grandmother. His grandmother, who had always been able to read Alex like a very short book, had easily anticipated his plan to find a much younger, more attractive and more easygoing replacement. Knowing that Alex was certain to have extremely shallow criteria he would miss that, at twenty five, Miss Harris already had a formidable reputation in society circles for strictness, discipline and getting results. Alex realised his unfortunate mistake within thirty seconds of his first lesson, but it was too late. As his grandmother was quick to remind him, a deal is a deal.

"I do hope you've been keeping up with your practice." said a voice from behind him.

Snapping back from his daydream, Alex jumped up so quickly his legs caught under the stool. He stumbled into the piano, hitting the fallboard which slammed shut, only narrowly missing his fingers. The discordant sound of tightly strung piano wires reverberated noisily around the room. He turned and saw a very attractive young woman dressed head-to-toe in black, leaning in the doorway, arms folded, smiling at him.

Sara.

Alex tried to speak, but the words caught in his throat and instead a gurgled squeak came out.

"What are you doing here?" he coughed, sounding a lot less suave than he'd hoped; a sudden rush of adrenaline was making him feel very odd and he could feel himself blushing.

"Well it's nice to see you too, Alex," said Sara still smiling.

She unfolded her arms and started to walk across the room towards him. He couldn't help but stare. Her hips were moving from side to side with every step, like the world's smoothest metronome; it was hypnotic. Realising where he was staring, he immediately flicked his eyes up to see her looking directly at him.

Alex felt himself go an even deeper shade of red; if it carried on, his head would probably burst. Shuffling out from behind the piano stool he tried to regain some of his composure, but leaning nonchalantly against the piano was a mistake. Slowly but surely, it began to roll away from under him across the smooth wooden floor. Feeling the support suddenly go from under his elbow, he very inelegantly staggered sideways after it, regaining his balance just in time to avoid a nasty fall.

This is not going well.

Thinking it better to just stand there casually, he went to put his hands smoothly into his school blazer pockets. However, it suddenly dawned on him that he hadn't been wearing his blazer since he left school, so he had to rest his open palms just above his hips giving him the appearance of an angry housewife. Sara reached the middle of the room and stood before him, radiant as ever. And there he was, hands pressed to his sides, elbows out, and shoulders pushed up towards his bright red, cringing face.

Alex hadn't seen her in two years, but she was exactly as he remembered, only perhaps more beautiful. At 5'10" she had always appeared very tall to the younger Alex, but in two years he had caught up. Now they stood eye to eye.

Her hair was a rich chocolate brown and hung perfectly straight to the small of her back. She had a gentle heart-shaped face that belied her strict nature. But it was her eyes–her big, bright blue eyes, shining out beneath her finely sculpted, heavy eyebrows–that always got him flustered. They seemed to look straight through him.

Her skin had a soft olive tone, giving her a natural glow that had enthralled Alex the first time he watched her long, slender fingers dance across the stark white piano keys in their first lesson. As he took a deep breath, trying to compose himself before speaking, he caught the scent of her light perfume. In an instant he was as mesmerised as he always had been.

"I… I was just thinking about you," he faltered, trying to sound casual.

"Oh really? And why's that, Alex?" she said, smiling.

Alex felt the heat inside him raise a couple of degrees. Sara always said his name when she asked him a question and it always made him feel like he was still at school, or that he had just said something stupid.

"I was just thinking about our first lesson… and that I'd made a mistake in choosing you to be my tutor."

She raised her eyebrows in surprise; her smile faded slightly.

"Oh, no–I didn't mean that," Alex spluttered, "I just meant that you were a lot stricter than I thought you were going to be. And that maybe one of the others would have been a bit easier on me."

Sara's expression softened. "Yes well, as I'm sure your grandmother told you, you should never judge a book by its cover, should you, Alex."

"Yes, yes I know. Very amusing. Her little plan worked brilliantly, didn't it." mumbled Alex, looking down at his feet, still annoyed that he had been tricked so easily.

"It didn't work out too badly though did it, Alex?" she said quietly.

He looked up and saw she was looking straight at him, head tilted slightly to one side with a feigned look of sadness on her face. "Well no… no of course it didn't," he replied, quickly looking down at his feet smiling.

She suddenly stepped forwards, arms outstretched, and hugged him tightly. Finally having something to do with his awkwardly placed hands, he raised his arms, but immediately felt the dampness of his armpits and quickly lowered them again, hoping she wouldn't notice.

This was the first time in years he'd been so close to Sara and it was wonderful, the feeling of her body pressed against his, the smell of her hair. But before he knew it, she let go and stepped back, a huge grin on her face.

"So Alex, you're probably wondering why I'm here?" she said excitedly.

"Well… yes actually. Why are you here?" He said, wondering why he hadn't asked that question before.

Oh yes, you were making an idiot of yourself, that's right.

"It was your granddad's idea actually."

The last thing Henry had mentioned about new arrivals suddenly made sense and Alex made a mental note to thank him later.

"He called me last week to say that you were coming home, and that you'd probably like to start your music lessons again. He mentioned something about a surprise?"

Alex laughed, "Yes, my surprise! Well, you're standing in it,"

Sara looked back at him confused, "You mean this *room* is your surprise?"

"Yup, I guess," he said, shrugging his shoulders, "Mum was showing me round, but then she got a call from old Snaggletooth."

"Alex! You shouldn't call her that. It's rude!" said Sara reprovingly, but she was trying not to laugh.

"Yeah well, she is an old Snaggletooth and Granddad reckons she's got big plans for me this summer. Which probably means she wants me to get a bloody *job*."

"Oh how the other half live," said Sara, "The thought of having to work to get paid must be terrible."

Alex scowled, "I didn't mean that, I just meant I wouldn't mind a few months off before I start work properly, you know? Some time to relax after my hard life at school."

He could tell Sara wasn't buying it. She was giving him the look that she always did when she thought he was being a spoiled little brat. Alex smirked, knowing full well what she was thinking.

"And there I was, thinking I'd missed you," she said, shaking her head but with a small smile on her face. "Shows what I know doesn't it?"

Alex crossed his arms, thinking of his slowly spreading sweat patches; but he was careful not to lean back on the piano again.

"So, err... do you want me to show you round my new room of wonders then?" he said with a cocky grin on his face.

Sara's eyebrows raised once more and the smile disappeared from her face.

"No, you're alright thanks, Alex," She said, "in fact, I should probably be going. Lots of other students to see."

She turned and began to walk back across the room towards the door. Alex watched her walking away–metronome in full swing–cursing himself for ruining the moment, but not sure what exactly he could say. He closed his eyes, hoping that something charming would appear magically out of the floor just as the pop-up library had.

"Anyway," came Sara's soft voice from across the room. Alex's eyes sprang open. She was standing by the door smiling at him again. "There'll be plenty of time for you to show me round during our lessons, won't there?" She winked.

Stepping out of the room and making her way down the stairs she called back over her shoulder, "First lesson is the day after tomorrow, Master Wolf! Don't be late, or there'll be trouble."

Before Alex had time to reply, she was gone.

CHAPTER 6

SANCTUARY

Feeling a little weak-kneed from his encounter, Alex returned to the piano and flopped down on the soft, leather-topped stool. His mind wandered back to his past piano lessons and the possibilities of the future. It was making him feel a little giddy. Slightly dazed, he lifted the piano lid and began to play the Rachmaninov piece he'd originally intended to play, before being so pleasantly interrupted. Despite the fact that it was one of his grandmother's favourite pieces, and that he'd been forced to learn it more or less from day one, he couldn't hold that against this beautiful piece of music.

Rusty though he was, he slowly made his way through the sweeping opening section from memory and within seconds was lost in his own world; just him and the music. After several minutes he played the final chord, holding it until the reverberating sound eventually died. He sat silently at the keyboard for a few moments, just smiling to himself. When he finally looked up, he was shocked to see how dark it had become outside.

There were no lights in the room, or at least none that he could see. Looking out at the quickly darkening sky, he could see clouds rolling in thickly overhead, ready to shower the vast terrain with another downpour. Without sunlight to reflect off the curved glass room, the wall and ceiling seemed to completely disappear, giving Alex the eerie feeling of sitting alone in a huge, dark garden. He felt suddenly very exposed.

Slowly getting to his feet, he picked up his bag and jacket and made his way to the door. With every step, the distance seemed to increase. He quickened his pace, desperately trying to ignore his heart beating faster and his moistening palms. More or less bounding the last few feet, he reached the door, grabbed the handle and swung it open.

Bright light bathed the small stairwell and he stepped into it, shutting the door behind him to block out the darkness. Letting out a long, slow breath he laughed nervously to himself, but then realised how dry his throat was. He coughed and licked his lips.

Get a grip. It's just your imagination getting the better of you again.

Having escaped the non-existent threat, an idea popped into his head. He reopened the tall white door and stepped back into the silent room. Peering into the darkness, he raised his arms high above his head and clapped his hands together hard. *Crack!*

Without any music to accompany it, a low mechanical hum began in the middle of the room. Sure enough the piano, silhouetted in the darkness, began to descend. Alex heard the soft clunk of the two half circles of wood reforming to create the solid floor. Grinning at the slickness of the operation, he raised his hands again and clapped once more. *Crack!* There was another low hum and he watched, captivated, as the tall black wall that wrapped around the entire space slowly began to retract into the floor. However, as he stared into the dark room, the stairwell lights flickered behind him. Bolting to the doorway, he watched as one by one the row of inset ceiling lights flared and went out. He froze in the darkness. The bookshelf had nearly reached its final position. As the last few inches of shelf flattened against the floor there was a soft *clunk* and then absolute silence.

Alex's heart beat harder and faster. He shut his eyes and pressed his back against the wall, desperately willing the lights to come on, but when he opened them he was still enveloped in darkness.

There was only one thing for it. He would *have* to go back into the big empty room and search for a light switch. Steeling himself, he slid very slowly past the door frame, back still pressed firmly against the wall. Raising his arm behind him he felt for a switch of some sort to end the impenetrable darkness. Searching up and down the wall, he felt nothing, but just as he moved his hand back down there was an almighty flash of light.

For a split second, Alex thought he had found an invisible switch, but as he looked up in relief he saw straight ahead, deep into the lightening-lit grounds. There, just on the other side of the glass wall was a dark figure. Hooded and cloaked, it was hunched over so that its black arms were touching the ground. Alex froze. The sheet lightening flashed again and as Alex stared transfixed, what appeared to be the dark figure's head jerked around, as if looking directly at him. Deafening thunder crashed down from the sky and reverberated around the room, before it went dark once more.

This was too much for Alex. Forgetting everything but his most primal instincts, he turned and ran screaming from the room, leapt down the steps in one, ran down the pitch black corridor, and didn't stop until he was back in the brightly lit entrance hall.

Breathless and terrified, he collapsed against the cold slate wall and sucked in great lungfuls of air. He could feel the beads of sweat running down his forehead and neck, dropping onto his still damp clothes. After a few seconds, he finally felt his breathing return to normal. Straightening up, he gave a huge, shuddering sigh. In the brightness of this room he felt stupid about running from the library like that. He knew that he had an overactive imagination, but he had definitely seen someone or *something* standing there. Wiping away the moisture from his face with the back of his sleeve, he ran his fingers through his damp hair. The only thing he could be glad about was that no one had heard him screaming like that.

Suddenly he heard the sound of footsteps in the corridor approaching quickly, getting louder. Then they stopped.

"Alex, what *are* you doing? I heard a noise? Are you alright?" It was Rebekka and she looked worried.

"No I'm *not* bloody alright!" He shot back in a slightly croaky voice. "I was in that stupid library room and all the lights went out. It was pitch black in there! And the lightening? And the thunder? And I've just seen a huge... *something* creeping around outside in the dark!"

Rebekka's look of panic dissolved and her hand flew to her face. Her shaking shoulders gave her away.

"It's not funny!" Alex bellowed. "Didn't you hear me? There's something out there! I could have been–"

The tall, wooden front door swung open. Preceded by a gust of wind and violent sprays of rain, a dark, cloaked and hooded figure walked in. Alex froze, a look of terror on his face.

"As requested Madam, the outside lights are now fixed and fully operational" came a familiar voice from beneath the hood.

The dark figure reached up to its head and with two large hands, pulled back the hood, revealing the smirking face of Archer. Alex glanced at his mother, who was still trying not to laugh, and closed his mouth.

"Oh Alex," she said softly, but still laughing, "we've been having a few problems with the outside lights since the new part of the building went up and I asked Archer to get on and fix them now that you're back. That's probably what made the lights go out."

"I'm very sorry if I scared you, Master Wolf," said Archer, shaking himself off and looking innocently at Alex.

Alex bristled, but then put his hands in his trouser pockets and strolled nonchalantly towards Archer.

"You didn't *scare* me, Archer," he said. "I was just raising the alarm about a possible intruder on the premises. That was all."

"Oh I see," said Archer, meeting Alex face to face. "It's just I thought I heard someone shrieking. I assumed that either there was a little girl running about the house whom I knew nothing about… or that I'd scared you?"

Archer made sure he said this quietly enough so that Rebekka couldn't hear him. Alex could feel the blood rising in his cheeks. He glared at Archer who just smiled sweetly back at him.

"Now, come along," said Rebekka, "it's time you went to bed, Alex. Busy day tomorrow and your granddad wants you up early too."

Alex continued to glare at Archer, but then turned and walked away, aiming a sly kick at Archer's leg as he did so. Just for good measure.

"Yeah ok," he said grumpily, still feeling stupid.

Saying goodnight to his mum, he let her hug him and eventually hugged her back. She didn't immediately let go, but when she did, she smiled at him.

"It's good to have you back, Alex."

Alex half smiled back but didn't say anything. Judging by the last ten minutes, he wasn't so sure he *was* pleased to be back.

Anyway, tomorrow's a new day.

He began to traipse slowly up the stairs. As he reached the top, Rebekka called up to him, "Oh and by the way," he stopped but didn't turn round, hearing the note of apprehension in his mother's voice, "your father's back tomorrow. He and your grandmother want to sit down with you for a few minutes first thing to discuss your plans for the summer."

Alex's shoulders slumped as he let out another long sigh and rolled his eyes, "Fine!" he called back, and began the long walk to his bedroom.

Although he knew that the discussion was inevitable, unavoidable and in every way unnecessary, Alex had hoped it would have been at least a couple of days before he had to endure the look of disappointment from his grandmother and grave tones of his father. He knew he didn't have much direction in his life, but he was 19 years old and had just left school. What 19 year old *did* have direction?

Of course, Lewis did. And as ever, he was being judged by his brother's standards. Lewis who was so sure of what he was going to do with his life, so confident in his actions, possessed of such business acumen, such wit and charm, such a brown nosing suck up. Alex began stomping down the landing rather pointlessly, his heavy steps barely making a sound in the thick, deep pile carpet. He was angry about Lewis, angry about the conversation he would have to endure tomorrow, angry about Archer making him look like an idiot.

A third of the way down the first landing he doubled back and walked up another flight of stairs to the third floor and stood at the end of the moodily lit corridor to his bedroom. What Alex saw made his jaw drop.

It wasn't just that the upper landing stretched over 100 feet–from the east side of the house to the west–it was more that the space appeared to have been attacked by a maniac florist. Every ten feet there was a small console table holding an enormous vase. Within each vase was a staggeringly elaborate floral display. Alex knew at once that this was his mum's touch. As a keen interior design enthusiast she always had flowers in every available crevice of their previous home; different flowers for different rooms, seasons, moods and guests.

Alex started heavily down the long hallway, his footfall still only kept in check by the thick carpet. As he made his way past the various flower arrangements and breathed in the strong scents, it seemed to relax him. By the time he reached the end of the corridor he was feeling positively drowsy. Reaching the last console table, nearest to his bedroom door, he smiled to himself. Placed on this one was a small display of fire lilies, his favourites. Finally, he had reached his bedroom. His sanctuary.

Although Wolf Manor was very old, Alex's room had only recently been refurbished. The devastating fire that had ripped through the house the previous year had been nothing to do with Alex, but the result of a faulty light fitting in the room below apparently. However, the opportunity to design his perfect bedroom from scratch had been too good to pass up. Ignoring his more important coursework, he had spent hours at school sketching out ideas and sending them back and forth with his granddad. Although Henry had kept him up to date with the progress, it would be his first real chance to enjoy the many luxuries he had spent so many meticulous hours planning. Alex paused in front of the dark wooden door, turned the brushed silver handle and walked in.

Situated on the far northwest corner of the building, he had always considered that room to have the best view in the house; it was exactly why he had chosen it. As he considered this, there was a break in the dark clouds and bright moonlight lit up the grounds. Walking straight across the solid walnut floor to the huge concertina windows on the far wall, Alex gazed out over his balcony. From his window, not only could he see the estate gardens, but also the beginnings of the lake and the tall imposing trees of the silver forest. The view was breathtaking and he stood for several minutes just soaking it in, before turning back round to admire his new quarters.

The room was a standard oblong, with high ceilings, intricate cornicing and beautiful metal fittings and fixtures throughout. A large section of the far wall was taken up by Alex's ridiculously oversized bed; low and wide, with more than enough room to fit six people side by side, it was covered with crisp white Egyptian cotton sheets and topped by a mountain of well-stuffed, silver-grey pillows.

Flanking the bed were two slimline bedside tables that appeared to float on a cloud of soft, yellow light, glowing from beneath.

On the right-hand wall was a wide, low-set oak-framed window and below that stood a beautiful rosewood desk that Alex had temporarily inherited from his father. Amazed that he had been allowed to even have it in his room, Alex had sworn that he would take good care of it. Making a mental note not to put any cold glasses of milk down on the delicate polished surface, as he had with his grandmother's rare Chippendale, Alex kicked off his shoes.

Noticing that his bags had been brought in from the car, Alex swung them up onto the freshly laundered bed sheets and slumped down beside them. He hated unpacking; it was almost as tedious as packing and that only escaped last place because it came with the promise of actually going somewhere interesting afterwards.

He stretched and fell back onto the luxurious coolness of his bed. Even he had to admit that for a single male of 19 years old, this custom-built bed was completely unnecessary. But it was, at least, supremely comfortable. He stared up at the high ceiling.

Like the walls, it too had been covered in exceptionally expensive, handmade wallpaper that resembled the grey slate of the entrance hall. In most rooms, this would have been too dark; too overpowering, but again the room still felt light and spacious.

He noticed the main room light: hundreds of miniature glass cubes clustered to look like a cascade of ice cubes. Rather than a cold blue or white light though, each cube emitted an ember-like orange glow in the half brightness.

Other than the huge clear windows that were framed by full-length cream silk curtains, the long north wall was dominated by the two imposing speakers that Alex had saved for several years to afford. The enormous cherrywood cabinets were topped by glossy teardrop shapes that glinted in the light. Alex couldn't wait to try them out in the morning, knowing that they were powered by a five foot stack of amplifiers sitting ominously in the corner alcove.

Finally out of distractions, Alex pushed himself back up and began going through his bags, unzipping one then the other. Inside was a complete mess. Becoming immediately frustrated, he upturned each and shook the contents out onto the bed. Once he could see everything, he spent a few minutes grouping the items depending on where they needed to go.

Starting with the easiest first, he sifted through the large pile and pulled out the various empty food wrappers, containers and boxes that had accumulated in his dorm room over the years. One by one he threw these over his shoulder towards the small leather dustbin by his desk. Each one missed.

Next were the various items of clothing that he had found under his school bed, having missed them on the first sweep of his dormitory room: one faded black t-shirt, one greying white t-shirt, a single monogrammed slipper, a pair of black silk pyjama trousers and three socks. He bundled them together and tossed them on the floor at the end of the bed.

Amongst the thinning pile of debris were three very large, very old and very heavy books. The first was an enormous dictionary that his grandmother had given him before leaving for school, some 8 years ago. She had suggested the eleven year old Alex would benefit from expanding his limited vocabulary.

The other two, which strictly speaking didn't belong to Alex, were both library books. One was about the insects and arachnids of the British Commonwealth, and the other was about the history of the Norwegian fjords. Alex didn't really care for either subject; it wasn't the contents that had caught his eye. It was the look of them. Both were thick and wrapped in old leather; one tan, one black. The wide spines appeared at one time to have had some very fine gilt detailing, but it had almost completely rubbed off, leaving small specks behind. The leather edges were shiny in places–no doubt from oily fingers–but they looked simply magnificent and they smelt wonderful. There was just something about old books that Alex loved. Knowing he would probably never read them he nevertheless decided that, for the time being, they would take pride of place on his bookcase.

Set in a recess in the wall to the right of his bed were five thick oak shelves. Originally intended as bookshelves, they were fast becoming a repository for nik-naks, curios and other objet d'art. Heaving the three books onto the third highest shelf, he spent a couple of minutes rearranging them at various jaunty angles, making sure they were just right.

Returning to the pile of detritus, he picked out an empty leather pencil case, an assortment of sketchbooks and notepads, and a chrome letter opener. Stacking them on top of each other, he began hunting for the pens and pencils that were supposed to be in the pencil case. Spotting his bright silver pen and pencil set almost at once, he rummaged through and picked out several orange biros and a small black metal ruler. Stuffing them into the worn old case he walked to the other side of the room and placed them delicately onto his desk.

Returning to the bed, he saw that he was at last getting to the good stuff. Carefully selecting the items he would keep on his bedside cabinet, he picked out his cream-faced stainless steel watch, his second pair of ridiculously large headphones, a small but very solid camera, and a selection of dog-eared and crumpled magazines. Taking a moment to arrange them all on his bedside cabinet, he returned for the last leg of his unpacking marathon. Waiting in front of him was a large wooden cigar box, an unopened bottle of expensive Vodka, the perfectly preserved photograph of Miss Green, a selection of letters from ex-girlfriends and a few more magazines. As these particular items were *not* for casual viewing, Alex decided that they would have to be kept in the most secure place he knew: his safe.

He wasn't a particularly secretive person, but after too many embarrassing school experiences he had learned the value of secure storage. Particularly since certain members of his family were often oblivious to the concept of privacy. So, when it came to planning his room, the very first thing he had thought of was a safe.

He remembered once, when he was much younger, he had seen his dad putting some thickly bound documents into the family safe in their old home. Morten hadn't seen him, but Alex remembered watching his father carefully dial in the combination, before yanking the big handle and slowly pulling out the heavy door. Something about it had really caught his imagination and he had never forgotten it.

Picking up all of the remaining items, he walked to the tall sliding wardrobe doors that ran along the wall adjacent to the main door. With a free hand he touched a panel on the wall. The door slid across in front of him to reveal a large, well lit square room. On the left and right hand walls were rows and rows of clothes, all neatly stacked or hanging from chrome rails. On the wall directly in front of him was a full length mirror set into a dark wood frame. Either side were at least a hundred pigeonhole boxes, each filled with shoes of various colours, styles and materials.

Alex walked straight to the far end of the room and, after a moment's thought, reached into a pigeon hole at chest height. He pulled out a ridiculous pair of purple suede loafers, placed them on the floor and reached into the empty space. Finding the small lever he had been looking for, he gripped it hard and pulled.

There was the sound of oiled metal plates sliding against each other and the mirror moved away from the wall by an inch along its right hand edge. Alex gripped the mirror's edge and pulled it away from the wall. Surprisingly heavy, it slowly rotated on hidden hinges, revealing a doorway just wide enough for him to step through.

Inside, the dark blue walls were dimly lit by a series of small yellow lights recessed into the wall at ankle height. Since it had been completed in such a hurry, and in secret, by Alex and his granddad he could still smell smoke from the fire that had started below. Careful not to let the door close behind him, Alex turned to face his pride and joy. Standing five feet tall and weighing around 1.5 tonnes was his gleaming black safe. He stood for a moment, imagining the real riches it would one day contain. Gently placing his treasures on the floor, he tried to recall how to get into the thing.

First, he pressed a small button on the top. A square panel set into the door slid down to reveal a brushed metal keypad and a black glass plate. Gently placing his thumb on the black glass, he waited for the sensor to make its customary beep, before he carefully entered the sixteen digit password into the keypad. A large elliptical plate began to slowly protrude from the door; he had remembered his password correctly. Coming to a stop four inches proud of the door, Alex turned it anti-clockwise ninety degrees and pulled. The door swung open, revealing four empty, felt-lined shelves.

He picked up his new additions excitedly from the floor. Gently placing them onto the top shelf he admired his secret haul, then pushed the heavy door shut once more. He turned the handle and once again typed his code into the keypad, watching as the handle retracted back into the door. Stepping out of the hidden room, he leant on the mirrored secret entrance until he heard a heavy *thunk* behind him.

Taking the chance to use his new changing room properly, he stripped right down to his favourite sky blue y-fronts and left his school clothes crumpled in a pile in the middle of the floor.

His unpacking *finally* over, he shuffled to his bed, climbed under the crisp white duvet and buried his head in the thick, fresh smelling pillow. He extended an arm from underneath the cosseting duvet and stroked the wall panel above the bedside table. The lights dimmed and went out, and within seconds the room cooled just how he liked it. The curtains, he left wide open. The storm was raging harder than ever outside, and with the lights off, the windows changed from mirrored black panels to beautifully clear views of the grounds and the night sky. He lay watching and listening to the storm gathering pace. Without noticing, he drifted off into a deep, dreamless sleep.

CHAPTER 7

AWAKE

Alex opened his eyes. He was lying on his back, staring at the ceiling and he could feel his body was wet from sweat. The room was deathly silent and the storm had stopped, but his heart was pounding and his chest felt unbelievably tight. There was a smell of damp in the air. From nowhere, a quiet ringing began in his ears. He tried to move but he couldn't. He tried to open his mouth, move an arm, a finger, but nothing. The ringing grew louder as he lay there, terrified. He could only look at the ceiling in horror as the dark wallpaper seemed to detach itself and form a black cloak that slowly fell towards him. He tried to scream but nothing came out. The ringing in his ears reached an unbearable pitch; then there was only blackness.

CHAPTER 8

SOFIA

Knock, knock. Alex stirred under the duvet, half awake. *Knock, knock.* He opened his eyes the tiniest amount. It was morning. *Knock, knock.* He was way too warm and comfortable for this.

"Alex? Alex, I'm coming in!" His mum's voice called from outside the room.

"Mmffine!" he shouted back, muffled by a face full of pillow. He heard the sound of the door opening quickly and footsteps moving quickly across the floor.

"Alex, what are you doing? You're supposed to be seeing your father and grandmother in a few minutes! I called you over an hour ago. They're waiting!"

"Oh sh…" Alex sprang from his bed in panic. Remembering he didn't have much on, he grabbed a handful of duvet and pulled it round him like a plump white ball gown.

"Come on, get dressed and get down there. You don't want to keep them waiting do you?" Despite his recently woken brain haze, Alex thought his mum sounded a bit anxious; if he was honest, so was he, knowing how these sorts of meetings usually went. "Grandma wants you to go to her office and you're supposed to be there in *two minutes* so get a move on!"

Rebekka turned and walked out almost as quickly as she'd walked in. As soon as Alex heard the door close, he threw the duvet ball gown aside and ran towards the wardrobe in a panic. He stopped dead suddenly, remembering the clothes he'd only just unpacked. Although they weren't entirely suitable for the occasion, he pulled on his black silk pyjama trousers and a faded black t-shirt and ran to the bedroom door. He stopped again. *Feet!*

Pressing the button to open the sliding wardrobe door, he dashed in and grabbed the first pair of shoes he saw. Springing out of his room, he ran as quickly as he could down the long corridor, bounded down the three flights of stairs, across the entrance hall and through the myriad of passageways. Once again he found himself out of breath outside the door to his grandmother's office. He took several long, deep breaths and tried to smooth down the front of his crumpled t-shirt. With a shaking hand, he knocked twice on the black painted door, turned the handle and walked in.

The room made Alex's bedroom seem tiny. It was easily as wide as his, but around five times longer. Just like the entrance hall, there was barely anything in it; the floor was made up of large black marble tiles, polished to a mirror finish, and the walls were panelled with what looked like smooth steel plates. A large array of silver-framed pictures lined the walls on either side. Each contained a photo of his grandmother standing next to someone famous; prime ministers, presidents, royalty and movie stars all featured in this rogues' gallery. At the far end of the room was a single large window that more or less filled the whole wall. Bright white light was streaming through the glass; so bright, in fact, that it made it difficult to see anything at the other end of the room. Alex couldn't even tell if he was alone. Squinting, he could just make out a wide glass-topped desk that appeared to have two high-backed chairs behind it. Their silhouettes looked like a pair of tombstones, planted side by side.

As Alex timidly approached, his eyes adjusted a little more and he saw a third chair in front of the desk. Unlike the other two, which were probably very comfortable, the third appeared to be a very uninviting looking wooden chair. He took a few steps more and then caught the unmistakable scent of fresh soap in his nostrils. *So, granny is here after all.*

He felt himself shrinking slightly in his ill-chosen clothes, as though the polished and immaculate room was punishing him for wearing such poorly chosen attire. The purple loafers he had picked felt like a particularly bad choice. He finally saw the two figures sitting stiffly in the tombstone chairs.

In the chair at the middle of the desk was his grandmother, Sofia Wolf. Her hair was a light silvery grey, which suited a woman of her years, but it had been cut into a severe long bob, which made her look even more austere and tightly wound than usual. It did have the benefit of covering up her craggy, wrinkly neck though, which Alex would often become mesmerised by if he looked at her for too long. He had never seen a photo of his grandmother looking younger; he supposed she would have been beautiful, like his mother. Perhaps. He had never known her to wear any make up, but since her eyes were an incredibly light, piercing grey, they often remained the focus of people's gazes anyway. As usual, she was dressed in her uniform of a black roll neck and black, wide-legged trousers.

Probably best she covers herself up, the wrinkly old bag. As Alex looked at his grandmother he had the same thought he'd had many a time: what exactly was it that attracted his Granddad to this woman?

He looked to the figure sitting on his grandmother's left. It was his father, Morten. As usual, he was dressed in a rather dour combination of a dark grey three piece suit and a white shirt. It was offset by his thick, wavy blonde hair–which Alex had inherited–and clear green eyes, framed with wide, black-rimmed glasses. Neither of them looked particularly happy. *Brilliant.*

"Hi… Dad," he offered, nervously.

"Hi Alex," replied Morten in his deep baritone, "it's good to see you back."

Could have fooled me. Morten smiled ever so slightly, stood up and walked around the desk. Misreading the signs, Alex moved in for a hug, just as Morten put out his hand. What followed was a fairly awkward wide-armed handshake, before Morten returned stiffly to his seat. Sofia hadn't said anything yet; she made a point of slowly looking Alex up and down.

"So, is that what everyone's wearing these days, Alexander?" she said.

He hadn't spoken to her in a long time. Her usual smooth-yet-haughty voice was sounding hoarse and rough, as though she'd caught something nasty on her trip.

"Err… no," he replied, "it's just what I found on the floor when I got up."

"Well, I'm glad to see you've made an effort." Her attention turned to a single blue piece of paper in front of her.

Intrigued and slightly apprehensive, Alex slumped down onto the hard chair. It was a lot lower than expected and he winced as his back cracked against the hard wooden surface.

"Why don't you take a seat," said Sofia still not looking at him.

Alex shifted uncomfortably. He tried crossing his legs but catching his father frowning at his shoes, he uncrossed them and tried to tuck them back under the chair instead. *Well, this is going well.*

"Alexander, the reason we wanted to see you this morning was to discuss several things," Sofia said.

Several? This sounds ominous.

"Firstly," she continued, "we wanted to discuss your trust fund." Alex sat up straight, excitement rising in him. He hadn't been expecting this at all. His eyes flicked between his Grandmother and his father several times, who were both staring at him. "As you know, the agreement we had in place was that you would receive a small percentage of your trust fund once you finished school, another percentage when you found suitable employment and further percentages at specific times thereafter." Alex wasn't paying attention; he was working out a new shopping list in his head. "However…"

No, no, no, no, no!

"Your father and I have decided that we shall be holding back the first two portions of your trust fund until further notice." Alex stared from one to the other. He couldn't believe what he was hearing. He felt the anger building inside him. "Do you have anything you'd like to say on this particular subject?"

Alex stared at her. She had the tiniest of smiles on her face. He could think of plenty of things he'd like to say but each one of them was pretty rude and would probably result in him never getting his hands on his money. He sat there fuming for a few more seconds then composed himself.

He forced himself to smile and asked in a ridiculous singsong voice, "Tell me, Granny," Sofia bristled. "Is there any particular reason why I'm not getting access to *my* money?"

"Well I'm glad you asked," she replied brightly, pushing her chair back and getting to her feet. Alex had forgotten how tall she was. "We feel that as you've decided to spend the next couple of months working with your grandfather on these various fun projects, you couldn't *possibly* need any money. After all, you're living here with us now."

Alex was taken aback. *How did they know about the plan? Has Granddad blabbed? Surely not. He promised he hadn't told anyone!*

"Of course when you find yourself a *proper* job we'll be more than happy to give you a little more, shall we say, financial support?"

Sofia smiled broadly at him. Alex looked to his father, but Morten was staring at the floor looking uncomfortable.

Without really thinking said through gritted teeth, "Well, what if I didn't work for Granddad and just went and got a job today?"

"Oh no, no, no," replied Sofia, shaking her head. "Your grandfather would be so disappointed. He's been looking forward to this for weeks now. And besides, you've made him a promise, and promises shouldn't be broken should they, Alexander?"

"No. No they shouldn't," he muttered gloomily, quite sure that he had been promised this money when he finished school.

It was no use though, he was trapped. There was no way they were going to let him have his money; they had decided. *Brilliant! Now I've got to spend the summer looking through old books and helping Granddad trace the bloody family history, without a penny to my name!* Alex slumped back in his chair looking miserable.

"Well, I'm glad we've got that agreed," said Sofia, still smiling. "We shall perhaps review the situation at the end of the summer, shall we? Now, moving on," She continued without waiting for an answer. Alex couldn't see much point in paying attention now. Whatever the other things were, it couldn't get any worse. "I'm sure you'll be pleased to hear that Lewis sealed a very important deal yesterday in New York."

Alex rolled his eyes and sighed, "Yes, I did see something about that in the paper."

"Oh excellent! I didn't realise you read, let alone the paper. Well in that case you will also have read that it has earned the company a rather significant profit, so we felt it only proper that Lewis should not only receive the agreed percentage of his trust fund, but also a bonus."

Alex tried to swallow back the comments rising in his throat. "What's that got to do with me?" he said, feeling himself descend into a full-scale sulk.

"Well, Lewis being Lewis," started Sofia with a look of sickly adoration on her age-worn face, "he has decided to re-invest his trust fund *back* into the company." Sofia paused as if to let this sink in. "Don't you think that's wonderful, Alex?"

"Wonderful." He said in a monotone. "Anything else?"

"Well just one thing," she said, holding out her hand in Morten's direction. "We wanted to thank Lewis for all his hard work. And for having such faith in the company by reinvesting." Morten slid open the desk drawer and took out a small glass and metal oblong. He handed it to Sofia. "We wanted to give him a nice surprise. Would you be so kind as to pass this on to him? I think he's on the veranda having breakfast if you'd like to go and find him?"

Sofia handed the object to Alex. He knew what it was before he'd even touched it. His stomach dropped through the floor. It was a key; a key to a car that was number four on his *Things to buy when I get my hands on my Trust Fund* list.

"Right. Of course." He said quietly, staring at the key sitting cold and heavy on his palm. He clenched his fist around it and looked up. Sofia was beaming at him. He looked to his dad who was expressionless but was at least looking at him now. "So is that everything? Or have you got any other nice surprises for me?"

"Yes, I think so for now. Yes it is. Thank you, Alex. Oh and enjoy your history lessons," smiled Sofia, even letting out a small chuckle to herself.

Alex stood up, turned and started the long walk back to the door. He could feel himself clenching the key in his hand like he was trying to crush it. He walked slowly, trying to at least retain some dignity. Reaching the door, he opened it, slid through quietly and slammed it behind him without looking back.

He could still picture the look of satisfaction on her face. She'd absolutely loved rubbing it in about the stupid company, stupid shares and stupid Lewis. He stomped down the corridor towards the main hall, thoughts flying round his head. There was no way he was going to take this lying down. He'd been counting on getting that money through. There were things he wanted to do, things to see, things to buy! And now what did he have to look forward to? Nothing! He may as well stay in his bedroom all summer. It would have to be better than watching Lewis swan about in his new car. *In my car! Lewis doesn't even like cars.*

Before he realised it, Alex was back in the entrance hall. He stood for a moment trying to decide what to do. Knowing that if he went up to his room he probably wouldn't come down again, he decided to find Lewis straight away to give him his present.

Noticing that the doors beneath the staircase were ajar, Alex assumed that Lewis was still out on the veranda. Storming through them, he marched silently through the gigantic kitchen, through the sunlit Orangery and out onto the warm, stone-flagged veranda.

Lewis wasn't there. *Great.* Not the least bit interested in searching for him, Alex called out in a high-pitched sing-song voice instead.

"Lewis? Oh *Lewis*? Where are you Lewis? I've got a *present* for you!"

"Al? Al, is that you?" A voice said from the far side of the veranda wall.

Alex would have bet his life that Lewis would be down there with a pot of tea and the business news.

"Yes it's me!" said Alex, dropping the girly voice at once and striding to the low veranda wall, ready to throw the key over the edge. "I've got something–"

As he looked down over the wall he saw that Lewis wasn't alone. He was sitting around a table with three of his friends: Hayden James, Lisa Manners and Chloe Hurst. All four were staring back up at him.

Hayden and Lisa regarded him like he was something nasty they'd just stepped in, and Chloe just looked embarrassed for him. He didn't really know which was worse. He felt his stomach lurch and knew that the customary reddening of the face wouldn't be far behind.

"Hi, by the way," said Lewis, sounding both confused and a little annoyed.

"Hi." mumbled Alex, mortified; his face felt like it was about to burst.

"The guys just came round to celebrate the end of school and… well, I'm sure you've heard about the business deal? You're more than welcome to come and join us if you like?

Typical Lewis. Showing me up by being Mr. Nice Guy.

"No I think I'll err… give it a miss. Things to do to… thanks though," he said awkwardly; very aware that Hayden and Lisa were still giving him dirty looks.

"Oh. Ok," said Lewis, sounding confused. "You were looking for me though, weren't you?"

"Oh. Yes. I just wanted to give you this," Alex said, remembering the reason he was here in the first place.

He looked down and saw that his hands were white from clutching the key so hard. Opening his palm he could see the moisture on the cool glass block.

"Present from the witch and Dad... they wanted me to give it to you." Alex threw the key gently over the wall down to Lewis who caught it effortlessly with one hand.

Lewis looked at it and realised quickly what it was. He shot a look up at Alex, half excited and half guilty.

"Thanks," said Lewis quietly.

"No problem," said Alex just as quietly.

He nodded quickly and started back across the veranda. As soon as he was out of sight he heard the excited chattering of the four friends over Lewis's new toy. Before he could make it indoors though, he heard something that made his blood run cold.

"Alex?" It was the voice of Chloe Hurst, the goddess of St. Bartholomew's who had left school nearly two years ago.

Somehow, even though he and Lewis were exactly the same age, Lewis had managed to become good friends with Chloe while Alex had not. In fact, Alex had only spoken to her twice in his whole life.

The first time had been during his very first week at school when, as a wide eyed first year, he got hopelessly lost and couldn't find his way back to the science labs. The very kind and very pretty third year who helped him was given the high honour of being offered one of his salt and vinegar crisps but she had declined, albeit very politely.

The second time had been only last year and was infinitely more embarrassing. Even thinking about it made Alex feel sick to his stomach.

At an end of year school party, after one too many cocktails, he vaguely remembered climbing up on stage and dedicating a song to his *favourite salt and vinegar girl* and requesting a dance. Once again she politely declined. Or, more accurately, her rather large boyfriend declined on her behalf.

Alex had always hoped that one day he'd be able to talk to her without making a fool of himself, to make up for last year's embarrassment; and now there she was, right after he'd made himself look like a total idiot. Again. *Isn't it supposed to be third time lucky?*

Alex could feel the crippling heat flushing his face. He slowly turned to see her walking towards him. With the morning sun behind her she practically glowed. She was wearing a light floral dress and tan heels, but it was her jet black hair that first caught Alex's gaze. It hung down past her shoulders in loose, thick furls and shimmered in the sunlight as it moved with her every step. Her lightly freckled nose and clear blue eyes caught Alex's attention next and he gulped. He tried to adopt a more casual pose, which proved difficult in silk trousers and purple loafers. She stopped in front of him and smiled.

"Hi," she said, more kindly than he had expected. "Is everything ok? You seemed a bit upset."

"Upset? Me? No, no not at all. Just messing around really, you know how it is."

She frowned slightly and tilted her head to one side. Alex caught the scent of her perfume and bit his lip, trying to prevent himself from saying something stupid. "Hey, why don't you come and sit with us for a bit? We could all have breakfast together? It'd be really nice to get to know you a bit better. Lewis is always talking about you, you know."

"I bet he is," Alex mumbled under his breath.

"Look," she continued, smiling, "I know Hayden and Lisa aren't the easiest people to talk to but I'll keep an eye on you if you like?" She punched him lightly on the shoulder.

"I... that's..." he could feel himself getting tongue tied and flustered, "I don't need keeping an eye on... I am 19 you know!"

Oh God. He wanted to bite his fist to stop him saying any more.

"Right..." said Chloe, who looked like she was trying not to laugh. "I just meant it would be nice to catch up. I haven't seen you since last year, remember?"

Alex smiled sheepishly. For a moment he considered joining Lewis and his friends; once he had got changed, of course. He didn't much care for Hayden and Lisa; they always seemed so superior and snidey. The thought of spending the morning with Chloe, though, was very appealing.

"And I know you two have a difficult relationship, but the more time you spend together then... well, it'll get better over time won't it?"

Alex's mood changed instantly.

"What *exactly* has Lewis been saying?" he said sharply.

"He... he hasn't said anything," said Chloe, slightly taken aback by the sudden change in Alex's tone. "It's just, it's the same with all siblings isn't it? Take my sister and I. We used to–"

"You wouldn't understand." Alex cut in tersely.

Chloe frowned, looking hurt and then angry. Alex immediately regretted his shortness; he really hadn't meant it to come out like that.

"No, you're right, Alex. I probably wouldn't." She sounded annoyed.

"Well, I'm sorry to have bothered you. Hayden said not to bother talking to you but I hoped he was wrong. I guess not."

Alex willed himself to apologise, but he was stung by Hayden's comment.

"Anyway, I'll let you get back to whatever it was you were doing." She looked him up and down, then said in a voice rich with sarcasm, "Nice shoes by the way."

Before he could say anything, Chloe turned and walked away. He wanted to cry out. *That is it! Enough!* It was time to retreat to his room and call an end to the whole day before anything else could go wrong.

Stopping only to snatch a leg of cold chicken from the fridge, he stormed back through the house, back to his bedroom; the place where he would surely be protected from any further disappointment or embarrassment.

Pleased that he hadn't passed anyone else on the way, Alex reached his bedroom door and found it slightly ajar. He entered to find his bed had been made and on top of it had been placed a book. Slamming the door behind him and locking it for good measure, he walked over to his bed and saw that a note had been left on top of the book that simply read, *a friend.*

Alex scowled. He really wasn't in the mood for his granddad's jokes. Alex knew he'd only put that there because he was feeling guilty about letting the details of the supposed *grand plan* slip. He picked up the book and slung it onto his bedside cabinet. An ornamental glass bowl that had been sitting near the edge fell to the floor and smashed. Taking a deep breath, Alex closed his eyes and tried to calm himself. It didn't work.

Remembering what he had always done when he was angry, he went to his bedside cabinet and pulled open the drawer. Rummaging around, he grabbed the two remote controls he was looking for.

First, he pressed the large green button on the smaller remote; there was the sound of a catch unlocking. Slowly but surely, the tall glass doors that formed most of his north facing wall began to concertina back, opening up the room to the dazzling sunshine and cool breeze.

Feeling better already, he hopped up onto his bed and crawled to the middle; propping himself up on pillows and leaning back against the wooden headboard. When he was comfortable, he pressed the largest button on the second remote control and gentle music began to float from the enormous speakers either side of the open window. Still feeling annoyed, he pressed down hard on another button. Within a few seconds the music was thundering from the speakers in powerful cannon-blasts of sound. They were so loud he could feel them coursing through his body, so clear that if he closed his eyes for an instant it felt like he was right there amongst the orchestra. Alex felt the hairs on his arms raise and his whole body tingle as the music surrounded and enveloped him.

Within minutes, as expected, there was a hammering on his bedroom door, barely audible above the music. It was his grandmother.

"Alexander? Alexander Wolf! Turn that down this instant! Alexander!"

As he nestled himself back into the thick comfortable pillows he took an enormous bite of cold chicken and chewed slowly. Closing his eyes, he thought to himself how the small victories were sometimes the best.

CHAPTER 9

THE STORM

Alex woke with a start, then lay still for several moments. Sitting up, he looked around his room, confused and disorientated; something had woken him.

With his memory slowly dropping into place, he remembered that when he had fallen asleep it had been bright outside and his music had been on extremely loud. Now, however, it was pitch black and there was no music. Even so, he couldn't seem to think straight.

What was that noise?

In his dazed state he fumbled for his watch on the bedside cabinet. As he blinked the fog from his eyes, he saw that it was 11.20pm. Slumping back onto his pillow, Alex screwed up his eyes before yawning loudly.

Must have slept all day. That would explain the dark… but the noise?

He crawled off the bed just as the sky suddenly lit up. Looking out into the grounds he could see that last night's storm had returned for a second run, with a vengeance. He had never seen rain or gales like it. The huge concertina doors were still open to the elements, but thankfully the balcony above had protected his room from the rain. He walked to the huge open void and stared into the black sky, breathing great lungfuls of the air that smelt of wet grass and stone. In the distance he could see the taller trees of the silver forest swaying violently in the wind. According to Henry, the forest was over 800 years old, so Alex was sure they must have survived batterings far worse. Even so the wind must surely have been pushing them to their limits.

Deciding that he'd had enough storm-watching, he pressed the control pad that glowed gently on the wall. The huge glass panels slowly began to unfold themselves and within seconds had reformed into a solid transparent wall, blocking out the sound of the storm.

Silence. With the spectacle of the storm raging outside it was several moments before Alex suddenly became aware that he was standing in the dark again. Just as he was about to sort out some kind of lighting, there was an almighty crash of thunder. Sheet lightening lit the sky for a split second and there, standing inches from him on the other side of the glass partition was a tall, black, hooded figure. Alex's heart almost burst from his chest and he stumbled backwards, tripping over the rug on the floor behind him.

Sitting down hard seemed to jolt something in his memory. *Archer! It's Archer playing his games again. Well this one isn't funny. Not funny at all.*

Alex pulled himself to his feet and strode back to the window, ready to give him a piece of his mind. But as he reached the window and peered out into the darkness he couldn't see Archer anywhere. *Knows he's been rumbled and probably run off laughing to himself.* Alex shook his head bitterly, still feeling uneasy.

A second burst of lightening lit up the sky, even brighter than before. But in this flash the black figure appeared again. Alex froze, rooted to the spot. The black figure's hood had slipped down and it most certainly was not Archer.

A man, older than any Alex had ever seen and ghastly in appearance, stood before him, separated only by an inch of glass. What was left of his long thin hair whipped about his face in the buffeting wind and his eyes, deep-set into his skull-like head, were as black as the clouds rumbling overhead, but wide and bulging with intensity. The face, that was snarling and grimacing like an old Hyena, was lined so deeply that Alex couldn't tell if it was from extreme old age or some kind of hideous scarring.

Alex's mind had shut down in terror. He couldn't move, he couldn't speak, he just stood and stared through the glass, terrified. The man began to raise his right arm. As his ragged, black sleeve slipped away, Alex could see his arm was covered in scars, partially covered with several silver bracelets and wide leather bands. The man's mouth parted in what looked like an enraged scream. The black cavern that opened before Alex's eyes revealed a bluish, lumpen tongue, framed by crooked teeth, rotten and broken.

The arm was fully outstretched towards him. Alex could only gawp at the gnarled and liver spotted hand protruding from the ragged sleeve under the man's black cloak. A thick, bony finger that ended with a long, yellow, cracked nail was pointing directly at Alex. Or was it?

The old man still appeared to be screaming but was looking past Alex and into the room. With all the courage he could muster, Alex managed to slowly turn to look back into the darkness. As he turned, he saw exactly what the man was pointing at.

The book, which he had found earlier placed on his bed, was standing upright on his bedside table, engulfed in flames; bright blue flames. Alex stared open mouthed at the unnatural dancing flames, completely mesmerised.

Suddenly, the blue fire died and Alex spun back to the window. The old man had disappeared. Forgetting his fear, he pressed his face to the window. As he looked out into the dark, the rain stopped in an instant. The deep rumble of thunder died and the black and grey skies that had blanketed the earth just moments before slowly began to roll back towards the horizon, as if recalled by an unknown force. Alex's bedroom was instantly filled with dawn light, as though the sun was about to break over the trees.

Confusion replacing his fear, Alex looked at the clock hanging above his bed. 4.20am. *That can't be right, I only just looked at my watch and it was 11.20!* He stood in his room completely dazed, not really sure what to think or what to do. At least he knew he wouldn't be leaving the concertina doors open again. Deciding that bed would be the safest place, he quickly returned to the strangely cold mattress and pulled the heavy duvet over himself. He pressed several buttons, turning on every light in the room to full brightness. Even with the dawn light beaming through the windows, he wasn't taking any chances.

Burying his head in his soft pillows he tried to sleep. But there was no drifting off. Not surprising, with his heart still pounding heavily in his chest.

Ten, twenty, thirty minutes went by and still sleep wouldn't take him. He pulled the thick duvet over his head. Forty minutes, Fifty minutes, then an hour went by; it was no good. He rolled over onto his front to see if that would make any difference but as he did, the book that was still resting on the bedside table caught his eye. He sat up and eyed it suspiciously.

From what Alex could see, it was clearly very old but still in pretty good condition. It was a bit bigger than an A4 notepad and maybe an inch thick. The tan leather cover was wrapped around the pages like an envelope, before being tied with a much thinner piece of leather like a shoelace. There appeared to be some sort of embossing on the leather too, but he couldn't quite make out what it was. Looking at the paper edges that were visible Alex could see that quite a few of them were crinkled as if they had become wet at some point. Swallowing hard, he reached out and touched the book with a single finger before pulling it away quickly.

Nothing happened. No fire, no bursts of light, no old men peering in through the window. Very gingerly Alex placed his whole hand on the book, firmly on the lookout for erupting blue flames. Still nothing. Very carefully he reached out with both hands, picked up the book, and placed it on his lap. The first thing he noticed was how heavy it was: far heavier than a book that size ought to have been. *Maybe they used thicker paper back then? Wait… no that's stupid.*

The second thing that struck him was how soft and supple the leather was, although it was scratched, battered and torn in a couple of places. He slowly began to undo the thin, rough, leather cord that had been wrapped around the book.

As he unwound it, the book seemed to expand in his hand like a sponge in water. He unwrapped the cord some more; and watched in amazement as the book seemed to grow in length and width. Alex blinked several times, wondering if he'd fallen asleep after all. *This cannot be happening. Books do not grow in size.*

Unable to resist, he undid the last full loop of cord and the book rapidly expanded to its full size. It was the size of an A3 notepad and at least three inches thick. He decided to take the final leap and open the book.

Slowly pulling back the soft leather cover, he saw that the first page was blank, except for a tiny scribbled inscription on the bottom right corner.

Frederik Johan Halverson - born. 1210 - died.   :
V24 - DoV

He turned the next page. That was blank too. Propping the book up on its corner he flicked through all the pages. Besides the musty smell of old paper puffing in his face, there was nothing on any of the pages. *All that for a blank book? What the hell did the old man want with a blank book? Was he trying to show me something?*

Alex's head started to pound; this was all too much to take in. It was almost 6am on the first day that he was meant to be working with his granddad. If he didn't get at least some sleep he would be useless. As much fun as his granddad was in small doses, a full day of him was something else entirely. And since he wasn't going to be getting any of his trust fund money, the thought of spending two months working together didn't seem quite as appealing as it had done before.

With this thought in his head, sleep finally enveloped him and he slowly slipped back down under the covers. He half noticed the heavy leather book slip off the duvet and hit the floor with a dull thud, but a sleepy twitch of indifference was the best Alex could muster. Within seconds he was fast asleep. If he'd taken a moment to put the book back on the bedside cabinet he might have seen it slowly shrink back to it's original size, burst into thick blue flames and then finally disappear into thin air.

Barely 150 feet away, a very old and very wet man was sitting on a stone chair, muttering angrily to himself. A sodden black cloak hung to his left, drying over a small fire. His thin, straggled hair clung to the rough contours of his haggard face. His yellowing, claw-like nails were slowly turning the pages of a thick, soft leather-bound book and his black, deep set eyes twitched from left to right as he began to read the tiny, scrawled text that filled every page.

CHAPTER 10

THE DIARY

When Alex woke he felt absolutely dreadful. Looking at the clock he saw it was just after 10am. Why did he feel so tired? After all, he had slept right through from yesterday lunchtime. *Perhaps too much sleep?*

What was more astonishing was that no-one had tried to wake him up. He reasoned that his mum and granddad would probably be feeling guilty about spilling the details of the grand plan, that his grandmother would still be too angry with him for his loud music and his dad probably didn't care whether he slept in or not.

As for Lewis, Alex was sure he was out playing in his new toy. Probably with Hayden, Lisa and Chloe; or maybe just Chloe. Maybe he was out with her now, roaring around the countryside in his new car, showing off how fast he could drive.

Alex stood up, avoided the half-eaten chicken leg on the floor and walked to the window. It looked like it was going to be a lovely day, although judging by the wetness of the stone balcony, it had rained overnight.

With a final stretch he began his morning routine, spending a leisurely hour showering, shaving, moisturising, preening, plucking and eventually getting dressed. Learning from the day before, he spent a further half an hour choosing a suitable outfit for the day's activities.

Despite still being miffed at his grandfather's indiscretion, Alex was going to take the opportunity to practice his Henry-ness as planned. When he was finally ready to leave his bedroom he took several moments to check his outfit in his full length mirror.

Even though it was clearly going to be a warm day, Alex had opted for a very smart fitted tweed suit with contrasting sky blue woollen waistcoat, a crisp open-necked white shirt, set off with an electric blue cravat he'd actually

74

forgotten he owned. Careful to accessorise correctly, he picked out his favourite tan leather long-toed brogues, a tan leather belt, and his favourite watch with the tan leather strap.

Admiring himself in the mirror for longer than was strictly necessary, he ran his fingers through his hair one last time before leaving his room and making his way down the long corridor, thumbs tucked firmly into his waistcoat pockets. As he sauntered down the cool hallway he took on a certain swagger that only came from the wearing of a well-made suit. He positively skipped down the staircase and made his way through the kitchen. As he passed through the kitchen he picked up the bacon sandwich on the sideboard which, he assumed, someone had left out for him, before hopping down the small flight of stone steps in the kitchen alcove that led to his granddad's study.

He had never understood why, in a house with over 40 rooms, his granddad had chosen a relatively small study more or less in the basement. Alex had a sneaking suspicion it was to avoid bumping into his wife too much; Sofia Wolf had always had a thing about going below ground. Munching on his bacon sandwich, Alex reached the dark green door of Henry's study. There was a yellow sticky note stuck to it.

Alex,
Thought we'd work in your new library today - that is what it's for after all! Meet me there when you're ready.
Granddad

Alex took the note off the door and grinned. Following yesterday's disappointments he'd actually forgotten about the new library; it would be much nicer working in there than in his granddad's stuffy study. He made his way back up the stone staircase but before entering the kitchen he stopped. He could hear someone moving. Peering round the stone doorway he saw Archer bent over, peering suspiciously at the empty plate that had previously held the freshly made bacon sandwich.

Realising that he may have made a small error in his assumptions, Alex quickly stuffed the remaining half of the sandwich in his mouth and started to chewed vigorously. Choking slightly on the last chunk of sticky white bread, Alex coughed; Archer looked up. Covering his mouth to cough again—and checking for crumbs—Alex swallowed the last mouthful, licked his teeth, and walked breezily into the kitchen.

"Morning, Archer," he said brightly.

"Where's my sandwich?" Archer's said gruffly. He was staring at Alex with one hand on the granite counter, the other with an index finger hovering over the empty plate.

"Oh that's nice isn't it," started Alex, figuring attack could be the best line of defence. "No 'Morning, Alex', 'Everything ok, Alex?', 'How are things, Alex?' Oh no. Just 'Where's my sandwich?'"

Archer held Alex's gaze. "You didn't answer my question. Where's my sandwich?"

"I haven't got your bloody sandwich, I don't even like bacon!" said Alex.

He realised his mistake the moment Archer ran at him. Alex only just jumped aside in time to avoid being knocked over. Alex shrieked and ran round the other side of the counter, putting it between himself and Archer, who now looked absolutely furious.

"Make me another sandwich." Archer said through gritted teeth.

"Why should I?" said Alex laughing with nervous excitement. "Besides, I'm so full after the last one, I don't think I could bend down to get the bacon out."

Archer lunged at him across the counter, both hands outstretched, but the worst Alex got was a face full of stale alcohol breath.

"Soaking up last night's drinkies are we? No wonder you want your sandwich so badly."

This wasn't the thing to say. Archer leapt up onto the counter with surprising agility. Screaming in fright, Alex moved just in time to avoid Archer crashing down on him. Picking that moment to leave, he dashed for the kitchen door, his would-be attacker running close behind him. They chased through the entrance hall, but instead of running for the maze of corridors, Alex went for the front door. Luckily for him it was unlocked and it swung open easily as he grabbed the handle. He dashed through and jumped down the stone steps at the front of the house. Stumbling slightly, he regained his balance in time to glance over his shoulder. Archer was still chasing after him. Alex dashed across the grass around the outside of the house and didn't stop running until he was the other side of the west wing. He was relieved to see that Archer was bent double, clutching a stitch in his side.

"Old age and too much drink!" shouted Alex, unable to resist adding a slow shake of his head in mock disappointment.

Straightening up and flattening down his waistcoat, Alex continued to walk around the edge of the house, rather than risk going anywhere near Archer. Taking his time to cool down from his sudden exertion, Alex meandered lazily through the flower beds, fountains and water features, stopping briefly to skim some flat stones across the calm fish pond. Having never been very good at it, he quickly gave up and continued on his way.

Walking through a small pocket of tall trees, he saw the new library in the distance. From the outside it didn't look at all as he had expected, rising like one of the enormous, domed gas towers he was used to seeing in cities. But rather than being dull grey steel, this was brilliant silver, dazzling in the sunlight. It was almost too bright to gaze at directly, but it looked spectacular. As he walked along, admiring the gleaming structure, something caught his eye in the grass.

It appeared to be a thin metal band; as he crouched down to get a better look, he realised it was a fine silver bracelet. Picking it up, he saw that it was about three inches in diameter and quite roughly made. It was ingrained with dirt, as if it had been buried in soil for some time. He could just make out a small mark on the outside. It looked like three letters:

AsF

A sudden thought came to Alex. *Maybe it's valuable. Maybe I could sell it to make some money. Maybe I should try and find its owner...* Remembering he really ought to get a move on, he dropped the bracelet into his pocket and carried on towards the library.

With no idea if there was actually a way in from the outside, he cut back across the lawn and made for a small door in the side of the building; he knew it would bring him close to where he needed to be. Just as he was about to open it, he heard the catch click and it began to open from the inside.

Leaping to one side, fully expecting Archer to come barreling out, Alex slid behind the opening door with his back against the wall. What he heard next was the last thing he had expected.

"You *cannot* be seen here, you do know that don't you?" It was his grandmother's voice and she sounded nervous.

"You saw the storm didn't you, Sofie? You know what that means don't you?" The second voice was a man's. Calm, slow and measured but very commanding, it sounded vaguely familiar. Alex just couldn't place it.

"Of course I know what it *could* mean, but maybe it was just a normal storm and nothing else," said Sofia sounding more as if she was trying to reassure herself.

"Tell me, Sofie, what were *you* doing between 11.20 and 4.20 this morning? Because *I* was watching the skies and I can assure you–"

"I know what you think, but I find it hard to believe–"

"Believe it, Sofie. *One* of them is back."

"Enough! That is enough. You must go. Now." hissed Sofia sounding angry.

"I will go. But you *will* be hearing from me."

Alex stood stock still and watched as the door began to close. Knowing that he would be exposed at any moment, he slid further back against the wall. But when the door had closed, there was no-one to be seen.

He assumed that his grandmother had gone back inside, but where had the other voice gone? Surely not back inside with her. *Wasn't he supposed to be leaving? But more importantly, who was he? And what was that conversation all about?* There was only one thing for it. He would have to ask his granddad.

It was nearly midday. He waited prudently for a few more moments to be sure the coast was clear, then carefully turned the handle of the door and stepped into the corridor.

There was no-one about, just a lingering smell of cigar smoke, which he assumed had come from the mysterious man. Trying to remember his way, Alex began to stalk down the winding passageways until he came to the long underground corridor leading to the library. He pushed the door open and walked straight into the enormous space of the library room. With the midday sun shining in, it looked magnificent; even more so than the first time he had seen it.

Henry was nowhere to be seen. Wondering if he hadn't arrived yet, Alex waited by the door to listen for him coming down the hallway. As he looked at the room more closely, however, something told him that his granddad was there somewhere. The bookshelves had been raised, the piano was out and there was that unmistakable smell of pipe smoke wafting around the air.

Due to the shape of the room, Alex assumed that he could see everything in it, but then it struck him. *Of course!* The gigantic circular bookshelf that rose from the floor didn't extend completely to the glass wall; there must have been a four foot gap to the windows. Alex would have bet the house that Henry would be hiding behind the shelves, ready to jump out at him.

Quietly he closed the door and stepped lightly into the room. He stepped behind the shelves and began to walk round the outer perimeter. It was quite a strange sensation, walking around the edge, as if being on a never ending right hand bend. Alex continued tiptoeing round, expecting to see his granddad any second.

Ten, twenty, thirty feet… still no sign of him. Alex guessed he must have passed the middle point. Forty, fifty, sixty feet… still nothing. He was certain he was over half way around. Seventy, eighty, ninety feet… but this would put him on the other side of the room and still there was no sign of Henry. It was then that he heard the appalling piano playing.

Running the last few feet to the end of the bookshelf, Alex looked to the middle of the room and saw his granddad, beaming away at the piano, long pipe in his mouth, playing an awful rendition of *We'll Meet Again*.

'Nice of you to turn up, young Alex… even if you are a day late!" he shouted over his own dreadful playing. "I hope you're not going to do this every time or this is going to take us years, not weeks!"

Alex strode over to the piano. "And where exactly did you come from?"

"Oh magic, dear boy, just magic!" Henry winked and then switched to what was supposed to be *Camptown Races*. "I think I'm getting better you know!" He pounded the keys with his thick fingers.

Alex broke into fits of laughter as his granddad began flapping his elbows in time to the music. Without warning, Henry stopped playing and slammed the piano lid down shut.

"Right!" he said, jumping to his feet. "First things first, let's fix ourselves a drink, shall we? This history business is thirsty work you know!"

"But we haven't even done anything yet," said Alex.

Henry had already walked over to the bookshelves. He was peering at the floor as if he'd lost something small. "Aha!" He said suddenly.

He raised his hands above his head and clapped out a short rhythm that sounded suspiciously like Morse code: two slow claps, one fast clap, two taps with his foot, one slow clap and one fast clap. Alex looked at him like he'd gone mad, but then suddenly a piece of the floor in front of the bookshelf began to rise up. Henry turned and grinned excitedly at Alex. When the piece of rising floor finally stopped moving he could see why.

It appeared to be a drinks cabinet. Shaped like a segment of larger circle, it stood about four feet tall and was split into three sections. The bottom section looked like it was carrying chilled bottles, the middle was carrying other various spirits, and the shorter top section was carrying an assortment of glasses. Alex couldn't help but laugh, not least because he'd never seen his granddad looking so pleased with himself.

Henry sniffed and his moustache twitched, "So, young squire, what can I get you? Bearing in mind it's only just gone midday, what?"

Alex, putting on his poshest voice and bowing slightly to his granddad replied, "I think I shall have a snifter of your finest lemonade please, landlord."

"Lemonade?" Cried Henry indignantly. "No, no, no, no. That won't do at all."

"Well I don't know then. Surprise me." said Alex, wondering if they were ever going to get started.

With a wink, Henry reached down to the bottom compartment and pulled out a narrow, cork-stoppered, green bottle. Plucking a small glass from the top compartment, he pulled out the cork and poured out a small measure of rich, golden liquid. He handed it to Alex with a reverent look in his face.

"What is it?" asked Alex peering at the syrupy liquid.

"That, my boy, is the drink of kings and gentlemen. It is the finest sherry that money can buy."

"*Sherry?*" said Alex, unimpressed. "Isn't that what old ladies drink?"

He saw his granddad's moustache protrude menacingly as he pursed his lips. Thinking it prudent to at least try some, Alex took a sip from the glass. He had to admit that the chilled, sweet liquid was rather nice. Henry's moustache returned to its former resting place as he resumed his air of placid knowing.

"Aaaand for me… hmm. Let's see, let… me… see…" he tapped his chin while he considered his options. "Gin and tonic!" he exclaimed, finger raised to the sky.

Replacing the sherry, he reached into the middle compartment and pulled out a short, squat clear glass bottle. Pouring a sizeable slug of gin into a heavy bottomed glass, he looked over at Alex and winked. "You'll like this bit."

Reaching to the top of the drinks cabinet, he flicked open the thin piece of wood that had, until a few minutes ago, been the floor. He pulled out what looked like a chrome shower hose with a nozzle attached to one end. Pressing a button on the top, a thick stream of tonic water topped up the glass.

With a drink apiece, Henry rapped the drinks cabinet sharply on top and it slowly descended back into the floor. Henry gestured to two comfy leather chairs that Alex immediately recognised from his granddad's study. Heading for the more padded of the two, which Alex knew was his granddad's favourite, he plonked himself down onto the soft dark leather upholstery. Careful not to spill his drink, he crossed his legs then sprawled leisurely in his chair, drink dangling lightly in one hand. Henry, sat down opposite Alex and squirmed uncomfortably, as if trying to adjust the thin cushion padding with his backside. Eventually he seemed to find a comfortable spot, raised his glass. "Cheers!" He took a big glug of his drink and said, "I must say, I do like your get up today, young fellow. Very smart indeed. Reminds me of the sort of thing I used to wear back in the day."

Alex looked at his granddad, who was wearing an almost identical outfit, but didn't say anything. He just smiled back and took another sip of his sherry.

'So, you're probably wondering what we're actually going to do today. What this is all about, hmm?"

"Well," said Alex, suddenly remembering he was still supposed to be angry with his granddad. "Seeing as though Dad and the dragon already know about what we're supposed to be doing, I wouldn't mind being let in on the secret as well?"

Henry looked confused. "What do you mean they know about it? How can they?" Alex ignored the look of disbelief from his granddad and scowled. "Well *I* haven't told them anything, if that's what you think?" said Henry, sounding hurt.

"Oh really? Well that's funny, because I was hauled up in front of Tweedledee and Tweedledum yesterday and they seemed to know all about it. They've even frozen my trust fund because after all, *Why would you need any money when you're living here and learning History?*" Alex did an accurate imitation of his grandmother's voice.

"Honestly, old chap," said Henry, sounding genuinely put out. "I didn't breathe a word to them. The only people that knew about it were me and your mum."

There was an awkward silence, in which Henry seemed to stare vacantly into the distance deep in thought. Alex began to feel bad for suspecting his granddad; he seemed genuinely surprised that Sofia and Morten had known about the plan.

"Look, don't worry about it," said Alex. "I was just annoyed that they knew. Caught me off guard, that's all. And to have my trust fund cut off before it had even started…"

Henry seemed to come to and his eyes snapped back to meet Alex's. "Ah well, don't worry about that." he said, suddenly buoyant again. "You need anything, anything at all, you come to me! The old dragon hasn't got her hands on all my purse strings just yet!"

Alex wondered how generous Henry would actually be if he asked him for the Lamborghini he'd placed at number three on his list. Maybe that could wait.

Henry tipped back his head and poured the remainder of his glass down his throat; Alex couldn't help but notice that his hands seemed to be shaking slightly.

"Right! As I said before, you're probably wondering what we're actually going to do today." Henry said, then dropped his voice to a serious whisper. "Well let me tell you." He leaned forward in his chair, gripping the arms. "As you may or not know, the Wolf family is one of the oldest in the world, going back centuries."

Alex smiled to himself. He loved it when his granddad got into history mode: all very serious, as if he was lecturing to a rapt audience. He wouldn't be surprised if Henry stood up soon.

"What you definitely will not know, however," continued Henry, pushing himself to his feet and plugging his thumbs into his waistcoat pockets, "is that the Wolf family originated from Norway."

Rebekka had actually told Alex this several years ago; thinking better of spoiling the moment, he kept his mouth shut. Henry had begun to pace around the room, head slightly raised and eyes shut as if deep in thought.

"I myself am not a true member of the Wolf family, as I took your grandmother's name when we married. However, I probably know more about the Wolf family history than anyone else in the country."

Alex had often wondered why Henry had taken the Wolf name. His granddad had always claimed it had been for tax purposes, but Alex had never bought that; especially when he learned his father had done the same thing. Henry was now striding around behind him.

"With that in mind, I thought it would be useful for you to learn more about the family history… whilst I am still around." Henry sniffed theatrically and Alex rolled his eyes. His grandfather got like this sometimes, as if to make out he was on death's doorstep and wanted to pass on his legacy. "But before we start on the actual historical research side tomorrow–"

"Tomorrow?" said Alex excitedly, sitting up in his chair. "You mean we're not going to be doing this all day?"

"*Before* we start on the historical research side tomorrow, I am going to give you a task. A task that you need to keep up for *at least* the two remaining months of the summer. If not longer."

Alex slumped back in his chair. *This sounds ominous.*

"Go on then, what is it?" He sighed, knowing there would be a catch.

Henry had disappeared behind the bookshelves, but soon reappeared holding a slim black box. Alex sat up in his seat and craned his neck to see what it was. Sitting down in the leather armchair again, Henry placed the black box on his lap and then held Alex's gaze as if to build the tension. Alex's mind wandered off into unrealistic expectations once again.

What task could I possibly need to keep up for two months? Perfect my driving skills? Go on a long holiday to learn how to really relax properly? Learn how to get my hands on my trust fund from annoying grandmothers that won't cough up?

"Your task is…"

"Yes?" said Alex excitedly.

Henry ran one of his fingers under the rim of the lid ready to yank it off, "to…"

"Yes, yes. Come on!" said Alex more urgently.

Henry lifted the lid some more. Alex slid down in his seat trying to see through the crack between lid and box.

"Keep a diary!" Henry whipped off the lid and flung it over his shoulder in one smooth movement.

As Alex stared into the box, his face dropped. On a cushion of black cloth was a plain, brown, leather-bound book. He looked up at Henry in disbelief. "You want me to keep a diary? What's the point in that? I thought it was going to be something *good*!" Ever since he had come back from school it had just been disappointment after disappointment.

"Now, now, young Alex. There's no need for that," said Henry, eyes fixed and smiling at Alex's downcast face. "This is an exact replica of the diaries that *all* of your Wolf ancestors have kept for over 800 years. This is a big honour, my lad. An important moment!"

Alex still couldn't see why he was supposed to be getting excited about writing in a stupid book every day. They used to make him do that sort of thing at school and he had hated it. Every Monday morning they would have to write their weekend diary. After making up all sorts of nonsense, Alex would invariably be hauled before the house tutor to be scalded, not only for his incessant lying, but also for his appalling lack of vocabulary. This was not an experience he particularly wanted to repeat.

"You want *me* to keep a diary?" said Alex looking disbelievingly at his granddad.

"Absolutely! But not like those awful things they made you keep at school," said Henry smiling. "There shall be none of that nonsense. No, I want you to write exactly what *you want to write*, what you *feel* like writing." Henry leaned forward and his voice dropped to a whisper. "You can write anything you like, but you just need to make sure that you do it. Every. Single. Day. That is all I ask."

"You are kidding me?" sneered Alex.

"I most certainly am not! Your ancestors were great diary keepers, writing down all sorts of useful information that could be passed on from generation to generation!"

"Sounds like a group of crusty old bookworms if you ask me," retorted Alex, snorting with laughter.

Henry fixed him with a surprisingly stern gaze. Alex looked down at the diary and then back at his granddad. There was something serious and intense in Henry's stare that Alex hadn't seen before and it was making him feel uncomfortable. He reached out to take the journal but before he could touch it, Henry seized his wrist and Alex flinched in surprise.

"Alex, you must promise to write in this every day. I'm serious now, boy. Every day for the next two months. Do you promise?" Henry's gaze was fixed and unmoving.

"Yes–yes of course, I promise, if it's important." Alex said quietly.

Henry smiled broadly. He released his grip and gently tossed the box over to Alex. He jumped to his feet and wrung his hands together as if he was trying to grind some invisible ball of muck into his palms.

"Right! That's today's lesson over then, I think. Another drink, perhaps?"

"Err, no… thanks. Still not finished the first one yet," said Alex looking down at the half empty sherry glass, taken aback at the sudden change of atmosphere.

"No–no quite," said Henry reaching into his jacket distractedly and pulling out his gold pocket watch. "Well I should probably wait a bit as well then. Don't want to be sozzled before lunch, do I? Devil to pay and all that. Right, well if we're done for today then I'll be off. Things to do, people to see!"

Henry strode off at such a pace that within a few seconds he was at the door. He turned quickly and barked back to Alex, "Same place tomorrow, but let's make it a few hours earlier shall we?" Without waiting for an answer, he disappeared through the door, pulling it closed behind him. Alex could hear him humming Camptown Races all the way down the passageway.

Knowing full well that Henry neither had anything to do, nor anyone to see, Alex sat in the huge room and pondered his sherry. The sudden change in his granddad had made him feel quite odd. It was so unexpected.

Why is he so intent on me keeping a diary? The black box lay open on Alex's lap. He looked down at the leather bound book inside. The deep brown leather appeared brand new and unblemished; it certainly smelt new. He picked it up and examined it more closely. There were no other adornments on the book, save for a small silver buckle on the front that held it closed.

Already censoring half of the thoughts and feelings he would be writing in such a poorly secured book, he flipped it over in his hands a couple of times. He went to undo the buckle, but as his fingers touched the metal he felt a powerful jolt of electricity. The hairs rose on the back of his arms and neck, and his skin suddenly felt extremely sensitive. Every movement of his clothes made his body tense and he dropped the book to the floor.

That was odd. Must be static from all this tweed. After a few seconds his skin returned to normal and he delicately picked up the book. He half expected the same response, but there was nothing. Relieved, he quickly undid the clasp and fanned through the pages from the back to the front; enjoying the cool breeze and the smell of new paper. Reaching the front page, he saw an inscription written in a silvery ink.

Alexander Gunnar Wolf - born. 1991 - died.   :
V1 - DoSW

Alex stared at the inscription with the strangest feeling of déjà vu. He'd seen something like this before, but for the life of him he couldn't remember where. The wording itself was odd too. Obviously his name and the year of his birth were correct, but why did it need a space for the year of his death? *That seems rather morbid.*

Trying to put it from his mind, he looked at the last part of the inscription: V1 - DoSW.

He had seen 'V' used to signify 'versions' of computer files sometimes, so perhaps it meant 'Version 1'. It was his first diary, he supposed, so that would make sense. But what about the DoSW?

Dignitary of Supreme Wealth? Dictator of Seven Worlds? Despising of Sophia Wolf? Alex gave up. He would ask his granddad during tomorrow's session.

He returned the diary to its black padded box, without bothering to do up the buckle, and tossed the whole lot into the leather chair opposite him. Looking around, and realising he didn't really have anything else to do for the day, he thought he'd take the opportunity to have another play on his new toy.

He walked around to the front of the enormous grand piano, running his fingers over the smooth, black bodywork. It was an amazing piece of engineering. He lifted the heavy lid, propping it up on its thick support, and gazed into the wondrous satin-gold cavern inside. It was like staring into the open chest of a huge mechanical beast. Every component, small and large, was crafted and aligned with the express purpose of creating beautiful sound.

Tearing his attention from the complex internals, he carefully sat down on the leather-topped stool and noiselessly lifted the lid. The black and white keys gleamed invitingly and he felt a welcome sense of relaxation return after the morning's bizarre events. He raised his hands above the keyboard, wrists high, fingers loose, and began to play.

In moments, Alex was in a world of his own, lost in the music. The room had near-perfect acoustic feedback; whether performing or listening, you could stand anywhere and feel like the music was surrounding you and only you. It occurred to him that this was an odd feature for his father to have designed into a library, but the music swiftly banished the thought from his head.

For over an hour he sat and played nothing in particular; he just blended one piece of music to another, letting his fingers decide what sounds would be created next. Chord after chord rose and fell, one after the other, and the melodies soared and swept around ever more complex arrangements of his favourite music.

Such was the detachment of his mind when he played, he felt as if he were drifting in and out of reality. Even so, he suddenly became aware of someone sitting down gently beside him as he played. Glancing sideways, he saw that it was Sara. She was beaming at him, her face lit up with excitement.

Ordinarily, he would have stopped instantly, flushed and embarrassed, but for some reason he didn't seem to care. Her intoxicating smell, mixed with the music, was like a drug; he felt sedated, calm and peaceful. He continued to play and Sara sat silently at his side, barely a sliver of light between them.

He closed his eyes. Deep from his memory he pulled a new melody and began to play. Sara's eyes moved between Alex's face and his hands, which were dancing over the keys. He felt like he was in a trance, but sensed her move closer to him; her rich perfume intensified with every chord, his playing became ever more fluid, ever more elaborate. Beginning to feel light-headed, he opened his eyes and glanced down at the black and white keys that were rising and falling under his delicate touch; keys that were covered in thick droplets of blood.

Alex's playing faltered as he looked down at his chest and saw the shimmering red liquid had soaked his front as well. Not sure what was happening, he turned to Sara. The smile fell from her mouth to form a scream that he never heard. His eyes clouded and the piano fell away from him into darkness.

CHAPTER 11

TIME TO WRITE

When Alex opened his eyes and saw that he was in his own bed it took him several seconds to remember why. He sat bolt upright, then very quickly slumped back down again onto the hot, clammy pillow.

He felt terrible: light-headed, woozy and sick to the stomach. With some difficulty he turned his sodden pillow over, the coolness of the cotton came as some relief to his spinning head. Hearing a noise to his right he saw the door to his bathroom was open; someone was humming inside.

Despite his condition, his first thought went to the preservation of his modesty. Rummaging quickly under the duvet, he was relieved to feel the soft cotton edging of his Y-fronts and he breathed a sigh of relief. After all, whoever it was in the bathroom, they had more than likely undressed him.

The humming grew closer and Sara appeared in the doorway holding a bowl of water. He threw her a weak smile but she didn't smile back, instead rushing over to him with a concerned look etched across her face. She placed the bowl of water clumsily on the floor before sitting down on a chair that had been placed by the bed.

"You're awake!" she said, almost in a whisper, reaching down to the bowl and pulling out a flannel.

Alex didn't reply; he was still trying to process that Sara was in his bedroom and he was mostly naked. Half expecting to wake up any second, he watched as she wrung out the flannel, folded it in three and placed it on his forehead. Expecting warmth, he gasped as the ice cold material was stretched out across his brow; it instantly brought a cooling relief to his hot head.

"Sorry," she winced. "It's just you've been so hot these last few hours."

"Hours?" Alex said quickly. He was almost convinced he wasn't dreaming.

"Yes, hours. It's gone midnight. You've been passed out all afternoon and evening." *Great. Another day gone with me doing nothing but lying in bed.* "We were both so worried, Alex. Your granddad too." Sara continued, the look of concern on her face returning.

"We?" said Alex "Who's we?" He could feel himself making the same worried look as Sara.

"Well me and Archer," said Sara. "He carried you up here and got you undressed."

Alex died a little inside.

"When you fainted I didn't know what to do, so I ran for help. The first person I met was Archer coming out of his office. He called Henry and came to have a look at you. Alex you were in such a state..." her voice trembled. "You were covered in some sort of blood. And then– "

"What do you mean some *sort* of blood?" Alex felt hot, flustered and more than a little embarrassed. "Blood is blood, isn't it?"

"Well yes, but this looked... different." Sara's voice trailed off, but it didn't matter; Alex wasn't really listening anymore.

"I suppose everyone else knows by now, do they?" He said sulkily. "It was just a nose bleed. Happens all the time, probably?"

"Oh no, no one else knows," said Sara quickly, her eyes wide. "When Henry came in and saw you, he said we weren't to tell anyone. He said he didn't want to worry the rest of the family. Archer brought you straight upstairs and got you into bed. Then Henry asked me if I wouldn't mind looking after you until you were awake. I said... well, I said I didn't mind." She looked a little red around the cheeks.

"Thanks," he said quietly. "I'm sorry, I didn't mean to be rude. It's just that I don't really know what happened. One minute I'm tinkling around at the piano, the next I'm waking up in bed having emptied half of my brain all over the place. It's just a bit weird." He chanced another glance at Sara but she was smiling and gently shaking her head in disbelief. "What? What's so funny?"

"Well, you!" she replied.

"What about me?"

"Well that you think you were just *tinkling around at the piano*? Alex, your playing was incredible! I just find it strange that you're so modest about it, that's all.... when you're not about most other things." Alex shifted in his bed. "By the way, what was that last piece you were playing? Just before you had your nose bleed. I don't think I've ever heard it before."

Alex flushed. He had hoped this question wouldn't come up.

"Well..." the room suddenly felt a lot warmer. "It was just something I started to write a few years ago for someone... I never finished it though, just...

well, I never finished it." Not for the first time, Alex felt like sliding under his duvet and hiding.

Obviously deciding that he was beginning to feel better, Sara's usual confident, playful look returned. "And may I ask whom you were writing that particular piece of music for, Alex?"

Alex paused and then, not really knowing what came over him, he took a deep breath, looked her straight in the eyes and said quietly, "You actually. I was writing it for you."

He expected himself to look away at any second, but he felt surprisingly calm and just held her gaze. He saw her mouth open slightly and heard a short inhale. It was Sara's turn to look away and she stood quickly. Knocking into the bowl of ice cold water, she busied herself with her cardigan and belt, all the time with the tiniest hint of a smile on her lips.

"Well," she gave a small cough. "As you're awake now, I should probably leave you to it. I've got to get home anyway and you probably need some more sleep. So, anyway Alex, I'll see you in a couple of days for our first proper lesson. Ok? Alright well I'll see you then… then."

Sara had said all this in such a rush, Alex hadn't had time to reply. In a whirlwind of curves and perfume she more or less pirouetted towards the door in an emerald haze. Before Alex had said goodbye, she was gone.

He lay there for a few minutes, not really sure what to think about their last exchange. He couldn't help but feel quite pleased. For the first time in recent memory he'd actually managed to say something nice to someone he liked without making an idiot of himself.

Suddenly feeling quite sprightly, he pulled back his duvet and was relieved to feel the cool, refreshing breeze over his body. Planting his feet on the warm, walnut floor, he pushed himself up and stood tentatively by his bed for a few moments. He still felt light-headed, so he walked carefully over to the long wardrobe mirror to take a look at himself. He could see the faint outline of a blood stain that still marked his chest; someone had obviously wiped most of it off. Thinking it must have been some amount of blood to have soaked through his thick clothes and formed a stain so big, he moved closer to the mirror for a better look.

He couldn't see anything unusual or different, like Sara had suggested, but then a thought struck him. He swung round to locate his bloodied clothes. Immediately realising that wasn't the best idea, he stumbled slightly, barely regaining his balance before falling lamely into the mirrored door. Cursing himself, he scanned the room more slowly, but his clothes were nowhere to be seen *Archer must have taken them to be cleaned, The one time I* want *him to be useless and he isn't.*

There was a knock on the door and it immediately began to open. Realising he didn't have time to get back into bed, Alex did the best he could to cover himself up by placing both hands over his nether regions and crossing his legs.

For a split second after it appeared round the door, Archer's face appeared mournful, respectful and even the smallest bit sad. On seeing Alex, however, standing in the middle of the room like he was posing for a life drawing class, Archer's face split into a wide grin before bursting into such raucous laughter he almost dropped the tray he was holding.

"Archer!" shouted Alex. "What the *hell* are you doing? Don't you ever wait for an answer before entering a room?"

Creased up with laughter, Archer couldn't reply. Staggering to the bed, he only just managed to set the tray down without spilling its contents. Alex stood in a silent, seething rage.

Finally managing to pull himself together, Archer pulled a grubby looking handkerchief from inside his black suit jacket and wiped away the tears that were still streaming down his cheeks. Looking Alex up and down, he walked to the end of the bed and pulled a cosy-looking thick, grey dressing gown from under the duvet. He threw it to Alex who caught it with both hands, revealing his blue pants. Archer snorted again as Alex quickly robed himself.

"I *am* sorry Master Wolf," said Archer, clearly not sorry at all. "I've just seen Ms. Harris downstairs and she said you were up and about, so I thought I'd bring you some supper. A bacon sandwich, in fact, as you seem to like them so much?"

He lifted a plate from the tray and turned around to display a very tempting looking sandwich.

"Brown or red?" Alex asked suspiciously.

"Brown, of course,"

Alex was still angry, but nonetheless rather moved by this unexpectedly thoughtful gesture. Remembering he hadn't seen Archer since the previous sandwich incident, he thought it best to tone down his angry rhetoric.

"Well in that case," he started haughtily, "I shall accept it."

He gently took the plate from Archer with both hands. Trying to regain some dignity, he walked slowly to the bed, sat down and began to ravenously devour the sandwich. Archer watched on with a wry smile on his face. Within a minute, the sandwich was gone and Alex was wiping the excess brown sauce from around his mouth with the sleeve of his dressing gown.

"Enjoy that, did we?" said Archer, eyebrows raised.

"Hmm, yes it wasn't bad thank you, Archer. I don't suppose you'd rattle off and get me another one could you, old chap?" Alex grinned at Archer, clumps of white bread lodged between his teeth.

Archer's smile disappeared. "Don't push it."

Alex suddenly remembered about his clothes.

"Archer," he wasn't really sure how to proceed with this one. "You know earlier?"

"You mean when you had a nose bleed and passed out?" Archer said.

"Well, yes, when I had my near-death experience." Archer rolled his eyes but Alex continued anyway. "What happened to my clothes? I wanted to check something but I couldn't find them anywhere."

"Your grandfather took them. Said he would sort them out." replied Archer stiffly.

"He took them? He's not going to clean them is he?"

"I'm not sure what he's going to do with them. I think he just wanted to avoid any *more* embarrassment for you, that's all."

Well this has all turned out rather well. As far as Alex was concerned, he was perfectly happy for the incident never to be mentioned again.

"And by the way," continued Archer, "We've decided not to mention this little episode to anyone else. Do you understand? *No one* else."

Archer sounded so serious it made Alex suspicious, despite his relief. "Well I don't have a problem with that, but why? Why all the secrecy?"

"There's no secret, Alex." Archer moved closer. "We just thought you'd prefer it that way, that's all. If you start telling everyone now, they might wonder why *we* didn't tell them about it first." He was almost standing over Alex and a little too close for comfort.

"Ok–ok fine. Well I'm hardly going to tell anyone, am I?"

"Good!" said Archer. "Then that's the end of it. Oh your grandfather did suggest that this whole experience might make a good first entry in your new diary. I've put it on your desk, in case you were wondering."

Archer glanced over Alex's shoulder. Alex turned to see the black box sitting on top of his desk. He felt oddly compelled to say something highly unusual, assuming it didn't catch in his throat.

"Thanks for helping me out earlier, Archer." he said quietly, followed by a small cough. "It was good of you."

It was Archer's turn to look taken aback. Alex saw a flicker of surprise in his eyes before he straightened up and said stiffly, "My pleasure, Master Wolf. Just doing my job."

With a nod, Archer picked up the empty plate, placed it on the tray and walked out of the room, closing the door quietly behind him.

Alex lay back on his bed and stared at the walls. It was nearly 1am. Not feeling in the slightest bit tired he got up, walked to his desk and stared at the open black box. He rolled out his high backed desk chair and slowly took out the diary.

He decided that he didn't like the look of it. It was far too plain and new. Maybe if he did keep up with the promised diary-keeping it would become more tatty, battered and worn over time, just like the old Norwegian fjords and British insect books that sat on his shelves.

Opening the cover, he pressed down hard on the spine to try and make it lie flat and did the same to the first two pages. He then sat blankly in front of this plain canvas, not entirely sure what to do next.

He had never written a proper diary before and didn't really know what he was supposed to be writing about. His granddad had said *anything at all* but this seemed very vague and unhelpful. He told himself that he should just give it a go and write about the events of the day. But not before he had prepared properly.

Doing a quick sweep of his room, he gathered an assortment of items: headphones, remote control, a small black notebook, a glass of milk from the small fridge under his desk, a pair of comfortable slippers, an old pipe belonging to his granddad and his favourite pen that he had found in his desk drawer.

Sliding his feet into his open-backed leather slippers, he sat down comfortably on the desk chair, pulled a coaster from the desk drawer and placed the cold glass of milk on top of it. Then he slid both to the left hand side of the open diary. Refreshments in place, he dropped the large, comfortable headphones over his head, adjusted the headband slightly and plugged the long cable into the socket at the back of his desk. Choosing some of his more subtle music, he listened carefully as it began to pipe directly into his ears. The mood set, he opened up the small black notebook and pulled the lid from the pen, revealing an ink-covered nib. He scratched out a few practice words on the notepad. Finally, he took the old pipe and placed it firmly in the corner of his mouth, as he had seen his granddad do so many times before. The slightly bitter, musty taste in his mouth didn't exactly tally with the sweet, woody aroma that plumed from the chamber of his granddad's smoking pipe, but it was pleasant enough. He imagined that he probably looked rather distinguished and important.

Sadly, he found that he was no more ready to write than when he had started his short preparation ritual. He sighed loudly and shifted in his chair.

As bizarre a task as this was, he had promised his granddad that he would do it, so there was no going back.

He clicked the volume up with his remote a couple more notches. Instead of the music being merely a background noise, it filled his head and began to separate him from the surrounding world. He looked at the stark, blank page in front of him and once again smelt the rich leather binding, the paper, and the old pipe's tobacco. Finally he began to write in his best handwriting.

Yesterday I was woken up by my mum and I had to get dressed really quickly because I was really late for going to see grandma and dad in a meeting I had with them that I had been told about the night before. I put on some stupid clothes, not on purpose but because I was rushing and then I ran downstairs to see them but it didn't go very well because when I went in they said that I couldn't have any of my money then they gave my brother a car which I wanted.

Alex paused, carefully thinking about what he should write next. As he sucked on the end of his pen, staring at the page, desperately willing more words to come, the words began to slowly un-write themselves. It was as if they were made from a long line of tautly strung black cotton that was slowly winding itself back onto a reel.

Alex stared, not quite believing what he was seeing. He couldn't take his eyes off it. The incredible un-writing had almost finished. As it reached the first 'T' the globule of black ink that had collected on the page sat still for a second and then vanished. Staring at the blank page, Alex reached for the glass of cold milk, took out the pipe and took two big gulps. He placed the pipe back into his mouth and decided to try again.

Yesterday morning mum woke me up and I had to get dressed really fast because I was really late for going to see dad and grandma in a meeting I was supposed to be having with them. I put some clothes on but because I was in a rush they weren't very clean and smelt a bit

But the same thing happened again, only the words retracted faster than before. It was if the page was trying to shed itself of his writing as quickly as possible. He racked his brain for an explanation.

Of course! This is one of his Granddad's little tricks. Vanishing ink or something. No wonder he'd been so serious about me writing in it. He wants me to get caught out with his funny book. Well, I'll show him! Alex tried again, scribbling his words across the page as quickly as he could. No matter how much ink he used on the page, the book was faster at removing it. Alex felt ridiculous.

How is it doing that? He sat back in his chair and let the music settle his increasing annoyance. Glancing over his shoulder at the clock on the wall he saw it was nearly 2.00am. He wasn't feeling even close to being tired.

Rocking back gently in his chair, he slid both hands behind his head, as if trying to massage an answer out of his confused brain. Briefly feeling something hard and rough, he stopped. He began to burrow carefully through his thick hair. With some deft finger work, he located the lump. It felt like a clump of dried blood; Sara must have missed it when he'd been lying on his back.

He began scraping at his scalp and within seconds had pulled away the scabby lump, with a yelp and several hairs. Although the dried blood had clotted almost black, there was something odd about it. It shimmered as he turned it in the light, as though it was slightly metallic. Feeling a wet trickle down the back of his neck, he touched the soft skin below his hairline and his fingers slid across his nape. He looked at them; they were covered in bright red blood that must have been sitting under the hard dark carapace. The wet blood had the same reflective sheen, but it was so much more pronounced. As Alex moved his fingers in the light his blood glistened and danced; the silver mixing with the red like coloured mercury.

Just as he was starting to become unnerved by this strange and unnatural substance he caught sight of his pen. It rolled slowly across the desktop and dropped off the edge. Without thinking he shot out his hand and caught it before it hit the floor, instantly cursing himself. Silver-red blood was smeared over the pristine pen's barrel. But there was something else. The pen had begun to glow bright yellow. Alex stared, mesmerised at the pulsating light. Without warning, the pen burst into flames; intense white flames.

Alex shrieked and tried to throw the pen across the desk, but he couldn't. It was stuck resolutely to his hand and was getting hotter by the second. An intense pain began to course through his outstretched open palm and he watched in horror as the flames grew higher and higher. With every inch taller they burned, the pain in his hand intensified. Tears of pain and panic began to flow down his face and in desperation he grabbed the open diary with his free hand, trying to beat down the ever growing inferno. Through a haze of watery eyes he realised that the diary had burst into flames as well. But they were no longer white; the fire had turned black.

Alex felt a growing sense of calm and curious wonder. Although the fire burned ever higher, it was no longer hot. The pain had all but disappeared and he sat mesmerised in his chair, book in one hand, pen in the other, both engulfed in dancing black fire.

Gently, he placed both items onto his desk, somehow knowing that the fire wouldn't burn the wooden surface. His heart was racing and he could feel the blood pumping through his veins and arteries. Almost sensing what he should do next, he picked up the fiery pen. Its curiously cold metal body sent a pulse racing over his skin and the lights in the room flickered and died. Turning to the first white page of the burning diary, Alex pressed the pen nib to the smooth white page and began to write.

Words seemed to just form on the page before him. Although he didn't know how he was doing it, or even what he was writing, it felt right. It was as if the words were being drawn from his mind and translated directly onto the page, bypassing his consciousness altogether. He didn't even feel he had to move his hand; it was moving of its own accord, as if he was a strange motorised automaton.

He watched page after page go by, all the time trying to read his own words as the pen darted across the open diary, but he couldn't keep up. He caught a word or two, a half sentence here or there. He read the names of people he knew, snatches of feelings and thoughts he'd had but never shared. The intensity of the writing increased with every page, drawing more energy from him with every stroke of his pen. He tried to focus, but he could feel his eyes begin to drop; a blanket of tiredness was being drawn over him and he was swept into deep sleep. His writing continued.

CHAPTER 12

RAGE

The withered old man had been perched on his throne-like stone seat for two days, trying desperately to sleep. As he sat slumped against the hard surfaces, his ragged black cloak the only source of warmth in his dark and miserable cave, he felt a sudden and painful twinge in his right leg. He tried to shake it out, putting it down to cramp and old age and cursing his old joints that creaked and cracked with every movement. The twinge spread to his left leg and then up through his whole body. A slow realisation dawned on the old man and a manic grin spread across his gnarled and scarred face, his chipped and blackened teeth barely visible in the darkness.

He waited for the twinges to subside and then snatched up the thick and battered old book that was sitting on the rough floor. Desperately riffling through the pages, he reached the last but one. He stared at the page as thin black writing began to appear from nowhere, letter by letter.

Alexander Gunnar Wolf - born. 1991 - died.   :
V1 - DoSW

He stared at the words in shock and let out a horrendous scream of rage and fury. This was *not* how it was supposed to be.

CHAPTER 13

SOFIA'S ROOM

At dawn the following day, and for the first time since he had left school, Alex awoke peacefully and without fuss. Feeling entirely relaxed and not in the least bit tired, he enjoyed the feeling of warm sunshine on his face as it streamed in through the tall bedroom windows.

He rolled lazily out of bed and walked to his bathroom. Once under the shower, he spent far longer than was strictly necessary, savouring the hot powerful jets of water on his body. As he closed his eyes and washed his hair under the large shower head, the last signs of the previous day's nose bleed swirled down the chrome drain hole, unseen.

After showering, he spent a further half hour in his cavernous bathroom admiring himself from different angles, until he was completely satisfied. It wasn't until he came out of the bathroom and glanced over to the desk that everything came flooding back.

The nose bleed. Sara. The writing. The fire! He dashed over to his desk and picked up the diary. Flicking through it, he found nothing but blank empty pages; there was no writing there at all. He looked across the rest of his desk. There was his empty glass of milk on a coaster next to his headphones; next to them lay the remote control. Lying behind them all was the pen. He picked it up and looked at it closely. There wasn't a trace of blood on it, nor any sign of the black fire that had engulfed it. He stood in his towel, deeply confused.

Did last night really happen? He clearly remembered the wet blood on his head that had caused the fire. He also remembered writing page after page of words so quickly that he couldn't keep up. But what he *couldn't* remember was falling asleep, or even going to bed for that matter.

Running to his wardrobe he pulled out some dark jeans, yellow trainers and a white V-necked t-shirt; there was no time for tweed. By the look of the bright blue sky, he guessed it was probably going to be a hot one, too.

Quickly checking himself in the mirror, he grabbed his diary and pen and left the room, being careful to lock the door behind him. He walked briskly down the cool hallway, past the newly arranged floral displays, and down the first flight of stairs to the hallway below. He heard the sound of muffled giggling behind him.

Alex froze to the spot, listening intently. Nothing. He began to creep theatrically back down the lower landing, stopping outside the room he thought he had heard the noises coming from. It was Lewis's bedroom.

He leant in closer to the door. There it was again; by the sound of it, Lewis had someone in there with him and unless Alex was very much mistaken, it was a girl. A mischievous grin spread slowly across his face.

If Lewis has let a girl stay over in his room he's going to be in so much trouble. Brilliant! Alex's mind was already working furiously on ways to relay this information to his staunchly traditional grandmother, dropping Lewis right in it. Crouching down, being careful not to drop his diary and pen, he positioned himself right in front of the solid door and leant forward, trying to peer in through the silver keyhole. Unable to see much, he carefully adjusted himself so he could see further into the room. He could just about see a figure on the other side of the door…

"Alexander Wolf! What *do* you think you are doing?"

Alex shrieked, fell forward and head-butted the door which, unfortunately, swung open. He tumbled headlong into Lewis's bedroom and lay sprawled prostrate on his front. He heard the sound of muted footsteps on the thickly carpeted floor; when he eventually turned himself over, he was greeted by three looming faces: his brother, Lisa Manners and, worst of all, his grandmother. Lewis looked confused, Lisa looked haughty and arrogant as always, but his grandmother had a face like thunder.

"Get up this *instant*," she hissed.

Before the sentence had even left her mouth, Alex had scrabbled to his feet. He stood, red-faced and sheepish, between the three of them. Not knowing where to look, he chose straight down.

"Well, explain yourself, Alexander," started Sofia brusquely.

Alex racked his brain desperately for something that would explain why he'd been caught listening at Lewis's keyhole.

"I… I was just coming to see how Lewis was and…" He stammered.

"And?" His Grandma said.

Alex knew she still didn't believe him about the girls' changing room incident; to her this was probably just further proof. He thought for a moment more and then he had it.

"*And...* I wanted to give him his pen back," he said triumphantly and with a flourish he whipped the pen from his hand, holding it up high as if it was some sort of beacon of truth.

"His pen?" Said Sofia, snatching it from him and eyeing it suspiciously.

"Yes, I err... found it earlier. Thought it was his," said Alex quickly.

"I knocked on the door but no-one was in, so I, erm... crouched down to put it under the door–which is why I was crouching down, you see–but then I heard someone laughing and I thought it might be burglars... oh, and then you startled me, so I fell through door." Alex's eyes darted nervously between each member of his three panel jury.

"That's not even my pen, Al," said Lewis quietly.

"Oh," said Alex in mock surprise. "Oh yes! You're right, well no bother. My mistake. I'll just be going then–" He turned to leave.

"Not so fast, Alexander. I think you owe your brother and Miss Manners here an apology, don't you?" Came his grandma's soft yet dangerous voice.

"But I didn't do anything wrong, did I?" Said Alex innocently. "If I'd realised Lisa had stopped overnight and was in Lewis's bedroom I wouldn't have gone anywhere near his door."

Lewis bristled slightly and Lisa–entirely unnecessarily in Alex's opinion–gasped loudly in feigned shock. Alex wouldn't have been surprised if he'd seen her faint into his brother's arms. Alex could have sworn he could see her hackles raising. His lame attempt at deflecting the issue onto Lewis had not been wise.

"I can assure you that Miss Manners did *not* spend the night, Alex. Lewis knows the rules of my house, even if *you* think he does not! Miss Manners here came by invitation to have breakfast with us this morning, which you would have known, had you been up at a reasonable hour. I think that you owe both your brother and Miss Manners an apology."

"But–"

"*Now!*" Sofia said.

"It's alright, Al. You don't have to apologise to us. If you say you were giving me my pen back, I believe you. It's not a problem. I'm sure Lisa feels the same way too."

Alex looked up at his brother; he had a look of almost encouraging pity on his face. He chanced a glance at Lisa; she clearly wasn't satisfied with the lack of an apology but was keeping quiet nonetheless, no doubt just to keep Lewis happy.

"Well," Sofia said in a tone of respectful pride. "That's very magnanimous of your brother, but of course I would expect nothing less of him. Even though *you* do not deserve it."

"Mag-what?" said Alex before he could stop himself.

"It means generous and forgiving." said Lisa.

"Exactly, Miss Manners," said Sofia.

Alex rolled his eyes.

"Anyway, we'd better get going," said Lewis, addressing his grandma. "Lisa and I are heading out for the day, thought we'd take the car out for a drive."

Alex's eyes darted to Lewis's hands, where the glass and metal key was dangling loosely on one finger.

"Yes of course, dear. You two had better get going then. Enjoy yourselves, won't you." Said Sofia, all the time smiling nastily at Alex.

Lisa brushed past Alex, giving him a dirty look before Sofia joined her out in the hallway, leaving Alex and Lewis alone in the room.

"You can come with us too if you like, Al. I'm sure Lisa wouldn't mind."

"You sure about that are you?" Alex mumbled.

Lewis looked disappointed. As he walked past Alex he patted him gently on the shoulder. "Maybe some other time then, eh."

Lewis left the room. Alex stood there silently, feeling like a complete turnip. Thinking everyone had gone, he turned around and recoiled in shock. Standing right behind him was his grandmother. She was smiling at him like he was that evening's dinner.

"I want a word with you, young man," she said quietly. "Follow me."

Alex didn't dare disobey or answer back so he followed her silently, closing Lewis's bedroom door behind him as he went. They walked out into the hallway, past the main staircase and began the long march to the end of the west corridor.

In all his years of visiting, Alex couldn't remember ever venturing as far down that particular corridor. It was the way to his grandmother's private rooms and he had never had any inclination to go anywhere near them.

Maybe it was his imagination, but as they moved further down the corridor Alex was sure the temperature was dropping. He reasoned that it was probably kept that bit chillier since, after all, rancid old corpses tended to get a bit whiffy when they warmed up. He chuckled to himself, but then quickly put it out of mind. Laughing out loud would probably be the last mistake he ever made.

Unlike Alex's upper hallway which ended abruptly in a stone wall, this one ended in a large set of double doors. Sofia pushed both of them wide open and swept through; they swung closed behind her. Alex hesitated, not sure if he was supposed to follow her inside or not. Her voice called out from the other side, "Come in, Alex. It's quite safe."

Far from convinced, he pushed on the tall black doors which opened surprisingly easily. Whatever he'd been expecting, it was *not* what greeted his eyes.

CHAPTER 14

UNDERGROUND

Knowing his grandmother's penchant for stark, clean, minimal spaces, her private room came as a bit of a shock.

It was certainly bright enough inside, but it looked and felt old; really old, as though it hadn't been redecorated since the house had been built, hundreds of years ago. The first thing that struck Alex was the height of the room. If he hadn't known better, he would have said it was at least twice the height of his own. Although the ceiling was grubby and crumbling, it was beautifully framed with elaborate cornicing and a spectacular ceiling rose, all covered in very fine gold leaf.

The room was square, with alcoves of all sizes adding interest to every wall. Not that they needed it; every available inch seemed to be covered by paintings. There were hundreds of them. In fact, there was hardly any need for wallpaper at all. There were portraits of men, women and families; landscapes of countryside, mountains, lakes and rivers; and abstract images, some colourful, others faded and dull.

Still in the doorway, Alex noticed something else; there was hardly any furniture. A small desk sat in front of the large window on the far wall and next to it, an elegant old wooden chair. A battered and frayed chaise longue was positioned neatly in the corner and an elaborately-carved wooden wardrobe stood on the nearside wall. It felt as though someone had moved out years ago and the new occupant hadn't bothered to bring much furniture with them.

Sofia was sitting at the desk with her back to Alex. As he drew closer she craned her neck around to look at him, sliding a small black notebook into the desk drawer. She gestured for him to sit on the chaise by the desk. It creaked loudly as he perched in the middle, so he positioned himself closer to the more solid edge of the seat, worried the cushioned part might suddenly give way. His grandmother turned slowly in her chair to look directly at him. She held up his pen.

"Oh," he said, surprised. "I'd forgotten about that. Thanks."

He leaned forward and reached out but Sofia didn't move.

"I thought you had," she said, not taking her eyes off Alex. "And may I ask where you got this pen from?"

Alex was taken aback, not only by the question but also by the sudden pleasantness of his grandmother's tone.

"Erm..." he thought for a moment. "Birthday present, I think. Or Christmas maybe. One of them, anyway."

He laughed nervously at his grandma's quizzical look. She stared at him without speaking for a long while before placing the pen softly back down on her desk. Alex began to feel very uncomfortable. Fidgeting on his seat, he heard it creak and crack underneath him. His grandmother opened another drawer of her desk. Although ridiculous, the image of his grandma pulling out a gun and shooting him suddenly popped into his head. When she pulled out her hand though, it held a piece of light blue paper. Alex leaned forward to see what was on it but couldn't make anything out.

"Right," said Sofia, suddenly smiling. "I think it's about time that you signed this, Alex."

"Err... what is it?" He eyed it suspiciously.

Although he wasn't particularly good at business, Alex had learned a long time ago that it was not a good idea to go signing things without checking them first. Sofia smiled broadly at him, which didn't ease his paranoia.

"It's a legal document that authorises the immediate release of 10% of your trust fund directly into your bank account."

Alex nearly fell off his chaise in surprise. "What? It's *what*?" He said, trying to keep an enormous smile from forming on his face.

"I think you heard, Alex." said Sofia quietly.

"But... but you said I wasn't allowed any?" His voice was filled with barely contained disbelief.

"Well, I've had a change of heart. I was perhaps a little too hard on you before and, all things considered, I feel that you may deserve this small treat."

She leaned forward, holding out the form in one hand and pointing to the bottom of the page with the other; her long, manicured talon gently scratched the paper. In his excitement, Alex missed the slightly awkward smile stretched across Sofia's wrinkled face.

"All you have to do is sign here and the money can be put across to your account right away."

Alex reached out and slowly took the piece of paper from her. Reading it through, it seemed to be a fairly standard legal document; meaning he hardly understood any of it. But it was the headline figure that he was most interested in.

...I hereby do agree to the amount of £1,000,000.00 being transferred to a bank account of my choosing. This sum represents 10% (ten percent) of the value of my trust fund and will be deducted from the total to be received hereafter...

Alex could feel his pulse racing and he squirmed excitedly on his seat.

One million pounds! Visions of cars, expensive toys and ever more elaborate safes flashed through his mind. What would he buy first with all this lovely money?

Remembering what he was supposed to be doing, he scanned to the bottom of the page and saw three signature spaces: one for him, one for his grandmother and one for his father. Sofia had already signed hers but the other two were blank. Alex looked up at his grandma.

"And Dad's agreed to this as well, has he?"

"He will do when I tell him, yes." She said stiffly.

Alex thought it was odd that she hadn't discussed this with his dad yet; but then, she was the boss and who was he to complain? Without another word, Alex took his pen, placed the paper securely onto the leather-topped desk and signed the document.

Sofia whisked it out from under his hand, folded it twice and slid it into the desk drawer.

"Done!" she said briskly. "Now if you could leave me, Alexander, I have things to do."

She didn't look at him but simply turned in her seat, pulled out her small black notebook and began to write. Alex sat in silence for a few moments, confused by the abrupt ending of the meeting.

"I'll just... go then," he said.

When he didn't receive any sort of response he waited for a few more seconds, stood and hurried to the doors, trying not to appear as if he was running. Closing them behind him, he stopped briefly on the other side, took a long deep breath and began the long walk down the hallway. Faster and faster his feet carried him, eventually breaking into a silent, leaping run; his fists punched high into the air in mute celebration.

This is brilliant! No more relying on handouts. No more relying on pocket money. I'm independently wealthy and ready to spend! He descended the main staircase three steps at a time, running his hands on the carved bannister rail as he went. On the second-to-last step, however, he tripped and lost his footing. He fell hard onto the cold stone floor of the entrance hall.

Something cracked in his wrist and an incredible wave of pain flooded his brain. He tried to cry out, but his tongue seemed to be lodged in his constricted throat. Through tear-drenched eyes he saw his hand hanging limply, almost at a right angle to his forearm. The pain was excruciating and the sight caused a wave of nausea; there was nothing he could do to make it stop.

Clutching his forearm, he gritted his teeth and rolled onto his back. Above him he could see the bright sunshine flooding in through the tall entrance hall windows. Images of driving along sunlit country roads with Sara at his side flashed unexpectedly into his mind, as if his brain was trying to distract him from the agony. As he squinted against the bright sunlight the vision seemed to fade. The sky outside had suddenly become black, as if time had leapt forward twelve hours. Alex stopped his gentle rocking, the pain momentarily forgotten at the shock of this sudden change. He blinked rapidly, trying to clear his eyes from the tears. He sniffed loudly. A nasty aroma caught in his nostrils.

Something foul-smelling was nearby and getting closer by the second. With a great effort, Alex pushed himself to a sitting position and sat nervously for a moment in the dark room.

Without warning, the ground beneath him began to move and he found himself slowly rotating on the spot; as if he had fallen onto the platter of an enormous record player. The huge Wolf crest on which he was sitting was rotating. What's more, with every half turn it seemed to have risen several inches. In his panic, Alex shuffled off the rapidly rising platform, using his feet and one good arm to push himself as quickly as he could.

The stench in the room was becoming overwhelming. Alex dropped from the rotating disc and onto the floor. His wrist jarred with the impact and he winced again in agony.

The family crest stopped moving. Raised around 2 feet from the floor, all Alex could see beneath it was a dark, shadowy void. One thing was certain though; it was clearly the source of the gut-wrenching odour.

He didn't know what compelled him, but Alex pushed himself closer to the black space. Leaning over the vast emptiness, he timidly peered into the darkness. A wrinkled and scabbed hand darted out from the hole and grabbed Alex around his broken wrist. He screamed out in fear and pain, but these were nothing compared to what he felt when the strong hand began to drag him slowly towards the shadowy opening.

His head was spinning and he tried desperately to break free. He heard his fingernails scraping against the hard stone floor and his own desperate pleading whimpers, but they did nothing to stop his progress. Whatever waited for him in the dark was too strong by far. Bit by bit it pulled him ever closer to the rim of the broken seal.

Finding his voice, Alex cried out for help, but the sound was deadened, as if it was stuck inside his head and wouldn't reach any further than his own ears. His broken arm had been completely swallowed in darkness and inch by inch his face was being drawn towards the edge. Despite the pain, he twisted and writhed, arching his body upwards. As he did, he glanced down and saw directly in to the hole. A twisted, withered face of evil, wide-eyed and panting, was grinning up at him as it pulled mercilessly on his arm. Inhaling a great lungful of foul air, Alex desperately screamed again. He thought he heard the faint sound of running footsteps, but he knew it was too late. He was dragged headlong into the void.

CHAPTER 15

FEAR

In total darkness, Alex was being dragged along the ground by his broken wrist. He could feel the rough stone floor beneath him; every bump seemed to be magnified tenfold. He tried to stand, but he was being pulled along at such a rate that he couldn't get any kind of firm foothold. Desperately he tried to yank his arm away, but that only brought further pain. The long, thick nails of the thing that was dragging him cut into his skin. He felt warm blood begin to trickle down his arm. Every breath Alex took filled his lungs with the foul stench of his captor. Just as he managed to catch a breath, the thing started to chant words that poured pure, cold fear into his heart.

"Beneath the ground in corners dark, a terror waits inside your heart, that makes you want to call out loud, to join the safety of the crowd. It walks at night, fear stalks about. One cut, one slash, the lights go out. Though please don't count on daylight hope, for hanging by the blood stained rope, a body swings, a victim dead, the monster takes another head..."

Alex began to scream loudly; it must have had some effect. The thing that had been dragging him instantly released its grip and Alex's head cracked against the hard stone floor. Slipping into unconsciousness, he heard a horrible, low cackle and saw a rough, yellowing hand coming towards him. A silver bracelet hung loose around its wrist. Once again, the darkness swallowed him.

CHAPTER 16

AN OLD TALE

Someone was drilling into his head; drilling a huge hole into the side of his head and then stabbing his brain with needles. Or at least that's how it felt.

Alex half opened his eyes, not entirely sure where he was going to find himself or what horrors he was about to see. He needn't have worried though; he was in complete darkness. Strangely, he couldn't feel any pain either.

Sitting in the dark, he pondered mournfully that his wrist must be so badly damaged that it had gone beyond normal pain. But as he moved his hands slowly he found he could actually move them both perfectly well. He held them both up in front of his face but couldn't see them, no matter how much he squinted. He wiggled the fingers on his left hand and gently examined his wrist. It felt completely normal, as if it had never been broken. Ever so quietly he sniffed the air. Nothing.

At least the foul stench of that monstrous man has disappeared. Maybe he's left me alone in his lair to go and find another victim to drag into the darkness. A shudder ran down Alex's spine. He could feel that he was sitting on some sort of hard chair. Slowly reaching out in front of him, he found what felt like a glass table. He squinted into the darkness again, waiting in vain for his eyes to adjust. He coughed. The way it echoed, suggested he was in a large space; but where?

With a start, Alex heard the short, unmistakable scratch of a match being struck, and barely two feet in front of him, a dazzling flash of bright yellow flame. The flame descended slowly and disappeared for a second, replaced by the pulsing red glow of newly-lit shag. The triple pop of someone sucking noisily on the end of a mouthpiece followed. In the small glow from the smouldering tobacco, Alex saw the grinning features of Henry Wolf, sitting directly opposite him.

Alex gasped, ready to exclaim loudly, but Henry swiftly moved a finger to his mouth, warning him to be quiet. The light from his pipe was still too dim to reveal anything other than his grandfather's head, floating mysteriously in space.

"Thank you for joining me, dear boy," said Henry in a barely audible whisper, his eyes twinkling in the ebbing light. "It would seem you've met a friend of mine."

"*What?*" said Alex loudly.

Henry's eyes widened and Alex saw the end of the pipe droop a couple of inches. "Keep your voice down old chap!" he wheezed, his eyes flicking from side to side.

"What do you mean *a friend of yours*? You know what that thing is?" hissed Alex.

"He's not a *thing*," choked Henry, swallowing a cough. "He's a person!" He placed the pipe back in his mouth; the lit end continued to hover just below his nose. "Granted, he's not the ah… best-kept of chaps, or the most subtle for that matter, but he more than likely saved your life earlier."

"Bullsh–"

"I tell you it's true, Alex." Henry said gravely.

"Well then he's got a funny way of saving my life. I go and break my wrist– nearly *dying* in the process–and he appears from the depths of the earth like some stinking old mole and drags me into this filthy pit with him!"

Henry rolled his eyes and shook his head, chuckling. Alex watched the embers of Henry's pipe glow from red-black to bright orange and back, each change accompanied by a fresh breeze of sweet tobacco.

"You know, I'm amazed you haven't ended up on the stage, the way you carry on sometimes." said Henry, still chortling to himself.

"Very funny," said Alex, half stung and half imagining himself standing under bright spotlights with an audience all chanting his name. "Well what was he doing if he wasn't trying to kill me? And how do *you* know him?"

"One thing at a time Alex," started Henry, sounding panicked. "And for goodness' sake keep your voice down. You don't know who might be listening."

Henry's eyes shifted from side to side, uselessly peering into the pitch black to check that there was no-one else here with them. He leaned in, over the table, and Alex instinctively did the same.

"I don't know everything. Far from it, in fact. But I know that his name is Frederik and he is very real. He's also very old, very bitter and very, *very* angry. And from what I know about this business, he has every reason to be, so you'd do well not to cross him. If you ever encounter him again there should be no answering back and *no* cheek. He has a grudge to bear, that's for sure. But not against me and not against you."

Henry paused to let these words sink in for a moment. Then, as if he had plucked it from the dark itself, he produced a large, green, leather-bound book. Even in the low light, Alex could see it was incredibly old; far older than any book he had ever seen. It was very plain, but the edges were cracked and the leather looked dry. Many of the pages looked like they'd been damp, the edges crinkled like layers of pastry. A single piece of taut black ribbon was tied around it, keeping the contents together.

"I want you to read this," said Henry quietly.

"Where did you get it from?" Alex said suspiciously.

"I got it from the family library, albeit far down in one of the deeper vaults. Frederik suggested I would find it there. Here, take it."

Henry held out the book. Despite his misgivings, Alex took it very carefully in both hands. It felt unnaturally heavy and it gave a dull thud when he placed it on the table. He quickly untied the ribbon, being careful not to damage it, and slowly opened the cover. The first few pages were indeed water-damaged, but blank all the same. On the fourth, however, there was some writing. It was very faint and too small to read from a distance. He looked up, about to say something, but Henry was already holding out a pocket magnifying glass and a small torch on a keying. Raising one eyebrow, Alex took them both.

"Prepared as ever, are we?" said Alex.

Henry didn't say anything, merely harrumphing quietly and sucking loudly on his pipe. Alex leaned in close to the page, clicked on the torch and placed the magnifying glass barely an inch above the page. He began to read.

Annelise & Frederik, sent from the Norse gods, were gifted with immortal life. Of these facts, neither was aware. As lovers and friends they lived their favoured life between the mountains and fjords of Norway, amongst the mortals of a small village. They enjoyed life without fear, regret or worry.

While their home was in Norway they would spend many months travelling, taking in nature and all of the world's beauty, recording all the things that they would see in books of great worth. They carried these books everywhere they went so that they could always record their experiences, their thoughts, their feelings, sights, tastes, sounds, and smells.

Little did they realise, this was exactly the task for which they had been created - to keep a record of all things and to seek out the most enchanting experiences for every human sense. The gods wanted to better understand man so they could control him. Knowing how to stimulate the senses of the world's mortals would let the gods rule unchallenged.

Annelise was a most talented artist and Frederik, a master of words. Together, these skills enabled them to record rich tapestries that would allow the reader or listener, for they often shared their tales with others, to easily conjure vivid images in their minds.

They travelled all over the world safely and without any troubles, protected as they were by the gods. However, upon returning home from a trip that had lasted many years they found their village at war and their community in despair, victims of an unknown force that could not be overcome.

In the chaos that ensued, Annelise and Frederik were attacked. After a short fight, Annelise lay dead.

Frederik was lost. He did not understand the nature of death and what it meant, for in all their years they had never experienced death. Death was so incomprehensible to Frederik that he sat with Annelise for many months in their home, waiting for her to wake up. He brought food and water every day and would talk to her as though she was asleep, her eyes just closed momentarily.

For many years Frederik did not write in the books of feeling, but in time he was compelled to express what he was experiencing. Death, grief, loss, devastation, anger, betrayal were now the subjects of his writing.

The books he had written with Annelise were to remain untouched so he began again, writing a single book that held all of his new feelings. With nothing to stop him, he wrote unchecked for many years, pouring everything he had into the pages. Never leaving the house, he shut out the light of the sun.

Overwhelmed by his own feelings, he forgot about Annelise. He didn't check on her, he didn't speak to her, he didn't look at her.

One morning he awoke to find his Annelise nothing more than bones. Tormented by grief at the sight of his love he had neglected, Frederik tore at himself to release his pain.

After many more years, with his home overgrown and black inside, Frederik discovered that the bones of his loved one were gone. Knowing then the true nature of grief and suffering, having written about it for so long, it gnawed at him from within.

Having failed to care for Annelise in death, her soul was trapped between worlds and began to haunt Frederik's waking hours, sending him visions of destruction and devastation, of life on Earth bereft of the good and pure things that they had spent so many years documenting.

Frederik feared he was succumbing to madness but in that moment, he was visited by Loki.

Loki talked to Frederik about what had happened with Annelise. He told Frederik that the only way to conquer his grief and release Annelise was to reveal to him the secrets of the books. Loki wanted to learn the five elements of the senses so that he could control mankind alone, and become the most worshipped of all gods. In return for the books' secrets, Loki would not only release Annelise from her turmoil, but also give Frederik the name of her murderer.

Frederik read the chronicles to Loki over many years and revealed all the secrets he and Annelise had discovered; but in doing so, he became weaker until eventually he could read no longer. Loki became stronger as he learnt more about the life of humans and their finest experiences. Finally, each of the chronicles had been read and Frederik was spent.

True to his word, Loki set Annelise free to rest in peace forever, then whispered the name of her killer in Frederik's ear.

But Frederik was too weak to act, as the reading of the chronicles had stretched him beyond his means. He had the knowledge but not the means to avenge his dearest Annelise.

This was a torment greater than any he had felt since Annelise's death. Laying broken in the dark, he vowed to return and seek revenge on those that had caused him such pain. He would grow strong and bring vengeance with him.

As he finished the last sentence, Alex felt a strange emotion come over him. It was partly pity for the pain the man in the story had suffered, but mostly it was a rising incredulity that the Frederik in the book could be the same man he had met earlier. He looked up at Henry who was staring at him as if he had read his mind.

"I know what you're thinking, my boy, and I understand why. But I tell you, it's all true."

"How can it be true?" Alex said, forgetting to lower his voice again.

"Alex, be quiet!" Henry whispered almost as loudly as Alex. He was looking out into the darkness, his eyes moving rapidly across the empty space like he was following an invisible fly. "First things first, close that book and tie up its ribbon. It shouldn't be left open for any longer than is strictly necessary."

Alex did as he was told.

"Right, now turn off your light and follow me. Keep close now."

Without a moment's hesitation, Henry stood up and walked away from the table into the pitch black. Taking only a second to fumble with his light nearly cost Alex the ability to see which way his granddad had gone. Spotting the small bobbing orange disc barely 10 feet in front of him however, he slid out silently from behind the table and quickly followed.

He was still unsure where they were, or where they were going. He glanced around, hoping for clues, but there was nothing that would give their location or destination away. He sensed his granddad stop in front of him and did the same. A door handle was turned and they continued on a few paces, but Alex must have walked too far; suddenly he heard Henry's voice whisper behind him, "Stand still and don't make a sound."

He sounded worried, perhaps even scared, and it gave Alex the creeps. His mind raced with the possibilities.

"When I say run, just run." came Henry's voice, low and quick.

"Run where?"

"Ahead. Just straight ahead until I say stop. Ok?" Alex didn't have time to respond before Henry's voice in his ear said, "*Go!*"

Alex ran as fast as he could and in as straight a line as possible. He felt a cold breeze on his face and realised he must be outside. *But where outside?* He had no idea which side of the house he was on, assuming he was even still at the house, or where he was heading; He just kept running, following his granddad's orders. Despite his reeling senses, he wondered how Henry was going to tell him to stop, when there was no way his granddad would be able to keep up with him. The air seemed to change and Alex sensed that he was surrounded by trees or vegetation.

If I'm this close to trees I must be at the back of the house! Seeing a faint light up ahead he scrambled towards it, assuming it must be Henry. The trees were getting thicker the further he ran and his body was slowing down, completely unprepared for unexpected sprints.

As well as the light ahead, Alex began to notice a slight glow was coming from the trees themselves. Out of nowhere he heard his granddad whisper, "Over here."

Alex stopped and staggered towards the voice. He felt tired and light headed. Another light appeared several feet ahead but this one was a familiar reddish-orange colour. Confused and panting, Alex stopped just in front of the glowing light to see his granddad's face smiling broadly and not the least bit out of breath.

"Enjoyed your early morning jog did you, young chap?" laughed Henry loudly.

Alex, bent double, stared up at his beaming granddad. He could feel a painful stitch burrowing into his side. "How the *hell*… did you get here so fast and *why*… aren't you out of breath?"

"Ha! Well some of us know the grounds better than others, don't they? Anyway, follow me. We're nearly there."

Alex tramped on after Henry, still struggling to stand fully upright; the pain in his side pushed out across his ribs. They passed several more large bushes and a copse of tall trees, before they eventually came out into a wide open space. For the first time since Alex had found himself outside, the dark clouds parted and the moon shone through.

They were standing on the near side of the glass lake house, only feet away from the edge of the lake. From their viewpoint it looked more like a river as it wound far off into the distance like sleeping, silver snake. It seemed so peaceful and still in the quiet night. Henry beckoned for Alex to follow him and they walked to the front of the great glass cube. They stepped up onto the thick wooden ground floor platform, through the almost invisible front door and into the glass structure itself.

Despite their hurry, Alex couldn't help admiring the delicate metal castings that appeared to be holding the entire building together. Bolted between the brilliantly clear glass panes, the four-pronged limpets seemed to float motionless in the night sky. A very fine-looking leather wingback chair had been placed haphazardly by a tall pile of old papers and maps. It looked comfortable. A large part of him now just wanted to be back in bed. He felt cold, tired, confused and his brain was still addled from so many strange events.

Henry, on the other hand, was clearly enjoying every moment of this adventure. He strode confidently straight through the glass structure and out onto the far side of the building, stopping at the edge of the dark wooden mooring platform. Alex caught up just as Henry placed his hands on his hips and inhaled two huge lungfuls of fresh air, swelling his broad chest. As the two of them gazed out onto the vast mirror of moonlit water, Alex caught the look of pride etched clearly on Henry's face and half expected him to erupt into song. It wasn't until he looked down, however, that he saw what his granddad was so excited about.

He felt his stomach lurch. Sitting in the water, bathing serenely in the moonlight was a very low, very long and very sleek motorboat.

"Isn't she a belter," said Henry in the same tone Alex had once heard him use to describe a particularly fine steak he'd once had.

"Please tell me we're not going in the water in *that* thing?" Said Alex, trying to hide the apprehension in his voice.

"Of course we're not going in the water in that thing," Alex breathed a short sigh of relief. "But were are going *on* the water in it! I shall be admiral of the fleet and you can be my sub-lieutenant! Huzzah!"

Alex could tell Henry was far too excited for his own good and that he would have no choice but to go along with it.

"Fine. But can you please tell me *where* we're actually going?" Said Alex moodily, feeling his tiredness might erupt into an enormous sulk at any moment.

"All in good time. All. In. Good. Time. Right, hop in and I'll ah… *cast off* or whatever it's called."

Stepping down from the solid wooden platform, Alex immediately felt uneasy as he clambered into the gently rocking vessel. He quickly sat in one of the small leather seats, pulled the meagre-looking lap-belt as tightly as possible and grabbed hold of a sturdy looking chrome hand rail.

Henry was dancing around on the platform, elegantly undoing the mooring rope and twisting it into an enormous fibrous sausage before dropping it heavily to the wooden floor with a thud. Alex hadn't failed to notice there was a suspicious lack of limp from his granddad at this particular moment. *Must be one of his good days.*

Henry more-or-less pirouetted into the boat and dropped down hard into the captain's chair. He pressed the red start button. The twin engines burst into life, then settled down to a low burble.

Peering over the low windscreen, Henry gently turned the thick steering wheel, navigated slowly away from the platform and turned the boat ninety degrees until it was facing clear, open water.

Thinking it would be wise to mention his fear of water, Alex only just managed to utter, "You're not going to go too f–"

Henry, grinning like a small boy with a toffee apple, winked at him and yanked the chrome throttle lever right back on its stops. The engines erupted with the roar and the bow of the boat seemed to lift skywards.

Alex just about heard an exhilarated cry of, "*Rumpy!*" as the boat shot forward, sending a wave of white water over the mooring platform towards the lake house. Alex was pinned in his seat. With his eyes closed and the wind whipping through his hair, he managed to squint to his right to see his granddad sitting bolt upright, looking as though he hadn't a care in the world. The wind was sweeping Henry's hair back to reveal his whiter sides. Alex couldn't help but think of ridiculous go-faster stripes.

Unfortunately it wasn't enough to distract him from the insane speed at which they were travelling. Even the smallest changes in direction pitched Alex violently from side to side, sometimes perilously close the water's edge. Eventually, on one particularly sharp left hander, Alex felt the stomach lurch he had been waiting for, immediately followed by a violent bout of sickness that splattered into the deep dark water.

Even with the wind battering his exposed ear he could hear Henry laughing loudly, shouting something about scurvy dogs and landlubbers. Feeling worse than he had in a long time, he managed to wipe his mouth on his bare arm before slumping back heavily in his seat.

After what seemed like an age, the boat stopped weaving; after a few minutes more, Henry began to slow down. Alex craned his neck around, searching for a possible stopping point. In the distance he thought he spotted a recess in the heavily tree-lined bank. Sure enough, as they drew closer, Henry killed the engine and slowly nursed the boat to the left hand bank. Almost at snails' pace, he managed to glide the craft expertly through the tight gap in the trees. As they pulled to a gentle stop, Alex looked up; they were in front of one the strangest buildings he had ever seen.

CHAPTER 17

BLACK BLOOD

Henry immediately leapt out the boat and began pulling on a thick rope that lay on the jetty. As he busied himself tying it around the mooring post of the speedboat, all Alex could do was stare at the building in front of him; not really sure what to say.

The structure appeared to be another perfect cube of a similar size to the glass lake house. Instead of thirty foot tall panes of glass forming the outer shell, however, this one appeared to be made entirely from woven twigs. Even more unusually, wherever there were gaps in the twigs, a soft yellow light shone out. It was as if the twigs were acting as a natural camouflage for an entirely unnatural glowing yellow cube.

"So, what do you think of my bachelor pad?" said Henry, catching him unawares.

Alex was speechless. He couldn't decide what was more surprising: that the secret building existed at all or how it looked. Slowly he clambered out of the boat, relieved to feel firm ground beneath his feet, and walked up the short jetty. Henry was already through the front door before Alex had had chance to reply.

Reaching the door, Alex caught the wonderful smell of roasting meat and suddenly realised how hungry he was. He hurried inside after his granddad and pushed the door closed, leaving the nausea behind him.

The space he had entered was completely open-plan. In contrast to the modern exterior, the interior was very traditional: or more accurately, it was very *Henry*.

The dark wood floor contrasted beautifully with the hot pink walls, which were covered in hundreds of framed photographs. Alex was reminded of the many photos that lined his grandmother's office. But as he looked closer he saw that unlike the rich, powerful and famous people in his grandmother's, Henry's pictures seemed to be of him and his friends.

One thing that did strike Alex was how much younger and happier his granddad looked in all of the photos. He couldn't have been more than thirty in most of them. Even back then Henry seemed to have a drink and some sort of smoking implement hanging from his hand or mouth.

Wandering slowly around the room, Alex ran his fingers gently across the battered old chesterfield sofas, past the low glass tables full of racing memorabilia, and up to the elaborate polished steel hi-fi stand in the corner. Placed on top was an enormous record player that Alex vaguely remembered from the main house years ago. Lifting up the cover, he peered at the label on top: *'Rhapsody On a Theme of Paganini, Op. 43: Variation 18: Andante Cantabile - S. Rachmaninov'*. Alex smiled, knowing this piece all too well. He pressed the small round power button and watched the platter spin quickly up to speed. Gently, he lifted the delicate head and swung the tone arm out to hover over the spinning black vinyl. Flicking the lowering mechanism, Alex watched with anticipation as the tone arm slowly lowered onto the platter.

A few seconds of crackles and pops were all he had to wait before the music seemed to glide gently towards him. He felt his whole body tingle and as the music built, he sank down quietly into the closest armchair.

Henry appeared from the rear entrance of the building and, on hearing the music, immediately raised his arms as if conducting an imaginary orchestra, sashaying around the kitchen with his eyes closed but still managing to pick up a carving knife to use as his conductor's baton.

Despite his tiredness and stress, Alex couldn't help but smile at him. Eventually, Henry put down his makeshift baton and opened the heavy oven door. He recoiled at the burst of escaping steam, then reverently pulled out an enormous covered roasting tin, placing it gently onto the island unit. Alex was instinctively drawn to the smell. As he pushed himself up from his comfy armchair, Henry grabbed the tinfoil cover in a gloved hand and flamboyantly pulled it off, revealing an enormous leg of slow-cooked lamb.

"Care for a spot of baa-baa, young squire?" said Henry in a very solemn voice.

Alex could only manage a wide eyed nod. Chuckling, Henry quickly pulled out knives, forks and plates from the various oak-panelled cupboards and drawers. Reaching into another cupboard he pulled out a jar of mint sauce and spooned a great dollop onto both of their plates.

"Right then, no standing on ceremony. Get stuck in, you must be starving."

Alex didn't need asking twice. Sitting on a tall bar stool next to the counter he began to fork off great chunks of the tender meat, dunk them in the mint sauce and unceremoniously shovel them into his mouth. After several minutes of grandfather and grandson going at it with knife and fork they sat and listened to the music, enjoying the contented feeling of being stuffed to the gills.

"Right," said Henry suddenly. "It's time you and I had a serious chat."

Alex looked past Henry's shoulder at the pendulum clock on the wall behind him. It was nearly four o'clock in the morning. He placed his fork noisily on the large plate and gave a big sigh. "Do we really have to do that now? I am pretty tired you know."

"Well you can't go to bed on a full stomach, so now's as good a time as any I think, young man!"

Alex could tell that Henry wasn't going to take no for an answer and that it would be pointless for him to argue the point. Giving another loud sigh, Alex stood up from his bar stool and stretched, yawning loudly for emphasis.

"Shall we retire to the drawing room then?" Henry said, gesturing across to the large battered sofas.

Alex was already drifting towards the very comfy armchair he had been sitting in previously.

"And just so you know, the armchair's mine," came Henry's voice from the kitchen, just as Alex was about to sink into the soft padded seat.

Choosing a sofa that looked just as inviting, Alex dropped down and made himself comfortable.

"So what is this place, anyway?" he said, looking around. "And are you the only person that knows it's here?"

"Ah well, they're two very good questions," said Henry, pulling out his pipe from his jacket pocket and lighting it slowly. After a few long puffs, smoke began to curl from its bulbous end into thick, heavy clouds that lingered on the ceiling.

"As for *what* it is, well, let's just say it's my little, ah… bolt hole. You know, for when things get a bit tense with the dragon" He stabbed at the air with his fingers as if he was fending off an imaginary beast. Alex chuckled lazily. "And as for *who* knows about it, well you make the fourth. Archer knows about it. He's the one who put dinner in the oven when I told him I'd be bringing you back here." Henry paused and took a long slow puff on his pipe, making the embers glow yellow. "And then, there's your dad."

"*Dad* knows about this place?" said Alex, sitting up a little more in his seat.

"Every inch of it," smiled Henry. "He designed it for me. Thought you would have guessed, to be honest. What with the shape and all. Yes, he sorted it all out for me *and* undercover as well. Good sort, your dad… despite what you may think about him."

Henry's eyes were narrowed as he watched Alex intently, but Alex was too busy gazing around the space. The more he looked, the more he noticed his dad's signature details. Not for the first time, he thought how strange it was that his dad had more-or-less given up architecture to work for the family business.

Despite having never been as close to his father as Lewis was, Alex knew that his dad had loved what he did and was, by all accounts, extremely talented at it. His awards shelf was testament to that. Nevertheless, Morten had decided to pack it all in and work for the family firm instead; a move which seemingly made him very miserable. Alex often wondered if it had been motivated by money, but it couldn't have been. Married to Rebekka Wolf, heir to the second largest fortune in the country and son of Konrad and Veronica Steen, custodians of the *largest* fortune in the country, he was never going to find himself short of cash. Alex wondered if he'd simply stopped enjoying it. As he thought about how much of a mystery his dad was to him, he tried to remember the last time the two of them had really spoken. The only really strong memory that came to him was over four years ago on his 15th birthday.

In all seriousness, Alex had asked his dad if he could borrow one of his cars and take it out for a drive. Morten had actually laughed at the question, but had at least tried to soften the blow by telling Alex when he reached 18 he could choose whichever one he liked and take it for a drive.

On reaching his 18th birthday, however, and with Morten claiming to have no knowledge of such an exchange, Alex decided to take matters into his own hands. Despite Lewis pleading with Alex not to, he had covertly borrowed the keys to his father's McLaren and taken it for a quick spin around the winding country roads of their old home. On reaching the long road heading out of the village however, Alex had floored the accelerator. To his great surprise he suddenly found that he had no control of the vehicle whatsoever and promptly crashed it into a large cluster of Elm trees. Two days later, Alex had woken up in hospital to find a copy of the estimated repair bill next to him on his pillow. Since then, the two of them had barely spoken.

As he sat looking around at his dad's creation, he considered that in hindsight, the joyride hadn't been worth it at all.

"Now then," started Henry, "I imagine you have some more questions for me?"

"Eh?" said Alex, caught slightly by surprise.

He'd half expected to just be talked at for the next half hour, as was customary with his granddad, but that didn't seem to be how it was going to work this time. His head was still hurting, but he remembered that he did indeed have questions; a lot of them.

"Alright then, well first of all *how* do you know that thing? This Frederik person, or whatever it's called. And *who* exactly is he after, if he's not after me? *And*, if he's not after me, then why's he dragging me underground like some deranged lunatic and singing songs about cutting off my head? Actually, that's a point, *why* was he wearing that bracelet thingy I found? And where did he get it from? And *why* isn't my wrist broken any more, *and*–"

Henry held up a hand. He was sitting back in his chair with his eyes closed, as if he was sleeping. After a few seconds, he slowly opened them and let out a long sigh.

"What?" said Alex, concerned. "What is it?"

"Alex, I'm going to tell you everything I know and you'll need to make up your own mind what you do with this information. Do you understand?"

"I suppose?" Alex said, not entirely sure what he was going to hear.

Henry gave a smile and took a few more long sucks of his pipe, slowly expelling another large cloud of smoke into the atmosphere.

"Firstly, what you have to realise is that, despite appearances, Frederik is not a bad person. He is here for a reason, but I can assure you that the reason is not to put the frighteners on you or to *get you,* as you put it. As I mentioned before, and as you read earlier, he's known a lot of pain and suffering in his life. I think it's fair to say that it has left him with a somewhat… hmm, *threatening* manner."

"You've got that right!" snorted Alex, his lip curling in disgust at the thought of Frederik's horrible face.

"What you also have to realise," continued Henry, "Is that the reason he dragged you underground earlier was to save your life."

"Save my life? You are kidding?" Alex laughed. "I know I go over the top sometimes, but it was only a broken wrist. A quick trip to the hospital would have sorted that out."

"Well if he *was* trying to kill you, why would he have delivered you safely back to me with a mended wrist? Why not just finish you off when he had you, hmm?" Henry was tapping his finger impatiently on the arm of his chair.

Alex had to admit his granddad had a point. Even as he looked down at his wrist he began to slowly rotate it, as if he was trying it out for the first time. It felt absolutely fine; almost as if there had never been a problem with it in the first place.

"But *how* did he fix it? It was in a pretty bad way you know? It was all bent over and was so pain–"

"We're not here to talk about your bloody wrist!" cut in Henry loudly, making Alex sink suddenly back into his seat. He watched as his granddad sucked moodily on his pipe several times before speaking again.

"Sorry... sorry, old chap. Didn't mean to snap like that."

Alex had never seen his granddad like this before. After several seconds Henry seemed to compose himself and continued.

"Do you remember a few days ago, the day I picked you up from school, you saw something when we came through the gates. *A shadow*, you called it."

"Yes... you told me it was the vicar in his hot air balloon."

"Well that *shadow,*" continued Henry, lowering his voice, "is the very reason that Frederik came to me in the first place. So that I, or I should say *we*, could begin to start taking certain... steps."

"What do you mean *steps*? What was the shadow?" said Alex.

Henry leaned forward, his eyes quickly flicking from side to side as if to check that they were alone.

"What *makes* the shadow, I don't know. I keep asking Frederik, but he won't tell me. He just keeps saying that all I need to know is that it's incredibly dangerous. More dangerous than any other living thing on this planet, in fact. He keeps telling me that if I ever see it, I should just run for my life and never look back. I suggested to him one time that I might have a pop at it myself. He said... well, he just said that I would be dead before I'd even blinked."

Alex was beginning to feel uncomfortable.

"Anyway, he's been keeping an eye on the grounds for at least six months now, checking everything's ok, keeping me updated. But the night before last, he apparently had a run in with this thing. In these very grounds, in fact, and *that* is when he lost his bracelet."

"But that was the bracelet I found in the grounds, on the way to our first history lesson," said Alex, confused. "I remember putting it in my jacket pocket so that I could ask you about the markings on it. But–"

"But you had your nose bleed, didn't you." Henry cut in. "Yes, well after you had your little incident, I had to do something with all your clothes. In a right old state they were. When I was sorting them out I found the bracelet in your pocket. I knew it was his the moment I saw it. I'd seen him wearing it before. He was in a dreadful rage when he lost it, you know." Henry said with a small shudder that made his moustache twitch. "I'm pretty sure it belonged to his wife you see, Annelise, and it's likely that's the only thing of hers he's got left. So you can imagine how he felt when he lost it."

Alex tried to collect his thoughts. "So... hold on then. If he had a fight with this shadow thing in the garden, does that mean that it's gone now? Or dead?"

Henry gave him a very grave look, before placing the pipe back in his mouth and taking three short puffs.

"I'm afraid it does not. In fact I'm fairly sure that the shadow was in the library with us earlier. That is why we had to leave in such a hurry and that is why I made you run. You were running from the shadow."

Alex sat up straight and felt his heart returning to its all-too-familiar rapid pattern. He looked desperately at his granddad for the smallest sign that this was some sort of joke, but there was none.

"It was *in* the library?" Alex just about managed to whisper.

"Yes. Or it was at least just outside. But that's not all." continued Henry.

Alex noticed the sense of hesitation in his voice.

"Going back to your incident with Frederik, did you notice anything strange happen just after you'd broken your wrist?"

"You mean apart from the floor opening up and your psycho friend dragging me underground?" Alex muttered. "Oh no, it was all fairly normal."

"Alex," said Henry seriously "*Think*. Did you notice anything else, before Frederik took you?"

Listening to his granddad, Alex realised what it was that was making him so uncomfortable. There wasn't even a hint of humour in Henry's voice. For the first time in his life, his granddad sounded deadly serious; even a little scared.

"Well, I remember falling down the stairs… then the floor started rotating and it got a bit darker. Actually it got a *lot* darker. Really, *really* quickly."

Henry finally leaned back in his chair taking another long puff on his pipe.

"Well, it sounds to me like you had a very narrow escape then. Frederik probably saved you just in time."

"What do you mean?" asked Alex, worried by this new revelation of a near death experience.

"Frederik told me that this *thing* doesn't really go out during the day, instead preferring to do its work under cover of darkness. Sometimes though, it needs to go out in daylight, so it creates a darkness of its own. The fact it went dark so quickly more than likely means that it was moving towards you. And I'm afraid it was more than likely just about to attack."

Even in the comfort of Henry's secret bachelor pad, Alex had to admit he felt scared. He must have looked it too, because just as Alex was about to ask another question Henry cut in.

"Look, I know it's easier said than done, but you really shouldn't let any of this worry you now. I'm only telling you because I want you to be aware, that's all. Keep an eye out for anything strange."

Not worry? What am I supposed to do with Death's bad-tempered cousin running round trying to bump me off?

"The point is that whilst Frederik is keeping an eye on things you're more-or-less safe. So just try not to think any more about it. Ok?"

Alex didn't really think that *more-or-less* was a very satisfactory answer when murderous lunatics were involved, but his granddad seemed to trust in Frederik's protection, so he supposed he would have to as well.

"But what's this thing after though? And why's it after me?"

Henry paused a while longer before he spoke, still in his whispered tones.

"I'm not sure of that either I'm afraid, Alex. Again, I've asked Frederik but he won't tell me."

Alex got the impression this time that his granddad wasn't telling him the truth, or at least not all of it. He decided to change subject.

"Ok, well if you don't know any more about this shadow thing, then tell me more about Frederik. When did you meet him? And *where* did you meet him?" Alex was surprised to hear his granddad actually laugh out loud. "What are you laughing at?"

"Sorry, sorry, I shouldn't laugh really. It's just that you've reminded me of the first time I met him. Bloody fellow damn near gave me a heart attack!"

Alex still wasn't sure why this was funny, but Henry's laughter had at least lightened the mood. Still chuckling to himself, Henry started rummaging around in a small wooden box that was sitting open on the coffee table. He pulled out a good pinch of dark, curling weed and stuffed it into the end of his pipe. Striking another long match, he plunged it into the overflowing bulb. As the rich smoke billowed into the air Alex watched his granddad lean back in his chair, swing both feet up onto the low coffee table and wriggle himself into a comfortable position.

"I remember it was just over six months ago. I'd been in my study all day looking over some old family papers, you know, family trees, old wills, that sort of stuff. Anyway, before I knew it, all the lights went out. Pitch black it was. Of course, I just assumed it was a power cut so ever the boy scout, I rummaged around in my drawers and pulled out that fancy lighter your mum bought me for my birthday. I'd just managed to make my way to the door with the aid of this small light, but when I reached it, I found that the bloody thing was locked!

"Now, I'm no coward but I have to admit that even I got a bit of a sweat on at this point, even more so when I heard something move behind me. Needless to say I'm not one to be intimidated in my own home, so I swung round quick as a flash with my trusty lighter in hand to confront whatever intruder was there.

"Only thing was, when I saw him, with that face, sitting casually on my chair as if he'd just popped in for a visit, I dropped the blinking lighter and was left standing in the dark!"

Henry took several more long puffs on his pipe. "As you can imagine, I was bloody terrified. But I needn't have worried. The lights came on a second later and there he was just sitting there, bold as brass. How he'd found his way in I don't know—still don't know to this day actually—but I didn't have any choice but to sit there and listen to what he had to say.

"I can tell you that it was such a sad story, you can't imagine, Alex. This poor fellow seemed to have been through so much misery in his life that I was amazed he'd been able to keep going. But as I listened to him talk, it soon became clear that the only thing *keeping* him going was his plan for revenge. As you will have read in that extract I showed you in the library, he'd been terribly betrayed, his wife had been murdered and he was left facing an eternity of loneliness. All he's been thinking about for all those years is how to punish the one who killed Annalise. And that's what he's here to do."

Alex had been sitting mesmerised, but suddenly realised what his granddad had just said. "So Frederik's here to kill the shadow thing? That's who betrayed him and killed his wife?"

Henry shook his head slowly. "That's what I thought at first but..."

"But what?" said Alex, leaning forward.

"But... well, I asked him the same thing and he wouldn't really give me a straight answer. It was like he was holding something back. Almost as if the shadow isn't his main concern, merely a distraction."

Alex stared at his granddad for a moment, before finally shaking his head. "Come on... how much of this is there? Mad old men skulking about the house, magical shadows, I'm not a kid anymore, Granddad. What's *really* going on?"

Henry stood and walked slowly to the large walnut sideboard underneath the staircase. He opened the door and very carefully took out what appeared to be a thick, wide slab of burnt wood. He placed it very carefully on the coffee table between them and returned to his armchair. Sighing, Alex leaned forward to examine it more closely.

He guessed it was just over a foot long, about ten inches wide and about an inch thick, but there wasn't a straight line on it. The rough edges looked as if they'd either been hacked, snapped, sawn or burnt. As he stared closely at the charred surface of the wood he could just make out an emblem embossed in the middle.

"If you're wondering what that is," came Henry's low voice, startling Alex.

"It's the Wolf family crest."

Alex squinted at the blackened wood. "So what is this then? An antique dinner tray? The world's oldest chopping board?" Henry said nothing, staring at the object. "And anyway, why's it so burnt?"

Henry leaned forward and placed his hands gently on the sides of the wooden block. There was a small *snick* and he carefully lifted the top piece clear of the bottom. Inside was a small and delicate-looking piece of paper.

"It's a blank piece of paper," he said.

"What you see here before you," Henry said, "is the only remaining page from the five books you read about earlier. Frederik very kindly lent it to me in case I needed it for a… hmm, demonstration."

"Demonstration?"

"Yes, for some reason he thought that you might not believe any of this. As for the reason it's so burnt, well, we'll come to that later." Henry passed the piece of blackened wood to Alex who seized it roughly.

"Alex, you must be very careful with this page!" blurted Henry quickly, a look of genuine concern on his face. "It's extremely old and *incredibly* dangerous."

Alex looked up into Henry's eyes, a smile spreading across his face. "Dangerous? Pull the other one, there's nothing on it! How can it be dangerous?"

Now that it was closer, he saw that the wood wasn't black at all, but a deep reddish-brown colour. It only appeared black from the soot that had permeated the two halves and pressed into the surface.

Although it was blank, Alex had to admit the page did appear to be very old. Apart from its yellowed colouring, its only other notable feature was the rough edge down one side; as if it had been torn quickly from a book.

"How old did you say this was?" Alex asked lazily.

"Oh, about seven hundred and eighty-seven years old, I think," came Henry's slow, measured reply.

"Seven hundred and eighty-seven?" laughed Alex. "That's a bit precise isn't it?"

"Ah well, if we're being precise, I would say it's seven hundred and eighty-six years, four months and twenty-one days old." said Henry.

"You know how old it is to the *day*?"

"Of course I do."

"How?"

"Because the author told me."

"Frederik?"

"Yes, Frederik. And now, he wants *you* to have it."

"He wants me to have it, does he? Oh well, I'm so grateful for this sheet of blank paper. You'll have to pass on my regards." Alex burst out laughing. "I'm not being funny, but this isn't the best practical joke in the world is it?"

Rocking back into his seat, Alex watched as Henry gave a big sigh, got slowly to his feet and walked the few steps towards him. Alex then heard the ominous sound of cracking knuckles.

"I'm afraid you're going to have to pass on your regards yourself, Alex." said Henry quietly in a voice of disappointed resignation.

"Why? What do you mean?" said Alex, staring up at his granddad.

"I really didn't want to do it this way, old chap, but I'm afraid you've left me no choice." Smiling sadly at his grandson, Henry punched him square in the face.

Alex reeled in shock and pain and heard his nose crack under the force from his granddad's powerful fist. Clutching at his face with both hands, Alex looked up at Henry through tear streaked eyes, but he was in so much pain he couldn't even find his voice to speak.

He doubled over, trying to escape from the throbbing feeling reverberating around his head. He felt a familiar warm sensation running through his hands and down his wrists. As he took his hands away from his face, he saw that it wasn't the bright red stream of blood he was expecting; it was the dark reddish-black liquid with a shimmer of silver he remembered dropping onto the white keys of his piano.

Several droplets of the silvery stuff dripped from his open fingers onto the old torn piece of paper. It immediately glowed yellow and Alex saw hundreds of tiny words appear from nowhere on the page. He felt a strong blast of wind as if a door had suddenly opened somewhere and glanced up to see his granddad fading slowly into blackness. There was a blinding flash and then darkness.

CHAPTER 18

THE TOWER

The man was standing 800 feet up on his penthouse balcony, looking directly into the eyes of the shadowy figure opposite him. Softly, he spoke three words.

"Follow him. Now"

He gently touched the silhouette's shoulder and a yellow pulse of light shone briefly at the point of contact. The menacing form turned, and vaulted over the guard rail, disappearing into the night.

Reaching into his tailored jacket pocket, the man pulled out a long, thick cigar and returned to his desk inside to light it.

Leaning back in his chair, he stared out into the dark night, considering his next move.

CHAPTER 19

FREDERIK

Still clutching his nose, Alex shivered and felt goosebumps rising on his arms. He could hear a strong wind blowing outside and rain lashing against the windows. Cold air was surrounding him like a chilled blanket.

Wondering why he kept finding himself sitting in the dark, he sat for a moment, waiting for his eyes to adjust. He could make out the shape of the window and the night sky beyond. Realising he was still holding the charred piece of wood, Alex felt with his left hand that the page was still on the board. He picked it up and tried to examine it. Squinting through the gloom he could see that the words had vanished again.

He moaned as the heavy, dull throbbing in his nose returned in a wave. Feeling the wet blood on his fingers the anger rose in him.

"What the hell did you hit me for? That really hurt, you know!" Alex shouted, screwing up his eyes against the pain. "And why have you turned the lights off? I want to see your face when you apologise!"

There was no answer. He moved his head from side to side but he couldn't see anyone. He felt a slight unease growing in him. *Why would he have left me here on my own?*

"I know you're here somewhere." He called out, less confidently than before.

Even though his nose felt painful and swollen he caught the smell of something that greatly added to his unease.

"Granddad?" his voice was a lot smaller and higher pitched than he had expected. He coughed. "Granddad, can you… can you turn the lights on please? I can't see."

"Your *granddad* is not here, boy," came a low, rasping voice from the other side of the room.

Alex went rigid in his chair. He recognised that voice. It went hand in hand with the rotting, festering smell that was beginning to fill his nostrils. It was the same voice that had spoken that awful verse as he was dragged underground. Fear pumped through his veins once again. Squirming in his seat, Alex realised it was no longer a soft, comfortable padded chair, but one of cold, hard stone.

"Do not fidget, boy. I will do you no harm. Not unless you deserve it. I can only assume that you are here because you still do not *believe*, hmm? Well, we shall see what we can do about that."

Alex barely heard the words, he was so terrified; not least because he couldn't tell where the voice was actually coming from. At first it had been to his side, but it seemed to have moved behind him.

"And how is your arm?" came the same creaking voice, directly in front of him.

"My... my arm?" said Alex, his throat dry and constricted.

"Yes your arm, *idiot* boy! You broke it, did you not? I fixed it for you."

Alex reached down and rubbed his wrist again, but all he noticed were the hairs that were raised along his sticky forearms; only partly caused by the cold wind.

"Are you... are you Frederik?" he asked nervously, peering blindly into the gloom.

Without warning, a fire sprang up in front of him. He caught sight of a face thrown into sharp relief by the crackling flames. Alex let out a little yelp. He desperately wanted to close his eyes from the sight, but he couldn't help staring in horror; the man was standing directly in front of him.

The deeply lined and scarred face was barely a foot from his, with its jet black eyes peering savagely into his own. Alex recoiled in his seat, trying to keep as far from the abhorrent creature as possible; the foul stench coming from the creature was nearly unbearable.

"Yes. I am Frederik," came the hoarse response, the man's vile breath gassing noxiously from between his crooked and blackened teeth. "And this is my home." He waved a cloaked arm vaguely into the darkness.

Alex was about to point out that this was actually his granddad's house, but the sight of Frederik's face had put any sort of backchat out of his mind.

"I have been watching you for some time, Alexander," said the man. "Yes, for some time indeed. In fact, I think you may have seen me too on one occasion?"

"I... I don't think so?" Alex stutteringly replied.

"You don't remember seeing me on your balcony? During the storm two days ago?"

"Storm? What storm?" The raging wind outside seemed to increase in intensity even as he spoke.

"Idiotic child!" spat the man angrily, almost to himself.

Alex was surprised and annoyed to see the man roll his eyes and push his hands to his forehead as if he was in pain. Frightened though he was, Alex's fear was being dampened by rising indignation at the regular insults.

"I'm... I'm sorry, but I don't quite understand what's going on here."

"I *know* that you do not understand!" screamed the man violently, suddenly pointing a gnarled boney finger at Alex. "You know nothing about *anything*! Idiotic, *useless* boy!"

"Now wait a minute–" started Alex rising angrily from his chair.

"*Shut up*!" screamed the man rushing forward again, bringing his face back to within inches of Alex's.

Alex immediately dropped back onto his hard seat. He could do nothing but stare into the black eyes in front of him.

"Of *all* the people that has to make things right," said the man, almost to himself. "The one to help my Annelise, the one to save everything, and it is supposed to be this boy? *This one?*"

Frederik's tone had turned from fury to utter despair in the space of a sentence. He turned and stalked back into the darkness of the room. Alex heard a soft, thud as if Frederik had sat down hard into a chair. As the flames in the fireplace crackled, Alex could just make out a figure slumped miserably in his seat, still muttering to himself and tugging loosely at his black ragged cloak.

They both sat silently for a few minutes. Alex listened quietly to the howling wind and the low crackle of the fire; it seemed to be giving out no heat whatsoever. He could feel the deep cold beginning to chill his bones.

"I'm *not* an idiot," said Alex moodily under his breath.

"Whether or not you are an idiot remains to be seen, Alexander, but the fact you are here with me now proves that you do not yet believe. Not yet."

Alex couldn't say for sure, but he thought he could see Frederik grinning nastily in the dark. Alex scowled but then added, with a hint of desperation in his voice, "Can you *please* just tell me what this is all about? I don't understand what's going on."

"No, well I'm not surprised by that," came the voice from the shadows. "You don't seem to be aware of much do you, Alexander? Not unless it has to do with your own reflection in the mirror, or getting your hands on lots of money, or perhaps Miss Sara Harris?"

"How do you know about..." started Alex, completely taken aback at this accurate insight into his personal life. All he received in reply was a low, mean laugh.

Silence descended on the room again, lifted only by the slow crackle of the fire and the ever-growing winds outside. Alex sat quietly. Despite his best efforts, his eyes were still drawn to the face of the wretched old man. Frederik was staring into the fire, seemingly in a world of his own. There was incredible sadness etched clearly all over his horrible, scarred face and filling his sunken black eyes. Frederik lifted his head and in a much softer tone than Alex had ever heard, began to speak.

"Alexander, there are… *things* I need to tell you, things you need to know about. I know that you have no idea what you are involved in but if… if I don't tell you now then it will be too late."

Not knowing quite what to say–and not wanting to be called an idiot again–Alex thought it best to keep quiet.

"As you know, my name is Frederik and I am from Norway. As it said in the story your bestefar–sorry, your *grandfather*–showed you, I have been alive for many, many years. Too many years, Alexander. I have seen such things…" Frederik seemed lost to the crackling fire again, but Alex still didn't interrupt. "The story said that I lost someone very close to me. That is true. Her name was Annelise and I… I loved her more than you or anyone could ever possibly imagine. She was as much a part of me as I am myself. I… I cannot explain this in any other way than to say she was the other half of me." Frederik seemed to choke on his words slightly. Even in the darkness, Alex could see that his black eyes were glazed with tears, reflecting the dancing yellow flames in the fireplace.

"She was taken from me. Murdered by something so cruel and evil that its very existence on this earth puts *everyone* in danger. It *must* be stopped Alexander. If it is not… if it is not dealt with, then we are talking about the end of humanity!" Frederik's voice had grown quickly in anger and his mouth was curled, hissing the least few words, almost as a plea. "For some reason that I do not know, it seems it is *you* that I need to help me do this. To stop this thing, to stop all this war and fighting and death. It is *you,*" he looked Alex up and down with barely-concealed disgust. "It is you that is supposed to put things right, to bring an end to all the terrible things that have happened and *are happening* around you now."

Alex sat in stunned silence. There was no doubt about it. The old man, whoever he really was, was completely unhinged. Alex's only thoughts now were of how to get out alive and to find his granddad. Frederik sat looking at the fire again and was flicking his bony fingers with his nails as if he had some sort of angry twitch.

"I don't mean to be rude," said Alex. Frederik's eyes flicked towards him.

"But this all sounds a bit far-fetched, don't you think? I mean… all this end of the world, bogey-man stuff. I mean come on, I'm not twelve."

Frederick shifted in his seat and blinked rapidly several times.

"Look, I'm sorry about your wife and everything. Annelise was it? She sounds really great and all that, but she's dead isn't she? So don't you think it's time to move on? You're not getting any younger, after all." If he hadn't been so busy trying to think of something else to say, Alex might have noticed that Frederik had stopped clicking his fingers and was clutching the sides of his chair. "I mean, maybe you ought to find someone new? Get yourself out and about a bit? Find someone who's not, you know... dead."

Alex had barely uttered the last few words when he felt himself lifted from his chair and slammed hard against the heavy wooden wall behind him. The breath was knocked out of his lungs as a rough, crooked hand around his neck pinned him to the wall. He struggled and writhed against the incredible force, but there was nowhere for him to go. Frederik's hideous face was now barely an inch from Alex's and his hot, foul breath was coming in short, panting waves.

"Do *not*… speak of her… that… way," he seethed. "She was… my *life*!"

With every syllable, Frederik dug his claws deeper into Alex's throat. His eyes were streaming and he could barely see, let alone breathe, but beyond Frederik's manic flashing eyes, Alex's terror grew as he saw that the room had begun to burn, with intense black flames. Frederik pushed harder into Alex's neck and with every hideous, panting breath the black flames rose until they surrounded them both. Alex thought he was about to pass out, but suddenly Frederik released his grip and Alex fell to the floor in a crumpled heap. Clutching at his neck, trying desperately to fill his lungs with oxygen, he rolled over and saw Frederik walking back across the room.

Unsuccessfully trying to ignore the pain in his neck, Alex seized his chance and crawled towards the door. Still struggling to see through his streaming eyes, he reached out blindly for the cold metal handle that he had pushed on barely an hour ago. Instead, he found what felt like a short, rough length of rope. He pulled it strongly towards him. As he staggered to his feet the door swung open hard and a pummelling blast of icy wind struck his face, making it hard to catch his breath. The moon, still high in the sky, illuminated the surroundings vividly but it was a second or two before Alex realised something had changed.

The sleek, gleaming speedboat he had been expecting to see tied to the small jetty had been replaced by a small area of rocky ground. And beyond that, there was nothing. Alex rushed forward, battered by the rain and wind, but in a few steps found he was standing at the edge of a cliff. He almost lost his footing as the harsh, cold wind blew around him and felt his stomach lurch as he peered over the edge. At least 100 feet below him was a wide, black, swirling river and on the other side, a sheer dark grey rock face stretching high into the sky. Alex slowly backed away from the cliff edge. Turning back, he saw that the house from which he had just escaped, appeared to be nothing more than a single wood-panelled wall; set flush into the side of a sheer and ragged cliff face. Alex was merely standing on a small ledge. To his right and left, above and below, there were only the flint edges of raw black stone. There was nowhere to go.

Frederik was standing in the doorway. His long, straggled hair whipped mercilessly around his face and his black eyes, filled with anger, glinted brightly in the moonlight. A forgotten memory flashed into Alex's mind and he remembered where he had seen the man before. *The balcony. The storm. Of course!*

"There is nowhere to go, Alexander," shouted Frederik over the howling wind. "There is nowhere to go except inside with me. Come in and we shall talk. There is much to discuss and… I have much to explain!"

Frederik was beckoning him inside with a long bony finger. Realising he had no real choice, Alex slowly walked back into the strange building and closed the door behind him.

CHAPTER 20

HOW & WHY

Alex stood in the doorway, his head swimming. Maybe it was the release of finally leaving school. Maybe it was because he hadn't been to bed all night. Whatever the reason, he was clearly having some sort of breakdown.

He closed his eyes and began to count slowly in his head, hoping more than anything that when he opened them he would find himself back with his granddad in the bachelor pad on the lake; not stuck on the side of a cliff with an 800 year old lunatic. He opened his eyes slowly.

Worth a try. Alex could make out Frederik walking slowly towards the fireplace with what appeared to be a long stick in his hand. He lit the end in the fire and used it as a taper for a series of wall lamps that Alex hadn't even noticed. Slowly the room grew brighter.

With all the lamps lit and every corner of the room illuminated, Alex felt more confused than ever. Although the chair he had been sitting in was clearly made of stone, the room itself was exactly the same size and shape as his granddad's house. However, the furnishings were quite different. Aside from the two chairs, there was no other furniture at all. There were no photos, no carpets, no paint, no electricity and not even the faintest hint of roasting lamb. In fact it wasn't even built of the same materials. Concrete and glass had been replaced by stone and mortar and where Henry's apartment had a suspended steel mezzanine, here there was a very rickety-looking wooden platform that looked like it would fall down at any second.

Frederik spoke suddenly, making Alex jump. "Alex, I must apologise for my behaviour just now. My temper sometimes… gets the better of me." Alex said nothing, his neck still stinging where Frederik's claws had sunk in to his skin. "I would… appreciate it if you would not mention this to your grandfather. It is not the first time that we have had words about my… how did he say it, my *bad form."*

Putting it down to his tired brain giving up completely, Alex actually laughed out loud at the fact that this withered old man was talking like his granddad.

"I also want to thank you," Frederik paused as if this was going to take more effort than the weak apology he had just given. "Your grandfather told me how you found my bracelet in the grounds."

He held up his arm and pulled back the ragged and frayed sleeve to reveal a dull silver bracelet sitting high atop multiple leather bands and straps.

"I cannot thank you enough for retrieving this for me. It belonged to my Annelise and is all that I have left of her on this earth."

Alex, who was now feeling more tired than ever and past caring what really happened next felt it prudent not to mention that he had been planning to sell the bracelet for cash. "That's no problem," he said, looking at the floor feeling slightly embarrassed.

He looked up to see Frederik staring directly at him again, his eyes narrowed as if he had guessed Alex's true intentions or because he was waiting for Alex to say something else. Searching for anything else to say, Alex suddenly remembered something his granddad had told him earlier.

"Oh and I should probably say thanks too!"

"What?" said Fredrik, taken aback.

"Granddad told me that you may have saved my life earlier. When you dragged me underground? He said that some sort of shadowy thing was coming to get me or something and you got there just in time?"

"*Ssshhh!*" hissed Frederik, looking genuinely scared and holding his bony finger up to his lips.

"What? What did I say now?"

Frederik didn't respond, but instead walked to his own chair. With unnatural strength he slid the great stone lump across the floor to just in front of the fireplace. Doing the same with the chair Alex had been sitting in, he beckoned for Alex to sit down.

As they both sat in front of the fire, Frederik reached into his cloak and pulled out what looked like a small glass tube. He crushed it in his hand and threw it directly into the fire. Alex half expected a great puff of smoke, but instead he felt a gentle wave of warmth from the fire. It was as if a great invisible fireguard had been removed and all the built-up heat was spilling out. Feeling his shoulders relax a little, he realised how tense he had been against the cold. Alex settled as comfortably as he could into his chair and looked to Frederik.

"You may ask me anything Alexander," he spoke quietly, without looking up from the fire. "But you may not ask about the shadow. He is too dark a thing for you to be concerned about right now and I told your grandfather the very same thing. That verse I spoke to you when I dragged you from his clutches was about the shadow. In all truth you do not need to know any more than that. Do you understand me?"

Even though the room had become as warm and cosy as Alex's own bedroom, he felt a shiver at the thought of this unknown thing. He couldn't help but look back over his shoulder.

"I asked if you understood me Alexander?"

Alex turned and his eyes met Frederik's. "I… understand."

"Good!" said Frederik. "Then let us move on."

"Ok then," said Alex. "So I'm still a bit confused as to why I'm halfway up a cliff face, locked in a shack with… well, whatever you are. Would it be too much trouble for you to tell me exactly where we are?"

Frederik scowled, but obviously chose to ignore Alex's slight, instead choosing to wrap his cloak more tightly around himself.

"As I told you before, Alexander, we are in my home."

"So you say," started Alex, "But *where* are we? Last time I looked I was in England. At home. By a lake!"

"Ah, well you are not there now. We are in my native country of Norwege. We are in the house where I spent many long years, set in the fjords of Knallust."

Alex stared blankly back at Frederik, itching to mention that travelling thousands of miles in an instant was impossible, but he was too tired to bother. Instead he decided to just go along with the old man's story.

"Fine. So we're in *Norway* then. Can you tell me how we got here exactly?"

"Alexander, calm yourself." Frederik said impatiently. "How we got here is not of any concern at this moment and if I told you how, your little, tiny brain would likely go *pop*." Frederik flicked open his gnarled fingers to demonstrate this sound.

Before Alex had time to object to this further slight of his intelligence, he continued. "So. You want to know what all of this is about. Correct?"

"*Yes*! Please, can you *just tell me* what is going on? Once and for all!"

"Fine. I shall tell you all you need to know, so listen carefully and do *not* interrupt."

Alex watched sulkily as Frederik adjusted himself once more in his chair. After he had wrapped his cloak around himself once more, he placed his hands on his knees and began to speak; still quietly but at a faster rate, so that Alex had to lean in to try and catch every word.

"The story that you read in the library about Annelise and I was only *partly* true. It is often the way when a story is told many times over a number of years that a certain amount of... *embellishments* are made to make it seem more interesting.

"The parts about Loki and other such gods, for example, are nonsense. That never happened, of course. But what *is* true is that we did write those books. However, we wrote far more than five.

"Over the years we must have written many hundreds of books. Hundreds and hundreds! We would write about every little thing, Alexander. Every little thing that we saw or did, or touched or smelt or tasted. Everything! Such things we wrote, you cannot believe, and of course the more we experienced, the more we wrote, and the more we wrote the more we wanted to experience. So we began to travel the world looking for the best and finest experiences for the senses you could ever imagine. Those days were good, Alexander, those days were the happiest of my life, just the two of us." Frederik gave a long sigh. His eyes were glazed with tears once more.

"It wasn't until much later on, when we had travelled all over the world, that we returned home to consolidate those many books into just five.

Agreeing that only the very purest and best experiences would make it into the final books, we spent many more years sorting, writing, editing and reducing until we had our five, one to represent each of our earthly senses: sight, hearing, taste, smell and touch.

"Only after completing these books did we realise our mistake. We should not have put all of these feelings and thoughts into one place!" Frederik leapt to his feet and began pacing the room in an agitated manner. "There was too much power, Alexander. Too much energy in these books and we started noticing changes right away. It started that just by reading these books a person would begin to experience what was written on the pages. It was no longer that you even had to do these things any more, merely reading about them meant you could experience it and for some time both Annelise and myself enjoyed these experiences. It was like reliving our travels but without having to leave the house.

"But soon, soon it became–how do you say–*addictive*. Like a drug. We were spending all our time in these books, experiencing these incredible things, but doing nothing else. It was Annelise who first noticed it and she became scared of the books, almost as if they were too pure, too special.

She tried many times to tell me to stop but I would not listen. I did not *want* to listen. I did not *want* to be away from my books for one moment. I do not know how much time passed when I was engrossed in these books. It may have been months… it may have been *years*… but when I finally tore myself away from them, the place where we lived was in such trouble. And I had not even noticed.

"As with all things of great power or value, Alexander, they will attract much stronger forces. This is what happened with the books and that is when the shadow came to my village. It came to take my books, but of course I did not want it to. So I fought it… and not just me, but the whole village fought it.

"But it was too strong, Alexander. The shadow was too strong and it beat me. And then it began to kill. It killed every single person in the village before finally, it killed… my Annelise."

Tears were flowing down Frederik's cheeks and falling silently onto his lap as he once more sat gazing into the crackling fire. Alex, who had been listening intently recalled the feeling of sadness he'd felt when he'd read the story in the library; but to hear it now from the man who had lived it was something else entirely. Frederik seemed to pull himself together and wiped at his eyes on the haggard sleeve of his robe before continuing.

"Of course, after Annelise was killed I did not know what to do with myself. I had all but ignored her for such a long time, but without her I was completely lost. All of our friends in the village had been slain. The only thing I could think to do was get rid of the five books that we'd spent so many years writing. Even though we'd created them as something good, there was too much in them for any human being.

"So I decided to destroy them. I *had* to destroy them. The very night that Annelise was killed I built a pyre, placed the books around her sleeping body and set fire to the lot. They burnt so incredibly hot and bright that I couldn't stand close to them. I couldn't even look at them. It was like the heat and light of the sun was pouring from that fire…

"Eventually it died away, leaving nothing but ash. A pile of soft, white ash for ten lifetimes' work and my darling wife."

Frederik's voice faded and Alex had to swallow the lump that had risen in his throat from the poor wretch's tale. Frederik turned and Alex saw the fury return to the old man's eyes.

"It was then that *he* came."

"Who?" said Alex enthralled, completely forgetting he wasn't meant to be interrupting.

"The one who told me how I could find and kill the shadow. I didn't know where he had come from but he vowed to help me. And I was so pleased to have company that I gladly accepted his offer. But he tricked me, Alexander.

"After many days of talking of this and that, I told him about the books and he was very interested. So I told him all about them and what they had become and why I had destroyed them. He wanted to know as much as possible about the kinds of things I wrote in them, so I told him.

"But the more I told him, the weaker I became and the happier he grew. Eventually, I was so weak I could barely move and I think was close to death. That is when he told me that it was *he* who controlled the shadow and that it was *he* who had ordered it to kill the villagers and my Annelise.

"You cannot believe the pain Alexander. To have my dear Annelise's killer in front of me, but being too weak to do anything about it. He then told me that he'd heard about the books and at first had wanted to take them for himself. But after realising I'd destroyed them, he tricked me into teaching him how to make his own set of books.

"That is why I am here now, Alexander. I think this person is going to, or already *has,* made his own set of books. I need to stop him and if I can also stop the shadow from doing any more damage then so much to the better!"

Even through his sleep muddled brain Alex realised what Frederik was saying. "So you're telling me that this guy who, by all accounts, is a nasty piece of work and who controls this shadow thing you're terrified of, is not only still alive *800 years on*, but might also have made himself a set of these books?"

"That is correct, yes."

"And you're going to try and stop him and his shadow?"

"With your help, yes."

Alex's eyes bulged. "With *my* help? What have I got to do with all this?"

"Believe me Alexander, I would rather it wasn't you either. But unfortunately for both of us, it would appear that you are more important than even I had previously thought."

"Based on what exactly?"

"Based on the fact that the shadow has tried to attack you on three separate occasions now. And based on the fact that your blood is not entirely… normal."

Alex sat back in his chair thinking hard, his head felt on the verge of shutting down completely.

"Ok… ok, you might have a couple of good points there, but… but… ah! How do you know that it's not supposed to be *Lewis d*oing this stuff? He's the one with the brains and the business head! He's the clever one! It might be him that you need to talk to rather than me?"

Frederik's eyes narrowed again. "Believe me, Alexander, I would prefer it if it was your brother I had to deal with. But unfortunately for me, brains don't always come into this type of thing. And besides, he is busy with your grandmother is he not? Making deals and swelling the family coffers? If you like, we could put you both outside for a few nights and see which one the shadow takes? Then at least we'll know if I'm right or wrong."

"Oh very funny," said Alex, annoyed even more since Frederik seemed to be enjoying himself again. "Ok, let's suspend reality for a minute here and say that I *am* the one that's supposed to help you. I've got two questions for you."

Frederik raised his eyebrows.

"Firstly, *how* would I help you? And secondly, *why* would I help you?"

Frederik's smile broadened as if the questions were easier to answer than he'd anticipated.

"The *how* is simple. You need to do as your grandfather told you, as you promised him you would. You need to write in your diary. Write and write and write."

"Yeah well I tried it, but the words kept disappearing off the page didn't they? I tried twice and gave up. I just assumed it was some sort of joke."

"Joke? This is not a joke, Alexander. This is very serious. Did your granddad not mention this to you?"

"He may have done, yes. But what's the point of writing on a page if it's just going to disappear again? It's pointless!"

Frederik looked agitated again. "There *is* a point to this, Alexander. You need to practice your writing. If it disappears, then so be it. You have to keep writing until it sticks. That is what is important. Out of interest... what *exactly* were you writing about?"

Alex thought for a moment.

"Well, I was just writing about getting up in the morning, I think. Mum woke me up, I went downstairs–"

"*Achh!*" exclaimed Frederik, throwing his hands up in disgust. "This is useless! How can it possibly be you? Do you not understand what you need to do? Of course it won't stick if you're writing like a *child*. You need to write better, write with feeling and with passion!"

Frederik waved his hand dismissively and turned back to the blazing fire but Alex was on his feet again.

"Write with passion? I'm not sodding Shakespeare! How the hell am I supposed to write with passion? And write about what exactly? My favourite socks? What sauce I have on my bacon sandwiches? The music I listen to? How I–"

"What was that you said?" shot Fredrik, swinging round to face Alex with a look of keen interest on his face.

"What was what?"

"What you said just then."

"Bacon sandwich?"

"No! Achh! About the music? What did you mean?" Frederik's eyes were fixed on Alex's, making him feel very uncomfortable.

"I don't know what I meant. Just that it's something I do a lot... listen to music. I could write about the music I listen to."

"Then you *must* try that, you must *try* and write about listening to your music! Write about how it makes you feel, what emotions it gives you, what it makes you think about! Forget this day-to-day nonsense, write about the music. Do you understand?"

"Ok, ok I'll try it. But say I manage to do it like you say, what good is it going to do?"

Frederik sighed and looked like he was forcing himself not to lose his temper. "*If* the master of the shadow has worked out how to make his own set of books, we will need something to counteract them. We need you to create your own set of books that can work against his."

"But I still don't understand what good these books are. I mean what are we going to do - throw them at each other? Surely then it's just down to who's got the better aim?"

Expecting to see Frederik flip out at this intentionally stupid comment, Alex was surprised to see him looking almost excited.

"*That*, my idiotic little friend, brings me onto the *why* you would help me." Frederik leapt to his feet and stooped behind his chair to pick something up from the floor. When he straightened up and turned around, Alex saw that he was holding the charred block of wood in his hand. On it was placed the single sheet of paper.

Alex had completely forgotten about it, which he realised wasn't all that impressive since he'd been expressly told to guard it with his life. Frederik was already on his way out of the door. Cold air ripped through the room and the fire was blown out in an instant. Alex could see that dawn was coming and even in the harsh weather, the light blue-grey sky was beginning to reveal itself behind the tall dark cliffs. Frederik turned in the doorway and beckoned for Alex to join him outside. Reluctantly, Alex made his way to the door and out into the biting wind.

Frederik walked the few steps to the edge of the cliff and Alex followed, being careful not to get too close to the edge. Frederik turned and shouted over the noise of the buffeting wind, "This is the only remaining page from one of the five books. I should not have done, but I had to keep something back. This is a page from the book of hearing. The book of sound!"

Alex looked down at the wooden slate with the page placed on it. He saw nothing but a blank piece of old paper.

"We do not have much time, Alexander for the dawn is nearly here but it is important that you watch very carefully."

Alex tried to shout back over the noise but the strong wind took his breath and he simply nodded instead. Frederik held his gaze for a moment more before holding out the black wooden tablet in front of him. Alex was worried the delicate page that was placed on the wooden slate would be blown away, but it didn't seem to be affected by the wind at all. Raising his other hand high in the air, Frederik shook his arm and his sleeve dropped down to his elbow; revealing the numerous leather bands around his arms that were topped off by the silver bracelet. Frederik lowered his arm so that the bracelet hung a couple of inches above the page. At once, the bracelet and page glowed blue at the edges. Alex watched in amazement as the page started to grow on the blackened wooden board. Not only did it grow, but words formed on the page as well; words made up of tiny letters, filling every square inch of the blank paper. They were so small that Alex couldn't make out anything that was written. Frederik moved both hands to the edges of the board and raised the whole thing high above his head.

The sound of the wind stopped at once. It still raged on, because Alex could feel it on his skin and see it in Frederik's hair and cloak, but there was no sound until Frederik spoke softly. "This is what I can do with one single page, Alexander. Perhaps you can imagine that the power of a whole book would be devastating."

Frederik swung the wooden panel down through the air. A shimmering wave of what looked like heat blasted from the wooden panel down towards the black and swirling water below. As the translucent wave hit the water, there was a thunderous boom that seemed to shake the mountain, but more shocking was the sight of the water in the river below. It was being pushed out to the sides of the mountain, as if someone was pressing an enormous bowl deep in to the water. The circle grew bigger and bigger and seemed to go deeper, until eventually Alex could make out a huge, exposed circular section of the river bed.

The water crashed and foamed around this invisible obstacle until Frederik raised the tablet once again over his head. The black water came crashing back down on itself, returning to its usual riding torrent. At the same time, the sound of the wind returned and Alex put his hands to his ears.

"As you can see," shouted Frederik over the noise. "If someone else even has a chance of wielding this kind of power, we cannot be left with nothing! You need to get to work, immediately!"

Alex stared back at Frederik, a small part of understanding beginning to dawn on him.

"We will talk again soon Alexander. I will come for you. Believe me when I say that this is *real* and that if you do not follow what your granddad says, then I shall not be held responsible for my actions."

"Fine!" Alex shouted back over the melee. "I'll do whatever he says! So I can go now can I? Are we done?"

"You can go, Alexander. Go back inside my house and you will be home!"

Not needing to be asked twice, Alex walked the few steps back to the door of the cliff house. Taking one last glance over his shoulder, he saw Frederik standing bolt upright, clutching the board to his chest. Alex took a final step through the open doorway. The sky suddenly went dark, followed by the same rush of wind that Alex had felt when he had arrived. When the lights returned, he was standing back in his granddad's house. Henry was wringing his hands together nervously and looking very sheepish indeed.

CHAPTER 21

RETRIEVAL

"So did you ah, have a good trip then, old chap?" began Henry, almost apologetically.

"Old chap… *old chap*? You *punched* me! What the *hell* did you do that for?"

"Necessary evil, old boy. Needed some of your blood you see, to ah… get things moving." Henry looked very uncomfortable and was still wringing his hands and bouncing on his toes as if he couldn't keep still.

Alex walked back to the sofa and slumped down into the soft leather seat. Tiredness washed over him in waves and in the warmth of Henry's house, he realised just how cold he had been. He reached over the back of the sofa to pull a large, soft throw around him, before sinking back into the warm leather cushions.

"Have you *any* idea what I've been through tonight? What I've seen?" he said, still not looking at his granddad.

He hated to admit it to himself, but he suddenly felt very confused and more than a little scared. Henry's hands finally parted and he stopped bouncing. Hitching up his trousers, he settled into the seat beside Alex.

"I feel like I'm going mad with some of the things that have happened over the last couple of days, and I'm still not sure what's going on. Frederik explained some but I–"

"I know, I know," said Henry soothingly. "I don't understand everything myself, if I'm completely honest with you. It is all so very strange, after all. But then I suppose…"

"Suppose what?" Alex said after a few moments.

"Hmm? Well, I suppose that I've had longer to get used to the idea than you, haven't I."

Alex didn't say anything. He was still going over things in his head, trying to rationalise everything he had seen and heard. Henry was once again rooting around in his jacket for his pipe which he pulled out and lit. The smell of the smoke comforted Alex somewhat and he felt himself begin to relax. After several minutes of Henry puffing on his pipe and with Alex finally starting to warm up, Henry finally spoke again.

"So, first things first. What exactly did Frederik tell you?"

Alex paused before answering, thinking that his granddad sounded far too excited to hear this part, almost as if he'd been putting off asking Alex for fear of annoying him. But he supposed it wouldn't hurt to talk it through some more and maybe his granddad would be able to explain everything some more.

"Well, after we got past the initial pleasantries," Alex instinctively rubbed his neck, "he told me the truth about that bit of story that you showed me in the library. He told me about all the books he and Annelise had written over the years, how they'd cut out all the rubbish and just put the good stuff into these five *super-books* and that it had started to go a bit wrong from there really."

Henry merely sucked on his pipe, so Alex carried on.

"That's when he said that Annelise had been killed by the shadow thing, so he'd burnt the five books. But then this other person turned up and Frederik reckoned that this other person controlled the shadow *and* that he's still alive somewhere."

Henry was taking ever more ponderous sucks on his pipe, each one followed by great billowing clouds of smoke from his mouth.

"He did say though that even though he'd burnt all the books, he'd actually kept one page back, which is that page you showed me earlier."

Finally this seemed to stir Henry into speech. "And did he show you anything with this page?"

Alex's eyes narrowed. "Yes… he did actually. That was the really weird part. He took me outside onto that cliff ledge, which was supposedly in Norway, and then started waving this page around in the air! It kind of took all the sound away and then he somehow managed to control the water in the river below."

Henry was chewing on thegutt end of his pipe, deep in thought again.

"And did he say anything about your writing in the diary?"

"Yeah, he did. In fact, he told me about that before he showed me his water trick. He basically said that he thinks the guy that controls the shadow might have made his own set of books and that I need to start making my own, so that if this guy *has* made his own set we've got something to fight back with."

Even as Alex heard himself speak the words, he realised how ridiculous it all sounded.

"So… he wants you to create your own set of books," said Henry quietly, almost to himself.

"Well that's what he said, yes. He said I should write about music for a start. He thinks that'll work quite well. Said I should write about how I feel when I listen to it… or something like that."

Henry chuckled to himself.

"What's so funny?"

"Oh nothing, nothing. It's just nice to know that he's sticking to what he told me, I suppose."

"What do you mean?" said Alex. Henry looked back at him and smiled.

"Well, it was Frederik that suggested you might want to start your music lessons again, you see? And it was he who suggested we make the glass house a music room for you to work in. He obviously thinks that you and music go together quite well."

"But I thought they were both your idea?" said Alex, taken aback.

"Well, getting Sara to help you was my idea, yes. I thought that if you were going to be doing a lot of music based… *activities,* then you'd rather have Sara with you than anyone else? Was I right?"

It was Alex's turn to laugh now and he felt himself going slightly red before mumbling a few incoherent words into his blanket. Henry merely winked before patting a heavy hand on his knee.

"Anyway," said Henry through an enormous yawn. "It sounds like you've had a right old time of it tonight, but at least you've got a task now. You *must* write that diary of yours. Do as Frederik told you. Write about the things he told you to write about."

"Don't worry, I'm going to," said Alex earnestly. "The last thing I want is that freaky old man coming to visit me again in the middle of a thunder storm."

Henry laughed. "Yes, he is rather intense, isn't he?"

It was then that something stirred in Alex's memory about the storm the other night, but he couldn't remember what it was. Finally it came to him.

"The storm! I heard grandma talking about the storm to someone the other day."

"Well that's not surprising is it?" said Henry, leaning back in his chair with his eyes closed. "It was quite a belter you know."

"No, I mean she was talking to someone about the storm as if it was something unusual."

Henry's eye's flicked open and he sat upright, a look of grim curiosity on his face. "When was this exactly?"

"Err, a couple of days ago. Yeah, it was when I was coming to meet you for the first time in the new library. I'd just found Frederik's bracelet thing, then I'd walked round the side of the house. That's when I heard them talking. It's ok though, she didn't see me. It just seemed a bit odd that was all."

"Do you know who she was talking to? Do you know who it was?" Henry looked stern.

Alex looked at his granddad, once again unnerved by this sudden change of attitude. "No. Like I said, they didn't see me but… well I couldn't see them either. It was a man though. He sounded… old. Oh, and he called her *Sofie*, which I thought was weird too…"

Alex's voice tailed off at the look of cold fury that seemed to have come over his granddad's face.

"What *exactly* did they say?" Henry said in a low voice.

For the first time he could remember, Alex felt nervous in the presence of his granddad. This wasn't helping his efforts to remember a whispered conversation from two days ago. Especially with everything that had happened in between.

"Err… well they said something about the storm… um, and watching the sky between two times, half past eleven to half past four, or something? Then the man said that *one of them* was back. And then grandma told him to go. That was it really. Hey, you don't think this is something to do with Frederik, do you? Grandma doesn't know anything does she?"

Henry stood up and walked to the kitchen area, without a word. There was a light jangle of metal on marble and Alex looked up in time to see Henry throw some keys towards him. Catching them in cupped hands, Alex saw that they were the boat keys. He looked back to his granddad, confused.

"Take the boat and go back to the house. Go on." said Henry flatly.

"You want me to leave?"

"Yes. Please, I need some time to think. Don't worry I'll come and find you soon enough and then we'll talk some more."

Alex didn't like this one little bit. This didn't sound like his granddad at all. Maybe he should have kept his mouth shut about what he'd heard, but then why should he? He hadn't done anything wrong. It was his grandma's fault if she wanted to sneak around with people she shouldn't.

"I'll see you soon then?"

Alex stood to leave and waited for his granddad so say something, but Henry had his back to Alex and had already lit another pipe. The familiar swirls of smoke were surrounding Henry's outline. From behind it appeared he was slowly catching fire. Alex stood up, dropped the rug onto the sofa and walked to the door.

"One more thing, Alex," Alex turned round to see Henry facing him, his eyes red and glazed with tears. "Whatever Frederik told you to do, do it. Do not mess with him. Do not be cocky with him. Do not antagonise him. And do not tell anyone about any of this. Do you understand me?"

Not knowing how to react, Alex nodded. Then, pulling on the long silver door handle, he left the house and walked along the deck-way to the boat.

Never, in his whole life, had he seen his granddad like that. It just didn't suit him at all. He was so used to seeing him as upbeat, ready for a laugh and a joke, that seeing him this way was almost more worrying than the experience he'd just had with Frederik.

Clambering down into the boat, Alex suddenly realised he didn't actually know how to drive the thing. Trying to remember what Henry had done on the way out, he inserted the key into the slot and turned it a full ninety degrees clockwise. The lights on the dials lit up a pale blue before Alex thumbed the chrome start button. Once again the engines grumbled into life. Rather than launch off at top speed, Alex gently pushed forward on the double levers and the boat pulled away gently from the mooring into the still water of the lake.

The sun was beginning to break over the top of the trees that edged the lake. He looked at his watch; it was almost 6.30am. The boat was gliding effortlessly through the still waters and it wasn't long before he could see the glass boat house reflecting jewel like in the morning sun.

Finally with time to himself, Alex thought about all the things that had happened in the last 24 hours. There was so much to take in; he wished he hadn't had to leave his granddad, so they could have talked some more.

Deep in his thoughts, Alex soon found himself back at the house. It all looked peaceful and quiet from the outside, so he made his way to the side entrance on the west wing of the building. The door was unlocked as usual and he slipped in quietly, closing it behind him and turning the key in the lock. Creeping through the house he marvelled at how quiet and peaceful it was. Eventually, he was back in his own bedroom and some sense of normality.

Within moments of being inside, however, there was a knock at the door. Alex froze. *What now?*

He gazed longingly at the thick white duvet; so inviting and soft. Thinking he may still get away with catching a few hours' sleep, he quickly kicked off his trainers, whipped off his socks, jeans and t-shirt and pulled on the grey silk robe that hung on the back of his door. Rubbing his hands quickly over his head to mess up his hair, he pulled his best sleepy face and opened the door; eyes half shut. The door was barely open an inch when Archer pushed in, closing it behind him with a smirk on his face.

"Very convincing, Master Wolf, but you can drop the sleeping beauty act with me."

"I don't know what you…" Alex gave an expansive yawn for good measure, "…mean, Archer."

"Oh yes you do. I've just followed you back from the lake house. I take it you didn't see me? Your granddad called ahead and told me to meet you there." Archer was still smirking in a very annoying manner.

"If you must know," said Alex, annoyed but far too tired for an argument. "I've got *rather* a lot on my mind. So I don't have time to be looking out for members of staff lurking about in the bushes."

Archer's eyes narrowed. "I wasn't *lurking*, I was told to come and find you to check you were ok after everything that happened tonight, that's all."

"And what would you know about it?" asked Alex aggressively.

"Enough to know that you've got some important work to do on a certain book? And, that if you don't get on with it, there'll be trouble. You wouldn't want another visitor in the night would you?"

Alex's mouth dropped slightly in surprise.

"Wha—well fine then! If you would just leave me in peace, I might be able to get on with it mightn't I? I can't work with you loitering around the place like a bad smell." Alex pointedly sniffed the air in front of Archer.

Archer's chest swelled; he looked like he wanted to throttle Alex more than usual, but instead let out a long, calming breath and walked out of the door, slamming it behind him.

Alex slumped down onto the bed, absolutely exhausted. His head was swimming again and he tried to clear his mind, desperate for sleep, but he couldn't stop the strange image of his granddad and Frederik both shaking their fists at him as if he'd already broken the promise he'd made to write in his diary as soon as he got back. Resigning himself to the fact he'd better do it sooner rather than later, he went to his desk and pulled his diary out of the drawer. He slid his hand back in to retrieve his pen, but it wasn't there.

Racking his brain for several moments, he suddenly remembered that he must have left it in his grandmother's room after signing the release form. Letting out a long sigh he cursed loudly, dropped down heavily onto the desk chair before beginning to swing moodily from side to side thinking about what to do next.

He had to write; that much was certain. If he didn't, he thought that his brain might explode. He pulled out a black biro from his pencil case, but as soon as he touched it he knew that he needed his other pen. The biro just didn't feel right. If he was going to be writing such important matters down, he really should have his favourite writing instrument. There was only one thing for it; he would have to go and retrieve the pen from the dragon's lair, even if it meant waking the dragon up herself.

Just the thought of this made his heart beat that little bit faster. Steeling himself, Alex quickly assembled an all-black outfit that he thought appropriate for the mission and quietly left his bedroom.

It wasn't long before he found himself hesitating once more in front of the black double doors that marked the entrance to his grandmother's personal rooms.

Should I knock? Should I just walk in? It wasn't like there was a doorbell after all. Deciding to play it safe, he took a few deep, steadying breaths, knocked three times and waited. After a full minute there was still no reply. He tried again; harder this time, so that the doors vibrated slightly after each impact. Still nothing. He tried again once more; a lot harder. Three loud bangs echoed down the hallway and he cowered slightly at the noise, but still there was no answer. Deciding that he had now given fair warning–and getting bored of waiting like a lemon–Alex slowly turned the cold brass handle. Half expecting the door to be locked, he was surprised when he felt the catch release and the door glide slowly open.

Cautiously, he poked his head around the edge of the door and was relieved to find the room empty. He quickly stepped inside and closed the door behind him, not wanting to stay a second longer than he had to. He darted across the room to the desk where he'd signed the wonderful document only yesterday.

The pen wasn't on the top of the desk where he thought it would be, so he searched through the desk drawers, one by one. The first drawer was empty, save for a metal glasses case embossed with the letters 'SW'. It was empty, so he dropped it back into the drawer and slid it shut. Next he opened the middle drawer; this had nothing but paperwork inside it and he knew better than to start looking at his grandma's private documents. He closed that too. In the third and final drawer, however, he hit the jackpot.

Inside lay his gleaming silver pen which he snatched up immediately. But then he stopped. The pen had been resting on a piece of familiar light blue paper that had been torn in half.

With a strange sense of foreboding, he gathered the pieces and laid them out on the desk. As he suspected, it was the trust fund release that he had signed yesterday. Alex's stomach dropped through the floor.

The old witch! All that money! Snatched away from me, again! But then another thought occurred to him. *Maybe the torn papers are meaningless. Maybe they're just not needed and that's why they've been torn up? There's only one way to find out.* Returning the torn pieces of paper to the drawer, he quickly slid it shut, checked everything was in order and made his way back out across the room to the door. Just as he reached for the handle, however, he heard heavy footsteps coming towards him.

No, no, no, no! Alex froze to the spot, his brain too tired to think clearly. He spotted the tall wardrobe near the door and instinctively lunged for the small brass handle. Pulling it towards him, the large, heavy door opened just in time. He slipped inside and with his fingernails, gently pulled it shut behind him.

He heard the gentle *swoosh* of the door being opened quickly and closed again, with the awful sound of a key turning quickly in the lock.

Alex pressed his ear against the wardrobe door. He heard footsteps and then the heavy desk chair being rolled quickly across the floor. Assuming it must be his grandmother, there to do some early morning business, he risked pushing open the wardrobe door a fraction. He squinted out into the brightly lit room.

From his hiding place, he could see his grandma sitting at her desk. She was facing away from him with her legs crossed. But then he heard the familiar creak of the chaise longue, as though someone was sitting on it.

Surely there's no-one else in the room? I would've heard two sets of footsteps. Alex carefully adjusted his position, but he still couldn't see. Then his grandmother spoke.

"I'm assuming you have some news if you've risked coming here?"

"Oh I have news, Sofie, but it is not good."

Alex froze. He recognised that voice, but how its owner had got there, Alex had no idea.

CHAPTER 22

A MEMORY

Henry Wolf was leaning against the counter in the small kitchen of his bachelor pad, sobbing quietly. One hand was clenched in a fist to his mouth as if trying to stop himself shouting out, whilst the other held a small black and white photo of an attractive young couple.

The woman in the photo was beautiful with a kind face and large, bright eyes. Her mouth was open, like she was laughing and her long dark hair was blowing in the wind. With one hand, she was trying to hold onto her hat whilst her other arm was wrapped tightly around the middle of a tall and much younger Henry Wolf. They looked very much in love. Several tears fell silently onto the glass of the picture frame that shook gently in Henry's hand.

CHAPTER 23

THE LIST

Alex was leaning as close to the wardrobe door as he dared without falling through it, desperately trying to hear what his grandma and her mysterious visitor were saying. From the moment the visitor had spoken, Alex had recognised the voice; it was the same man he had heard his grandmother talking to in the grounds, just after he'd found Frederik's bracelet. But there was something else familiar about his voice that Alex just couldn't place.

"He is alive," he said casually.

"But how can he be?" Sofia said, a note of uncertainty in her voice.

"I don't know how… but we are, aren't we? Isn't it the same thing?"

"Yes, but I thought he'd been dealt with." Alex could just make out his grandmother holding her hands up to her mouth, as if she were praying.

"So did I, or at least that's what I'd been informed. Either that person was lying or they were mistaken. It doesn't matter now. It's just another problem that needs… resolving."

Alex saw his grandmother's hands drop to her lap and she seemed to stare directly at the source of the second voice. "That isn't the easiest thing to do though is it? He's survived this long for a reason."

"Yes, I suppose so," said the man thoughtfully. "But he hasn't ever faced *her* before has he? Not in the true sense anyway."

Sofia didn't reply.

"You still have access to her I imagine, Sofie? You still have her on side?"

"Of course I have, but I choose not to use–"

"Anyway," said the man. "How we do it is neither here nor there, but something must be done and soon."

There was a long pause. Alex adjusted himself once more to try and discover the identity of the mystery man, but it was no good.

"What *else* did he say?" asked Sofia finally.

"Oh not much, just that he was seen around here."

"*Here?*" said Sofia loudly. "You didn't tell me he'd been seen around here!"

"Oh didn't I?" Said the voice lazily. "It must have slipped my mind. Anyway he was seen lurking at the edge of your estate, a bit further up the hill."

"So you mean he was as close to *you* as he was to *me* then? Maybe he was coming for you first after all?"

Alex just caught what he thought was a nasty smile slide across his grandmother's face. He had been on the receiving end of it too many times not to recognise it.

"Do not worry, Sofie, the thought had crossed my mind as well."

There was another long pause before Alex's grandmother started again sounding terse. "Well, what else did he say? Anything?"

"Nothing much. He did think that he seemed to be protecting someone though. Interestingly he said he followed your dear old husband through the grounds late last night as well. Just around the time that he made his visit to the old country."

Sofia's smile disappeared. "Henry? What's Henry got to do with this?"

"Maybe nothing… maybe everything," said the man quietly, almost to himself. "I don't honestly know, Sofie. He followed him to that secret shack of his, but he couldn't get close enough to see who was with him. There was certainly *movement* of some sorts. And then he said he saw the boat return from Henry's house to the bank. All by itself." There was a long pause. "You wouldn't know anything about this would you, Sofie? You aren't doing something with one of yours and not keeping me informed?"

Alex saw his grandmother bristle at this suggestion and sit up stiffly in her chair. "Of course I'm not! I don't know anything about this!" How dare you suggest that—"

"Well I think that's probably enough to be going on with, don't you?" said the man. "The fact is he's *here*. He's alive and he's up to something. Whichever way you cut it, that's not good news for us. Is it?"

"It may be worse news for *you*," shot Sofia, "because let's not forget, that it was *you* who did it!"

Alex saw his grandmother lift her gaze; the man must have stood up.

"As far as I'm concerned—and as I'm sure he's concerned—we're both in this together. And if you think—"

There was a sudden hammering at the door. Alex saw Sofia spin round then turn back to the hidden figure. "You must go. Go. Now! *Beskytte og ære!*"

She stood, straightened out her clothes and strode towards the bedroom door, her face returned to its usual impassiveness. Alex heard the key turning in the lock and then the door being opened.

"Morten?" Sofia sounded surprised.

"I… I want to speak to you. About Alex's trust fund." Alex noticed his father's nervous tone.

"Ah yes, I thought you might. Well let us go down to my office, this is no place to be discussing business matters, Morten."

There was the sound of the door being closed and then very faint footsteps heading quickly away. Alex let out a sigh of relief, but then stopped mid breath; the mysterious visitor must still be in the room.

He eased the door open a touch more, giving him a wider field of vision. He couldn't see or hear anyone, so he opened the door further. Still nothing. Confused, Alex pushed the door fully open, ready to take whatever consequences came his way, but there was no-one there. He stepped out into the room and swivelled around, looking for signs of the recently departed visitor. Despite the size of the room there were actually very few places to hide.

How could he have just disappeared? Pausing momentarily to consider his luck, Alex moved silently out of Sofia's study and back to his own bedroom as quickly as his tired body would allow.

He slumped on his bed, feeling the first throbs of a powerful headache pressing on his brain. He still had to write. He had to get it all down.

Scrabbling off the bed he sat down hard at his desk, nearly toppling over in the process. Quickly undoing his diary's silver buckle, he opened it up and pressed down the spine before pulling out his cherished pen and laying it delicately next to the open book.

Taking several long, slow breaths to clear his mind, he stretched out his fingers, coughed and then finally picked up the pen. It could have been his imagination, but he thought he felt a small pulse travel down his arm and into his hand. He considered where to begin. A vague memory swam into his head, something his dad used to say: *when in doubt, start with a list.* Wondering if this was perhaps too simple for this seemingly high-maintenance diary, he cautiously put the pen to the paper and began to write.

Alex Wolf's List of the Strange and Unexplained

Never one for simple titles, he sat and admired it for at least two minutes before realising excitedly that it hadn't disappeared. Encouraged, he began his list in earnest.

1) I come home from School and saw a shadow at the gate which turned out to be something really dangerous - great start to the summer.

2) On my way to see Granddad in the new library I found a silver bracelet which turns out to belong to an 800 year old man called Frederik. I have a vague memory of seeing Frederik during a storm but can't quite remember that...

3) Just after I found the bracelet I hear Grandma talking to a mystery man in the grounds about a storm and SOMEONE being back - do they mean Frederik?

4) Granddad gives me a diary to write in - says it's important.

5) I play the piano then have a huge nosebleed when Sara turns up - it turns out that my blood isn't red, it's black and silver. V. weird!

6) Sara more than likely sees me in my pants.

7) When I wake up I try to write in the diary but the writing disappears. Then I get some of my weird blood on this pen which starts to glow and I start writing all sorts of stuff. The writing isn't there in the morning.

8) Grandma pretends to be nice and gives me £1,000,000.00. Good news!

9) I break my arm and then get pulled down underground by Frederik - but it turns out that he's saving my life from that shadow thing!

10) Wake up in the library in the dark then Granddad shows me a story about Frederik, which is MOSTLY true. Turns out Granddad's in on all this and knows Frederik. We have to run from the library because that shadow thing might be about again.

11). Also turns out that Granddad has got a hidden bachelor pad (which Dad helped him build). We go there and Granddad explains some of what's going on then shows me a page from a really old book - one of the ones Frederik wrote.

12) Granddad punches me in the face and Frederik appears - now we're in Norway on the edge of a cliff!?!?!

13) I annoy Frederik but he tells me that even though the special books he made were destroyed, he thinks the person who controls the shadow AND killed his wife might be making another set.

14) Then he says that I need to write in my diary a lot about music so that I can make another set of books to work against this other set.

15) Frederik then shows me what one page can do in the water... scary but pretty cool!

16) Go back to see Granddad who gets really annoyed when I mention Grandma talking to this strange guy then he tells me to leave.

17) Run into Archer who ALSO seems to know more than I realised. AND he knew something about my nosebleed too! Archer is really starting to annoy me now.

18) Go to get my pen back from Grandma's room but get stuck in a wardrobe. The same mystery man appears and talks to Grandma again - they seem to know something about all this. They mentioned Granddad and 'him' and 'her. Who are they? Why can't they just use names like everyone else?

19) Now writing a list in my diary and so far it hasn't disappeared - brilliant news!

Alex sat back in his chair and pondered the list, trying to think of anything he may have missed. His brain was pounding. He rubbed his hands over his face to try and wake himself up a bit and shake some of the tiredness from his mind. He yawned and then read the list again. Out of everything, there were only two things that really unsettled him.

Firstly, that he had been so close to having access to a million pounds, only to have it torn away from him. Secondly, that if his grandmother knew *anything* about this whole situation that suddenly made it very real and a lot more scary.

Frederik, he could deal with, but his grandmother? She was a whole other proposition.

Realising that he was more bothered about his grandmother than an 800 year old lunatic, Alex leaned back in his chair and laughed.

He suddenly remembered the torn blue form in his grandmother's study. The laughter must have helped as he felt a sudden wave of optimism. Reaching into a desk drawer, he pulled out a thin touchscreen tablet. After a few taps and one very long password he found himself staring at his bank account, powerless to stop the huge grin that began to spread across his face.

A. Wolf Main Account: 48601787 - 18-00-02 £1,000,008.02 credit

So, despite the fact she tore up that contract I still get the money? Alex gave up trying to ponder the hows and whys of his grandma's labyrinthine brain; he was far too excited for that. Leaping to his feet, the tiredness seemed to fall away as if his sudden wealth had invigorated him and reset his brain.

He began to pace the room at great speed, broken by the occasional happy hop, imagining all the things he could buy for himself; all of those things on all of those lists that he'd been making for years. But then he stopped.

In a moment of common sense, which took him entirely by surprise, he decided that he really should wait until he had slept before starting shopping; it would be sensible to let the reality sink in first. After that he'd be able to spend a lot more quickly and with much more precision. Another small squeak escaped from his grinning mouth. Alex glanced over at the time: 8.02am. He felt ravenously hungry but truly happy for the first time since he'd been home.

Enjoying a refreshing shower and change of clothes, he sauntered downstairs to see what he could find for breakfast. He failed to notice the words in his journal flash bright blue for a moment.

CHAPTER 24

BREAKFAST

Alex could smell the invigorating scent of coffee in the open entrance hall. Following his nose, it wasn't long before he picked up the unmistakable aroma of fried food. With an extra spring in his step he bounded into the kitchen, nearly knocking over his mum in the process, who had her head buried deep in a cupboard looking for something.

"Is that you, Alex?" She said as she removed her head from the jar-filled void. "I didn't see you at all yesterday. Where were you hiding all day?"

"Oh… just around," said Alex, shrugging his shoulders. He walked to the centre island and picked up a piece of toast that was sitting lonely on a plate.

"Would you like some breakfast then?" She asked, following him to the huge gas range. "It's nearly ready if you're hungry?"

Alex lifted his chin and nonchalantly inspected the contents of the frying pan. Knowing that his mother wasn't the best cook in the world, he was surprised to see bacon, sausages and fried bread in the frying pan; scrambled eggs in a saucepan next to it; and under the counter top grill, tomatoes, mushrooms and hash browns.

"Hmmm… yes I think I will actually, Mother," said Alex, affecting a very haughty voice. "And don't hold back on the sausages, will you."

The smell of it was amazing and he wanted to be sure he got his fair share. Just as he reached out to grab a particularly crisp looking hash brown from the top of the grill, Alex heard footsteps behind him on the tiled floor. He turned quickly to see his dad standing right behind him.

"Morning, Alex," said Morten softly, reaching past Alex to turn off the grill.

"Morning…" said Alex, surprised to see his dad in the kitchen, not just for breakfast, but obviously having cooked it as well.

"I just thought it would be nice for the four of us to have breakfast together. You don't mind, do you?" Said Morten quietly.

Alex's brain took a moment to catch up. "Four of us?" He spun around to check he hadn't missed anyone sitting behind him.

On the long wooden table at the far end of the room, Alex spotted a neatly folded copy of the financial papers, topped off with a set of car keys. Before he had time to sigh, the tall glass side door opened and Lewis strolled in, dressed head-to-toe in running clothes and smiling brightly.

"Morning, Al. You alright?" He said, only slightly out of breath as he began to stretch. "I haven't seen you in days!"

"Why does everyone keep saying that?" Alex muttered.

"Sorry mate," said Lewis. "Wasn't keeping tabs or anything. It's just I knocked on your door this morning to see if you wanted to come for a run with me. Maybe tomorrow eh?"

Lewis wiped his forehead with a towel. Alex watched him fold it neatly and place it over the back of the chair.

"Running? No thanks. Rather drive to be honest..." He couldn't help but look at the car keys again and Lewis caught his eye.

"Hey, well why don't you take mine out for a spin?"

Alex was taken aback for a moment. "Err, no… thanks, no. I've got some big plans today actually and besides, I'll probably have my own car soon enough."

Alex smiled inwardly at the thought of arriving at the house in something much bigger and faster. Lewis raised his eyebrows, then shrugged, pulled out a chair and sat down at the table.

"Big plans?" Said Rebekka from the other side of the room. "You mean you've got something planned for the dinner party tonight? Oh how wonderful!"

Alex looked up at Lewis. "Dinner party?" He said quietly. "What dinner party? What's she on about?"

Lewis looked confused. "You know? The dinner party we have *every* year? Just after we've finished school? Lots of people? Lots of food? A party… with dinner?"

"Yes, I know what a dinner party is. I'd just forgotten that it was tonight that's all!" He hissed at his brother. "It's not my fault nobody reminds me of anything around this place."

"Well to be fair, mate," said Lewis, reaching for his paper. "You've not exactly been around a lot since you've been back have you? Anyway you'd better sort yourself out because this one's the *big one*, apparently. Now that we've both finished school and all that."

Alex knew only too well why Lewis was looking so pleased with himself. He relished these occasions as they were a perfect opportunity for him to grease his way around as many people as possible.

They had been going on for years, dressed up as an occasion to celebrate Alex and Lewis's returning home from school, or to celebrate their latest exam results. Alex had never understood why though, since they were always home at Easter and Christmas and their exam results had never arrived in time for the party. Unless they miraculously arrived that morning, a month early, that year would be no different.

Alex knew full well that the parties were just an excuse for his grandma to do business with the parents of influential friends Lewis might have picked up; they always followed the same pattern:

Sofia would invite a lot of her rich business associates and talk shop all night whilst trying to screw them out of more money. Lewis would suck up to them as well, saying how everything was *wonderful* and *hilarious*. His mum would be the perfect hostess but not rest for a minute, whirling around in a flurry of activity all evening. His dad would chat to a few people but more than likely end up sitting by himself in the corner. The only bright spark would be his granddad who, without fail, would get roaring-drunk and start telling obscene jokes to anyone within earshot. As for Alex, if last year's party was anything to go by, he would get stuck into the food, try and snag a couple of bottles of something bubbly then make a sharp exit before being asked to perform for his parents' friends; or something else equally horrifying.

The sound of ceramic on wood pulled Alex from his bitter memories and he looked down to see an enormous white plate, piled high with food. Alex glanced up to see his dad standing over him with a somewhat curious expression on his face. For some reason he didn't feel that hungry anymore.

"Come on, Alex, tuck in!" Said Rebekka, who seemed to be waiting for everyone else to start eating before she did. "Are you having some too, Lewis? There's plenty to go round."

Lewis looked up from his paper and caught Alex's eye again. "No, no thanks, Mum. Not after a run. Think I'll just stick to the healthy stuff if you don't mind."

Alex scowled at his brother until Morten sat down next to Alex with a small bowl of muesli. Deciding he would make up for his breakfast tomorrow with some form of exercise, Alex assessed his plate for his first target. Although the gleaming sausages looked particularly appealing, bathed in hot oil and tomato ketchup, Alex decided on a beautifully crisp piece of fried bread instead.

"Well, this is lovely isn't it," said Rebekka, who was standing by the table, beaming down at her family. The only response was the sound of chewing and the rustling of turning newspaper. "What time did you tell your friends to come round tonight, Lewis dear?"

Alex's skewered piece of fried bread stopped en route to his mouth.

"I told them all to come for around seven, for dinner at eight. Hope that's alright?"

"Perfect, perfect!" Said Rebekka sitting down opposite Alex with two pieces of lightly buttered toast and a glass of orange juice.

It seemed Alex was the only one subjecting himself to a good artery-clogging. "We're supposed to bring friends tonight? I didn't know that!" He said stiffly, although he was pleased to see his mother look slightly uncomfortable.

"Well I just thought Lewis might want to bring some friends along that was all and I wasn't sure who you'd–"

"Don't worry, Al," said Lewis. "It's only the usual lot. Hayden, Lisa–"

"Chloe?" Said Alex, trying to sound casual.

"Yes, Chloe too," said Lewis with a smile on his face.

Rebekka laughed out loud. "Oh wonderful, wonderful." she said almost to herself before biting into her toast.

Maybe tonight is going to be a bit more fun after all. Alex pictured himself whisking Chloe Hurst around the dance floor; he would finally be able to make up for the end-of-year party incident and sweep her off her feet.

"I think Sara's coming too, isn't she Mum?" Lewis watched the piece of fried bread fall from Alex's fork.

"Oh yes, that's right! Your granddad invited her. There you go, Alex, Sara's one of your friends isn't she?" Alex felt queasy again. "Speaking of whom, I haven't seen your grandfather in a day or so either. You haven't seen him have you, Alex?" his mum said, wiping several crumbs from her front and sipping on her glass of orange juice.

Morten's head turned slightly towards Alex, but he didn't notice.

"What? No, no–not seen him at all," Alex said.

In truth he was completely distracted by the fact that his two favourite women in the whole world were going to be at his house that very evening and he hadn't even begun to prepare.

"Right, well I'd better get on. Lots to do for tonight!" said Rebekka standing up suddenly. "If you two could be ready by half past seven then you can help me with any last bits before the guests start to arrive."

"No problem, Mum," said Lewis, without looking up from his paper.

"Yeah," said Alex quietly, imagining kissing first Chloe and then Sara.

She whisked out of the room. Hearing the tinkling of a spoon, Alex glanced at his dad and the empty bowl in front of him.

"I suppose I'd better get going too then," said Lewis, who folded up his paper, finished his mum's orange juice and stood up.

"Catch you later, Al. See you later, Dad." Lewis called over his shoulder as he walked quickly from the room.

Morten barely looked up, still gazing at his seemingly fascinating bowl. Alex felt the uncomfortable silence growing with every heartbeat. Lately, he had rarely found himself alone with his dad; when he did, it always seemed to be an uncomfortable experience.

He tried to distract himself from the obvious silence by spearing a slightly deflated sausage and poking moodily at his egg with it until it popped. The velvety golden liquid, oozed out slowly onto the white plate.

"Alex, I want to talk to you about something." Morten said quietly, still looking at his bowl. Alex could feel his shoulders tense up instantly. He had never known a conversation that started with these words end well. "It's about your trust fund."

Alex rolled his eyes and gave an overly-dramatic sigh, "Oh here we go. Let me guess, you want it back now, do you? First I'm having it, then I'm not, now I am, now I'm not? Make up your minds–"

"Alex," said Morten quietly but firmly. Alex stared at his plate.

"No, I don't want it back actually," said Morten. "I just want you to be careful with that money, that's all.

"I know it seems like it's a lot. But I don't want you just to blow it all on rubbish. You never know when you might need some of it."

Alex shifted in his seat. His father was always trying to lecture him about being careful with his money; he was sick of it.

"It's only a million. What's a million to us? I'm pretty sure I'm not going to ever be short of money am I? Heir to the second richest family in the country, only out-monied by–let me think–oh yes, your dad! I don't think being careful really comes into it does it?" Alex gave a humourless laugh, strangely satisfied by the rising colour in Morten's face.

"That's not the point, Alex. If I'd known your grandmother was going to give it to you I would have come and spoken to you about it first, given you some advice but–"

"But she didn't come and speak to you, did she? And she doesn't have to," said Alex angrily. "Because *she's* the boss! She doesn't actually have to tell you what she's doing at all, does she?"

Morten looked as though Alex had just punched him and silence descended again for several moments. Eventually Morten got to his feet and quietly made his way out of the room only turning at the doorway.

"Yes, she is my boss, Alex... but I'm supposed to be your dad."

Alex felt a surge of guilt. He wasn't even sure how things had escalated so quickly. He hadn't meant to say those things at all and the look that his dad had given him made him feel awful. He tried to block the image from his mind.

I am right though. Grandma is the boss and if she wants to dish out a minuscule percentage of her wealth to me then who am I to complain? I'll spend it how I like and that's the end of it.

Thinking that this kind of incident would be perfect filler for a diary, he felt an odd rising panic as he pictured it open and unattended on his desk.

He leapt to his feet and raced out of the kitchen, back through the entrance hall, up the various stairways and down the landing. Barging through the heavy bedroom door he found the brown leather diary still on his desk, exactly as he had left it.

He considered the various people who may have just happened to wander into his room and see the things that he had written. Whether they believed them or not, it probably wasn't the best idea to leave something so important out on public display. Making a mental note to be a lot more careful in the future, he picked up the diary, put it back in its black box and took it quickly to his safe.

After he'd finished the long-winded opening and closing process, he stood in his voluminous wardrobe trying to decide what to wear that evening. His mum always liked everyone to get dressed up as if it was the party of the century. Considering that Chloe and Sara were both going to be there, he thought he'd better make a special effort.

After some careful thought, he picked out one of his single-button black tuxedos and hung it carefully on the clothes stand. Next, he chose a crisp white herringbone dress shirt; which he planned to combine with a black silk paisley cravat, rather than a bow tie. He knew his brother and father would be wearing bow ties, as would most of the other male guests, so that would definitely make him stand out. Being careful to choose suitable undergarments (black silk socks and banana yellow Y-fronts), he decided to leave the cufflinks, shoes and wristwatch until later. He looked down at his dressing stand, entirely pleased with his selections.

It was almost 9am; he had been up for twenty four hours. Yawning loudly, he walked contentedly from his wardrobe and crawled into his soft bed, only just remembering to set an alarm before his head hit the pillow. Within seconds he had drifted off into a deep but restless sleep.

CHAPTER 25

THE DINNER PARTY

Having completely ignored his alarm, Alex shouldn't have been surprised to have been woken by his harassed looking mother. Even so, being yanked out of a particularly enjoyable dream involving Chloe and Sara with threats of Archer and his grandmother wasn't the ideal start to the evening.

Looking more than a little flustered, Rebekka had told him to be downstairs and ready by 7.30pm or else there would be serious trouble. Blearily looking at his clock as his mum left the room he saw that gave him just under 15 minutes. Thinking that he could do with at least another hour or two on top of that, he nevertheless took his mum's threat as genuine and lazily rolled out bed.

Slightly dazed, he still managed to be washed, dressed and standing at the bottom of the stairs in the main entrance with thirty seconds to spare. Even though that was already a personal best, he knew he could have been quicker if he hadn't spent so long choosing his watch. Glancing at his heavily weighted wrist, he admired the oversized circular watch face and the fluorescent yellow second hand, ticking slowly round to the twelve o'clock position.

7.30 pm exactly. Outstanding!

As though the clock reaching 7.30 had triggered a doorway release mechanism, the whole of the entrance hall was suddenly flooded with bodies. There were people carrying boxes of flowers that were taller than he was; some carried lights that trailed behind them as they walked; some carried huge ice sculptures; others carried buckets of ice, cases of drinks, chairs, chair covers, trays of cutlery and finally platters of food. Alex's eyes bulged at the sight of so much food and his stomach began to growl.

As he gazed longingly at the roast pork, cold meat terrines and piles of profiteroles that were gliding past him like a gastronomic conveyor belt, Alex noticed something odd. None of them were going up the stairs to the grand reception room. They were all heading out of the front door and onto the driveway. Spotting a man carrying a tray of enormous king scallops, Alex quickstepped behind him and followed in the line of people marching like uniformed ants out of the house.

Following down the steps, it wasn't long before Alex realised where they were all heading. He stepped out from the tray-bearer's slipstream and walked briskly past the ant leaders. Within seconds he was striding through a single white door into the wide open circular space of the library.

His library. As he entered the huge, domed room, ready to vent his anger at such an invasion of his personal space, he looked around at what had been achieved. His rapidly rising annoyance fell away instantly; it looked incredible.

The bookshelves had been lowered and the piano was nowhere to be seen so that it was all one wide open space. Or at least it would have been, were it not for the single long table that neatly bisected the room. It was covered in white linen that hung all the way to the floor and there must have been at least fifty chairs split between the two sides. Down the centre of the table were five silver candelabras, each with holders for ten tall black candles. A long, snaking floral arrangement wove in and out of the dining paraphernalia scattered across the never-ending white surface.

It seemed the staff had been instructed to use the second set of slightly less expensive silverware. The first was reserved for use only if royalty visited. Since this had never happened in the history of Wolf Manor, Alex thought that this was rather a stupid rule and had said so on many an occasion.

Someone called his name from across the room. Amidst the flurry of activity he could just make out his mum on the far side of the circular room, bending over as if she was picking something up off the floor. Casually he wandered over to her past the various catering staff, all the time keeping an eye out for any unattended plates of food, but there didn't appear to be any. The staff seemed to be scurrying around faster than usual; Alex wondered if they were on as tight a deadline as he had been. His stomach groaned again.

"Alex could you help me get this sorted please? I can't seem to get it to work and we need it for tonight. Thank you dear," said Rebekka as he reached her.

She sounded flustered and distracted and didn't even wait for an answer before disappearing off into the swirling melee of people. Alex looked at where his mum had been crouching; a section of the floor had been lifted and underneath was some sort of computer control panel. Remembering when his mum had clapped the music on and off, Alex figured that this must be what controlled it all.

Turning the volume dial up just a touch, he intuitively tapped a couple of switches. Music began to float down from the ceiling, just as it had done before. Closing his eyes and entirely forgetting himself, Alex began to silently conduct the imaginary big band.

Lost in the music, he began moving his head from side to side in ever more extravagant motion and raising his arms ever higher and more elaborately as the music built to a crescendo. It wasn't until he swung around and opened his eyes, still waving, that he realised that Lewis, Hayden, Lisa and Chloe were all standing behind him watching.

He put his five-fingered conductors' batons into his pockets, as he felt the instant flush of blood heading directly to his face. "Can I help you?" he said, raising his eyebrows.

"I think we should be asking you the same thing, shouldn't we Alex?" Hayden followed his high pitched sneer with a glaring smirk.

"Hayden, the kitchen's that way if you're wondering?" said Alex pointing vaguely towards the house.

Hayden and Lisa looked blankly back at him.

"Oh sorry," Alex said. "It's just I assumed that coming dressed like *that* you'd be more comfortable serving the food rather than eating it?"

"Alex!" said Lewis.

Hanging off Hayden's arm, Lisa looked appalled. Chloe looked like she was trying not to laugh; that or her shoes had suddenly become very interesting.

Alex grinned, the rising tide of redness in his face abating. "Sorry, Hayden. No offence, just a joke."

Looking more than a little red himself, Hayden scowled but said nothing.

"You look nice tonight, Alex," said Chloe, looking him up and down and smiling.

"Thanks," said Alex still grinning, caught slightly unawares. He coughed nervously. "So do you."

Chloe's long dress was a shimmering midnight blue that was cut high at the side. Her hair was extravagantly arranged and held in place with a small silver flower. Alex struggled to focus on anything but her sparkling blue eyes though.

Before he could pull his gaze away, Chloe frowned slightly. "Hold on, Alex, your cravat's a little crooked. Here, let me…"

She took two steps towards him and was suddenly so close that he lost his breath for a second. He felt her gently tug at the black silk.

"There, that's better." she said quietly, looking straight into his eyes.

Alex could smell her perfume, her wonderful scent and quickly felt himself go red again. He had to look away; her eyes were burning him up.

"I'll see you later then shall I, Alex?" said Chloe, stepping back towards the others.

"Yes, that would be… yes."

She gave him a broad smile and turned back to the other three whose attention had turned to the beautiful room.

That went pretty well. You didn't offend her, you didn't make yourself look stupid and you made her laugh at Hayden. All in all, not too bad Alex, not too bad at all. Feeling rather pleased with himself, he wandered over to the other side of the room on the hunt for his granddad. Even before the party had started, his granddad would usually have been telling rude stories and throwing drinks down his neck; but he was nowhere to be seen. After the previous night's events, Alex was beginning to feel anxious.

Making his way outside and back to the main entrance hall, Alex noticed the number of people in black polo necks had decreased dramatically, replaced by new people in smart white jackets; no doubt they would be serving the meal. Once more, he felt his stomach tighten and release a low unstoppable growl.

Bounding up the steps, Alex then leant casually against the wide open front door, enjoying the warm summer air. In the distance he could see numerous cars arriving, as if they were in formation. He watched in bemusement as Archer desperately tried to direct all the geriatric old fools around the driveway. He wasn't doing so well.

To his credit, in most circumstances shouting *Could the driver of the black Rolls Royce please make their way over here!* would be a fairly distinctive way of addressing someone. Unfortunately, it seemed that every guest had arrived in a black Rolls Royce. Alex considered in their rich business fraternity it must be part of the uniform.

Archer happened to look round and notice Alex standing in the doorway with his hands in his pockets. Alex smiled and waved, followed by a swift two finger salute behind Archer's back.

Searching for something a little more individual in the long line of ubiquitous black saloons, Alex grinned as his wish was granted. Making its way down the long driveway and glinting in the evening sun, Alex spotted a low, wide car that stood out like a silver sore thumb. Not knowing anyone who owned a Bugatti, Alex's mind started to clunk in action as to the owner. It wasn't long before one name came to mind. He only knew of one person rich and extravagant enough to have one of these magnificent cars.

But surely he wouldn't have been invited to the party. Surely someone would have mentioned it.

As the car pulled round to the front of the house, the deep burble of the powerful engine grew louder and louder. It pulled gently to a stop directly in front of the steps to the main entrance, barely ten feet from where Alex was standing. The engine died and the long, low door opened an inch before slowly swinging fully open. Out stepped Konrad Steen; Alex's other granddad.

It was like the world had stopped as everyone turned to watch him. Dressed in a tailored black tuxedo, Konrad cut an imposing figure. Although Alex hadn't seen him in a long time, he guessed that he was at least as tall as Henry, but noticeably slimmer. His neatly trimmed short white beard was in stark contrast to his tanned face, but he had the well-cared-for look that Alex had often noticed in friends of the family.

Konrad closed the car door with a thud and ran his hand roughly through his thick, short white hair. He checked his watch, walked around the car, and strode confidently up the steps towards the main door, where Alex was standing perfectly upright.

He hadn't seen his granddad in a very long time. Alex wasn't entirely sure what to do. He didn't have anything like the same relationship with Konrad as he did with Henry. In fact, he didn't have any sort of relationship at all.

As Konrad bounded up the stairs two at a time, it was clear that he was about to walk right past Alex, no doubt assuming he was the hired help.

"Granddad?" Alex said timidly, just as Konrad was about to walk past him.

Konrad stopped and looked at Alex, frowning as though he was annoyed at being stopped in this manner. Alex looked for a second into his granddad's shining black eyes, before Konrad's face split into an enormous smile and he threw his head back in loud laughter. Alex stepped back at the sudden loud outburst.

"Alexander? *A-ha-haa!* Of course it's you! I didn't recognise you at all, please do forgive me. It's been so long."

Before Alex knew it, Konrad had grabbed him and was gripping him in a tight bear hug. Being several inches taller than Alex, this felt as embarrassing as it probably looked. Eventually he was pushed back, still held by both his arms as Konrad looked him up and down.

"Well, well. It's been too long, Alexander, but it's good to see you. So very good to see you!"

Konrad was smiling broadly, but his large and perfectly straight, white teeth couldn't distract Alex from a sudden rush of panic. He recognised that voice. It was the voice he had heard in the garden, and in his grandmother's room as he hid in the wardrobe.

Alex swallowed hard, his mind racing, trying to remember what he had heard the pair talking about.

Konrad was now frowning at him. "Alexander? Are you ok?"

"Is… is that your car?" Alex asked quickly, immediately feeling stupid.

Konrad's eyes narrowed conspiratorially. "It is one of them, yes. Do you like it?" Konrad put his hands in his pocket and pulled out a key. "Here. How about you park it for me, hey? I need to go and find your mother and father. I'm not sure if they got my RSVP or not. We'll catch up later then, Alexander."

Without waiting for a reply to either of his questions, Konrad patted Alex on the arm before striding into the house and down one of the side corridors as if he owned the place.

Alex stood for a moment. His knees felt slightly weak and he still couldn't think straight. He needed to get away, he needed space to think. He looked as the large lump of leather-bound metal, embossed with a large EB, in his hand. Despite himself, he couldn't resist a smile.

Skipping down the steps and round to the other side of the car, Alex grabbed the shapely door handle and pulled. He slid into the low, tan leather seats and breathed in the rich aroma that only came with a high quality motorcar. He inserted the key into the ignition and pressed the satin 'Start' button. The enormous engine barked into life.

From the panoramic windscreen Alex could see Archer looking on in disbelief whilst trying to direct the cars that were still arriving. Managing to give him a wink, he ever-so-cautiously pressed the accelerator and felt the car slowly move off, the gravel drive crunching under the wheels.

Archer was waving him into a space next to a dark blue Bentley at the end of the row. Alex pulled the car in a wide arc towards it, but then he had another idea.

Driving slowly past it, Alex carried on and began to make his way out onto the long straight driveway that led away from the house. Glancing in the mirror, he could just make out Archer waving his arms, but Alex just laughed. It was then he decided to press the accelerator a little harder.

Without a split-second of hesitation, the car launched up the driveway like a pinball and Alex was pushed back hard into the seat. His breath caught for a moment at the violence of the acceleration. Quickly lifting his foot from the pedal, he felt adrenaline and excitement coursing through his veins. Thinking it might be wise to keep a light foot, especially with more and more cars coming directly towards him, Alex continued slowly up the long, snaking drive that took him out towards the main gate.

It was still a light evening and as he passed the stream of cars making their way to the house he began to notice that all of the passengers were craning their necks, trying to see who was driving this car. Knowing full well that they were probably expecting an old Konrad Steen, instead of young Alex Wolf, he smiled and waved like he was royalty.

Reaching the main gates, he was relieved to see that they were both still open. Being careful to navigate his way through the narrow gap, he pulled to a stop on the other side.

Decision time. Alex knew the sensible thing would just be to turn around and drive straight back into the estate, but he didn't want to. He felt annoyed and confused. His mind was all over the place and that he needed somewhere to think. But above all he was feeling reckless. Checking both directions, Alex smiled to himself before slowly turning left onto the wide country road.

Even after several minutes of travel, he could still feel his whole body tingling with excitement. He wasn't even going very fast but the sense of power that he knew was under his right foot was intoxicating. As he pressed a little harder on the accelerator the thick bands of trees that lined the roads turned from a lumpy green patchwork to an emerald green blur as they whooshed past the window. On he went, taking bend after bend, gaining in confidence until finally he was within sight of the place he was looking for.

About a mile from Wolf manor was a long, wide stretch of quiet road. It was around four miles long and arrow straight. Alex had often daydreamed about driving a car down that road at ridiculous speeds; this was his chance.

As he slowly made his way around the last blind bend and onto the start of the long straight, the sinking sun behind him lit up the straight grey tarmac like a runway.

Alex couldn't help but be reminded of his last joyride. His foot seemed to lift from the pedal of its own accord and the car began to slow down naturally. It seemed the part of his brain that knew this was a very, very bad idea had won. But a sudden feeling of recklessness came over him as he looked up the straight; the sight of a long, clear road and this car was all too tempting after all.

Decision made. Alex gripped the steering wheel tightly, gritted his teeth and shoved the accelerator hard into the thickly carpeted floor.

The car exploded forward with such ferocity that it took Alex's breath away. It was the same feeling he'd experienced in his granddad's speedboat, being punched towards the horizon, only multiplied by a hundred. The force of acceleration was pushing Alex deep into his seat and his eyes flicked down to the speedometer.

100… 120… 140mph. Alex could feel his heart pounding in his chest. Every one of his senses was heightened; his heart felt ready to burst.

160… 180… 200mph. He was gripping the steering wheel so tightly it looked like he was wearing thin white gloves.

210… 220mph… *That's enough!*

He lifted his foot from the accelerator and instantly felt the speed decrease. Through the rearview mirror Alex saw the large spoiler flip up to act as an air brake and felt the car decelerate even faster. Alex's heart was still pounding but he was wide-eyed and laughing manically. Finally applying the brakes a little he brought the car down to a much more manageable 60 mph before pressing down on them harder, slowing down completely and finally pulling to a stop at the end of the straight, just off the road. He felt alive with energy. He was buzzing.

Alex sat for a few minutes and let the adrenaline-fuelled laughter subside, enjoying the feeling running through his body, waiting for his heart to slow. Lifting his hands from the steering wheel he could feel them shaking slightly. He wiped his top lip, which felt moist with perspiration, with the back of his hand, but as he did he noticed it was a lot wetter than he'd expected. His hand was smeared with the black and silver blood that he had seen before in the library.

Swearing quietly he flipped down the illuminated vanity mirror and checked his reflection. His top lip was a deep red where he had wiped it and both nostrils were bleeding slowly. Without a handkerchief, Alex used his jacket sleeve to remove as much of the dark stain as possible. He caught sight of the time on his watch. Not only was he dangerously close to being late for the party, he had also been absent for over half an hour in a car that wasn't his. If he didn't return soon people would be sure to notice.

Alex quickly turned the car around and set off back up the long road, but as he pulled back on the shift paddle to change up a gear the car stalled and died, coasting to a silent stop.

Just as he was starting to panic that he'd broken a £1,000,000 car, it suddenly jolted and burst back into life. Sitting quietly on the road for a minute listening to the engine, Alex couldn't make out anything particularly unusual and just put it down to a glitch of some sort. Even so, he decided to take it a lot easier on the return journey.

Finding that the four mile straight took a lot longer to complete when you weren't travelling over 200mph, Alex's mind wandered back to Konrad.

Konrad had met with his grandmother at least twice, that much Alex knew. But that in itself was odd, as Alex had always assumed they hated each other. He knew that they had always been bitter rivals in business, despite the family links, but now it seemed they were closer than anyone else knew.

Maybe that was why granddad was so annoyed when I told him about grandma talking to someone else that called her 'Sofie'. Maybe he knew it was Konrad all along? Alex then had a horrible thought.

What if Konrad and grandma were together before Henry came on the scene, like a young romance or something? Imagining his uptight, austere grandmother dating anyone, let alone Konrad, was making him feel quite ill so he moved on.

Trying to recall the conversation between his grandma and Konrad in the garden, he remembered the list he had written only that morning.

When I heard them in the grounds, Konrad was talking about the storm. The first time I saw Frederik was during that storm. Perhaps Konrad knows something about Frederik? But Konrad had made Grandma so angry talking about it, she'd sent him away. Although he seemed to disappear straight afterwards. How the hell had he done that? He thought about the second time he'd heard Konrad with his grandmother. That had been a much more cryptic conversation, but it still proved that they both knew something of Frederik and, more than likely, the whole strange situation. Alex could easily believe that his grandmother was involved, but how much?

What if Konrad and grandma were involved in the killing of Frederik's wife? Alex tried to push this thought from his mind as well. He knew his grandma was an old battle-axe but he really didn't think she'd be involved in murder. Besides, she'd have to be as old as Frederik if that was the case and she didn't look, or smell, nearly as bad as he did.

Before he knew it, Alex was pulling back through the gates to Wolf manor and beginning the drive back down towards the main house. As he approached the final stretch of descending road he saw that the lights were on in the house and the driveway was packed with row upon row of gleaming cars. Thinking he may just have got away with his unauthorised test drive he continued slowly down the driveway, onto the gravel in front of the house and parked the car in the only spot left.

He couldn't see anyone around, so he quickly hopped out of the car and walked towards the steps to the front door, clicking the key as he went to make sure the car was locked. Just as he was about to walk through the main door he heard fast footsteps coming towards him. With barely enough time to stuff the heavy key in his pocket, he saw Konrad striding towards him with a face like thunder. Without thinking, Alex stepped back against the thick doorframe.

Again, it wasn't until Konrad was almost past Alex that he seemed to realise he was there. He stopped, towering over Alex, and fixed him with an intimidating stare.

"Ah Alexander, just the man. I'm afraid our reunion will have to wait for now."

Alex had actually forgotten they were supposed to be catching up but was quietly relived. "Oh, that's a shame…"

"Yes it is. I'm afraid I got the reception I'd expected, but not the one that I had hoped for." Alex wasn't sure what the correct response to this was so he didn't say anything. "I'd still like to see you though, if that's ok with you? I'd like you to come and see me tomorrow at my house."

"Err… yeah, ok."

"You know where I live, don't you. Up on the hill. Your father will know if you need directions." There was a bitterness in Konrad's voice that didn't ease Alex's feelings. "Good. Be there for 10:30 and we shall talk some more."

Konrad was already down the steps and walking towards his car before Alex had a chance to reply. As he reached his car, Konrad pulled the door handle but then stopped, as though frozen. After a few more seconds, he turned slowly with a smile on his face.

"Alexander?" He called out across the gravelled space.

"Yes?" Said Alex, feeling very uncomfortable.

"Keys. I need my keys."

"Oh–yes!" Alex laughed weakly at his stupidity.

He fumbled around in his trouser pocket and pulled out the large key. Reluctantly, he tossed it over to his grandfather. Konrad, who was still staring at Alex with that same smile on his face, raised his hand and caught them without looking. He blipped the key, got in his car and within seconds was roaring up the long driveway out of the estate.

Alex checked his watch again; 8:30pm, the party would be about to start. Pulling the two huge front doors shut behind him, Alex ran down the steps, across the gravel and round the house to the library. When he got there he found the space packed with groups of people, still milling about and chatting to each other. A floating soundtrack of his mum's orchestral favourites wafted down from above. He strolled into the room, deciding it would be best to act as if he'd been there all the time.

With a glance he could tell the night was going to be completely as he'd expected. The average age of the guests must have been in the high 60s at least and he could hear the ringing of fake laughter and the jangling of gold watch handshakes at every turn.

Looking around for a familiar face, he first spotted his mum and dad standing together; his dad looked stressed and angry. Combined with the way his mum was trying to calm him, Alex guessed that the conversation with Konrad hadn't gone well at all. Next he spotted his grandmother, surrounded by a group of rather rotund, piggy-faced men. Typically, they were all simpering in front of his much taller grandmother. Recognising at least two of them as the family accountants, Alex wondered blithely at what point someone's wealth outweighed the fact that they looked like a crusty old dragon. His grandmother's black sequinned dress only added to his vivid imaginings; making her look covered in small black scales.

Lewis was not far away from his grandmother and was standing with Chloe, Hayden and Lisa. Although he looked like he was enjoying himself, Alex was pleased to see that not only was he missing the pointed glances from his grandmother, obviously wanting him to circulate more amongst the rich and influential, but also that Chloe looked somewhat distracted, as if she was looking out for someone. Alex tried not to hope that it might be him, but the thought didn't seem to want to leave his head; at least, not until he saw the woman standing on the other side of the room.

It was Sara. Alex could have sworn that his heart had stopped. She was standing by herself, holding a glass of champagne in one hand and a small black purse in the other. The short blue dress she was wearing was making it very hard for Alex to take his eyes off her; not that he was making that much of an effort. She looked over and caught his eye, her face breaking immediately into a big smile. Taking his cue, he began to move through the crowd towards her, just as there was the tinkle of metal on glass.

Silence fell in an instant and from somewhere towards the back of the room a voice announced, "My lords, ladies and gentlemen, if you could please make your way to your seats, dinner will be served shortly."

There was a sudden buzz of noise followed by bodies moving in every direction. Alex lost sight of Sara in the muddle. He stood on his tiptoes to try and see her but the sound of 100 chairs being slid across his pristine wooden floor distracted him. Still unable to locate Sara and not actually knowing here he was supposed to be sitting, he waited until more or less everyone else had sat down and then looked for the empty chair. There appeared to be only two chairs that weren't occupied. One was between Sara and Alex's dad on one side of the table, and the other was between Chloe and Hayden on the near side of the table. A few people had turned in their chairs to look at Alex. Like sheep following the flock, more and more people were twisting round in their seats.

"Come on Alex, darling," called out his mother, smiling graciously over at him. "Sit yourself down so we can get started."

Alex's eyes flicked from his grandmother's glare to the two empty seats. Both Sara and Chloe were looking at him, both smiling. This wasn't making his decision any easier.

"Torn between a rose and a lily are we, my boy," whispered someone in Alex's ear.

He spun round to see Henry beaming at him. Wide eyed, Alex burst out laughing then stood back and looked him up and down. Henry was dressed in a claret velvet evening suit, salmon pink dress shirt and a large white silk bow tie.

"Where have you been? I didn't think you were going to make it tonight?" whispered Alex.

Henry looked at the floor rather sheepishly. "Yes, well I'm sorry about that, lot on my mind if I'm honest. Just needed a bit of time out, if you know what I mean. Anyway, I'm here now so let's make this a night to remember, shall we? And as for your little floral dilemma, don't you worry. I'm going to make this one easy for you!" He winked at Alex and then limped off towards the table using his silver-tipped cane as a support.

Assuming Henry would take a seat next to Sara, he was surprised when he actually sat himself down between Chloe and Hayden. Alex couldn't help but notice the look of disappointment on Chloe's face but also the way that Sara looked down at her lap, blushing slightly.

Alex walked around the far side of the table, pulled out the chair and finally took his seat between Sara and his father. Catching his eye, Henry winked at Alex in a very unsubtle way and started to tell Chloe a joke that Alex knew had a particularly rude and very inappropriate ending. Hayden, who was given the pleasure of Henry's furry red back, turned and sat looking put out.

"Hi," whispered Alex quietly, half looking at Sara.

"Hi," replied Sara looking directly at Alex. "How are you feeling?"

"Good actually… thanks." Alex turned and smiled, then laughed as he heard the punchline of Henry's joke. Chloe was in fits of laughter but Hayden and Lisa looked horrified.

"I wondered if we were going to have our first music lesson at some point this week?"

"I'd really like that," said Alex.

There was another ringing of metal on glass. At the end of the long table, his grandmother was standing up to say something. A hush fell on the room again.

"Now that we're finally all here," she said, directing withering looks at both her grandson and her husband. "I'd like to congratulate Rebekka on putting on another wonderful dinner party. Well done, dear."

Alex saw his mum smile eagerly, then laughed as Henry began banging on the table with the end of his knife shouting, "Here, here!"

"Secondly," she began, slightly louder. "I'd like to congratulate Lewis and Alex on completing their schooling. I'm sure we're going to see great things from Lewis in the not too distant future."

Alex rolled his eyes at this obvious slight but couldn't be bothered to dispute it. Even so, he caught Henry's eye who silently raised a glass to him and mouthed, "Cheers".

"And finally, I'd like to announce that I shall be retiring from Wolf Enterprises next month to focus on my family. An announcement about my succession will be made in the coming weeks. Thank you everyone. Now we should eat!" Sofia sat down and took a long, slow sip of her wine.

The white-jacketed waiters began to stream into the room, each carrying trays. It appeared that this announcement wasn't just a shock to Alex. Confused glances were being traded around the table in every direction and Alex could actually see the other guests' minds working as to how this announcement might affect their own businesses. If his grandmother's intent had been to direct attention away from Alex and Lewis, this had definitely done it. Alex looked across at his mum. She seemed just as surprised as everyone else, yet putting on a brave face. As he glanced sideways at his dad however, he saw that he looked absolutely miserable.

At that moment, Alex felt a strange touch of pity for his dad. Alex at least knew that *he* would never run the family company; nor would he want to. But it was clear to Alex, his father and everyone else around the table that it was Lewis who was being primed to take over the company. Where would that leave his dad? Working for his own son?

Lewis was deep in conversation with Lisa and Hayden. He didn't seem phased at all. Had Lewis known this was going to happen? Or was it as much of a surprise to him as everyone else?

Alex took a long drink of chilled white wine. More than anything else, the most worrying part of his grandma's speech was her comment about spending more time with her family. Could this have something to do with her meetings with Konrad? Sofia spending time on anything but the family business could only be a bad thing, in his opinion.

"The pâté or the scallops, sir?" said a dry voice over Alex's shoulder.

Startled and without thinking, Alex said, "Erm... both?"

"Very good, sir." Said the waiter, placing two generous portions of sliced pate and five enormous king scallops onto his plate.

Alex glanced sideways at Sara, hoping she wouldn't notice his apparent greed.

"That's the ticket!" Henry shouted from the other side of the table, looking excitedly at Alex's mountainous plate. "Need to keep up your energy to fend off all these ladies that are after you, don't you boy!"

"All these ladies, Alex?" Sara said softly, cutting delicately into her pâté. "I didn't realise I had any competition?"

Alex inhaled a scallop that he was in the process of swallowing. He coughed and watched as a small piece of it flew out onto the pristine white table cloth. He looked up to see Chloe frowning slightly at him and began to feel hot under the collar.

"Competition?" He mumbled, skewering the half-chewed mollusc and putting it back on his plate. "Don't worry, no one's after me, I'm sure." *Unless you count scary shadow people, anyway.*

Course after course of the most spectacular food followed. As the drinks flowed, Alex began to relax and found himself totally engrossed in conversation with Sara.

They were reminiscing about their lessons several years ago; Alex admitted to playing badly on several occasions just so he could make the lessons last that bit longer. This had caused Sara to throw her head back in laughter. As Alex watched her smiling, open-mouthed and eyes closed, he found himself smiling back and reaching out to touch her hand. When she finished laughing, she placed her other hand on top of his and silently held his gaze. For a moment, Alex felt as if the rest of the room had just slipped away.

The sound of a breaking glass distracted them both; at exactly the same time they broke eye contact and their hands slid apart. Alex grinned down at his plate, which appeared to be covered in fruit sorbet, topped with an elaborately spun sugar cage. He wasn't sure if it was the food, but his stomach felt like it was wrapping itself in knots and his heart was beating a little faster than usual. Although it wasn't an unpleasant feeling, it was certainly different.

Suddenly remembering that he was in a room with seventy other people, Alex looked around the table to see what was going on. His grandmother was still in full flow about something or other, to anyone who would listen. To their credit, a lot of the people near to her were doing well at pretending to be interested.

His mum and dad were in deep conversation. Finally, his dad seemed to be smiling, even if only slightly. Alex realised that this was something he hadn't seen in a long time.

Lewis was chatting to a very serious-looking man to his right, who looked like he had something to do with banking; Lisa and Hayden were also talking between themselves, although neither was smiling. Alex wondered if they were trying to decide who they should go and suck up to next. That left Chloe and Henry.

Unfortunately Alex's granddad appeared to be nodding off after his dinner; or he'd at least closed his eyes and was bobbing his head slightly, which left Chloe sitting silently on her own. Alex felt a pang of guilt; he had no idea how long she'd been sitting there like that. Eventually she looked up, only to give him a weak smile before looking back down at her plate again. Feeling that there wasn't much he could do, Alex directed a swift kick at Henry under the table. Unfortunately he misjudged it and watched as Hayden squealed and winced in pain before bending down to rub his leg. Alex only just managed to look away in time.

Finally the plates were cleared away and coffee and liqueurs were brought round for everyone. Alex hoped that with dinner all but over, he'd be able to make a quick exit and, if his luck held, possibly with Sara in tow.

It wouldn't hurt to have a quiet stroll around the grounds and perhaps show her some of the sights. Just as he was about to suggest this idea there was a third unmistakable tinkle of metal on glass. This time though, it was his mum standing up and she had a big smile on her face.

"Thank you everyone, I hope you all enjoyed your meal. Now I have a favour to ask. Well, two in fact. Firstly, could we all stand up and move away from the table."

Everyone looked at each other slightly bemused but obliged in good humour, picking up their drinks and stepping away from the long table. As soon as everyone had retreated, thirty waiters and waitresses descended and within seconds the whole thing had been cleared of any evidence that dinner had taken place. Next, five rather large looking men appeared, whisked off the table cloths and began moving the individual parts of the table towards the edge of the room.

Something inside Alex told him that he wasn't going to like what was coming next. Sure enough, as soon as the tables had been moved away he saw his mum raise her hands high above her head and clap. The assembled crowds gazed in wonder as the floor split in two and the huge gleaming piano ascended from the depths.

"And now, for tonight's second favour," Rebekka looked at her son. "Your father and I thought it would be wonderful if you could perhaps play for everyone, Alex? We haven't heard you play for so long and I'm sure everyone here would love to hear you."

There was a round of polite clapping from the assembled audience. Alex's heart sank, not only because he hated playing for other people, especially when it was sprung on him, but also because the last time he played he'd ended up having a strange silver nose bleed and passing out.

Casting his mum and dad a pleading look, all he got in return was an encouraging smile from Rebekka and a blank stare from his father. Henry shrugged his shoulders theatrically, but was far too busy stuffing his pipe to be too concerned. Chloe was smiling at him with an interested look on her face. He instinctively turned to Sara, standing right behind him. She gave him a reassuring smile and then a shove.

"Ok, ok," he said, turning back to the crowd and holding his hands up in mock surrender.

Henry whistled and started clapping loudly. "That's m'boy!" He roared from the side of his mouth that wasn't stuffed with a pipe.

Alex just caught sight of his mum grabbing the bottle of Port that had found a home by Henry's feet and holding it behind her back. Alex walked to the piano, sat down on the leather-topped stool and began to breathe slowly, thinking about what he was going to play. Taking one last look at the expectant faces crowding around the piano, he decided on one of the only pieces he knew off by heart. Brushing the first keys gently with his fingertips he paused, then began. The moment he played the first chord the lights went out and there was a horrific scream somewhere at the far end of the room.

"Alex!" A quiet, desperate voice whispered in his left ear. "Take Sara and go now. Leave this room. Do not look back. Something follows you tonight!"

Without a moment's hesitation, Alex stood up and heard the stool crash to the floor. There was another wailing scream and pure panic in the pitch blackness. Alex glanced about, expecting to have to search for Sara, but saw her as clear as day in front of him as though she was lit from above. He grabbed her hand and she gasped in surprise, as though she hadn't seen him.

"It's me, it's Alex. We need to leave. Now!"

He tugged at her hand to follow him and moved quickly towards the door. The corridor on the other side wasn't lit either; feeling his panic rising, he looked about for another route. He could only see into the grounds beyond the glazing. It was then that he thought he saw something dark move towards him. That was enough for Alex.

Pulling Sara behind him, he ran as fast as he could in the darkness; through the winding corridors, through the main hall, up the two flights of stairs, along the landing and into his bedroom.

How is it all dark? Pulling Sara inside, but never letting go of her hand, Alex locked his bedroom door behind him and slid the mirrored panels aside using the edge of his shoe. Hearing the lock snick in the door he pulled Sara into his changing room and slid the mirrored panel back closed. Still in darkness he made a quick decision; rummaging around for the small lever, he pulled, releasing the hidden door. Pulling hard on the door's edge he grabbed Sara and guided her through into the small room where his safe was kept, sliding through himself before slamming it closed behind him.

In the blackness he heard a quiet sobbing noise and began rummaging around at the back of the room. He found the torch he was looking for and switched it on. All he could see was Sara's terrified face staring back at him.

CHAPTER 26

CONFUSION

Alex felt exactly as Sara looked. He'd brought her to the first safe place that came to mind; few others knew about it, it was relatively secure and it was so small that if anything did come for them it would be easier to defend themselves. Alex held felt the torch in his hand and wondered how useful it would actually be in a fight.

His mind was racing, not least because he hadn't recognised the voice that warned him to leave. Something told him that he could trust it, and in the panic that had been enough. It said something was following him; all he could think of was the mysterious shadow. It must have been coming for him again. That was why all the lights had gone out; so that it could strike.

But what about everyone else downstairs? What if the shadow attacked them? *Granddad, Mum, Chloe, Dad. Everyone!* He had left them all alone and run away. This wasn't good. He knew he should go down to check everyone was ok, but on the other hand, he had been told to leave and to take Sara with him.

Sara. She still looked petrified. Unsure what to do, he rested the torch upright on the floor and held out his arms. She rushed into his embrace and wrapped her arms tightly around his middle. Alex tried to keep his breath steady as her hair brushed against his face, but he realised that he'd simply stopped breathing. As she rested her cheek against his he could feel her warm body shaking slightly against him, either from fear or from the chill in their small, secure room.

Caught slightly unawares, he held her tightly. He couldn't help but feel calmer being with her; every breath he took filled his head with her sweet smell. The thought of everyone else in danger slipped away, replaced only by the feeling that he never wanted to let Sara go.

"Alex what happened down there?" Sara said softly.

"I… I don't know. The lights went out, I heard a scream and so I thought I'd better make a run for it… so I did."

She lifted her head and her tear-filled eyes looked directly into his. "You took me with you though. You saved me."

"Well not really, it just… seemed the right thing to–"

She kissed him and something seemed to explode in his brain. He felt her hands move up to the sides of his head and then her fingers run gently through his hair. As the initial surprise, he kissed her back. The temperature in the room seemed to increase instantaneously. It felt as if someone had plugged him into the mains as wave after wave of electricity seemed to pulse through his whole body. But as quickly as it had began, it ended.

Sara pulled away and smiled at him. He felt himself blush and looked to the floor. Despite the blood pounding in his ears he heard her soft laugh.

"Alex Wolf, are you blushing?"

"No! Of course not. I've kissed lots of girls," he said, immediately wishing he hadn't.

Sara raised both eyebrows, but she was smiling still. "Well I'm glad to hear it, I'd hate to think I was your first."

Alex mumbled something about the central heating then coughed, before sliding his shoe distractedly on the carpet. There was a long pause as Alex searched for something to say, but the silence was eventually broken by Sara.

"You know, we should really go and see what's going on, don't you think?

"Hmm? Oh… maybe," replied Alex, lost in thought.

"I don't mind going to check if you want to stay here?" said Sara earnestly.

"No! No, if anyone's going *I'll* go," blustered Alex before gently reaching out to touch the side of her face. She smiled. "Hold on, stay here a minute. I'm going to check something in my room first."

Sara didn't say a word, but looked confused as Alex pressed the door until he heard it click open. Moving very slowly into his dressing room he reached round the corner for the light switch. Flicking it on, the room was filled with a soft yellow glow.

At least the power is back on. Cautiously he moved to the far side of the dressing room. As he peered into his darkened bedroom he couldn't see anything unusual, so he slipped quietly out.

The room was bathed in moonlight; thankfully he hadn't closed the curtains. Alex walked slowly to the large windows, unlatched the small gold catch and gently pulled it open. Instantly his room was filled with noise, but not the chaos of shouts and screams that he had expected. There was the sound of music and laughter coming from outside, one floor down.

That can't be right? Sliding the window open fully, he stepped out onto the stone balcony and walked to the edge. To his surprise, a group of people were dancing on the stone veranda below, drinks in hands and music blaring; they seemed to be having a whale of a time. He could see his mum, Lewis, Hayden, Lisa, Chloe and at least forty or so of his grandma's friends. And to top it all, his granddad with a bottle of what looked like champagne in either hand and a long pipe bobbing up and down in his mouth out of time with the music. Halfway through a poorly executed pirouette, with his head looking up to the sky, he caught sight of Alex.

"*Alex!* There you are, old chap!" He shouted, flicking pipe ash all over himself. "Where did you run off to all of a sudden?"

A few of the others stopped to look around as well and several cheered, clapping their hands above their heads. Alex was speechless.

"Why don't you come down and join the party? And bring Sara too if you know where she is?" Henry punctuated this last comment with an enormously unsubtle flap of his elbows.

Alex stared at the partying crowd for a moment more and then turned and walked back into his bedroom. He pushed open the door to the safe room and found Sara leaning against the wall looking nervous. He fought the urge to step in and close it behind him.

"It's alright, you can come out now. Panic's over." He said moodily.

Sara followed him back to the edge of balcony and looked down to see the sight for herself. As soon as they both appeared Henry wolf-whistled and many more people turned to look back up at them. Alex couldn't miss the look of disappointment on Chloe's face; she quickly looked away and began chatting to a tall, dark haired man.

"I don't understand…" said Sara quietly, looking at Alex.

"No, neither do I," said Alex, desperately trying to think of an explanation.

They left the room quickly and began to make their way back downstairs to the party. As they reached the entrance hall they saw Lewis walk through from the direction of the kitchen, carrying two glasses of champagne. He stopped at the bottom of the stairs to wait for them both, smiling broadly.

"I know you didn't really want to play the piano, Al, but don't you think that was a bit drastic?" He said, half laughing.

"Drastic? What are you talking about? Didn't you hear the screaming? Everyone was terrified!" Said Alex incredulously.

"Screaming? No one screamed, Al," said Lewis. "Lisa shouted at Granddad, but that was only because he dropped his pipe onto her leg when the lights went out. Maybe that's what you heard?"

Alex turned to Sara looking confused, "You heard the scream didn't you?"

"Well... I heard *a* scream. Maybe it was Lisa? I just remember the lights going out and then you grabbed my hand and said we had to go..." Sounding apologetic, her voice trailed off at the look on Alex's face.

Alex could feel his cheeks getting hot. "Look, I didn't make it up," he said loudly, his eyes flicking between both of them.

"Don't worry about it," said Sara quietly, taking his hand. "It's not like it turned out so bad after all, is it? Come on, let's go and get a drink and join in with the party."

Alex moodily pulled his hand away from Sara's. He felt angry and confused and seeing everyone else dancing and having a great time was just making things worse.

"No. I think I'm going to give it a miss."

Lewis rolled his eyes. "Come on Sara, let's leave him to it. I'll get you a drink and you can come and meet the others if you like?"

"No, no thanks," started Sara stiffly. "That's very kind of you, but I think it's time I should be going too."

Despite his mood, Alex picked up on Sara's tone. He saw his brother staring at him as if to say *do something!* Sara was rummaging around in her handbag for her car keys.

"Do you want Al to walk you to your car, Sara? I'm sure he wouldn't mind.'

"No it's fine, I'll walk myself I think. Archer will be out there won't he? I'm sure he'll look after me in case there's any more ghosts and ghoulies out there."

Alex felt like he'd been slapped. He looked at Sara, trying to catch her eye, but she didn't look back. Instead she snapped her handbag closed and began to walk away. Alex racked his brain for something to call after her, but nothing came. Even his own brain seemed to have turned against him. He could only watch as Sara walked out the front door and pulled it closed behind her with a dull thud.

"You know something," said Lewis. "You really are a dick head sometimes."

Alex watched as his brother walked away shaking his head. He was ready to call it a night; the evening had not gone well at all.

CHAPTER 27

AWOKEN

One hundred years of peace. One hundred years of bliss. Time to be still. Time not to think. Not to have to deal with the battle. Not to see her. Not to see him.

That night was the first time Aurora had been out in 100 years and it had been one of the closest calls she had ever made. The boy had been in more danger than he could have possibly known, and escaped by barely a second; only because he had been near the girl though. The girl Sara.

And that scream. She recognised the thing that gave *that* scream. But why had Zephyr gone after that brother and not the other one? She knew that she could have saved the other one if he'd needed it, but she had sensed he didn't need her help. It was Alex who was in danger.

Something was beginning to happen and Aurora knew that she wouldn't have much longer to rest before she was called upon once more.

CHAPTER 28

A MEETING

Alex awoke the next day cushioned on a soft cloud of feathers, comforted under a warm, heavy blanket of sleep; and for a split second he felt content. Until, the sight of Sara's hurt face swam into his mind.

As much as he screwed up his eyes trying to wipe the images from his memory, it made no difference. Suddenly his duvet felt hot and oppressive and the soft plumpness of his pillows began to irritate him. Yanking back the covers he sat up and sighed heavily.

He'd have to call Sara and apologise; there were no two ways about it. But maybe he'd leave it until later. Much later, in fact, as there was something else more important he was supposed to being doing. His meeting with Konrad was at 10:30 and he couldn't be late.

He checked the time on the watch that was still on his wrist; it was only 9.00am. Walking to the windows, he pulled back the tall curtains and looked out at the view before him.

The grey sky seemed to blend seamlessly into the thick haze that was curling around the grounds of Wolf Manor. A light sheen covered everything, reflecting the limited light from the dense clouds. Wet, drizzly weather was going to be the order of the day.

After showering, Alex spent several long minutes standing in his dressing room deciding what to wear. It was certainly a day for looking smart, so he picked out a Navy pinstripe three piece suit, dark tan leather brogues, a light pink high-collared shirt, red and blue diagonally striped tie and a pair of thick, black-rimmed glasses. He felt the clear-lensed frames definitely gave him an air of intelligence and made him look older and more distinguished; which was no bad thing when he was due to meet with one of the richest men in the world.

Choosing an enormous wristwatch, he used the next few minutes for the obligatory self-examination in the mirror; before leaving the room feeling ready for business.

Making his way down to the kitchen, Alex was taken aback to find his whole family sitting down eating breakfast and chatting away quite normally. Aside from the dinner party, he couldn't remember the last time he'd seen his mum, dad, grandma, granddad and brother in the same room together. A feeling of unease at this unusual and unexpected scenario slowed his entrance.

As usual, his brother and grandma were in deep discussion over the financial papers, his mum and dad seemed to be silently staring into their respective cereal bowls and his granddad was sitting back in his chair comfortably, as though he'd just finished an enormous breakfast. Judging by the state of his plate, he'd done just that.

In fact it was Henry who looked round first, hearing the *clack* of Alex's hard heels on the stone floor. "Well look at you in your best bib and tucker!" He said, his eyes opening wide and eyeing Alex up and down. "Very businesslike."

The word *business* obviously had some sort of instinctive pull on Sofia and Lewis, as they stopped talking instantly and looked up at Alex too. His grandma eyed him suspiciously.

"You applying for Lewis's job or something?" Said Henry.

"Looking good, Al," said Lewis brightly. "What's the occasion?"

"Well," he said cautiously, predicting the effect his next words would have. "I was invited to go and see someone this morning."

"Who?" Said Lewis.

"Yes, come on Alex," said Rebekka brightly. "Are you going to meet Sara for breakfast? I'm sure she'll be impressed with how you're dressed–"

"Actually, I'm going to see Konrad."

Alex could have sworn he felt the temperature in the room drop a couple of degrees. Henry reached into his jacket and slowly pulled out his pipe, his eyes flicking around the rest of the table.

"You're going to see whom?" Said Sofia quietly, slowly tapping the end of her fork on the table and staring at Alex.

"I *said*," started Alex loudly before putting his hands up to his mouth as if he was talking to someone hard of hearing. "*I'm going to see Konrad. You know, my* other *granddad*."

Sofia's eyes narrowed, firstly at Alex and then at the barely contained snigger from Henry's direction. Alex was surprised she could still see him with her eyelids so close together.

"I know who he is, Alexander." She shot another withering look at Henry.

"What I'm keen to know is *why* you're going to see him."

"Why not? He asked me last night and as he said, he hasn't seen me or Lewis in years. He wants to get to know us a bit better, so he's invited me over."

"Lewis or *I*," Sofia corrected. "But shouldn't Lewis be going with you too?"

"It's fine, I'm sure I'll catch up with Granddad soon enough," said Lewis. "It'll be good for us to meet separately anyway, that way I don't have to be seen with Al looking like he's off to the bank."

"Very funny," said Alex in a bored voice, taking off his glasses and sliding them into his inside pocket.

"Well I think it's wonderful!" Said Rebekka, getting up from the table and collecting up bowls and plates. "It'll do you good to get to know your granddad a bit better. At least that way we might not end up with *two* pipe smokers in the house." She glared at Henry, who quickly put his pipe down before folding his hands across his stomach.

"How are you getting up there then?" Henry said, looking slightly hard done by.

"Oh, well that reminds me," said Alex, addressing his grandma again but with a much more polite tone to his voice. "I was wondering if I could borrow your car for the drive?"

A nasty look seemed to form on Sofia's face even before Alex had finished his sentence. "Oh, I'm afraid not, Alex. I need the car this morning so you'll have to look elsewhere."

Alex scowled but then tried a different tactic. "Lewis?"

"Sorry Al, Hayden and Lisa are borrowing mine for the day. Think they're off to the seaside or something."

Alex briefly looked to his dad, but he was still staring morosely down at his empty bowl. He didn't even bother to ask.

Henry was beaming at him, "You could borrow my push bike if you like, but I don't think it'll do your suit much good."

Alex sighed heavily again. "So you're telling me that in a family of billionaires we haven't *one* car I can use to drive to see my own granddad?"

"You can use mine, Alex?" Came his mother's voice from behind him.

Alex's heart sank. He'd forgotten about his mum's car. The last thing he wanted was to have to drive around in *that* thing.

"There you go, Alexander," said Sofia who was positively grinning. "Why don't you take your mother's car. That'll be much more suitable for you, don't you think?"

"Wait here a moment and I'll tell Archer to bring it round for you." said

Rebekka, smiling as she left the room. Within a couple of minutes she was back, jangling a set of keys in her hand.

Unlike his dad, Alex's mum didn't care for cars very much. She thought them merely a form of showing off; a point that she had made quite clearly when she bought her first ever car at the age of 19. It was second hand and, unfortunately, was still going strong.

She dropped the keys into Alex's hand before walking back to the table and sitting down. "Great… thanks," said Alex, with as little enthusiasm as he could muster.

Lewis and his grandmother had already returned to their discussions and his mum looked as if she was trying to catch his dad's eye. She gently stroked his forearm, but Morten didn't seem to react.

Henry, who had placed his unlit pipe back in his mouth, glanced to the door as if signalling him to leave. Alex took his cue and trudged out of the kitchen and through to the main entrance hall, the soles of his new shoes still clacking loudly on the stone floor.

It wasn't long before he heard a second pair of offbeat footsteps moving quickly behind him. He turned to see his granddad limping quickly towards him with a look of conspiracy on his face. Before Alex had time to say anything, Henry grabbed him roughly by the arm and pulled him quickly through the large front doors, closing them behind him.

"What are you–"

"When you see Konrad, I want you to be very careful." Henry was talking in a hushed, rough whisper but his voice had the same serious tone he had used in the boat house. "Do you understand?"

"What do you–"

"Keep your guard up and whatever you, do not tell him *anything* about Frederik."

"Of course but–"

"Do you understand, Alex?"

"Yes, but–"

"You must keep an eye out for anything unusual as well."

Alex stared at his granddad. "You think Konrad's involved don't you? You think he's part of this?"

Henry didn't say anything, but held Alex's gaze before putting his pipe to his mouth. Alex thought for a moment.

"I think he's involved too." Henry stopped chewing on the end of his pipe and his eyes narrowed, as if pushing Alex to tell him more. "Last night, when I spoke to him, I recognised his voice. I think it was *him* who was speaking to Grandma about the storm in the grounds. And I heard them talking again after I'd come back from your lake house."

"You heard them *again*?" Said Henry slowly. "What were they talking about?"

Alex had to think; his memory had never been very good under pressure. "They were talking about someone being alive. They were surprised he was alive. They must mean Frederik because they were both scared that he'd been seen around *here*. Then they were talking about someone dealing with him. A *him* and a *her*. Who do you think they are?" Henry didn't say anything but just listened intently. "Then they mentioned you, too."

"Me?"

"Yes, they knew that you'd gone to your lake house the other night and that you might be involved somehow."

"Did they say anything about *you* though?" Asked Henry sounding worried.

Alex racked his brains again. "No. No, they didn't. Konrad thought that the boat had come back from your lake house all by itself, so they *can't* have seen me."

"Konrad was there? Konrad couldn't see you in the boat?"

Alex thought again. "No, it sounded like Konrad had sent someone else to watch what we were doing. It sounded like he'd gotten a report from someone else who had been watching us."

"You mean… like a *shadow* perhaps?" Said Henry.

Alex froze, but his mind raced. "You think Konrad's this shadowmaster person? *You're kidding*? And I'm supposed to be going up to see him now? *I'll be killed!*"

Henry seemed to be pondering this last statement. "No… no I don't think that's going to happen, Alex. But I say again, be very careful and do not mention anything about Frederik."

"But what about Grandma? That means she is involved in this too. I know she doesn't like me very much, but I never thought she'd try to have me done in!"

Henry smiled. "Don't worry about your grandma for now. I've got a feeling that for once she's not the bad guy here. My main concern at the moment is Konrad. As I said, Alex, just be aware when you go and see him. Pay attention to your surroundings and don't say anything you shouldn't. Do you understand?"

Alex nodded quickly, but still felt uncomfortable at the prospect of spending time with the man who more than likely controlled the shadow; a shadow that had tried to kill him on more than one occasion. Just as he was about to suggest to Henry that he could perhaps postpone his appointment, he heard a muffled bang, followed by the lumpy chugging of what sounded like an old lawnmower engine.

Turning towards the gravelled driveway, both men looked down to see the vehicle that would be transporting Alex to his meeting. Alex felt his shoulders slump at the sight; a feeling that was only exacerbated by the heavy hands that Henry placed on top of them.

"Well, I suppose you can comfort yourself in the fact that even if Konrad doesn't do you in, the car might finish you off instead." Said Henry, smiling broadly.

Alex scowled as Henry chuckled to himself. The driver's door creaked open and out stepped a grinning Archer, closing it carefully behind him as though handling an antique. Alex slowly made his way down the steps towards his mother's rust-encrusted baby blue Fiat 500. Leaning against the front wing with his arms crossed tightly, Archer was grinning from ear to ear.

"Oh piss off, Archer," said Alex moodily. "Just open the door, will you."

Still grinning, Archer unfolded his arms and opened the driver side door for him.

Climbing into the cramped compartment, Alex tried for several seconds to get comfy in the threadbare seats before reaching into his pocket and pulling out his own key. Scowling at Archer, Alex put the key in the ignition and started the engine. It choked slowly back into life before settling into the same lumpy rhythm.

Archer leaned down to look at Alex's cramped body folded into the car.

"All ready for the off, Master Wolf?"

"Yes," said Alex dryly.

Archer slammed the door entirely too enthusiastically. Checking his watch he realised he only had twenty minutes to get to Konrad's. If he'd been driving any other car that wouldn't have been a problem; in that thing, he would have to put his foot down.

Piling on the revs and dropping the clutch, Alex expected at least some wheel spin, but instead just pulled away jerkily. Glancing in the wing mirror he could see Archer creasing over and Henry jubilantly waving his pipe. This was *not* how it was supposed to be.

The journey wasn't quite as bad as Alex had expected. The main problem was that the route to Konrad's all seemed to be uphill. After the initial drive through the dense, tree-lined roads around Wolf Manor, the trees peeled away to reveal vast expanses of oilseed fields, stretching out like a yellow-gold carpet far off to the horizon. Although he had never been to his granddad's house and didn't know the exact route, he only had to head in the general direction of the enormous tower that stretched high into the sky.

Finally after forty achingly long minutes, Alex turned off from the main road and began to drive slowly towards the tall gate of Steen Tower. The high silver gates were supported by two tall obelisks of dark grey stone. They looked as if they'd been carved from solid blocks, yet they were merely the end pieces to an equally tall stone wall that stretched out either side, far into the distance.

Pulling up to the gates, Alex was grateful that he didn't have to stop; the enormous silver barriers opened automatically as he approached. He continued slowly up the long, arrow-straight driveway that led to the tower.

Alex couldn't help feeling that the tower seemed incredibly out of place, set deep into the countryside, and that it would have been better placed in the middle of a big city skyline, surrounded by other tall buildings.

He peered up through the windscreen, but as much as he tried, he still couldn't see the top of the tower; it disappeared into the low grey clouds that were blanketing the sky. Eventually he reached the huge elliptical space that formed the foundation for the tower.

Apart from the tower itself, there were no other buildings in sight. Unsure where to park, Alex pulled up next to the two other cars that were parked along the edge of the ellipse. He recognised the silver Bugatti and felt another twinge of guilt as he remembered his short joyride. The other car was an immaculate black Lamborghini. Feeling like he was soiling sacred ground with his mother's rust-crippled contraption, he quickly unfolded himself from the car, slammed the door shut hard and began to flatten himself down. Driving in a car that compact was not good news for easily creased suits.

"Well, well, well," called out the instantly recognisable voice of Konrad Steen. "I did not think I would ever see this again."

Alex turned quickly and saw his grandfather walking across the smooth stone platform to meet him. He was smiling, but he wasn't looking at Alex; he was looking at the car.

"You've seen this car before?" Said Alex, taken aback.

"Of course I have, Alex. This used to be *my* car!"

"Yours?" said Alex, taken aback.

"Indeed. I owned it for many years before I sold it to your mother when she turned nineteen. It was quite funny actually. Of all the cars in the world she could have chosen, she wanted this one." Konrad was smiling at the car like it was an old family photo he hadn't seen in years. "Truth be told, I didn't want to let it go. But I could tell that it would have a good home with your mother. *Ha!* I honestly did not expect you would arrive in it today though. I thought you had a taste for the more expensive things in life?" Konrad nodded towards the two altogether more impressive cars that were parked nearby.

"I didn't think I'd be coming in it either, to be honest. But Grandma was being tight with her Rolls Royce so I got left with this."

Konrad threw back his head and laughed. "Your grandmother is a good woman Alexander… but I take your point. She is not one to be crossed, is she not?"

"You're telling me!" Started Alex, about to make a few other choice comments on the subject, before thinking better of it.

"Come, let me take you inside and show you around."

Konrad put out his large hand in the direction of the entrance before leading Alex back towards the tower. Alex's feelings of apprehension had diminished at the kindly welcome; but as they walked up the short steps, Henry's words of warning swam into his mind. He tried to refocus and keep his wits about him.

As they moved closer to the tower, Alex could see that the building was made from a combination of stone, glass, metal and wood. From a distance, he had always assumed it was entirely glass and metal, the way it caught the light. Up close, he could see that there was a lot more to it.

From what he could tell, the tower would resemble a tear drop if viewed from above, albeit a slightly softened one. Instead of a tapering point, there was a softened curve, and it was to this narrower side that they were walking.

The first thirty feet of the building looked as if it were made up from a series of thick steel rods, spaced at intervals around the perimeter of the tower with huge pieces of a curved dark grey stone in between. Above the rods, tall sheets of metal cladding covered the rest of the building. On the side that Alex was approaching it appeared to be aluminium sheeting, occasionally inlaid by foot-wide strips of a silvery wood. On the other side of the building, Alex knew, there was a perfect arc of glass forming the base of the teardrop shape. This ran the full height of the tower and Alex couldn't wait to see what it would look like from the inside.

As they passed through the main doors, he couldn't help but notice how modern and fresh it all looked; with the dark stone, reflective metals and geometric shapes. Although the tower wasn't meant to be an office space, it had that feel to it; at least on the ground floor.

Several years ago, Morten had told Alex that the original plan for the tower was for it to be a workplace as well as a home for the Steen family. The idea was that Konrad could run his company from this building without having to waste time travelling to and from the city every morning. However, Morten's mother had talked him out of it; saying that if he lived and worked in the same building then his work life would simply merge into his personal life. Konrad had eventually relented and settled on the plans just being for a family home.

Alex knew that his grandmother, Veronika Steen, had died fifteen years ago; leaving Konrad alone. That was when he had finally begun to build his new tower, but only after reverting to the original plan of a combined workplace and home.

Passing an unattended reception desk, they came to a single lift door that was set into the dark stone wall on the far side of the space. The doors opened silently. Gesturing for Alex to lead the way, Konrad followed him in and pressed the single glass button on the inside of the lift. The doors shut instantly.

"How come there's only one button in the lift?" Alex thought out loud.

"Because we only need to go to one floor," said Konrad, giving Alex a broad, dazzling smile.

Alex felt his stomach drop as they ascended quickly. He felt the slightest of jolts and with barely a whisper, the doors slid open again. Alex blinked in the bright light and stepped out into an enormous circular room.

He turned to look at Konrad in astonishment, who smiled back. "Welcome to my home."

CHAPTER 29

HIDDEN SECRETS

Alex was amazed; not just by the space, but that they'd travelled so high in such a short space of time. Without thinking, he walked right across the room to the enormous glass panels that formed the panorama of light. The room had to be at least 800 feet up and the view was breathtaking. Alex had been in skyscrapers before but the views always seemed to be obscured by other tall buildings. Even on such an overcast day, Alex could see for miles and miles. Scanning the skyline, it wasn't long before he spotted Wolf Manor far off in the distance.

"And I always thought that Wolf Manor was totally hidden." He said, almost to himself.

"It was," said Konrad who had moved silently behind Alex. "Until I built this tower, that is. I remember your grandmother was somewhat upset about that. But I assured her I would keep my telescope pointed in the other direction."

For the first time, Alex could see how vast the Wolf Estate really was. He could see the road leading to the main gate disappearing behind the trees; then the land gradually descend until it reached the house and slowly climb again until it was obscured by the Silver Wood. He could make out parts of the lake as well where the trees broke apart. The memory of moving across that lake at great speed merely two days ago suddenly came back to him, as did images of Frederik, glowing books and an 800 year old mystery.

"Would you care for a drink, Alex?"

Alex jumped slightly when he saw that Konrad was back on the other side of the room, standing by the lift door.

"Err... coffee would be good." Konrad raised his eyebrows. "Oh milk, one sugar please. Thanks"

Konrad spoke briefly into a small panel set into the wall by the lift.

"Bryson will be up with it shortly," he said to Alex. "Would you like to take a look around? I have to make a phone call so feel free to explore."

He nodded excitedly and watched as Konrad pressed the lift button and disappeared behind the two sliding chrome doors. Alex couldn't prevent a broad grin spreading across his face. If Konrad's taste in cars was anything to go by then he was bound to own some very cool stuff.

As he looked around the space, Alex realised there was something familiar about it, but he couldn't quite put his finger on it. Perhaps it was the room's shape; round with huge glass windows. It reminded him of his music room back at home, perhaps. Konrad's space though was split into two floors.

The second floor was a mezzanine that appeared to be a library. Underneath the mezzanine, Alex could see two boxy and rather uncomfortable looking sofas on the left hand side. On the right was an enormous collection of vinyl records, lined up neatly on thick metal shelves. Between the sofas and the records, on either side of the lift doors, were two enormous speakers. They looked as if they were pointing directly where Alex was standing, in front of Konrad's desk. They were very much like the ones Alex had in his own bedroom, only twice the size and, he noted, at least five times more expensive. Feeling a pang of jealously, he decided to take a look at the mezzanine level and stepped very lightly up the floating glass stairs that wrapped around the right-hand arc of the room.

The library covered a half-moon shape from one side of the room to the other, with shelves stretching right up to the tall ceiling. Each shelf was filled with books of all shapes and sizes, colours and ages; or so it seemed, judging by the state of some of the spines. Picking out one or two that looked interesting, Alex quickly found himself feeling quite ignorant; he didn't even recognise the language, let alone the titles. Sliding them back carefully, in case they were valuable, he wandered further around the arc until he reached what felt like the centre. That section of the library was quite different.

Instead of housing books, each shelf from floor to ceiling had a curved piece of black glass set into it. Curious, Alex cupped his hands over his eyes and leant forward trying to peer through the pane of glass set at chest height. The second he touched the glass, however, there was a small *hiss*. The glass turned from near opaque black to crystal clear and began to slowly move upwards. Alex gasped. On the other side of the rising glass sat an ancient book, propped up on a metal stand and lit from above. The cover was burnt and black. He could make out the subtle embossing of the Wolf family crest on the warped cover.

It looked *just* like the crest that Henry had shown Alex in the lake house. He thought about the single page that Frederik had used to such great effect. But Alex didn't see one page, or even two, or ten; in front of him was a complete book.

Alex struggled to remember what Frederik had told him. He had said that all his books were destroyed; and that the master of the shadow would be trying to create his *own* set of books. But this didn't look like a new book at all. It looked like it could even be one of the original five.

Is Frederik mistaken? Had Konrad stolen one of the original books without Frederik noticing and kept it all these years? Whatever the explanation, at the very least it proved that Konrad was involved.

Suddenly feeling very nervous, Alex looked around the edge of the opening for some sort of reset button, but he couldn't see anything. Instead, he began to wave his hands around in the air wildly to engage any invisible sensors. He must have done something right because he heard a small click and the glass began to descend. By the time it had resealed the book in the wall, the glass panel had also returned to opaque black.

Alex breathed a long sigh of relief and tried to compose himself. He could feel his heart pounding. It wouldn't do for Konrad to find him sweaty and uncomfortable when he'd only been gone for a few minutes; both sure signs that Alex had been up to no good.

Quickly, he made his way across the mezzanine and back down the glass staircase. However, in his haste he stumbled on the last step and had to grab Konrad's desk to steady himself. A split second after he'd touched the desk he heard a mechanical latch and an airlock being released. Alex could only watch in horror as a huge circular section of floor in the middle of the room began to rise.

Oh what now? Making a mental note to take the utmost care on stairs in the future, Alex's panic soon gave way to genuine wonder as the circle of stone rose ever higher, revealing what looked like a hidden bookcase.

It was unlike any bookcase Alex had ever seen before. After several seconds it came to a stop. At least a foot taller than Alex, it was packed with small red books that were roughly A5 in size.

Approaching the newly revealed obelisk but not even bothering to check the door to the room, Alex took one of the books closest to him and fanned through the many pages. There were lines and lines of text; interspersed with many hundreds of sketches and diagrams. Some were neat and ordered, some were scribbled, some were written along the page and some were written up and down. But as Alex flicked through further he did notice one consistent thing; all of it was in the same handwriting.

A sudden idea struck him and he flicked to the first page of the book. What he saw made his heart skip a beat:

KONRAD MYERSON STENNING - b.1610 - d.   : V17 – FWF

It was the same kind of label that Alex had in his journal.

Konrad was born in 1610? If he hadn't known better, Alex would have guessed that the book had been written by a relation of Konrad from years ago, and passed on as an heirloom.

He quickly put the book back in its place and picked up another from two shelves down; more writing, more images, more thoughts and ideas. Flicking to the front he read again:

KONRAD MYERSON STENNING - b.1610 - d.   : V08 – FWF

He checked three more; they too all had the same kind of contents and the same kind of label at the front. There was a flutter of movement and Alex noticed that a book on the top shelf had fallen across the empty gap next to it. He reached up and took it off the shelf.

KONRAD MYERSON STENNING - b.1610 - d.   : V20 – FWF

He flicked to the last entry.

Taking a trip to Wolf Manor for the first time in years to see my family. I'm sure Sofia will be as pleased to see me as my son will.

I must also find out if Alex is the one that needs to be dealt with. If he is, then I will send him to do it.

Alex nearly dropped the book.

Who is him, *the shadow? And what is* him *going to do to me?* Starting to panic, he quickly stuffed the book back on the top shelf and dashed to the desk, desperately trying to find the switch to make the bookcase go back down. Rubbing his hands over every available surface, he could feel his panic rising. There was a whirring sound and Alex's eyes shot to the doorway.

The long row of lights above the doorframe were moving at pace from right to left; signifying a rapid descent; Konrad had called the lift down to him and it would only be seconds before he returned. Heat flushed Alex's face and in desperation he turned back to the desk to try and find the switch again. He didn't know what he pressed, but without warning the book-filled column slowly began to retract down into the stone floor.

Eyes flicking between the lift lights and the column, Alex was convinced he would be discovered and promptly thrown from the top of the tower if it didn't hurry up.

With only a foot of distance remaining, Alex leapt on top of the stone disc to try and make it descend faster. 3 inches... 2 inches... 1 inch. There was a soft *ping*, the lift doors parted and in walked Konrad, busy reading a newspaper and followed by a tall man carrying a tray with two cups on it. Konrad looked up just as Alex had touchdown.

"Everything alright, Alexander? You look all hot and flustered." Konrad asked quietly.

"Me? Oh I'm fine," spat Alex quickly in a voice that wasn't entirely his own. "Absolutely fine, thank you. Well, I did trip down those stairs earlier, glass steps caught me out a bit you see... or not, as the case may be?" He laughed nervously and hoped that the other man would walk over and hit him around the head with the tray he was carrying so expertly.

There was a moment's pause while Konrad stared blankly at Alex without a trace of emotion, but then he smiled. "Yes, I know what you mean, I keep thinking about having them changed but I just never get round to it. Come, sit down here with me."

Konrad gestured for Alex to join him on one of the uncomfortable looking sofas and Alex didn't hesitate to oblige. The other man had already placed two cups of coffee on twin side tables and was making his exit via the lift doors. Alex took a seat on one sofa while Konrad sat down slowly on the opposite one. Surprised to find them more comfortable than they looked, Alex thought it best to sit back, keep quiet and just wait for his granddad to speak. For the first time in his life, he hoped he *only* appeared stupid.

For several minutes, he sipped his coffee, while Konrad returned to his newspaper. Just as the silence was beginning to reach an extremely uncomfortable pitch, Konrad threw the newspaper onto the table with a bang and clapped his hands loudly. Alex jumped slightly, spilling coffee on his trousers.

"So," Konrad boomed, smiling broadly. "Tell me all about yourself. I don't think I've seen you and your brother for at least ten years."

Unsure where to start with this question, Alex started with the first thing that came into his head. "Well, I've... I mean *we've* just finished school, so we've got the summer to decide what we're going to do from now... really. I'm doing some work with granddad... Mum's dad, I mean... and Lewis is... well, I'm sure you know about Lewis. Planning to take over the company when Gran croaks it, I think."

Konrad's laughter boomed out loud again. "Ah, but I suspect your grandma will go on forever, Alex." smiled Konrad, reaching for his coffee.

"Oh God, I hope not!" Replied Alex with a smirk which vanished quickly when he remembered who he was talking to.

"But what are *you* going to do after the summer? What job will you do? How will you make *your* name in this world?"

Slightly taken aback, Alex had to admit that he had never really given the topic much thought; the events of the last few days had certainly shifted his perspective somewhat.

"After all," said Konrad. "Your brother seems like he's got his plan all worked out. You could follow in your father's footsteps I suppose, but unless you've a passion for architecture that doesn't seem likely? What do you like? What makes you excited?"

Alex had to stop himself from saying, "fast cars, music and expensive watches". When he actually thought about it, he didn't know what he really liked doing. Konrad seemed to sense this internal dialogue.

"Forgive me, Alex, but the reason I ask all these questions is because I think it is important that a man tries to map out his own path in life. Or at the very least, have some idea of what he wants to do. Would you not agree? You cannot, for example, continue to live off your parents' name and wealth forever can you? You must make your own plans. Make your own mark!"

Thinking that he didn't see much wrong with living off his parents' name and money, at least for a little while longer, he nodded in agreement anyway.

"So, with that in mind I was wondering if you wanted to come and work for me?"

"For you?" Said Alex.

Konrad smiled. "Well don't sound so surprised! I'm not, if you'll pardon the pun, the big bad wolf that you've probably heard about on the news, or at home for that matter. I just thought some work experience with me might give you a bit more of a foundation for the future. I don't suppose for one minute you really want to have to work for your grandmother, or for your brother, do you?"

"Well no, but..." said Alex, not really sure what he was going to say next.

"You don't have to give me an answer now, but just have a think about it. I'm sure there's much I could teach you and who knows, maybe one day you'll be running a company to rival your grandmothers!"

Alex was speechless, not least because his brain was moving quickly into a daydream about sacking his own grandmother. He wondered how working for Konrad would sit with his own family though. Would they consider it high treason? Something seemed to click in Alex's brain.

What am I thinking? Work here? Not when Konrad's the one controlling the shadow! Shifting uncomfortably in his seat, he placed the coffee cup gently on the side table, avoiding his granddad's unblinking eyes. He had to try and get out of there promptly but politely. The last thing he wanted to do was raise suspicion. As if Konrad had read his mind, he too placed his coffee cup on the side.

"Now I'm afraid I have some things that I need to get on with, Alex, so we'll have to end our meeting here. But before you go, I want to give you something."

Alex watched intently as Konrad stood and walked to the wall on the far side of the lift door where the stacks of vinyl records were. Konrad leant forwards and said something under his breath. Without warning, a whole section of the curved wall moved out two feet and then began to slide sideways, revealing an enormous black safe set into the wall. Alex gasped in awe as Konrad quickly pressed a series of buttons. With a prolonged *beep,* the door swung slowly open.

As much as he tried, Alex couldn't see inside without standing up. When his granddad turned, he was holding a small black box. He swung the safe door shut and returned to the sofas, his tall frame towering over Alex.

"Here, take this," he said quietly. "It'll help you to think things over, I'm sure. In case you're having any doubts."

Alex took the box gently in both hands; it felt heavy. He began to lift the lid but Konrad stopped him. "I think you should open that when you get downstairs, Alex. Only when you get downstairs. Ok?"

"Err… no problem. Well thanks for this anyway, whatever it is." Konrad smiled and gestured for the lift. "Oh! Of course, sorry!" said Alex, glancing at the lift; forgetting he was supposed to be as keen to leave as his granddad was for him to go.

Alex put out his hand to shake his grandfather's, but Konrad had already begun to walk back across the room to the large windows that looked out over the surrounding land. Feeling slightly foolish, he lowered his hand and walked quickly to the lift doors, pressing the small button on the wall. The door opened instantly and he stepped inside. He was just about to press the down button when Konrad called out, "Just one more thing, Alex."

Alex looked across the room at Konrad's black silhouette against the bright morning sky. "I suggest that next time you go driving, it would be wise to keep your speed down. I think 200mph is probably a little fast for the public road, don't you? Especially when it's not your own car."

"I… but… how did you…" the lift doors closed.

Alex felt his stomach lurch again as it began its rapid descent. Feeling completely and utterly caught out, he swiftly exited the building and made his way out of the main door. Once on the steps outside he stopped to open his gift.

Cautiously, he stuck a thumb under each side of the lid and gently popped it off. Inside, on a soft bed of leather, was a solid block of expensive-looking black metal. It had no other markings, except for two rectangular buttons. Plucking it from the box, he examined it for a few moments, before pressing one of the buttons. Half expecting it to explode, he jumped at the small *bleep* that came from several feet away. He glanced up to see two narrow rear lights flash red against black bodywork. An immaculate scissor door ascended slowly like the wing of a powerful insect.

A wide grin spread across Alex's face.

CHAPTER 30

MISDIRECTION

Long after his grandson had driven away, Konrad stood looking out of the window, his gaze fixed on Wolf Manor. Bryson had returned to clear away the empty coffee cups.

"Did everything go as intended, sir?" He said stiffly.

"It did indeed, thank you, Bryson," said Konrad. "He saw everything that I needed him to."

"Very good, sir."

CHAPTER 31

LEWIS

With an unnerving lack of control, Alex pulled to a sliding stop in front of the front steps, spraying the house with gravel. After he regained the feeling in his hands, he burst into fits of laughter. Flipping the door handle, he slid out from the low seat and struggled weakly to his feet. He took a few wobbly steps backwards and then stood for a moment, admiring the mechanical beast that was still hissing and ticking in front of him.

If this is one of the perks of working for my grandfather then you can sign me up straight away! Shadow be damned.

"What the *hell* is—" came a shout from behind him.

Alex spun around to see his dad bursting through the front doors looking furious. Upon seeing Alex, however, Morten's fury seemed to change to bewilderment.

"Sorry… sorry, Alex. I thought someone was throwing rocks at the door." He was staring at the car sitting menacingly behind his son. "Where did you get this? Please tell me you haven't started spending your trust fund money already?"

"No!" Alex said quickly, holding his hands up. "Of course I haven't, I'm not stupid. This came from Konrad. I mean Granddad. *Your* dad, that is. He's lending it to me. He… offered me a job." Alex could see his dad stiffen, as if the air had been sucked from his body.

"He what?" Said Morten quietly.

"A job. He offered me a job?" Alex continued, slightly concerned by his dad's rapidly whitening complexion and tightening jaw. "I haven't said yes yet," he added quickly. "Just… thinking about it really?"

For some reason, every statement Alex made seemed to be coming out as a question.

"A job? But what are *you* going to do for Konrad?"

The tone of incredulity in Morten's voice made Alex bristle. "There's *plenty* I could do for him, I'm sure. I just need to come up with a few ideas, he said, then I can go and talk to him about it." Alex heard the anger in his own voice.

"But you don't know anything…" Morten said, but Alex's temper got the better of him.

"You don't know anything about *anything*? Is that what you were going to say?"

Morten looked shocked, "No Alex, I just meant–"

"It's alright, I know what you meant, Dad. *Alex who doesn't know a thing about business. Alex who doesn't show an interest in the company. Alex who's lazy and just sits around playing the piano all day.* I know what you all think of me."

"Alex," cut in Morten, sounding hurt. "I don't think any of that! I was going to say you don't know anything about *Konrad*. My father. You don't know what you're getting into with him! He may not have your best interests at heart, that's what I mean. I just want you to be careful."

"Don't worry about me. I'll be just fine," continued Alex bitterly. "Just because he doesn't like *you* anymore, doesn't mean he doesn't want to get to know me!"

Alex knew immediately that he'd gone too far. Morten's face dropped like he'd just been dealt a body blow. He just stared blankly at Alex.

"Dad…" he couldn't find any words.

"No Alex, you're right." Said Morten quietly, looking to the floor. "I know I'm a disappointment to my father. I just didn't need to be reminded, that's all." Something tightened in Alex's stomach as Morten looked back up at him. "You're your own man now and you have to make your own choices."

Alex went to say something, but again the words failed him. He just stood like a spare part. His dad squeezed him gently on the shoulder and walked back up the stairs towards the pebble-dashed front doors.

"Dad!" Alex called out, not really knowing what he was going to say next. Morten walked through the door and closed it gently behind him.

Alex felt wretched. The whole drive back he'd been filled with excitement about showing his new car off to his dad; his dad, who would be the one person to really appreciate it. More than that though, Alex thought how pleased he would be when he told him he'd found a job.

How had that gone so wrong so quickly? Alex slammed the heavy car door down and trudged morosely back up the stone steps, not even bothering to look back at his gleaming new ride. Pushing his way into the main hallway, he trudged upstairs and didn't stop until his was safe in his own bedroom.

He lay on the bed for several minutes, trying to put the bad feelings out of his mind. Instead of making him feel better though, the silence seemed to be making him feel worse. The more he thought about what he'd said, the hotter he began to feel, like there was a flood of frustration and anger welling up inside him and he didn't know what to do with it.

He got up and paced around the room, trying to walk out his frustration but that didn't help either. Neither did taking a kick at one of the heavy speakers, which only resulted in a cracking sound and a lot of pain in his foot. It was as he hopped up and down, clutching his right foot, that the idea came to him.

The diary! He limped through his wardrobe and extracted his diary and pen from his safe. Within seconds he was back at his desk with the diary open in front of him. Skipping the music, milk, slippers and perfect lighting, he just began to write.

He wrote about the incident with his dad, how it had made him feel, how angry he now felt about his day being ruined, and how guilty he felt for saying what he had. The more he wrote, the easier it became and the words seemed to naturally flow from short statements into longer sentences.

He wrote about his meeting with Konrad, what he'd seen and how his other granddad scared him. He wrote about Lewis and how he always felt like the stupid brother, how it wasn't necessarily Lewis's fault, that Lewis had never really done anything wrong. He wrote about the other events of the days since he'd been back at home; the dinner party, the trip to Henry's hidden home, meeting Frederik, the dark dreams he'd had and his first piano lesson with Sara.

Sara. When it came to Sara, the ink seemed to flow from Alex's pen like nothing he'd seen before. It was as if he just had to think of the words and they appeared on the pages in front of him. His mind lingered on the kiss they'd shared in the small room where his most treasured possessions lived. He wished that he hadn't been so scared and proud; maybe he could have kissed her again.

The words flowed as though a dam inside him had burst; one that had been holding back his feelings perhaps for his entire life. The more he wrote the better he felt.

The sky outside his window had grown overcast and a light rain had begun to pattern the windows. As he wrote, he heard it intensify and the light drumming on the glass became a constant drone. The darkened sky brought a gloominess to the room as the thick, heavy clouds roiled bleakly over the estate. Alex paused only briefly to reach forward and flick the switch on his desk lamp.

He wrote about playing the piano; how it made him feel as he pressed the keys in certain combinations, how certain chords and progressions made the hairs stand up on the back of his neck and across his arms, how he *hated* playing for large groups of people and felt annoyed every time he was made to do so. His playing was for him; for him and Sara to share and no-one else. The thoughts formed in his mind and the words appeared on the page.

He barely noticed the first flash of lightning as he began to describe the way he felt when he *listened* to music. Without thinking, he gently flicked on his music and listened intently. The first blasting strains of *O Fortuna* sung from the speakers, beautifully enriched by the accompaniment of nature's force that was growing steadily outside. Page after page went by in his desperation to express everything.

By the time Alex finally sat back in his chair, the storm outside had grown in intensity. Exhausted, he stared at the book and pen on the desk in front of him. Both were glowing faintly yellow; Alex felt so calm that he barely acknowledged it. He supposed that was just what happened when you wrote with such intensity; perhaps the books took on a life of their own in some way.

He flicked back through the diary pages and to his amusement, saw that he had written over thirty sides of small and sometimes illegible text. There were small sketches as well, most of which he didn't remember drawing. Yet there they were, interspersed between the text. He remembered Konrad's notebooks and how similar their scribblings looked. He moved his pen aside and closed the diary.

Alex got up from his seat and stretched. Nearly five hours had passed since he started writing. He felt that much better than when he'd started though, it didn't even register as unusual.

For the first time, Alex really noticed the intensity of the storm. Standing in front of the huge glass windows, he saw that the sky was almost entirely black and only far away on the horizon was there any sign of the sky brightening.

He pressed a small button on the wall and the huge doors began to concertina open. Every inch they widened brought the sound of the storm closer to him. He stepped outside and took a slow, deep breath, inhaling the smell of rainwater on stone and the wet grass from the grounds below.

Within seconds he was drenched and his clothes hung off him like rags. Regardless, he walked to the edge of the balcony and stood, barefoot, enjoying the sound of the storm at its most potent. As he stood in silence before the awesome power of nature, it occurred to Alex that it was only at times like these that he felt truly at peace. Contented. A tiny being in a huge world.

Sheet lightning lit up the grounds and Alex saw them at once. Someone was walking out across the grounds towards the edge of the forest. Squinting against the rain, Alex tried to focus on the distant figure but they were too far away. As the thunder rolled in above he ran back into his bedroom, quickly slid open one of his drawers and pulled out his camera. Flipping off the lens cover, he went back to the window's edge and held up the camera to his eye. Rotating the lens with one hand he quickly located the figure, magnified in his viewfinder. With quick precision he twisted the lens rings. The figure instantly snapped into focus; it was Lewis. Alone and walking into the forest. No jacket, no coat, just a T-shirt and jeans. Alex could see that he was carrying something in his hands, but even with the powerful lens, he couldn't quite make it out. He lowered his camera and frowned.

What is Lewis doing walking into the forest in this weather? Alex cupped his hands to his mouth and called Lewis's name; no response. He tried again, only louder. The wind and the rain were buffeting his words into silence before they'd even reached the end of the balcony.

He wasn't sure why, but seeing Lewis like that gave him a very bad feeling. He went back into his room and closed the windows behind him. Going straight to his wardrobe, Alex rooted round in one of the lower drawers and pulled out some clothes that he had once bought for a hiking trip but had never worn. Dumping his wet clothes in a sodden pile on the floor, he quickly threw on an all-black outfit of waterproof trousers and woollen jumper. Pulling on some thick socks and heavy-duty boots, he added a warm fleecy zip-up top and a long wax jacket. Thinking he might as well do the job properly, he grabbed a tweed flat cap from the top shelf, some thick, heavy gloves and a small silver torch. Despite it being summertime, Alex suspected it would be cold and dark in the shade of the forest where Lewis was heading.

Being sure to lock his door behind him, Alex hurried downstairs and out the front doors. There was no sign of anyone else, so he made his way along the side of the house and out towards the grounds. Cursing himself for not bringing his camera, he squinted into the distance and only just made out the figure of Lewis as he stepped beyond the tree-line. Fearing that he would lose him if he lagged too far behind, Alex sprinted to catch up. It quickly became clear that his fitness levels weren't as high as he'd imagined and it took him a lot longer to reach the forest than he'd hoped.

When he finally reached the spot where he'd seen Lewis, a feeling of grave concern began to creep over Alex. The rain had eased slightly, as had the thunder and lightning, but it was still dark and overcast. He knew that it would be darker still in the woods.

Should I really follow Lewis in there? Maybe he's just going for a walk. Maybe he doesn't want to be interrupted. He could of course turn back and no one would be any the wiser. The thought of heading straight back to his bedroom was incredibly appealing and Alex almost turned to walk away. Then he thought of the shadowy figure attacking his brother.

Lewis doesn't know! Sighing heavily, Alex buttoned his jacket to the top and stepped into the Silver Forest.

In Alex's bedroom, the diary slowly opened itself on his desk. As the pages fanned from right to left his words flashed brilliant blue, before turning back to their original black. The last page fell flat and the leather cover closed.

The diary lay still on the desk once more.

CHAPTER 32

THE SILVER FOREST

Even on their visits to the estate as children, Alex and Lewis had never been allowed to venture into the forest. Alex had imagined it was full of monsters; nonsense, of course, but those childhood fears were suddenly flooding back to him.

The forest itself was so tightly cultivated you were either in or you were out. Alex had often looked longingly at the boundary from the confines of his grandparents' house and thought it resembled a thick green wall, bordering the neatly mown lawns.

As soon as Alex stepped into the densely populated trees, the rain stopped immediately. The canopy was so densely packed above him, there didn't seem to be a single drop of rain coming through from the sky. Alex pulled back his hood, and let his eyes adjust to the strange green light. There was a chance that Lewis was still nearby, in which case they could both leave and be back home within minutes.

Unfortunately he couldn't see anyone or anything. He walked a few steps further and felt his feet pressing softly into the moss-covered ground. The sweet smell of rotting wood and fresh pine needles filled his lungs. Realising he'd underestimated just how dark it was going to be, he pulled out the torch and clicked it on. There was barely a flicker from it before it died. *Brilliant.*

Thick fern leaves brushed his legs and hands as he walked on but still no sign of Lewis. *Maybe he entered the forest further up? What was he doing in here anyway?* A feeling of annoyance was beginning to mix with his deepening concern. Although he couldn't feel the rain, he could still hear it along with the thunder above him. He tried to reason that it was just like he was back in the house listening to the torrent outside; just a very green and slightly scary room where he couldn't turn on the lights. He walked on, deeper into the forest.

The further he walked, the more he noticed a change in the general colour of the trees. At the edges of the forest, they were thick-trunked and mostly darker browns and greens. As Alex moved further in, the darker trunks were dispersing and making way for trees with a silvery-grey bark. He also noticed that along with the change of trees, the colour of the light was changing too. It was as if it was actually becoming brighter. Glancing over his shoulder, Alex realised that the place where he had entered the forest had become completely obscured. Grateful at least that the forest seemed to be providing him with its own light, he slipped the useless torch back into his pocket and carried on.

He had been so concerned by the thought of entering the forest he'd completely forgotten to shout Lewis's name. He was just about to call out, when a hand covered his mouth. He screamed into the warm palm, but no sound came, so he tried desperately to turn. A second hand gripped his right shoulder tightly, locking him in place.

"Be still, Alex. Danger walks this way," said a low, soft voice. Even in his panic, Alex recognised it at once.

It was the same voice he'd heard when the lights went out at the dinner party. He tried to turn again, but was held steady. There was no pain, but it felt like he was in an iron vice grip.

"I said be *still!*" The voice was whispering so close to his ear he could feel the hot breath on his neck.

They stood in silence for what felt like several minutes. All Alex could do was scan the trees in front of him, either for a sign of Lewis or of the supposed danger; he could see neither.

The hand on his shoulder loosened slightly, but the one over his mouth stayed where it was. As he turned cautiously in the dark, the hand over his mouth became just one finger, placed over his lips. When he saw who was standing behind him, his fear seemed to dissolve completely.

It was a woman, but unlike any Alex had ever seen. She was at least 6 inches taller than he was and dressed from head to toe in what looked like a perfectly contoured white jumpsuit. *Or is it white?* The way it shimmered and reflected in the half-light, it seemed to change colour with her every movement.

She was powerfully built and her long, black hair was tied in a ponytail, revealing a beautiful face. Sharp cheekbones sat below bright, almond-shaped eyes which, even in the dim light, seemed to shine brightly both green and yellow.

"When you've finished looking," came the cool voice of the statuesque woman.

Alex realised his mouth was hanging open slightly and closed it quickly.

"Who *are* you?" he said; the only vaguely relevant question he could think of.

"My name is Aurora. For now that's all you need to know. You are looking for Lewis, I think?"

"Err, Yes." Said Alex, remembering suddenly the reason he was there.

"Then follow me. Stay close and stay quiet. There is still danger." Aurora set off quickly.

Pulling himself together, he stepped carefully after her, keen to keep as close as possible. If there really was danger around, he would much rather be around someone bigger than him than be caught on his own.

Desperate to keep up, Alex stumbled noisily after his guide, crashing through dead branches and slipping on wet moss. Several times, Aurora glanced back and glared at Alex; he was paying more attention to the impressive view, striding several feet in front of him, than to where he was placing his feet.

Despite the distraction, Alex noted again how the light was beginning to change. It had begun to slip back into darkness. The canopy overhead was so thick that only the smallest speck of light was breaking through. From the view ahead, Alex also noticed that Aurora's clothing seemed to be changing to match the surrounding light. When he had first seen her, it had been a silvery-white colour, but now it seemed to be slipping into a dark, gunmetal grey. It still shimmered in the remaining light of the forest, but the further they travelled, the more difficult it was to pick her out from the surroundings.

They moved further into the woods and the light continued to decrease until it was more-or-less pitch black. Suddenly Alex collided with something solid in front of him and he fell backwards onto the soft mossy ground. It seemed that Aurora had stopped suddenly and Alex had simply bounced off her. He could only just make out her form turning in his direction. When she leant over, with hand outstretched, he saw that she was frowning at him. Embarrassed, Alex ignored her offer of help, scrambled to his feet and brushed himself down.

"Come, your brother is here." She said in a low whisper.

Without a sound she moved forward, positioning herself behind a large thick-trunked tree. She raised her hand slowly and pointed into the distance. Alex, who had moved behind her, followed her slender finger to see Lewis standing alone in a clearing barely thirty feet away.

He could see that Lewis was holding what looked like a small hatchet in his hand and was standing directly in front of an enormous silver-barked tree. He watched intently as he raised the axe and planted it firmly into the tree. Instead of a crack or a thud, there came a soft chime, as if a huge bell had been struck with a large felt-ended mallet.

Lewis shook the hatchet handle until the broad, shining blade came free, then he struck the tree again. Alex heard the same chime as before. Once more, Lewis shook the hatchet free; he raised his hand higher and brought down the axe with all of his might. Alex heard a sharper *ting* of metal on metal.

Reaching into his jacket, Lewis pulled out what looked like six flat pieces of wood and placed them on the ground. Quickly, he slotted them together, forming an open-topped box with a separate lid, barely six inches in each direction. Holding the box up to the tree, Lewis yanked out the hatchet and threw it to the floor. Alex watched in amazement as a thick, bright silver liquid oozed from the tree, slowly at first, but then it gained pace.

Within seconds it must have filled the box that Lewis was carrying. He held up his left hand and placed his palm over the slit in the tree. A dull yellow light flashed in the darkness and when Lewis removed his hand, it was like there had never been a slit there at all. He crouched down, putting the lid onto the box and sealing it tightly shut, before picking up the hatchet. Both items in his hands, he began to silently walk away.

Alex was about to tap Aurora on the shoulder to get her attention, but in the split second he reached up, Lewis changed in shape. Directly in front of them, his sodden clothes fell away and his body seemed to grow in height, width and colour until, standing by the tree, was a thing at least as tall as Aurora, even more muscular and dressed from head to toe in black.

It looked terrifying. The muscular form slowly moved the box up to its face and peered at it closely, all the time taking long, slow, breaths.

Alex desperately tried to pull himself to his feet to run, but he was pushed back hard against the floor as Aurora stood and let out a tremendous wailing noise. The black figure's head snapped towards them and a scream froze in Alex's throat. Dead, black eyes were surrounded by mottled, burnt flesh; stretched taut over an engorged and bony head. The lips of the beast pulled back and Alex saw its blackened teeth holding back a hissing, speckled tongue.

In a flash, the thing tucked the box under its arm and sprinted away through the trees. Aurora turned to Alex, their eyes locking for a split second, before she took off after the figure, disappearing into the trees.

Her voice came to him as she ran but seemed to linger in the air by his ear, "Go back to Henry. Tell him what happened but do not mention my name. Tell him Zephyr was in the forest."

Without a moment's hesitation, Alex pulled himself up and ran. Hoping he was going back the way he had come, he leapt over fallen tree trunks and the low-growing ferns. Adrenaline coursing through his veins, he passed the lighter-coloured trees. Although he was painfully out of breath, he pressed on into the darker and more densely-packed forest.

Struggling to breathe, Alex nearly cried out with relief when he saw the freshly mown grass of the Wolf Manor grounds. He fell heavily onto the wet lawn and rolled on to his back, gasping for air. His chest rose and fell like a young bird struck from its nest. The storm clouds had ebbed away, only to be replaced with the darkening evening sky. With a last effort, Alex pulled himself up, ran back to the house and in through the side door.

He stopped for a moment to think where his granddad might be. He ran through the kitchen, down the steep, narrow stairs and burst into his granddad's study, still panting heavily, his eyes wide with fear. Sitting quietly in his chair was Henry, who looked up surprised but with a smile.

"Alex! Just the man. Why don't you pull up a chair and I'll tell you the story I was just telling Lewis."

"*Lewis?*" said Alex.

"Alright, Al?"

Alex's eyes darted to his right. Lewis was sitting comfortably on a soft armchair in the corner of the room, biting into an apple.

CHAPTER 33

FALLING

Alex stood in the doorway, stunned.

"Granddad was just telling me about the time he got into a fight with the milkman over some missing Gold Top," said Lewis, chuckling. "You should get him to tell you it sometime. Hilarious!" He bit off another chunk of his apple.

"Everything alright, Alex?" Asked Henry, a look of growing concern on his face.

"No… no I don't think it is," he replied, his head spinning.

Lewis looked up at Alex, confusion etched on his face.

"Lewis, I think you should probably go and see if your grandmother's all set for your trip tomorrow. Check everything's in order?"

"Trip? What trip?" Asked Alex.

"Yeah, we're flying to New York. Gran's going to announce her retirement to the board. Not that she needs to after the other night. That ok with you, Al?"

"Lewis," said Henry, firmly still looking at Alex. "Go along and check on your grandmother, I need to have a word with Alex about a few things. I'll see you later."

"Yeah… ok," said Lewis quietly. He too was staring at Alex with a worried look on his face. "See you both later then." He patted Alex on the shoulder as he passed.

Alex flinched slightly and continued to watch Lewis as he left the room. The door shut with a thunk and he listened to Lewis's receding footsteps.

"Alex, what is it?" Said Henry quickly, but Alex didn't reply. "Come on, boy, sit down and tell me what's happened."

Slowly, Alex pulled out the chair from the desk, the hard feet scraping across the stone floor. Henry swivelled round in his chair and then returned with two small cut-glass tumblers in his hands. He pulled out a leather-wrapped hip flask from his jacket pocket, unscrewed the lid and poured two generous measures of amber liquid. He pushed one in Alex's direction.

Pouring the drink down his throat, Alex choked on the roughness and subsequent sting in his nostrils, but it seemed to do the trick.

"Right, now tell me what's happened. Go from the start."

Alex paused a few seconds before launching into his story.

"I was up in my room writing in my diary–"

"Excellent stuff!" Said Henry. "Glad to hear you're keeping–"

"I was up in my room, writing my diary," Alex said again, stressing each word. Henry fell silent. "When I saw Lewis outside, walking towards the forest. I called out to him from my room but he didn't hear me so I went downstairs and followed him. When I got into the forest I couldn't find him. I had to go in a lot further than I've been before." Henry shifted slightly in his seat. "Anyway, I was about to call out to him when–"Alex suddenly remembered he wasn't supposed to be mentioning Aurora. "When I realised I couldn't actually see him. So I... I didn't call out to him." The lie wasn't very convincing but he pressed on regardless. "I carried on walking a bit further and spotted him and that's when he started going at this big tree with an axe! He hit it a few times and then this weird silver liquid starts coming out of it which he puts in this box that he'd just made. Then, he turned into this enormous monster thing and ran off! That's when I ran back here to find you!"

Henry was looking at his desk, not saying a word.

"Well what do you think? Am I going mad or what? Lewis isn't really a huge monster in disguise, is he? I know there've been a lot of odd things going on recently but this was super weird!"

Henry sat still looking at the desk.

"Well say something then!" Alex said angrily, leaning forward in his chair.

"I think," said Henry quietly. "I think it's time we went to see Frederik. Only this time, we go together."

Alex sat back in his chair and rolled his eyes. "Oh not him again. He gives me the creeps!"

Henry stood up and walked around to the other side of the desk. Alex watched his grandfather suspiciously. "You're not going to punch me again are you?"

Henry gave a weak smile. "No, not this time, Alex. But I warn you to tell Frederik everything that happened and leave nothing out. Trust me, he'll know if you lie to him, and if you do... well it may be more than your nose you need bandaging up. Come on. Follow me."

Henry's tone reminded him of the time at his lake house; authoritative and unnerving. Without another word they left the office quickly and quietly. Henry led the way back up the stairs, through the kitchen and out through the darkened main hall. Just as they passed the huge stairway, they heard a voice that made them both stop in their tracks.

"And where might you two be off to in such a hurry?"

Alex and Henry both turned to see Sofia at the top of the stairs like a withered old spider about to descend on her prey.

"Music lesson, Sofia dear," called up Henry jovially. "Alex is going to try and finally teach me how to tinkle on the old Joanna!"

Alex thought his granddad sounded highly unconvincing. Even from a distance, Alex could see Sofia's eyebrow rise so high he half expected her eyeball to fall out.

"At this time, Henry? Surely it must nearly be time for dinner?" She said softly. The spider advanced towards them.

"Sorry, Granny," said Alex. "But I do find that Granddad is much more receptive to education just before dinner, you know. Must be the hunger keeps him interested. Anyway, we'd better be going. Why don't you shuffle yourself off to bed? Don't forget it's an early start tomorrow!"

Neither Henry nor Alex waited to see what reaction that last comment would receive. Both of them turned on their respective heels and quickstepped out of the entrance hall. Even in their serious situation Alex heard his grandfather stifling a snigger.

"Excellent work, m'boy," he whispered, winking. "We absolutely do not want your grandmother seeing where we go tonight, after all. She knows too much already."

Alex wasn't entirely sure what Henry meant, but they continued to walk quickly down the various corridors. Soon enough they were outside the library door, but before Alex could reach for the handle, Henry stopped him.

"Are you ready for this then, young man? Ready to find out what this is all about?"

"Of course," said Alex, already feeling the nerves and adrenaline pushing through his body again.

"Good. Just one moment then." Henry reached into his jacket pocket and pulled out a very old fountain pen.

He pulled off the lid and began to write on the white library door.

Henry Augustus Wolf MWF

The lights in the hallway went out, plunging them into near darkness. The writing on the door flashed yellow.

Henry turned the handle and opened the door. "In we go then, in we go."

Alex walked cautiously into the huge circular library. A small amount of moonlight was filtering in through the curved glass windows. Following Henry to the middle of the floor, they both stood silently for a moment. Alex felt his grandfather's strong hands grip both of his arms and move him first sideways, then back, ever so slightly, as if he were positioning him in some way. Henry then moved towards him so that they were literally standing toe to toe. Thinking that this was strange enough, Henry then began to hum.

As much as he listened, Alex couldn't place the tune; it sounded more like a chant. Whatever it was, it was certainly helping to dial up the eerie factor. Standing in the dark with his gently-swaying grandfather, Alex began to feel a cold draft rising up from beneath him. It was then that the floor began to tremble. Henry half-opened his eyes, but the shaking of the floor only seemed to spur him on.

There came the unmistakable grating noise of stone on stone. Alex felt the small circular section of wood on which they were standing begin to lower. He reached out to grab his granddad's arms to support himself, not knowing what to expect next.

One foot... two feet... three feet... the library floor was level with their waists when Henry finally stopped humming. He opened his eyes, reached forward and grabbed Alex tightly by the elbows.

Four feet... five feet... six feet... their heads passed below the level of the floor and Alex heard something sliding shut above his head. What little light there was in the library, went out.

"Are you ready then, boy?

"I... I think so?"

"Then hold on tight," said Henry, tensing. "I'm afraid you're really not going to like this."

The floor vanished beneath them and they fell into the darkness.

CHAPTER 34

INTO THE DARK

Alex could feel the acid burning his nostrils and smell the foul stench of his own vomit. He wretched again and the remaining contents of his stomach splattered on the floor at his feet. Thankfully it was so dark that he couldn't see it.

"Oh bad form, Alex, bad form," came Henry's gruff reply.

Alex could feel his granddad rubbing his back as he bent over double. If he hadn't felt so rough he would have swung for him.

"You could have told me what was going to happen, you know?" coughed Alex, wiping his mouth with his arm.

"If I'd told you you were going to climb into a small tube and plummet hundreds of feet below the earth, would you have hopped in? No, you wouldn't. Don't worry though, did the same thing myself first time I tried it!"

"Really?"

"Really. Although it ah, may have been from the other end."

Alex wretched again. Still bent over, he heard his granddad fumbling in his pocket, then a scratching noise and a small yellow flame burst into life. Henry's floating head appeared in the small circle of light.

"Now, before we go any further, Alex, I cannot stress this enough. Please do *not* make Frederik angry. Just *listen* to what he has to say and above all keep an open mind, ok?"

Alex finally straightened up, wiped his mouth with his forearm again and looked into his granddad's eyes. "Fine, I'll be good. As long as you promise there's nothing else like this to go through?" Alex swung his thumb up over his shoulder in the direction of the mystery elevator.

"I can *assure* you there is not," said Henry with a slight bow. "Now come along. He's expecting us"

"Hold on a sec!" Called Alex, but Henry had already set off quickly into the darkness.

From what Alex could make out, they were standing on bare rock. Suddenly fearing that they might be walking on some incredibly narrow pathway, suspended high above a bottomless crevasse, Alex stretched out both arms to reassure himself that there were some solid walls nearby. Worryingly, neither hand touched anything. The cool air of the slight breeze all around him gently tickled his fingers and began to dry his moistened palms. Alex was picturing the sheer drop on either side that would leave him spiralling downwards into nothingness. Keeping his eyes forward he trotted a little bit closer to his granddad.

After what seemed like an age of this precarious walk, Alex felt the ground begin to slope upwards. This coincided with an increase in the strength of breeze buffeting his sides; he put his arms out to steady himself. Eventually the floor finally levelled out. Sensing that they were passing under some sort of archway, Alex ducked.

When he looked up, he saw a faint glimmer of light ahead and wondered if that was where they were to meet Frederik. The ever-worsening stench of unwashed bodies certainly suggested that might be the case. He felt his pulse quicken slightly at the thought of seeing the old man again. Not because he was scared of him; he was, after all, with his granddad; but because of what he might learn about the events of the last week and with his brother.

The light in the distance grew stronger, as did the terrible smell. It was clear that the light ahead wasn't daylight; that would be impossible, so far underground. But it didn't exactly look like firelight either.

As it began to grow, Alex saw the structure they were about to enter. It looked remarkably like a giant stone igloo. He could just make out the edge of the dome in the surrounding gloom, but his eye was drawn immediately to the arched entrance. Even from a distance, Alex could see the interior was lined with some sort of reflective gold material, giving the illusion that the whole space was glowing.

Reaching the entrance, Henry stopped and turned to Alex. "You ready for this then, m'lad?" He wasn't smiling.

Alex wondered if his granddad was as apprehensive about meeting Frederik as he was, especially in such odd circumstances.

"Yeah. Course I am," said Alex weakly.

"Ok then, let's go and see what he has to say, shall we? Follow me!"

His granddad stepped through the arched entrance. A soft white light shimmered around him and then vanished. Henry stood inside the threshold, beckoning Alex. Taking a deep breath, he stepped through the archway and felt a strong pulse through his body; he was inside.

On the other side of the dome Frederik sat tapping his fingers moodily on the stone arm of his chair, glaring at the two visitors.

CHAPTER 35

THE TRUTH

Alex and Henry both stood for a few moments without saying anything. Frederik was still tapping his fingers on the side of his stone chair, but his expression softened. Henry was staring straight ahead, as if he was waiting for orders. Feeling ridiculous and annoyed at the complete lack of hospitality, Alex coughed and then spoke.

"So, are we here just for show, or are you actually going to tell me what's going on?"

A sly smile spread across Frederik's withered face before he finally spoke. "Come, sit. Both of you. Forgive my manners," he gestured to a stone plinth in front of him that resembled a medieval park bench. "Please, sit."

Alex sat slowly on the plinth, all the time keeping an eye on Frederik. After a couple of seconds, Henry joined him.

"So," said Frederik, addressing Alex. "I hope you didn't mind the manner of your arrival down here. I know it can be a bit of a shock the first time, no?"

Alex's eyes narrowed. "You could say that, yes," Henry nudged him. "But thank you for asking."

Frederik nodded, eyeing Alex knowingly.

"Well!" he said, putting his hands on his lap. "I must start, Alexander, by saying that I was most impressed by the work you put in to your diary today. I daresay I had my doubts about you, but you seem to be grasping the idea now, are you not?"

Alex looked blankly back at him. "My diary? How did you know that I've been writing in my diary?"

Frederik's eyes narrowed. "I know you've been writing in it, because every time you finish, I see a copy. Surely you have seen it flashing blue after you finish writing, have you not?"

"No," said Alex. "No I haven't! And why do you get a copy?" He felt the colour in his face rising rapidly and his voice was growing louder. "You haven't been… have you been *reading it?*"

He felt his granddad shift at his accusatory tone, but Alex didn't care. He didn't want the withered old man reading his personal thoughts. Frederik bristled and began to tap his fingers quickly on the side of his chair again.

"Of course I *read it,* Alexander. I have been keeping track of your thoughts this entire week. I had to know if you were suitable for the job I gave you."

"But that stuff's private! I wrote things in there that were only meant for me!"

"Alex," Henry warned quietly.

"When you have lived as long as I have, Alexander, and you have seen everything and done everything I have, nothing surprises you. You have nothing to be angry about." Said Frederik.

"But I *haven't* lived as long as you have. I *haven't* seen what you've seen. Those were my… my private thoughts!" blustered Alex, getting to his feet.

His mind raced to the things he'd written about his grandmother, about Lewis, about Sara. Fredrik's eyes flashed angrily before his expression softened and his hands gripped tightly on the stone arms of his chair, as if he was bracing himself for something. After some moments, Frederik spoke again, his voice strained.

"I… *apologise* Alexander. I forget what it is to have privacy… I forget what it is to be your age, so full of emotions and… feelings. Please, will you forgive me?"

Despite his embarrassment, Alex sat down.

"The reason I have read your diary," Frederick continued. "Is that I needed to see how you interacted with it, how you wrote in it, what effect it had on you. Alex it's so important that you too learn how to filter your thoughts and channel your feelings. It's important that you can accurately transfer them into your diary, so that you can make it strong. Just like the ones I made all those years ago."

"Oh not this again–"

"Yes! This again!" Spat Frederik, his temper rising as quickly as it had disappeared. "I told you before, you need to know how to write your own books in case the master of the shadows is making his own. If he has already done this, then we will have nothing to defend ourselves. He will take over. He and the shadow will take over everything. Is that what you want?"

Frederik slumped back down in his chair looking exasperated.

"Yes, I remember all that. You're looking for revenge on the person that killed your wife, but I still don't understand why *we* have to be involved in this."

"Come on, Frederik," said Henry somewhat timidly. "I really think it's time that you told him. It might make things easier?"

Frederik looked moodily at Henry, but then nodded. "Fine!" He sat up and roughly pulled his torn and battered robes around him in the same way he'd done in his shack. "Spanning many generations and many hundreds of years, your grandfather here has traced a link between your family of the Wolfs, or *Wulfs* as they were, right back to myself and Annelise–"

"So you mean we're actually related?" Said Alex, completely taken aback.

"In a way, yes." Frederik glowered.

"You're telling me that you're some sort of great, great, great, great granddad of mine?"

"Ach! Yes. Something like that," said Frederik. "The specifics aren't important. What *is* important is that when Annelise and I were granted the ability to live forever, our blood was altered. It was made to have something different about it. Something that would not only give us a longer life, but also an ability to see things more clearly, to think with more clarity and to have certain–how would you say–affinities with our feelings. You may have noticed your own blood is not as you might read in your science books, Alex?"

"It is a mixture of ordinary and extraordinary because, of course, over the many years the bloodline has been diluted."

A grin formed on Alex's face. He'd tried to stop himself but he couldn't. "Hold on, so you're telling me that I'm some sort of *immortal?* I'm going to live *forever?*" Alex puffed out his chest. "This. Is. Amazing! *Ha!* This is the best bit of news I've had all week!"

Alex didn't notice the cruel smile that had returned to Frederik's face. "Unfortunately for you, but perhaps more fortunately for the rest of mankind, that is not the case. Because of this dilution you are not immortal." Alex's chest deflated like a popped balloon. "But you are, for want of a better word, *different.*"

"How different?" Said Alex.

"Different enough for me to drag myself from my home and risk discovery. And different enough for the shadow to want to kill you. Forgive me if I am mistaken, but isn't that the reason you are both here?"

Alex went to argue, wanting to hear more about how special he was, but then gathered himself.

"Right. Then first of all, Alexander, you must tell me what happened this afternoon in the woods. And not that nonsense half story you told your grandfather this evening. And do not miss *anything* out, no matter what anyone might have told you to do."

Alex stared closely at Frederik, wondering how this old man managed to stay so well informed.

"Alexander," came Frederik's voice, softly breaking the silence. "Do you trust your grandfather?"

Alex instinctively looked to Henry. "Yes, yes of course I do."

"Then you can... in fact you *must* trust me."

Alex sighed heavily and slowly began to retell what had happened; he left nothing out.

"A woman?" Interrupted Frederik, half way through the story. His heavy brow furrowed above his dark eyes.

"Yes, a woman. Tall. White jumpsuit. Funny eyes."

"Aurora," said Frederik quietly, almost to himself. "Interesting."

"That's right! Aurora. She said her name was Aurora. Incredible looking, too. Really stunning, bit tall maybe, but when she ran–"

"You were saying, old chap?" said Henry.

"Oh right, yes..." Alex continued his story, mentioning Lewis, the hatchet and the weird chiming tree.

"And what did he do when the Silverblood came out?" Frederik said.

"The what?" Said Alex.

"Ach! The silver liquid you described. What did he do with it then?" Frederik began tapping the arm of his chair again.

"Well he had this wooden box thing that he'd put together on the floor and he kind of collected it into that. Filled it right up, I think. After that he pressed his hand to the tree, the whole thing glowed yellow and the cut he'd made with the axe just vanished... and that's when it happened."

"What? What happened, Alexander?" Said Frederik keenly, leaning forward in his chair.

"Well, Lewis... changed shape. He turned into this kind of monster thing. That's when Aurora screamed. Well, it was more like she was shouting in anger, really, but that's when the thing looked straight at us."

Alex shuddered at the thought of the face he'd seen in the woods.

"Tell me, Alexander," said Frederik slowly. "Did it see you?"

"Well it must have done, I suppose. It looked right at us. Its face though, it was like nothing I'd ever seen before, It's hard to describe but–"

"There's no need to describe it, Alexander. I know exactly what it looks like. Please, continue."

"Well, after it saw us it ran off into the woods with the box, really, really quickly and Aurora went after it. That's when she told me to run and tell granddad that Zephyr was here–"

"She told you to say that?" Henry cut in quickly. "You didn't mention that before. And who's *Zephyr?*"

"Sorry, I suppose I forgot. What with my brother turning into a monster and everything," said Alex shortly.

"Sorry, sorry old chap. Didn't mean to–"

"Quiet!" Shouted Frederik suddenly.

Both of them jumped slightly at this unexpected outburst.

"I need to think and I cannot do that with you two talking!"

Frederik slowly sat back in his chair and Alex watched as he once again resumed his finger tapping.

Silence fell on the room. Alex and Henry exchanged worried glances, not really daring to talk. Eventually Frederik clapped his hands together and sat forward.

"Well, gentlemen, I have good news and I have bad news," he said in a tone that sounded almost as if he was relishing this moment. 'The bad news is that the thing you saw, Alexander, the thing that Aurora called *Zephyr*, is the shadow I have told you both about. Zephyr is the one that has being trying to kill you."

Alex felt his stomach turn and heard a small moan from his left as Henry's shoulders dropped.

"You are both quite right to be afraid," continued Frederik who had stood up and begun to pace around the room. "As I told you before, Zephyr is one of the most dangerous people to have ever walked this earth. If he is here, it is because he has a job to do. That job is to kill you, Alexander."

"You said there was good news?" Said Alex, trying to ignore Frederik's long bony finger pointing directly at him.

Frederik stopped pacing and smiled nastily. "The good news, Alexander, is that at this moment you are still alive. And also that the person you saw walking into the woods was not Lewis, nor was it ever Lewis."

"What?" Said Henry. "But Alex saw him. He saw it was Lewis."

"Did you?" Said Frederik quietly, turning to Alex. "Did you ever see his face, or did you merely see his body?"

Alex had to think. He hadn't seen Lewis's face when he'd looked through the camera or when he chased him through the woods. Frederik seemed to have read his mind.

"I think what you actually saw was Zephyr in his other, more... acceptable state. That he may have resembled your brother is merely a coincidence."

"That's one hell of a coincidence!" Chipped in Henry, but Frederik merely shrugged his shoulders.

"When you say *acceptable* state…" said Alex.

"I mean that Zephyr can appear both the way you saw him when he went *in* to the woods or the way he appeared when he went *out* of the woods. He is an assassin, Alexander, and any assassin needs a disguise, do you not think? In the first case he looks like any normal man, although perhaps more handsome than most. He could walk amongst you and you would not notice him. But in the second case… well you have seen for yourself what he looks like."

There was another long pause before Alex spoke again.

"You told me before that this Zephyr thing is supposed to be after me. Trying to kill me, right?

"That is correct, Alexander, yes."

"Then what was it doing in the forest? Why didn't it come for me then?"

"Ah, well Aurora is the only one that Zephyr is afraid of, I think. She is easily as strong as Zephyr, but not quite as dangerous… perhaps. I wouldn't worry though, Alexander, for it sounds like Aurora has decided to keep an eye on you, as well as me, so that is also good news for you."

Alex had to admit he did feel slightly more reassured and then suddenly thought back to the dinner party. He remembered the voice he had heard when the lights had gone out urging him to leave with Sara.

Had that been Aurora too? He wasn't sure why but he didn't feel the need to mention this just yet.

"What he was doing in the forest," Frederik continued. "Was–I suppose you might say–*feeding.*"

"Feeding?" Said Alex, pulling himself away from his memory of Sara in the wardrobe.

"Yes, Zephyr feeds on the silver liquid that you saw. He needs it to survive, but there are, I think, only two places he can get it. One is in my home country of Norway. The other is here in England, in this particular forest.

"Judging from what you have said, he won't need to come back here any time soon though. If he has taken a box full then that should keep him satisfied for many, many years to come."

"Well that's reassuring to know!" Said Alex throwing his hands up in the air. "I'd hate him to have to kill me on an empty stomach."

Alex was on his feet again, pacing. Frederik sat back down on his chair moodily. Henry remained quiet, watching the pair of them.

Alex was still trying to make sense of it all; he'd begun to feel panicky and claustrophobic. It felt like it was getting hot in the small, domed room.

"Alexander, sit down!" Came Frederik's angry voice. "Walking around like that will not stop Zephyr from killing you." Alex shot Frederik a nasty glance but continued to pace. "But I do know a way you can stop him."

Alex stopped and looked to Frederik. "How? How can I stop him?"

"By killing the one who controls Zephyr, of course." Said Frederik casually, leaning back in his chair.

Alex suddenly remembered the conversation he'd had with Frederik back in his shack. *Of course! The shadow was controlled by someone else.*

"You mean Zephyr's master? As in the person who killed Annelise? Well? Who is it?"

Frederik's narrowed eyes moved from the floor to Henry.

"Zephyr's master is your grandfather, Alex. The man who killed my Annelise was Konrad Steen."

CHAPTER 36

REVEALED

Henry stared at Frederik.

"Konrad? *Konrad's* in control of Zephyr?

"That is what I said, yes."

"I don't believe it," said Henry, his voice sounded distant, as if he was thinking out loud.

"Do you not, Henry?" Said Frederik quietly. "Do you not believe that Konrad could be a man in control of such a murderous thing as Zephyr? Do you not believe that he could be the one who killed my Annelise all those years ago? Do you not believe that he may be making his own set of books of power? Indeed, that he could end up controlling the entire population of this world?"

"Of course!" Said Alex, jumping up and surprising both men. "I forgot! This morning!"

"What?" Said Henry, looking concerned.

"When I went to see Konrad, of course!"

"You saw Konrad this morning?" Frederik said slowly.

"Yes, he invited me to visit him when we spoke at the dinner party last night. He said he wanted to get to know me better as he hadn't seen me in years, so I said I'd go."

Frederik's hands gripped the sides of his stone chair again but he said nothing.

"Go on," said Henry.

Alex told them all about his visit to Konrad's tower, and finding the book with the rough leather cover and the Wolf emblem pressed onto the front.

"It was about this big," he said, demonstrating with his hands.

Henry looked towards Frederik who wasn't speaking. "What did Alex see in Konrad's office, Frederik?" His cool, gruff voice sounded angry.

For the first time, Frederik looked uncomfortable.

"What did Alex see, Frederik? You told me that everything, apart from that one page of yours, had been destroyed. The one you showed to Alex."

Frederik scowled. He obviously wasn't used to being told off as much as Alex was.

"Frederik, *tell* us!"

At last, Frederik looked up at both men. Alex saw a genuine sadness in the man's eyes. When he spoke, he sounded like a young boy that had been caught doing something bad.

"I *did* destroy them! I did... but you have to understand, these books are very, very powerful! After Annelise's death... when I realised that the books I had written were dangerous... I tried everything to get rid of them. I burnt them, cut them, tore at them and I managed to get rid of all five."

"So what's the problem then?" Said Alex.

Frederik looked to the floor.

"There was... a sixth book."

Alex heard his grandfather moan and slump back heavily in the stone seat.

"A *sixth?*" Said Alex. "You're not telling me you've got a sixth sense now, have you?"

"No, he's not," said Henry quietly. "He's talking about the other book from the story. Remember the story I showed you in the library?"

"It said," started Frederik. "That I wrote another book after Annelise died. One that I poured all my... bad thoughts and feelings into."

"But I thought that was just some sort of metaphor?" Said Henry in a whisper. "I didn't realise you'd actually written the bloody thing!"

"I am afraid so, yes. And the page I have... the page is not from the book of sound at all, but from this sixth book.

"I *tried* to destroy it as I had the other five but it would not *be* destroyed. Whatever I tried, it just kept repelling me with intense black flames. Of course, I knew I had to get rid of it somehow. So I wrapped it in many layers of fabric and packed it into a box, filled with many stones. I used all my strength to heave the box onto my boat and sailed it far out into the Northern Sea. It was there that I tipped the box over the side and watched as it sank into the depths, far out of the reach of anyone.

"I thought it was safe." Frederik stood. "But two days ago, I noticed something strange. I felt one of the books, this *black fire* book, be–how do you say–*awoken.*

"I know that it is the only one left, but it was the very worst. If it has been found... if it has been found by Konrad and he works out how it is to be used..."

then we, the whole of humanity, are lost!"

Frederik was pacing around the room, wringing his hands and scratching at himself; as if trying to purge himself of something.

Eventually, in a soft and reassuring voice, Henry said to Alex, "After you saw this book in Konrad's office, what happened next?"

Alex recounted how he'd struggled to return the glass case to its normal state, how he'd tripped on the glass stairs, and how he'd discovered Konrad's hidden archive of little red books.

"…and so, I read a few." He said.

Clearly unable to resist, Frederik sneered, "But *surely* you weren't reading other people's private thoughts, were you Alexander?"

"Well it's a good job I did, because it proves you're right and that Konrad's involved in all this. His red diaries had his name and birth date in them too, just like the one I've got!"

"Did you read anything else in his diaries?" Said Henry.

"Well lots actually, yes." Said Alex, feeling suddenly useful. "There were pages and pages of scribbled words. There were lots of sketches of funny-looking objects and some music notes in there too… and towards the end it said something about him coming to the dinner party to see his family. Then *right* at the end it said something about finding out if I needed to be *dealt with*, and that if I did then he'd send *him* after me…"

Alex's voice trailed off at the thought of being attacked by the monster he had seen in the woods. Frederik had closed his eyes as if in deep thought.

"Did Konrad see you looking at his things?" Asked Henry.

"No… no, I don't think so. I managed to make the bookcase go back down before he came back. That's when he asked me about a job though."

"A job?"

"Yeah, he offered me a job. At his company. He said that with Lewis getting all the action at home I could come and work with him if I wanted. Although, with what you've just told me about Konrad being a megalomaniac murderer with that crazy book in his possession I don't think I'll be handing my CV in anytime soon."

Frederik opened his eyes. "Oh, but I think you will be going to work with him, Alexander." He said quietly so that Alex only just caught what he said.

"Sorry? It sounded like you just said that I should go and work with Konrad?"

"That is exactly what I said, Alexander. You must go and work with him and you *must* get his book for me." Frederik was staring at Alex and was clutching the sides of his chair again.

"I'm not being funny, but if you're telling me that Konrad's the one who's got this really dangerous book as well as having control over an assassin who drinks liquid silver... I think I'll give it a miss if it's all the same to you."

"You will do as you're *told*!" Frederik nearly screamed this last word and both Alex and Henry jumped. He stood and slowly began to advance on Alex like a seething, rabid animal. "After *everything* I have told you, you still cannot see how important all this is? This evil man, who is in possession of a book *so dangerous* that he could use it to control the entire population of this earth, offers you the chance to work alongside him and you *won't take it?*

"Never mind that this chance would allow you to recover this book from him. Never mind that you would be saving billions of people. No. Why would you do this? I understand Alex. I understand completely. It is because you are a coward. No?"

With Frederik still advancing, Alex was backing away in fear.

"Selfish. Little. Boy," Spat Frederik. "Here you have a golden opportunity to save everybody and you won't take it because you're scared! You have so far done *nothing* with your life. Now you are given an opportunity. And you don't want it. Ach!

"Alexander, you know that you are different. You have felt it when you write, I know it! You have felt the way your thoughts are transferred into words. Only *you* have the power to create these books and defeat the shadow and his master. But if *you* do not retrieve the Black Fire book, it will be all but impossible." Frederik stopped and stared at Alex. He seemed to want to let his words sink in. His voice then dropped to one of soft indifference, "But, if that is your decision, so be it. There are others I can ask. Perhaps Lewis."

Alex's fear turned at once to anger. "Lewis? What's Lewis got to do with all this?"

"He's your twin brother for a start, Alexander. I'm sure he could easily do what I have asked you to do. He will have the same blood as you, I'm sure, and as he seems to be better at you than most other things–"

"We are nothing alike!"

"I agree with you there, Alexander. He's not as spineless as you for a start. I'm sure he would be more than willing to do this for the sake of his family. He seems to understand the ideas of loyalty and honour much better than you do. Perhaps I'll go and ask him now–"

"No!" Shouted Alex, before he could stop himself.

"No?" Frederik said with a low, callous laugh.

"No." Said Alex. "I'll do it. I'll get this book and I'll do it better than Lewis ever could."

"Good. Then we are agreed," Frederik said curtly. "Henry, take Alexander and go, please. I have had enough for this evening. You know what he has to do. Keep him writing, make him *feel*, and if you don't… I shall give him something to feel instead. And Alexander, above all… above your writing and any thoughts of your precious self… you must get me that book."

Henry quickly walked to Alex and took him by the arm.

"Alex? Alex, come on. Best get going I'd say, wouldn't you?"

Alex was staring intently into Frederik's eyes until Frederik finally looked away, turning his back on them both and returning to his stone seat. Alex saw the urgency in Henry's gaze and without another word, followed him out of the stone archway. Instead of heading down the steep slope from earlier, however, Henry took a right-hand path that hadn't been visible before.

They walked on for several hundred feet, all the time going downhill. Eventually they came to a small stone platform.

"Ok, hop on, Alex."

Alex sulkily looked down at the platform. "Please don't tell me we're going for another death drop? I'm really not in the mood."

Henry chuckled nervously, "No, indeed we are not. This time, we're going up, up, up!"

"Great," said Alex sarcastically, stepping onto the platform.

Once again the two men stood toe to toe, before Henry whispered something into the darkness. The platform began to rise like an elevator through a narrow black shaft that had been cut into the earth.

Several seconds later, it stopped. Henry pushed hard against the black roof above their heads. A thin sliver of light came through the narrow crack. With another huge push, the opening swung free. The platform began to rise, more slowly, and as their heads cleared the floor level Alex was amazed to see that they were back in the middle of Henry's lake house living room.

CHAPTER 37

AN OLD FLAME

The moon was high in the sky and Konrad was sitting at his desk, looking out across the softly lit landscape. Although there were a hundred things he could be focusing on, his eyes were locked on just one; Wolf Manor. He checked his watch and saw that it was nearly midnight.

He should be back by now.

Although Konrad was always supremely calm in any situation, a small part of him worried for Zephyr whenever he went out, especially when he was supposed to be bringing something back so precious. He turned in his chair to face his office. The moon outside passed silently behind a cloud, casting the room into near pitch blackness. There was a forceful knock on the door.

"Come." Said Konrad, not surprised by this interruption.

The doors opened and Bryson walked from the lift, followed by Sofia Wolf. She was barely a foot into the room before her protestations started.

"What is the meaning of this Konrad?" She strode towards him, her heels cracking loudly on the hard floor.

"Bryson," Konrad called lazily. "You can finish for this evening if you wish. I have no further need for you tonight."

"Very good, sir." Came Bryson's monotonous voice.

"Come, Sofia take a seat," said Konrad jovially.

"You can knock that off as well. I know you're as scared as I am." She said, slowing her approach.

"I don't know what you mean, Sofia."

Konrad stood slowly and walked back over to the door. He flicked two switches and a pair of side lights came on. They cast a yellow glow over the two leather sofas and Konrad gestured for Sofia to sit.

"You know exactly what I mean! Sooner or later he's going to come for us."

Sofia sat down smartly on the sofa, but didn't lounge back like Konrad, instead perching on the edge, her knees together. Konrad stretched out his arms and smiled back at her benignly.

"Oh I'm sure he will, Sofia, and *I* will be ready for him. But I'm sure you didn't come here to talk about our old friend?" Konrad raised his eyebrows.

Sofia pulled her shoulders back. "I had your boy storm into my office earlier. He wanted to know why one of his sons was being offered a job by his, until recently, estranged grandfather. To say *I* was surprised was something of an understatement. What the hell do you think you're playing at?"

Konrad was staring at Sofia but his smile had faded. "My boy? If you mean Morten, he's no boy of mine, Sofia. He made that decision a long time ago when he joined your family. He knows I will not forgive him until he retakes the name that was given to him."

There was an edge of anger to his voice that Sofia seemed to take great satisfaction in.

"Well I suppose Morten just thought the benefits of being a Wolf outweighed the benefits of being a Steen? I would tend to agree with him on that front. Not that Rebekka would have ever become a Steen, you understand. Not under my watch."

"Ah yes… and how is the lovely Rebekka? It was *so* lovely to see her at your little party the other night." It was Konrad's turn to smile at the look on Sofia's puckered face.

"You leave Rebekka out of this, Konrad. This has nothing to do with her! And that stunt you pulled the other night was completely unnecessary. I told you I was going to retire, didn't I? I didn't need you coming to remind me."

Konrad smiled. "The problem, Sofia, is that I've known you long enough to have learned that what you say and what you do are often two completely different things. I just thought a gentle reminder was in order, that's all. And besides, I thought it would be nice to catch up with the family."

"*This* time, Konrad, I intend to stick to my word. As promised, the company will go to Lewis, not Morten. And I shall keep my distance, for a while at least, until you can deal with Frederik."

"Excellent, Sofia! Well if you manage to keep to your word then I shall keep to mine and see that no harm comes to either you or Lewis."

"And the others?" Said Sofia, almost hesitantly.

Konrad didn't answer. He stayed silent for a moment, his eyes twinkling in the low light of the room, obviously trying to decide on his next move. When he finally stood he couldn't help but notice Sofia's hands moving quickly to the sofa seat, as if she was readying for action.

Walking to the centre of the room, he gazed out into the inky sky. In a moment, Sofia was standing back in front of him, barely a foot between them. Konrad smiled and his eyes narrowed.

"So, you wanted to know what I was doing with Alex, I think? I suppose I just thought the poor boy needed a better start in life. Better than the one his grandmother and father were planning for him, anyway. Correct me if I'm wrong, Sofia, but you don't have much time for the boy do you?"

"What on earth gives you that idea?" Replied Sofia, staring straight at Konrad.

"Oh I don't know," continued Konrad thoughtfully. "Maybe something he said when he was here? I can't remember now."

Sofia moved closer to Konrad and whispered, "I know what you're up to. And I know why you want him close to you. You think you can use him against Frederik. Well I'm fairly certain you've picked the wrong brother there, so I suggest you stop toying with him and send him on his way. Preferably back to us."

"Ah, Sofia, Sofia, Sofia." Konrad brushed Sofia's face gently with the back of his hand. "Well at least your intentions are clear now as well. Tell me, have you been teaching Lewis the old ways too?"

Sofia was breathing slowly, but she didn't answer. They both stood silently in the moonlight as if they were trying to read each other's thoughts.

"Konrad, if you hurt a single member of my family, I swear to you I'll–"

"I'd stop there if I were you, Sofia. I'm fairly sure Zephyr doesn't like it when people threaten his master."

Sofia spun round and immediately retreated several paces. Framed by the bright moonlight was the tall, muscular figure of Zephyr, dressed head to toe in black. The figure reached up with a gloved hand and pulled back the hood from its head. Sofia took several more steps back, her breathing faster.

"Isn't it unfortunate when it's not a level playing field." Said Konrad, reaching into his jacket and pulling out a long cigar.

Sofia shot him an angry look but then quickly composed herself.

"I was leaving now anyway." She said, backing away from the pair that were watching her intently. "Do as you will with Alex. But if you're doing what I *think* you're doing then you've picked the wrong one, Konrad… but you'll find that out soon enough, I'm sure."

Konrad merely shrugged his shoulders and lit his cigar, smoke billowing from his mouth. Reaching the lift doors, Sofia felt them open silently behind her and she backed in. The doors closed again with a whoosh and she was gone.

The moment the doors closed, Konrad stumbled slightly. Zephyr moved forward to help him but Konrad waved him off.

"I… shall be fine in a few moments, thank you. Have you brought what I asked you to? Was it there?"

Without a word, Zephyr walked to the desk and placed down the dark wooden cube. Konrad approached it slowly. Reaching out to touch it, he felt a surge of energy run through him. Gently running his finger nails under the top edge he slowly prized the lid open to reveal its contents.

Silver liquid filled the box to the brim, so thick and viscous it looked like a solid lump of metal. Konrad put his cigar back in his mouth, slipped off his jacket and began to roll up his right sleeve. With a quick glance at Zephyr, he plunged his right hand into the box.

He threw his head back in agony, as half of the box's contents rushed into his body. He cried out in pain, but remained standing as a bright yellow glow began to emanate from him, pulsing stronger and stronger before suddenly fading.

He opened his eyes. Staggering slightly, he collapsed into his high-backed chair; head swimming and heart pounding. He knew he would feel better soon enough, but that part was always so incredibly painful.

Eventually he refocused on Zephyr, who was standing quietly by the half full box, eyeing it carefully. Noticing Konrad watching him, he looked away immediately, eyes forward.

"Please, forgive me my friend. You should have your fill."

Konrad weakly raised his arm, gesturing to Zephyr to take it. Barely able to contain himself, Zephyr grabbed the box with both hands. Rather than placing his hand in the box, he lifted it above his head and tipped the contents into his gaping mouth. A yellow light blazed fiercely in his eyes.

As Konrad sat looking out of the huge glass windows, the moon slipped behind another cloud. His eyes had already returned to the same spot as before, even though it was obscured by darkness.

He half turned his head to his companion, before speaking the order he had been meaning to give all night.

"Do it."

CHAPTER 38

THE SPY

Henry handed Alex three thick slices of toasted white bread, each slathered with melting butter and coarse-cut marmalade. Alex rapidly devoured the first with barely any chewing. He needed food, and quickly. For the second and third slices, he took a more leisurely pace, savouring the crunch of the crust followed by the bitter tang of marmalade.

It tasted so good that when he was finished he was tempted to ask for more, but Henry had already walked in with his own plate. Feeling that he couldn't really be bothered to do it himself, he kept quiet.

Henry had put on some music and Alex sighed contentedly before sinking back into the sofa, thinking that he could happily drift off to sleep and forget everything about the last week. He'd been feeling more and more like it was all some sort of bizarre dream and that he'd wake up any moment to find himself in the back of his grandmother's Rolls Royce, just pulling up outside the house for the first time since leaving school.

"You look like you're deep in thought over there, young man," said Henry thickly, as he finished off a corned beef sandwich. Several crumbs and a bit of meat were lodged in his moustache, but Alex was too tired to mention it.

"Hmm, I am," said Alex wearily, letting out another big sigh and putting his head back on the cushion of the chair.

"I'm not surprised," said Henry not looking at him. "It's a lot to take in, I know. Took me long enough and even now I'm finding out things that I had no idea about. Konrad, eh? Always knew he was a piece of work."

Keeping his head on the cushion, Alex glanced over to his granddad; he was running his tongue over his teeth and picking crumbs from his face.

"You missed a bit," said Alex, pointing to a spot on his own face.

"That's the ticket!" said Henry, finding the errant piece of corned beef and casually flicking it back into his open mouth.

Alex laughed lazily and shook his head from side to side. "To tell you the truth… I'm not really sure what to make of all this."

"I know, boy," said Henry, searching for a pipe in his jacket pocket. "It's all so very strange isn't it? One minute you think you know what life's all about. The next, you're thrown a complete curve ball like this and you find out there's ghosts and ghoulies running around all over the place. People who are older than you'd ever believe possible. Trees with silver in them and right at the middle of it all… your own family. Ah! There it is."

Henry pulled out his pipe and began digging at the contents with a small penknife, flicking black flecks of burnt tobacco all over the floor. He leant forward and opened the carved wooden box on the coffee table. Humming to himself as if it was some sort of decisive rhyme, Henry finally settled on a compartment containing the darkest of the weeds and grabbed a big pinch. He stuffed it into the end of his pipe and packed it down with his ring finger. Adding a pinch more, no doubt just for luck, he pulled out a box of matches from his waistcoat pocket and sat back in his seat.

"I will tell you one thing though, Alex. *Two,* in fact." He pulled out a long match, struck it and lowered the yellow flame into his densely-packed pipe bulb. After a few sucks, thick white aromatic smoke puffed out from the side of Henry's mouth. He waved the match in the air a few times before throwing it onto the coffee table in front of him. "No matter what happens with all this strangeness that's going on, remember you've got your family. You know that, don't you?" Henry took a few more puffs on his pipe, infusing the room with more of the gentle aroma. "And you know if the doo-dah does really hit the fan, they'd all be there for you in a flash."

Alex took a moment to think about that. He wasn't entirely sure his granddad was right. *Sure, Mum and probably Lewis would step up, but Dad? He permanently seems pissed off with me. And as for Grandma…*

As far as Alex was concerned, his grandmother was a big part of what was going on anyway. He wouldn't be surprised if her and Konrad were in it together, just waiting for the right moment to take him out.

"So what's the second thing?" He asked, breathing in the luxurious smell that was wafting around the room.

"Ah yes, the second thing." His granddad had a definite glint in his eye. "The second thing is this. When you find the person you love–and they love you back, of course–whatever you do, do *not* let them go. No matter what the cost. Trust me on this one."

"What if it's a choice between the one you love and your family though?"

Asked Alex, laughing at the sudden switch of conversation.

"Don't be a smart arse!" Said Henry laughing back, pointing his pipe mouthpiece in Alex's direction. "You know what I mean. Just bear it in mind, is all I'm saying. I've seen the way you look at Sara."

Alex's eyes moved quickly to the floor; but he couldn't help himself smiling.

"She likes you too, you know. Told me herself."

"Did she?" Said Alex quietly, still looking at the floor but smiling even more.

"Well… not in exact terms, but I can tell! Always had a good eye for these sorts of things."

"I think I'm a bit young for all this though, old man. I am only young, remember. Plenty of time for all that, I reckon."

Henry chuckled and then coughed after inhaling too much smoke. "You've hit it on the head though, haven't you? That's exactly what I said myself when I was your age. Only problem was, before I knew it, fifty years had flown by and here I am like you say, an old man, wound up with someone…" Henry stood up slowly and walked to the window. "I just wish someone had told me what I'm telling you fifty years ago. When it comes to a girl, don't listen to anyone or anything except your own heart. The head… should never come into it." Alex noticed his granddad's voice seemed to crack and he barely finished the last word.

"*Hmmphh…* anyway, enough about all that." Henry coughed and Alex saw him wipe his face with the sleeve of his jacket. If it hadn't been for his earlier crumb disposal, Alex would have assumed that was what he was doing.

"Right then!" Said Henry briskly, turning round to face Alex again. "What are we going to do about you and your other dastardly granddad, hmm?"

"Oh who knows," said Alex, letting out a long sigh which turned into a yawn. "Can't we have a think about it in the morning? Too tired to think now."

"Well make sure you do think about it in the morning. Frederik's not going to be too happy if he thinks you're not taking this seriously. Reckon the bloke's a bit unhinged, truth be told."

Alex looked to his side to the place where, barely half an hour ago, he and his granddad had emerged from underground. The thought that Frederik was down there somewhere gave him the creeps.

Saying no more about it, on the off-chance that someone was earwigging beneath them, Alex decided to call it a night. He stood, swaying slightly.

"Off to bed are we? Not a bad idea. Up the stairs and second door on the left. I'm ah, I'm going to stay up for a bit longer if you don't mind. Finish off this pipe."

Too tired to do anything else, Alex flapped his right hand up in gesture of bidding his granddad a good night and began to traipse up the steep wooden stairs. Following his granddad's orders, he made for the second door on the left. When he saw what he would be sleeping on he let out an exhausted laugh, though he wasn't entirely surprised.

Flicking off his shoes, but not bothering to take off his clothes, Alex pulled back the duvet, balanced himself carefully and rolled sideways into his gently rocking bed. The pillow was incredibly soft underneath his head.

As he pulled the duvet back over himself, he could feel sleep caressing his eyelids down. His last thought before drifting off to sleep was about hammocks, and that even though he'd never been in one before, it was probably the most comfortable bed he'd ever slept in.

Downstairs, Henry turned up the volume on the amplifier a couple of degrees and his own thoughts drifted away, like the smoke from his pipe. He had some decisions to make as well; although, like Alex, he would probably be best leaving them until the following morning.

As sleep took the old man, he failed to notice that the small section of floor they had emerged from only minutes ago lifted slightly and a pair of bright yellow eyes peered out.

CHAPTER 39

THE WORST NEWS

Alex slowly opened his eyes. The smell of grilled meat was winding its way seductively from downstairs, bringing back a memory of devouring sausage sandwiches with Lewis on bonfire night. He remembered vividly standing around the blazing fire in the park with his brother and being brought the overcooked hotdogs by his dad. The three of them would stand in front of that fire every year for what seemed like hours, watching it crackle and burn; staring into its hot yellow heart, completely bewitched by the dancing flames.

Chuckling quietly to himself at the thought of writing this down in his journal for Frederik to see, he quickly decided against it, imagining the eruption of anger it would cause at something so insignificant.

After a while Alex rolled out of his hammock and made his way downstairs. He was surprised to see Henry lying flat out on the sofa, newspaper across his chest, snoring like a horse. He looked at the clock on the wall; nearly midday.

Confused, Alex peered into the kitchen. There was no one there, but the back door was wide open. Feeling that he could really do without something terrifying or unexpected happening first thing after waking up, he crept slowly to the kitchen counter and picked up the first heavy-looking object he could find, which happened to be a wooden meat mallet. Raising it above his head, ready to strike, he moved silently around the counter and made his way to the back door. Just as he was about to peer out, Morten Wolf came striding round the corner. Without thinking Alex screamed and swung the mallet with full force in front of them. Morten jumped backwards, dropping the armful of logs he'd been carrying and the mallet arced high in the air before hitting the soft earth with a heavy thud.

"What the hell are you doing?" Morten said in shock.

"Sorry... sorry!" Said Alex at once, looking sheepishly at his dad. "I didn't mean to swing at you like that. I thought there was an intruder or something, that was all. I didn't realise Granddad had invited you up here!"

"I wasn't talking about you attacking me with a mallet, I was talking about that scream of yours?"

"I… I…" Alex stuttered, feeling himself turn red.

Morten's face turned from one of blank indifference into a wild grin. So disarmed by the sight of his dad with a smile on his face, Alex burst out laughing.

"I can't help it. It just comes out like that sometimes that's all. I'll pick these up shall I?" Said Alex flustered, already bending down to pick up the random pile of logs at his dad's feet.

He was just about to ask what the logs were for, when his dad's face suddenly dropped. He dashed past Alex into the kitchen.

"No, no, no, no, no, *no!*" Came Morten's panicked voice from inside the smoke-filled room.

Alex had smelt the acrid whiff of charring meat coming from the grill too. Morten had made a leap for the oven and had seemingly pulled the sausages out just in time. They were beginning to turn from a dark woody brown to a dusty black.

"Forget those for now, Alex." Shouted Morten from inside as Alex once again went to pick up the logs.

"I'll get your granddad to do that later when he gets up." Morten was eyeing Henry suspiciously. The snoring was a little *too* loud, even for Henry. "Fancy a sandwich then? I know it's not bonfire night but what the hell, hey?"

Alex frowned.

"What's up?" Said Morten, looking bemused as he forked out sausages into thick white bread.

"Oh nothing, just something I was thinking about earlier. Anyway, what are you doing here?"

Morten passed Alex a three-sausage open sandwich and an extra slice of buttered bread. Alex placed it on the worktop and reached for the tomato ketchup. His dad shook his head as he squeezed out far too much sauce and pressed on the second slice of bread, causing the thick red liquid to ooze out onto the worktop. Morten squeezed three arrow-straight lines of brown sauce perfectly along each sausage before deftly placing the other slice of bread on top, making sure both slices were aligned. Without a word both men picked up their respective breakfasts and took enormous bites out of them. Ketchup continued to drip messily from the bottom of Alex's sandwich whilst Morten's stayed perfectly intact.

"Your granddad invited me," began Morten. "Told me he'd be up here this morning and asked if I fancied coming up for some breakfast? I didn't know you were here until I arrived this morning."

Alex took another large bite of his sandwich. "I take it you're here incognito then?" Alex said with his mouth full.

Morten didn't say anything, merely smiling before taking another bite from his own sandwich. When they had finished, both men wiped their hands; Morten on a clean cloth sitting on the side, Alex on his jeans.

A slight awkwardness seemed to fall on the room and Henry's snorting became all too apparent, grating on the silence with every other breath.

"Alex," said Morten and Alex could feel himself tense immediately. "I'm sorry about what I said the other day. It wasn't fair of me to talk to you like that."

Alex didn't say anything; his only thought was that it should really be he who was apologising.

"I was just a little surprised when Konrad—my father—offered you a job. That was all." There was a long pause. "But either way, I'm sorry."

Alex didn't say anything. His dad had apologised twice; he really felt he should say something, but he could feel himself getting hot again.

"Is there anything you want to say about it?" Offered Morten.

"I… well… I just don't see why it's so strange," started Alex quietly. "He is my granddad after all and he just said that with Lewis working with you and Grandma, I could maybe do with a bit of help?"

Morten frowned and looked to the ground as if he was searching for the best way to put his next phrase. Alex half-expected another argument any second.

"What you have to understand, Alex, is that Konrad Steen never has other people's interests in mind. He looks after himself. He did it with me… he did it with my brother and sister and he's probably going to do it with you too. I just… I just want you to be careful, that's all."

The conversations with both Henry and Frederik the previous night swam to the front of Alex's mind. If he did end up working with Konrad to try and get the book, he would have to be more than just careful.

"I will be, don't worry. And… I'm sorry too, you know," mumbled Alex, remembering how bad he was at apologies. "I shouldn't have said what I did about… well, I shouldn't have said it."

Morten didn't say anything but continued to look at the floor. There was another long silence only broken by Henry's ever-loudening snores.

"So," said Alex, not entirely sure if he should ask. "What actually happened between you and Konrad anyway? Why don't you two talk anymore?"

Morten sighed. His eyes were filled with such sadness that Alex immediately felt guilty for asking. "It's a long story, Alex. Well, actually it's not a long story. It's just… it's just complicated."

Alex didn't say anything; he wanted to give his dad the option of backing out if he wanted to. Morten looked down at the floor again.

"Basically, he wasn't very happy when I married your mum and took her family name. He saw it as a betrayal, as if I was killing off the famous Steen name" Alex remained silent; he could kind of see Konrad's point. "I never really understood it though. If I had been the last male Steen then maybe, I suppose, but I'm not." A dark look came across Morten's face. "Besides, I don't always see it as a bad thing that you never saw much of your other granddad. You and Lewis have been much better off growing up with the positive role models you've had," he looked at Henry, still asleep and snoring like a hippo with a cold, "than if you'd been influenced by someone whose only concerns are money, greed and power. Like my father."

Alex thought it best not to mention that he could have easily been describing his grandmother, Sofia. Morten seemed lost in thought for several moments.

"You won't remember this, Alex, but my mother died when I was twenty five years old. Father took it very badly, as you would expect. But it was more than that. Something in him seemed to change. He had always been very ambitious and successful. You only have to look at what he's achieved to see that. But after mum died something inside him seemed to snap. She was the best influence he could have had, even though he thought he didn't need it. When she was gone it was like the parts of him that she used to temper and keep at bay took over. He was making more and more cut-throat deals, putting other companies out of business, not caring who he ruined to get what he wanted. That's when he made the majority of his fortune, Alex. That was when he asked me to help him design his pride and joy for him. His tower."

"*You* designed it for him? I never knew that!" Said Alex.

"Oh yes, I designed it for him. I'm surprised you didn't notice when you went up there."

Alex thought back to the tower and realised there were several elements that he recognised from his dad's other building designs: the shape, the materials, the huge glass expanses. Then something occurred to Alex.

"But you can't have been very old when you designed it?"

Morten smiled. "It wasn't so much that, it was more that it was my first real solo job. Can you imagine working on a project of that scale, with full control and money no object. At first it was incredible! I had so much choice, it was almost too much. But it wasn't long before father started to interfere and bit by bit I lost control. Eventually I was just someone working for him. An employee. Eighteen-hour days for months and months on end. It nearly killed me."

A look of bitterness darkened Morten's face again.

"But… but it must have been amazing once it was finished though? To see a whole building you've designed?"

"Actually, Alex, we fell out before it was completed. I've never seen it. None of us have, in fact. You're the only one."

"I don't understand. Why didn't you ever go back?"

"I was sick of the sight of it, to tell you the truth. I'd spent so long working on it and had such a horrible experience, the thought of going back just makes me feel quite miserable. It was only after we fell out that I began to realise what he was really like. He'd basically used me for cheap labour on the pretence of helping me out. Which, of course, was crazy because he could've afforded a whole *firm* of Architects to do the job. And they'd probably have done a better job than I did anyway. The whole situation with the tower was just one of the reasons I decided not to take the family name when your mother and I got married."

"Konrad must have gone mad when you told him, didn't he?" Said Alex, trying to imagine his other granddad angry.

"That's the thing," said Morten with a sad smile. "He didn't go mad at all. He just gave me a look as if I was something he'd just trodden in and then he told me to leave his office and never come back. He said it so calmly, I thought he was joking. But of course, he wasn't. I only saw him once more after that. Until the other night at the dinner party, I hadn't seen him in person in over nine years. The last time he saw you and Lewis you were both ten years old. It was around Christmas time, I think. You probably don't even remember."

But Alex did remember. Ever since he had seen Konrad at the dinner party, Alex had been thinking about the few other times that he had spoken to his grandfather. Christmas nine years ago was one of the strongest memories he had of him. Even as he thought about it in his granddad's kitchen, the memory came back vividly.

It had been Christmas Eve and the whole family, apart from Sofia who had been grieving for her recently deceased husky, had been sitting in one of the smaller reception rooms in Wolf Manor, in front of a huge blazing fire. They had been enjoying the usual Christmas Eve rituals of board games, leek soup and the odd impromptu carol, but Alex had been awaiting the more exciting pre-Christmas tradition of opening one of his presents.

Lewis, who had picked his out first, had chosen a small box, flat and wide with gold wrapping paper on it. Alex, however, had immediately gone for the biggest and most extravagant box he could find. When Henry had shouted, "Go!" Alex had torn into his present and found a plain brown box. Inside was a remote controlled hot air balloon which, for several magical seconds, he had thought was the best present in the world. That was until Lewis, who had unwrapped his present very slowly, gasped in delight at finding a stunning blue portable Minidisc player.

Alex remembered looking back at his hot air balloon in disgust and then proceeding to throw the biggest tantrum of his life. The only thing that had stopped him was a loud knock on the door followed soon after by the announcement from Archer of the arrival of one Konrad Steen.

Even to that day, he could still picture the look of confusion on his mum and dad's faces when the tall figure of Konrad Steen had walked in, smiling broadly and bearing two large bags full of gifts like a pinstriped Father Christmas. He had placed them down on the table, wished everyone a Merry Christmas and then announced that he would be going away for a few years and that they wouldn't be seeing him for a while.

At the time Alex hadn't really paid much attention; he was too busy eyeing up the mountainous bags of presents. Konrad must have spotted Alex looking as he'd called him over and handed him one of the boxes. Morten had said that Alex shouldn't have another present, as he'd had just had one, but Konrad had brushed it off and told Morten to stop fussing. Without waiting another second, Alex had snatched the box out of Konrad's hands and torn open the black wrapping paper to reveal a wooden box. Inside this, he had found a beautiful pen, completely silver apart from a wide wooden strip inlaid along its full length.

Alex had put the box down gently on the table and picked the pen out of its black felt bed. He remembered that it had felt heavy and cold in his hand and he'd been mesmerised by it. Pulling off the lid, however, he had been slightly disappointed to find that it was a fountain pen; not because he didn't like fountain pens, but because whenever he used one of them in school he would always end up in trouble.

Being left handed, he always found that after writing a sentence or two, his hand would have smudged the wet ink across the page into a smeary blue mess. He remembered noticing something else on the nib; an emblem embossed onto the delicate metalwork.

"That is the Steen family crest, Alexander. The crest of your father's family." Konrad had said to him.

Alex had said thank you for his present and then, without much else said, Konrad had made his excuses and left, followed out by Morten. After Konrad's departure there hadn't been much more to the night. Sofia eventually came downstairs, Henry got drunk on eggnog, Lewis spent the rest of the evening listening to his minidisc player by the fire and his mum had sat quietly reading a book. His dad, however, didn't return and wasn't seen again until Christmas morning.

True to his word, though, Konrad had gone away for around six years. By all accounts he'd spent most of his time in Scandinavia, completing various deals with his company. After his initial departure there had been a lot of speculation in the news about what Konrad and his company were up to, but after the first couple of years even the media became bored by the lack of any real activity. Konrad's face had all but disappeared from the newspapers.

When he did finally make his reappearance, however, it wasn't in a quiet, low key or subtle manner at all. Alex remembered that day. Once again, the family had all been in the kitchen eating breakfast. Lewis had insisted the TV be on so he could watch the business news. Alex remembered the clatter of a spoon dropping into a cereal bowl and several large drops of milk splashing him in the face. Looking up to see who was to blame, he had been greeted with the sight of three open mouths sitting opposite him staring at the television screen. Turning round to look as well, he had first noticed the scrolling yellow ticker tape running along the bottom of the screen:

Breaking News: Konrad Steen returns from 6 year hiatus to announce new energy deals with Wolfwood worth £3bn.

Alex had then watched footage of Konrad and his grandmother Sofia, shaking hands over a boardroom table, sealing their deal. By all accounts the deals had broken down only weeks later, but even in that time there had been many explosive arguments within Alex's family over Sofia's secret meetings. Despite the deal falling through, from the day of his return neither Konrad nor his company had been out of the media spotlight; much to Sofia's annoyance.

"The point is," said Morten, bringing Alex back from his memories. "That I can't stop you from going to work for Konrad, and maybe in some ways it's not the worst idea in the world. I know you find things difficult here sometimes with Lewis and your grandmother working so closely together–"

"Don't forget that *you're* in that little group as well, you know." said Alex quietly, still keen to make the point.

"I just mean it can't be easy, that's all. Lewis seems to have this natural ability for business and I know that your strengths are in other areas. *That's* what I was trying to get at the other day when I saw you. I know that you can do all sorts of things that neither Lewis, nor I, nor your grandmother could ever dream of doing. I just wasn't sure how they were going to fit in with Konrad's business that's all. Have you given any thought to it?"

This had been weighing on Alex's mind as well. What would he be able to do usefully within Konrad's company?

"Not *really*," said Alex quietly, a thought suddenly occurring to him. "But, I was wondering if maybe you could help me with that?"

Morten looked slightly taken aback, but replied without hesitation. "Of course!" He said smiling.

There was a loud *harrumph* and a snort from behind them. Both Morten and Alex turned to see Henry fully stretching out along the sofa, fists clenched and toes pointed, before he began slapping his lips together like an old dog that had just finished its breakfast.

"I do believe I smell sausages? Don't mind if I do, to be honest. Woken up absolutely starving after yesterday's exertions!"

Alex looked back to his dad who had begun to laugh and shake his head. As he was reaching into the fridge for more sausages, there was a sudden loud hammering at the front door. All three of them froze.

"Well I hope that's Archer," said Henry yawning and walking stiffly to the door. "Otherwise we've been rumbled!"

Alex heard the door being opened slowly but in a second Archer was standing in the middle of the room looking directly at Morten, tears streaming down his face.

"You've got to come *now*. There's been an accident," he said, the words catching in his throat. "Morten, it's Rebekka. She's… she's dead."

CHAPTER 40

REBEKKA

For a second, no-one moved, as if they were trying to process what Archer had said. Alex's brain seemed to have shut down, but the creased look of pain and fear on Archer's toughened face sent a wave of nausea through his body.

The next moment, he felt himself being pushed and pulled towards the door. Within seconds he was in the waiting boat, the engine still running. It wasn't long before they were speeding towards the house.

Any conversation would have been drowned out by the roar of the engines working at full power. From the back of the boat Alex looked across at his granddad. With his hair streaming back in the wind, he was quickly shaking his head from side to side, staring blankly into space. His dad was looking straight ahead. Archer was pushing the boat as fast as it would go. They were skimming over the lake's perfectly smooth surface, but Alex couldn't imagine feeling more sick.

Panic began to overtake the numbness that had stifled his mind. Glinting in the sun, he saw the glass cube of the lake house looming into view. Archer kept the boat at full speed for as long as he could, before pushing forward on the lever to silence the engines. The boat's slow motion glide to the dock was painful, but as soon as the edge had bumped into its stops all four men scrambled out and ran for the house. The warm morning air rushed past Alex's face as the tears began to stream from his eyes. He was barely able to keep up with the others. Despite his years, Henry was moving fast but it was Morten who was leading the way. They ran across the gravel driveway, up the front stairs and in through the main doors, which were wide open; but Alex wasn't prepared for the sight that met him in the entrance hall.

A woman lay on the hard stone floor, her head turned towards them; her eyes open but not seeing. All four men stopped abruptly in shock. Only Morten walked to her side, a look of utter disbelief on his face.

"Bekka? Oh, Bekka!"

Alex's father dropped to his knees and screamed, as if his heart had been torn to pieces. The sound cut through Alex like a blade as he watched him fall across her then gather up her body in his arms, sobbing uncontrollably, shaking from the pain and speaking muffled words that she would never hear.

Henry was standing to Alex's left, grief etched across his tanned face. Alex could only stand and stare. He didn't know what to do or what to say. The numbness returned, as if he was watching the scene from outside, peering into another family's most intimate moment of grief.

His father held onto his mother's lifeless body like he was never going to let her go. Her eyes were still open, as if she was taking it all in, but Alex knew that she wasn't there.

He felt a heavy hand on his shoulder and turned to see Archer's tear-lined face. His eyes offered reassurance and understanding but these were meaningless to Alex. He just couldn't take it in.

"What happened?" Henry quietly asked Archer, barely able to get the words from his mouth.

"She fell… she fell from the top of the stairs. I think… she broke her neck."

As Archer spoke there was a sound from above. Alex looked up to see his brother at the top of the stairway sobbing heavily into his cupped hands.

"I've called the Doctor," came Lewis' broken voice.

"No!" Came another voice to their left, stern and commanding. It was Sofia and she was staring up at her grandson. "Lewis, call him back and tell him there was a mistake. Do it now!" She said, eyes wide and fearful.

Lewis stood for a moment at the top of the stairs, his eyes fixed on his mum, but then took off at a run back along the corridor.

Henry turned to his wife with a lock of shock on his face.

"What do you mean *tell him there was a mistake*? That's our daughter lying there. *Look at her!*"

Sofia held her husband's gaze. "Exactly. Look at her. The doctor won't be able to do anything to help her now."

"But she's our daughter, woman! What if he *can* do something? You don't know if he can do anything or not!"

"She fell and broke her neck. Died instantly. She's gone, Henry. I'm sorry, but she's gone."

It was as if his wife saying these words made Henry realise the awful truth. Alex could only watch as his granddad stumbled to Rebekka's body and fell to his knees opposite to his son-in-law.

"The last thing we want is the press finding out," said Sofia under her breath, almost as if she had forgotten anyone else was there.

The words seemed to pull Alex from his numbness and he felt cold fury rise inside him.

"The last thing we want? What do mean *the last thing we want*? Why do you even care about the press finding out?" Alex's voice was getting louder.

Archer was staring at Sofia too, a look of disgust on his face.

"You wouldn't understand, Alex. This is something you *cannot* understand," she whispered quietly, a menacing tone to her voice.

"What are you talking about?" He shouted.

Henry looked up from his grieving and Archer moved a step closer to Alex.

"My mum is dead! And all you're worried about is what the *press* will think? Trying to protect your share price are we? Worried about your *money*? Why don't you go and have another meeting with *Konrad again* if you're so worried about money?"

Alex had never seen such a look of shock before. Sofia seemed to reel from Alex's words but immediately regained her composure. "Do… do not forget it is *your* money I am trying to protect as well, Alexander."

His eyes were wide in disbelief and he felt his fists clench as he screamed, "I don't care about my money! My mum is *dead!*"

As soon as he said it, the reality of the situation finally struck. He felt winded. Gasping in short breaths, he tried to steady himself and once again felt a heavy arm around his shoulder.

He could do nothing but stare at the scene in front of him: Henry kneeling on the floor, holding the pale hand of his daughter; Alex's father rocking silently on his knees, holding his wife while heavy tears fell on her pale, soft skin. He didn't even notice Archer's arm around him as if gripping onto him for dear life.

CHAPTER 41

TAKEN

When Alex thought back on the days that followed his mother's death, much of it was a blur. Immediately after the confrontation with his grandma he had run to his bedroom and stayed there for the rest of the day, not wanting to see, talk to or be around anyone at all.

The following day, he had been aware of many people around the house. He assumed that they were relatives or friends, although none had been to see him. More than likely though, they were there on official business; to deal with his mother.

That afternoon he'd had a brief visit from his father, who had told him that everything was going to be ok. It would have been more reassuring if Morten had been able to get the words out; he'd simply broken down on Alex's shoulder and left, only minutes after he'd arrived.

On the second day, Henry had been to see him, no doubt with the intention of cheering him up. But both of them had just sat morosely on Alex's balcony for several hours, listening to mournful music. Henry had smoked his pipe while Alex just stared into the distance, neither of them saying a word. Later that same day, Lewis had called by too. For the first time since they were young children, the two brothers shared a hug and tears, but it wasn't long before Lewis withdrew, mumbling something about going to see his friends.

Archer was probably Alex's most consistent visitor, but he seemed to have the least to say. He would walk in with a slightly glazed and lost expression and the sour smell of alcohol in his wake.

Three days had passed when Alex heard a different knock on his door. He was sitting in a chair by the window, gazing out over the grounds and listening to a piece by Chopin on loop. Expecting Archer or his grandfather again, he simply called out, "Enter!"

He heard the door open, but when no one spoke he turned in his chair. It was Sara; the one person in the world Alex felt he could be happy to see. She was standing in his doorway, eyes filled with tears and a trembling lip that was straining to contain her emotion.

Before he knew it, Alex was out of his chair and standing in front of her. He fell into her tight embrace and for the first time, broke down utterly. For several minutes she held him, and they sobbed on each other's shoulders. As he shook against his will in her arms, she guided him over to the bed. For half an hour or more they sat quietly while he wept, all the time feeling her soft hands stroking the back of his head, gently trying to soothe away his pain. Eventually he felt his tears begin to subside.

"Alex," she said softly.

Alex, who felt as though he could have stayed holding her for ever; eventually sat up and looked at her. She smiled weakly; it was clear that she'd been crying as much as he had. Both wiped the tears from their faces, Alex on the back of his sleeve and Sara on a delicate white hanky.

"Alex? Alex, you need to talk to me."

Alex sniffed and wiped his eyes again. He felt exhausted and his stomach ached from his sobbing.

"About what?" He said pushing for time.

Sara's eyes narrowed slightly. "About what happened. You need to talk about what happened, Alex. You can't keep it bottled up, even though you've been having a good go these last few days, I imagine."

Alex laughed weakly and wiped his eyes. "There isn't much to it really. There isn't much to tell."

Sara just looked at him. He thought he saw one of her eyebrows raise slightly, but she was smiling kindly still, waiting for him. Slowly, he began to describe the events of the morning: how he'd spent it with his dad and granddad, how it had been the best time he'd spent with his dad in as long as he could remember, how Archer had arrived with the news and they'd then run back into the house and found his mum lying on the floor.

Alex felt Sara squeeze his hand as he struggled to describe what happened next, seeing his granddad, dad and even Archer breaking down in front of him. Finally, he described the conversation he'd had with his grandmother. Sara made no effort to hide her anger and joined in with Alex as they railed at Sofia's warped perspective.

Once he'd finished, they sat quietly for a few more minutes in a silence that didn't feel as though it needed to be filled.

"So," Sara said suddenly. "Have you been eating? Have you been sleeping at all?"

Alex laughed weakly and looked at her suspiciously. "Those sound just like the questions Granddad's been asking"

Now it was her turn to laugh. "Ok, well he did ask me to check you were alright. He's worried about you, you know. And I'm worried about you too." She squeezed his hand again.

"I'll be fine," Alex lied. "It's just..."

"I know," said Sara. "I know. It's ok. You don't have to explain."

Alex felt like he wanted to say so much whilst she was there but he didn't know where to start.

"It's... it's really good of you to come," he started weakly. "It's so good to see you."

Sara smiled warmly. "Well I just couldn't bear the thought of you going through this by yourself. And besides, I thought it would be nice to be in your bedroom when we're both not running for our lives!"

Alex looked at her slightly surprised. Realising what she had just said, she burst out laughing. Alex couldn't help joining in.

A part of him, unshackled by grief, knew that he'd never seen anyone as beautiful as Sara was in that moment. As she laughed, he leant forward and kissed her on the lips. Sara suddenly pulled away, taken aback.

"Alex—"

He immediately cursed himself. "I'm sorry, I didn't mean to—"

She leant forward and kissed him, both hands caressing his face. He felt the knot inside him being gently undone. Her fingers were running through his hair and he breathed in her perfume. His hands moved to her waist and he felt her move slightly towards him. He pulled her closer and she kissed him harder. Despite the warmth of his room he could feel the hairs on his arms rising and electricity raced through his body.

After a lifetime and yet the briefest of moments, Sara pulled away; but only slightly. Their noses were almost touching and he could only just focus on her smiling face. Alex felt the electrifying pulse run through his body again. Sara looked down; she too had goosebumps along her arms.

"We look like a couple of plucked chickens," she said in a slightly fumbling voice.

They both grinned. Alex moved in for another kiss, but Sara leaned back.

"Alex,"

"What? You didn't like it?" He said, slightly embarrassed.

Sara laughed, "Of course I liked it, silly! It was... it was wonderful."

"Then what?" He asked quietly.

"I just think I shouldn't be kissing you right now, that's all."

"*You're* kissing *me?*" He grinned. "I think you'll find it was *I* who kissed *you,* Miss Harris."

"Come on, Alex, you know what I mean."

Alex just smiled; he felt incredible.

Who knew that kissing could be so good? He'd never told anyone, but he'd only ever kissed three girls, and never quite so successfully.

There had been Sally Price when he was 13. But she didn't really count as she'd ducked at the last minute and he'd ended up with a face full of forehead. Then there was Marion Thorpe when he was 17, but she was so overzealous that he'd ended up with a swollen lip. He did manage a proper kiss with Jenny Grant on his 18th birthday though, which had been great until he realised she was doing the same with every guy at the party.

All in all, he considered, not a great track record for a 19 year old man; after his kiss with Sara though, none of that mattered anymore. He'd just found nirvana and he wanted more.

"I know, I just... liked it that was all. Much better than the other night in the safe room, when I was protecting you from a fate worse than..."

He pictured his mother's eyes, unblinking. Sara and the kiss had pushed it all from his mind, but suddenly it all came rushing back and he felt the most wretched person in the world.

Seeing the smile falter, Sara gently stroked his face. "Alex it's alright."

"It's not though, is it?" He said quietly, feeling his throat constricting again. "Mum's dead. She's dead and she's not coming back."

She looked at him, as though searching for the right thing to say.

"No. No she's not Alex."

Alex stood up and walked back over to the tall windows. It was raining again. Fitting though the weather was for his mood, he was beginning to tire of it. As he looked out over the grounds of the estate, he thought about everything that had happened to him in just a few days. It was all so much.

There was a knock at the door and Alex turned. Sara had already stood up and was straightening her clothes. Alex flashed a guilty grin. The door opened and Archer stood in the doorway, looking more solemn than ever.

"May I come in, Master Wolf?" He said stiffly.

"Of course you can, Archer, you don't have to ask."

Archer had been acting that way for the last couple of days, as if he was slipping into how he thought a butler *should* act. As much as Alex appreciated the sentiment, it was making him feel a bit uncomfortable. Archer walked slowly into the room and Alex caught the trademark whiff of booze.

"Good afternoon, Ms. Harris," he said, noticing Sara for the first time.

He nodded slightly and Sara smiled, giving a small nod in return.

"Master Wolf, I just wanted to give you this. It's being sent out to everyone, but I wanted to give you yours personally."

He reached into his jacket pocket and pulled out a small black envelope with a silver crest embossed on the front. Alex took it, knowing only too well what would be inside.

"Thanks for this, I'll… I'll have a look at it later."

"Very good, Master Wolf. I shall leave you in peace." He gave a small nod and then turned to leave.

"Archer wait," said Alex quickly. "I don't suppose you'd like to hang out here for a bit, would you? I've got some sherry in my… well in my cupboard if you want to crack it open?"

Archer's face moved from shock to gratitude to sadness in the space of a second. "Al–Master Wolf, that's very kind of you, but–" his voice caught and he coughed. "But I have a lot to do today, I'm afraid. I very much appreciate the offer though. Thank you."

"Any time," said Alex solemnly, holding out his hand.

Archer hesitated for a moment, before taking it firmly and pulling Alex into a rough bear hug. As quickly as it had happened, Archer broke away, turned and disappeared through the door.

Alex saw that Sara was smiling at him again.

"Alex Wolf, I do believe there's a kind young man in there after all."

He smiled, shrugged and then inspected the black envelope in his hand. Sighing heavily, he opened it and slid out the white card. Skimming over the formalities, Alex looked for the date and time of his mum's funeral:

Friday 28th July, 5.00am.

Two days' time. His granddad once told him it was Wolf family tradition to hold funerals very early in the morning. It had something to do with honouring the deceased over the whole day, and letting them lie in their own darkness for as much daylight as possible, before the night came. Alex thought it was more likely because the sooner the person was in the ground, the sooner the eating and drinking could begin.

He looked at the card and his mother's embossed name, he couldn't bear the thought of her being put into the ground. He handed it to Sara who looked at it briefly, before placing it on the bed beside her.

She looked at her watch. "I think I'm going to go–"

"No, don't go!" Cut in Alex. "You don't have to go do you? Can't you stay a bit longer?"

Sara smiled. "I was just going to say, I think I'm going to go and check on your granddad and then I'll come back?"

Alex blushed, before turning quickly to look out of the window.

"Yes" he started in a deeper voice than was usual. "Well that's what I thought you were going to say. Jolly good!"

He cringed and felt his face flush with heat. Before he could think of anything else stupid to say he felt a hand on the small of his back and turned to see Sara's face close to his again. Her eyes were rich and brown, reflecting the little light that was breaking through the hazy clouds.

"Don't worry, I thought that's what you meant," she said, grinning at his sullen face. "Besides, I don't want you being left alone for too long, who knows *what* you'll get up to."

"Ok, ok." He said, rolling his eyes but finally smiling.

She took both of his hands gently in her own and kissed him lightly on the forehead. Alex breathed in her scent one more time and closed his eyes. He wanted to remember the moment forever.

He felt her hands leave his, the final touch of her fingers on his skin lingering like an electrical charge. She was gone before he even opened his eyes.

Alex returned to his bed, waiting for the happy feeling to pass. As amazing as he felt when he was with Sara, there was always a feeling of guilt; as if he was somehow sullying the memory of his mum by feeling anything but grief.

He closed his eyes and lay back on his soft pillow, silently looking up at the ceiling. As much as he tried not to think about it, he couldn't shed the thought that somewhere in the house lay his mum's body: cold, still and alone. The thought seemed to fix itself in his brain.

He got up and had another shower, trying to shake it, but even as he stood under the water it came to him again. He could only picture her face, emotionless and white. He tried music, but song after song faded into the background. It wasn't until he slumped moodily at his desk, tapping his hand distractedly on the hard wooden surface that he realised what he should do; what he should have been doing for days.

He rushed through the tall sliding doors of his wardrobe and made straight for his safe. Punching in the combination, he swung the heavy door open and retrieved the soft leather-bound diary. Even as he touched it, he felt a slight tingling in his fingers. It felt almost warm to the touch. It felt right.

He quickly closed the safe and within moments was back at his desk; a pair of blank pages lay invitingly before him, almost willing him to write.

Why didn't I think of this sooner? A wave of excitement grew inside him, but his thoughts suddenly turned to Frederik.

Frederik had wanted Alex to get Konrad's book. Nothing else. He'd made that *very* clear. But there was no way, Alex reasoned, that he would be able to do that without a clear head. Yes, if he was going to get Konrad's book then he would need all of his wits about him, which meant emptying his mind of any distractions.

Fumbling in his desk, he found his silver pen and slowly began to write. As before, the first couple of pages he wrote began to disappear soon after he had finished them, but he pressed on, writing more and more until the words finally began to stick. The pen and diary soon began to glow yellow and it wasn't long before he was writing like a man possessed. Although he couldn't keep up with reading the words on the page, he could feel his thoughts being drawn from him and the cloudiness in his head decreasing with every page of text.

He wrote about the events since leaving school, about the time he'd spent with Sara, about the trip to see Frederik, and finally he began to write about the death of his mum.

He wrote about the pain, the anguish and the despair that could never be put into words, but to his surprise his deepest feelings were being translated into just that; words, sentences and paragraphs filled page after page. The more he wrote, the more his eyes glazed over and the pen began to move by itself once more.

The ink too seemed to be flowing more heavily from Alex's pen and the words became darker and thicker, wet against the page. As he slipped into another dreamless, writing sleep he failed to notice the yellow glow diminish to nothing; replaced by small, flickering, black flames.

There was a sudden knocking sound and Alex sat back in his chair, blinking. His left hand was shaking and the pen felt heavy. Despite his tiredness, he felt much better; happier, even. For the first time in days, his mind felt clear.

His clock showed it was almost midnight. He couldn't understand why, but he felt cold. As he placed his pen gently back on the desk, he heard the gentle pattering of light rain on the windows. Already, the glass was covered in transparent trails of water. He stretched out, and walked over to the glass doors and out onto the balcony. The scent of the rain filled his senses, calming him as the thunder began to roll overhead.

There was another knock and Alex jumped slightly. He realised it was someone at his door. It opened a fraction and he was relieved to see the smiling face of Sara looking at him. Alex beamed at her and watched as she quickly entered the room before turning to close the door quietly behind her. When she turned back to him, however, her perfect smile slipped and turned to one of abject horror. She wasn't looking at him, her gaze was focused about a foot above his head. Alex swivelled round and barely had time to register the muscular black figure towering over him, before he felt himself being seized around the middle and dragged towards the balcony ledge.

The last things he saw before falling were Sara screaming and his diary flashing a brilliant blue.

CHAPTER 42

UNMASKED

The fresh smell of the heavy rain vanished almost instantly, replaced by wet earth, then musty bricks and damp. Blind fear gripped Alex so firmly that he could barely breathe.

As he was pulled over the balcony, he knew they had fallen rapidly; being only two floors up though, he had expected an almost immediate jolt. There had been none.

Am I underground? The thought came to him in flashes between waves of panic. The sound of Sara's scream still rang in his ears. He tried to concentrate on something other than his impending death; the thing that carried him was so strong, he knew that it must be Zephyr. The shadow had claimed him at last.

Alex couldn't gauge how fast they were moving but he thought he saw flashes of silver, like lights in a dark tunnel. Was he imagining it?

Maybe we aren't underground. I've been fooled like this before, but then where is the rain? Despite wanting nothing more than to shut his eyes tightly and cry, he desperately kept them open in case of even a small chance to escape. He thought he saw openings to tunnels pass by, no doubt leading to even darker places of fear and misery.

His arms were numb and even though he tried to move his fingers, the only thing he could feel was the the hard body of the monster that carried him.

How am I going to die? How does Zephyr kill? A new panic gripped him and he began to struggle in the monster's arms as he remembered Frederik's rhyme. This did nothing, except cause the vice-like grip of the beast tighten.

After what seemed like an age, Alex thought they had begun to slow; the monster suddenly stopped. Alex was dropped to the ground, his legs buckling as they hit the hard floor beneath him.

This is it. This is where I'm going to die. His breaths pounded short and hard from his lungs and he rolled onto his back to look at his killer. The muscular black form was outlined by minuscule amounts of ambient light. Alex watched in dread as a hand moved slowly from the monster's side, up to its head. He knew that once it had revealed that face of horror beneath the black mask, the end would come quickly.

The huge hand gripped the material around its face and pulled the black shroud from its head. It moved closer towards him. Alex saw long dark hair falling around the figure's shoulders, and two bright, shining, yellow eyes. Alex's breath caught at the smiling face of Aurora.

CHAPTER 43

PARTNERS

"*You?*" He spluttered.

"*Ssshhhh!*" Aurora raised a finger to her lips and knelt down to Alex. "You must keep quiet, Alex. You don't know where we are."

"Well of course I don't bloody know where we are!" He hissed, anger quickly replacing his fear. "You've just kidnapped me. I thought you were Zephyr!"

Aurora's eyes glinted in the dark. "I know you did and I'm afraid that was my intention, Alex. It was a necessary measure. I am sorry for scaring you."

"Well... ok then," he said more softly, brushing himself down. "Where are we anyway?"

He could just about make out rough brickwork that curved up over his head. *So we are in a tunnel.* He imagined it must stretch out for miles in both directions, but as his eyes adjusted, he realised that they were in front of a smooth black wall.

"You asked where we are," came Aurora's low voice. "This is one of the entrances to Steen Tower."

"Steen Tower?" Alex said.

Aurora nodded slowly.

"There's a tunnel between our house and Konrad's?

She nodded again.

"Well what are we doing here?" His mind was racing at the realisation he was probably just feet away from his very dangerous granddad.

"I'm sorry, Alex, but I had to do this. We need to get Konrad's book and we need to get it now."

Alex's brain struggled to get into gear. "You mean *that* book? *The* book? But what do you know about it?"

Aurora's smile faded and her bright eyes seemed to dim. "I know enough, Alex. I know that in the wrong hands it is incredibly dangerous. If we don't remove it from Konrad tonight, there will be untold trouble."

"So… Frederik sent you to help me get the book then?"

"I was watching over you when you visited Frederik's tunnels with Henry, making sure you returned safely from the dark." She said softly.

"Because of Zephyr?" Whispered Alex, almost afraid to say the name.

Alex took her smile as a yes.

"Ok, well what's the plan then? How do we get the book? We can't just walk in there to get it can we?"

Aurora's smile broadened. "Yes Alex, that's exactly what we're going to do, but I need you to help me through this door."

Alex turned back to the wall and frowned. "What do you mean door? There *is* no door."

"Trust me," she said. "There is a door. All you need to do is touch the wall and it will open. I'm sure of it. Then you can show me where the book is and we can leave."

Alex was beginning to feel more awkward by the second. "I… I don't think this is a very good idea. I know Frederik wanted me to get the book and everything, but surely there must be another way to do it?"

"There isn't, Alex. We need to get that book tonight. There is no other option. Things are moving too fast to miss this opportunity."

"But what about Zephyr?" Asked Alex, feeling a shiver down his spine.

"You saw how he ran from me last time, Alex. He is afraid of me."

She had a point, but Alex still felt unprepared.

"Ok, well what about…" Alex said, hunting around for another argument. "What about the fact it's wrong?" He finished, almost triumphantly.

Aurora actually laughed and slowly shook her head. Her eyes beginning to glow stronger.

"Wrong?" she said, in a seductively silky voice. "Do you think taking something back from a man to whom it never belonged is wrong? Do you think stopping a man using this thing to do great evil is wrong? Do you think that it is wrong to remove a powerful object from the hands of a killer?"

The word hung in the air for a moment and Alex frowned, still having trouble believing his grandfather could be capable.

"He's had Zephyr try and kill you more than once hasn't he? And when Zephyr couldn't succeed with you, he turned his attentions to your mother."

Alex blinked slowly. He could feel his heartbeat increasing; the blood accelerating through his veins.

"What do you mean?" He said quietly.

"I mean your mother's death was not an accident, Alex. She was murdered."

"No!" He shouted. "No, she... she fell!"

The lump in his throat made his voice sound unnatural and small. He swallowed hard. Staring into Aurora's yellow eyes, he saw something flash across them.

"I'm sorry Alex, but she didn't fall. She was killed on purpose, at Konrad's bidding."

Alex stumbled backwards. "No! He wouldn't do that. Konrad wouldn't do that!"

"Is it so unbelievable?" Aurora shot back quickly. "He's the richest man in England. He's one of the richest men in the world. You don't think he hasn't resorted to violence before?"

"But... but why would he kill her? I don't understand? What does she have to do with anything?" He wiped his eyes with his sleeve.

"It was a warning. A warning to Frederik. Konrad knows that you've been talking to him, Alex and he doesn't like it. Konrad wants you for himself. Why do you think he offered you a position in his company?"

Tears had begun to roll down Alex's face. "Then... then what? You want me to *kill* Konrad?"

Aurora smiled again, but it wasn't kind, like before. "Can you see yourself doing that, Alex? Can you imagine taking a life?

"No!" he shouted, his voice dulled in the tunnel. "No, I don't want to kill anyone. Especially not my own family!"

"Even though Konrad did exactly the same?" Said Aurora quietly.

"But... but you haven't got any proof that he killed my mum, have you? I'm taking your word here. And now you're asking me to become a killer... to kill my own granddad? I don't think so!"

"Alex, these things I have told you are the truth," said Aurora, her tone quiet but forceful. "They have happened and they must be dealt with. *Now.* Either you trust me in this or you don't, it's up to you. I can help you get in. I can help you get past Zephyr and Konrad and I can show you proof that Konrad killed your mother."

"Proof?"

"Of course. You think Konrad wouldn't have written something this important down in one of his red diaries?"

Aurora was staring at him intently. She was right. If Konrad was responsible then he'd surely have written it down. That would be all the proof he needed; and if there was proof, well, then he would have to decide what to do about

Konrad.

"Ok." He said, finally. "Ok. So what do we need to do?"

Aurora smiled. "It's simple, you just have to place your open palm on the wall."

Alex frowned, but followed her command. Walking to the smooth black wall, he placed his palm against it and felt ice cold metal. For a moment nothing happened, but then he felt that all-too-familiar pulse surge through his body.

A yellow light began to glow beneath his hand, brighter and brighter until the whole tunnel was illuminated and the door almost looked golden. Unsure what to do next, Alex took his hand away from the wall. The light remained and where his palm had been, he noticed a small button. He pressed it, and the whole golden wall began to slowly swing away from him, revealing a long dark passageway sloping up and out of view.

Alex turned to Aurora. She was looking over his head, directly up the long passageway. "So, are you ready to face the man who killed your mother?"

She stepped past him and began to walk up the passageway and into the darkness. He took a deep breath and stepped over the threshold, still unsure what they would find on the other side.

CHAPTER 44

HENRY

For the first time in three days, Henry Wolf slept soundly. Propped against the soft leather wingback of his chair, he had been sitting quietly in his small study, pondering the events of the last few weeks.

There was so much going on that he didn't even begin to understand, and somehow his grandson had ended up right in the middle of it. For a long time, even he had doubted that Alex was the right one, but when he had seen his diary he had known in an instant that Frederik was right; it wasn't going to be Lewis who would change everything, but Alex. Henry had decided then he would do everything in his power to help his grandson, no matter what the cost.

Sleeping in his favourite armchair, a heavy bottomed glass of gin gently loosening in his grip, he clutched a silver-framed photo to his chest. Lodged in the corner of his mouth, his pipe glowed with a soft pulsating rhythm that matched his slow breathing, dispersing its delicate, sweet aroma into the room.

There was a sudden hammering on the door. The glass fell from his hand and smashed on the stone floor as Henry jerked awake, bleary-eyed but alert. The door hammered again and he stepped briskly to it, turning the heavy brass key in the lock. Swinging the door open, his eyes widened at the tear-stained face of Sara on the other side.

"What? What's happened?" Said Henry quickly, panic in his gruff voice.

"It's Alex, Henry. Something… *took him!*" She could barely get the words out as her sobbing chest heaved up and down.

"What do you mean something took him?" Said Henry, already fishing around in his pocket.

"I… I don't know. It was something huge… all in black. It took him through the window!"

Henry pulled a small grey cylinder from his trouser pocket and gripped it tightly before grabbing a set of keys from a leather-lined tray on his desk.

"I know where to find him," Henry's steely voice sounded almost calm. "Follow me."

He left the room and turned the brass key behind him. Henry led Sara back through the house and out of the front door. Archer was standing patiently next to a black Lamborghini that was gleaming in the moonlight.

Henry turned to Sara and said with a wink, "Are you driving then? Or shall I?"

CHAPTER 45

THE TRUTH

Following Aurora up the long passageway, Alex noticed that it seemed to be getting narrower. After a while he was able to touch both walls and the curved ceiling that had been several feet above him was almost within reach. In the low light it had begun to feel claustrophobic, exacerbated by the golden door swinging shut behind them.

The only light was coming from the end of the long corridor. A gentle yellow glow illuminated the passageway, reflected by the polished granite-like material that had begun to line the walls. Aurora was still confidently striding out in front. All Alex could do was follow after her.

As they moved further up the passageway the glow became stronger, the yellowish light pulsing slightly as if flickering at high speed. They came to a cross roads and without hesitating Aurora turned left, away from the pulsing light. It grew darker and her pace quickened. Alex was almost jogging to keep up when she suddenly stopped. He only just avoided running into the back of her again, stumbling into the hard wall to his right.

"Ow!" He hit his shoulder hard on the unforgiving stone.

The sight of her angry yellow eyes silenced him at once. Alex squinted into the dark as she reached forward and seemed to press something. There was a short mechanical whir and a handle slid out in front of her.

"In here, and be *quiet*." Aurora stepped forward, then stopped. She seemed to be standing in a small, square wardrobe. Before he had time to mention that he didn't think they would both fit, Aurora grabbed his shoulder with her large hand and pulled him into the small space. He heard the same mechanical whirring noise, followed by a small *clunk* and the unmistakable lurch of a rapid ascent.

Despite the unexpected pleasure of being pressed against his formidable partner in crime, the speed and claustrophobia was making him feel quite uncomfortable. He assumed that they must be in a lift shaft similar to Konrad's main one, so he wasn't surprised when they soon came to a stop. Aurora slid the door open. They were on the mezzanine floor that held Konrad's personal library.

Alex froze. *What if Konrad's here? What if Zephyr's here? What if we're caught?* He started to panic. His breathing was coming in shallow bursts and the small lift they were standing in felt suddenly much smaller. As if she had read his thoughts, Aurora stepped out onto the thick, soft carpet and Alex followed.

The lift was giving off a faint glow and Alex gently slid the door back so that it was almost closed. When he turned back, Aurora had gone.

"Aurora?" He barely whispered into the black room.

No response.

"Aurora?"

Still nothing. The panicked feeling returned.

"Aurora!" He chanced a louder whisper.

Outside, the moon passed from behind a cloud. The room was flooded with a pale blue light through the huge windows. Alex could view all of his surroundings, but Aurora was nowhere to be seen. Taking a few quick steps across the suspended floor, he called out again. Still nothing.

Maybe she's downstairs. He tiptoed further across the mezzanine and paused in front of the opaque black sheet glass that hid Konrad's stolen weapon, the Black Fire Book. He wondered whether he should simply take the book and run for it. *At least that would be mission complete.* The temptation to cut and run without Aurora was almost too great, but something stopped him. He knew he should find Aurora so they could escape together. He should do the right thing.

Staring at the black glass for a moment longer, Alex continued on, beginning to make his way down the clear glass staircase that led to the lower floor. After a few steps he crouched, peering into the far corners of the room below.

She's not there either. Where the hell is she? This isn't good. When he finally reached the bottom of the stairs he darted quickly across the floor, like a panicked insect. It was then that he heard a noise that stopped him in his tracks; the low hum of an ascending lift.

Alex's eyes flicked to the door. The single white light was moving rapidly from left to right. With barely a second to spare, he made a dash for the farthest, darkest corner he could find, to the left of the lift door. As he pressed himself into the shadows, he heard the *swoosh* of the metal doors and watched in panic as Konrad Steen stepped out.

Konrad strode purposefully across the room to his desk and swiped his hand across the flat, wooden surface. The black obelisk that Alex had seen on his previous visit rose slowly from the floor. Before it had even stopped, Konrad was peering at the many books lining the shelves, as if he expected one to be missing. After a cursory check he seemed satisfied and stepped back. He sat heavily against the desk and rubbed both hands across his face and through his short, white hair. He breathed what sounded distinctly like a huge sigh of relief.

The pale blue moonlight that was threatening to expose Alex's hiding place faded. Alex breathed his own sigh of relief as the whole room darkened once more. Thunder rolled threateningly overhead and he could hear the sound of heavy rain outside. Through the enormous window the sky looked as if it was being shredded to pieces.

With Konrad clearly satisfied, Alex desperately hoped that he might leave, giving him chance to do the same with the Black Fire Book. It was far too dangerous a situation for him to be in alone. The sooner he could leave, the better.

Before he had time to speculate on how he would get home without Aurora, a huge figure appeared outside. Lithe, sinewy and dressed all in black, it seemed to melt over the balcony rail like an enormous spider slowly advancing on its prey. Alex's fear of his granddad paled at the realisation that this new arrival was the *real* Zephyr.

Konrad seemed to sense Zephyr's presence too. He opened the tall glass doors, allowing the massive assassin into the room. The noise of the rain outside grew instantly. Lightning flashed menacingly overhead.

Trying desperately to stay calm, Alex watched as the two figures spoke briefly. He tried to remember which side of the door the lift button was on in case he had to run for it. But in that moment the bright yellow eyes of Zephyr flickered in his direction.

"You!" Konrad's voice boomed.

In the dark room he heard heavy footsteps advancing in his direction and saw the tall figure of his granddad looming over him. Alex tried to shrink into the shadows, but a sudden sheet of lightning confirmed his hiding place. Konrad had stopped just a few feet away.

"Come. Here. Now." Konrad said in a low, dangerous voice.

Alex stood slowly before taking several very small steps towards his granddad.

"What are you doing here, Alexander? Tell me the truth."

Alex couldn't seem to process the words; he had felt a swift movement behind him that had drawn his complete attention. Zephyr was no longer standing by the window. Alex watched as Konrad's eyes flicked above his head, confirming his worst fears. With just a look, Konrad seemed to signal something to the monster behind him.

It's going to throw me from the balcony. It's going to throw me high in the sky and off the balcony.

"I said, what are you doing here, Alex? If you don't tell me, I shall get Zephyr here to ask you instead, and I don't think either of us wants that, do we?"

Alex could feel the hot breath of the monster on the top of his head.

"I... I..." he said, beside himself with panic. His throat was so constricted it was a wonder he could breathe, let alone speak.

"Yes?" Said Konrad slowly, his eyes narrowing as he stepped closer.

"I... I came to get your book, if you must know." Said Alex, his own frank honesty taking him by surprise.

He saw a smile flick over Konrad's face and heard what sounded like a low growl from behind him.

"*My book* you say, Alexander?" said Konrad in a lighter tone. "Was there a particular book you had in mind, or will any book do?"

Alex was sure he shouldn't be telling the truth, but it seemed to be buying him some time. "I came to take back the book that you stole from Frederik. The one that you stole when you killed Annelise."

Konrad laughed and looked to Zephyr. "My, my. He *has* been busy hasn't he. Telling tales on his old friend."

"So you admit it then?" Said Alex, the words bursting from his mouth before he could stop them. "You're as old as he is!"

Konrad looked at his grandson and his eyes narrowed again. "I am old, certainly, but not as old as Frederik, no. And not nearly as evil either."

"Evil?" Shouted Alex.

His anger seemed to be fuelling his courage and he stepped forward to face his granddad. The impossibly strong hands of Zephyr seized his shoulders and he winced in pain.

"Frederik might well have a screw loose, but he never killed anyone! He wasn't the one that killed my mum!" He felt the emotion rise in him, his eyes welling with new tears.

Konrad's smile disappeared. He advanced quickly on Alex, who shrank back in fright, his body pressed against Zephyr.

"Rebekka's *dead*?" Konrad's voice had dwindled to a whisper.

His eyes were wide and seemed to search Alex's face, but the tears and hate in his grandson's eyes seemed to tell him everything he needed to know.

"No, no! She can't be dead. Not Rebekka, no… not Rebekka!"

"Oh, but I'm afraid she is dead, Konrad," came an instantly recognisable voice from the other side of the room.

Even through his streaming eyes, Alex could see Frederik standing calmly on the balcony outside; the wind from the growing storm whipped his long hair around his face, and his ragged black cloak billowed around him. As Alex felt a spark of hope, he couldn't help noticing that Frederik looked more intimidating than before; taller, broader and somehow younger.

"Send the boy to me, Konrad." Frederik said over the noise of the storm. "Send the boy to me with the book and we will not have to let things get nasty."

Frederik was staring directly at Konrad but with every word, Zephyr's grip had tightened on Alex's shoulders; he winced at the increasing pain.

"If you think I'm going to let my grandson anywhere near *you*, you have another thing coming." Konrad's tone seemed to give away his fear.

Frederik took three slow steps forward. Zephyr retreated with his prize in tow. Without thinking, Alex suddenly made a break for it. Dropping to his knees, he felt the grip on his shoulders disappear. He scrambled to his feet and darted towards Frederik.

"Alex, no!" Shouted Konrad as Alex moved swiftly behind Frederik's billowing black cloak.

He didn't care what Konrad had to say. Behind Frederik he knew Zephyr wouldn't be able to hurt him. Thunder and lightning crashed overhead and the open balcony doors began to rattle on their stops.

"Very good, boy," said Frederik quietly over his shoulder. "Now I want you to get me the book you told me about. Do you understand? Remember how important this is."

Alex didn't hesitate. He quickly made his way to the staircase, but as he reached the first glass step, he heard a voice that was so sad and yet filled with such desperation. He stopped and turned to see Konrad holding out his hand to him.

"Alex. *Please* don't do this. Do not trust this man over me. I am your family! Remember that, Alex. I am your family!"

Taken aback for a moment, Alex regained his composure, shouting, "My mum was my family, and you *killed* her! You're *nothing* to me!"

He bounded up the rest of the steps and quickly made for the middle of the mezzanine. The whole time, he could hear Konrad below, protesting his innocence. Alex was only focused on one task though. He walked straight to the glass panel. Pressing the cold plate, it gave the familiar hiss and began to rise. His hands were poised to reach in and seize the old book, but he quickly realised it was no longer there.

"Do you have it, Alexander?" Came Frederik's impatient voice from below. "Do you have the book?"

Alex didn't know what to say. *Where is it? Did Konrad move it before I got here?* But then another horrible idea came into his head.

Aurora. Alex turned and ran to the balcony rail. He looked down to see Frederik's expectant eyes fixed resolutely on him.

"Well? Do you have the book, Alexander? Do you have it?" He shouted over the thunder and battering rain.

"It's not here!" Alex called down. "The book's not here!"

Frederik flung back his head and let out a terrifying roar of anger that mirrored the flashes of lightning across the night sky.

"Where is that book, Konrad?" Spat Frederik, advancing on Konrad and Zephyr. He didn't seem the least bit afraid. "I want that book now! I know that you have it, your grandson here told me all about it!"

Alex couldn't explain it, but despite everything he suddenly felt very afraid for Konrad. Frederik seemed to be in a towering rage and was still advancing on his granddad with a positively murderous look on his face.

"I... I think Aurora took it!" Called out Alex in a desperate attempt to deflect the situation.

It certainly worked. Frederik stopped in his tracks and shot a look of pure anger up at Alex.

"What did you say?" Even over the noise outside, Alex could hear the venomous tone in Frederik's voice. "What has Aurora got to do with this? What have you done boy?"

"I... well, she brought me here!" Alex called down nervously, half glad he was at least some distance from Frederik. "She said she was underground listening to us when me and granddad came to see you. She said she could help me get the book from Konrad that you wanted. So I came with her-"

Alex's voice trailed off as he saw the rage and fury rise in Frederik's face. He let out a terrifying wail that almost sent Alex dashing for the tiny lift, but then he heard the most unusual sound.

Konrad had begun to laugh. It had started as a low chuckle but grew quickly into a full roar of laughter.

"Oh bad luck, Frederik! It would seem that she's outplayed you *again*. I guess you'll have to find another book to use if you want to regain your youth!"

Frederik looked ready to kill, his eyes flicking between Konrad and Alex.

"What does he mean?" Called out Alex from his high vantage point.

But it wasn't Frederik who answered Alex's question, it was Konrad.

"What I mean, Alex, is that Frederik here wanted his book back so that he could make himself young again, make himself strong."

"But… but I thought the book was supposed to give you power! That's why he wanted me to steal it from you!" Said Alex, feeling strange admitting his plan to his would-be enemy.

Konrad laughed loudly again. "Oh he didn't want the book to stop *me* using it, he wanted the book so that he could use the power again himself. But all that power would be useless, I think, if he hadn't first made himself young enough to use it. The book can do that you see, Alex. Isn't that right Frederik?"

Frederik, who was still looking at Konrad with a murderous expression slowly raised his head towards Alex and a hideous grin split his face.

"Your grandfather is right, Alexander. Yes, he is right. You think I wanted to get the book just to keep it from him? To then *destroy* it? If you truly believed that then you are as idiotic and mindless as I always thought!" Frederik was pointing his long, bony finger directly at Alex with a look of disgust on his lined face. "Your tiny mind cannot understand the power of the Black Fire Book, boy! A book that is filled with such pain and sorrow is *infinitely* more powerful than some pathetic books full of sights and sounds and other such things! They can never match the power of the black fire!"

Frederik seemed to be panting heavily and his eyes looked as though they had begun to burn.

"But even though you may have lost me my book for now, you have at least helped me to regain some of my youth, I think." He said with a gurgling laugh.

"What? What are you talking about?" Alex called over the raging wind outside. But even as he spoke, Frederik's long, ragged cloak slipped from his back and dropped to the floor.

Alex gasped. Frederik's arms that were once withered, frail and bony looked thick and muscular. The leather straps that had hung loosely around his wrists were stretched taut around his bulging forearms. Shining brightly from his wrist was the bright silver bracelet Alex had recovered in the grounds of Wolf Manor. He looked grotesque, like some aged, wrinkled bodybuilder, but it didn't diminish the ferocious look of anger and hatred in his eyes.

"I must thank you, Alexander. Those words you wrote about your poor mother, such despair and anguish, really did help me to regain some of my strength of old. In fact, I think it was more than worth the effort it took to kill her."

Without warning, Zephyr tore across the room at the cackling old man. There was a flash of lightning as the two unnatural beings collided.

Alex fully expected Frederik to be smashed across the room by the powerful assassin, but it didn't happen. Frederik stood his ground and seemed to absorb the shadow's full force with ease. He gripped Zephyr around the shoulders and Zephyr did the same in return.

The two men were locked in a battle of brute strength. They were barely moving, but Alex could see the enormous power they were both exerting as they grappled and fought against each other.

Frederik suddenly twisted and made a swipe for Zephyr's face with his long, bony fingers, but Zephyr landed a powerful blow to the side of his head that sent Frederik reeling into the wall. Frederik shrieked in pain and rage but was immediately on his feet and ready for Zephyr's charge. The two beings clashed again. The rain outside began to fall harder and faster, whipped against the windows by the ever increasing winds.

Frederik's huge arms moved quickly and Alex gasped as he saw Zephyr lifted off the ground and thrown clean across the open space, into the glass staircase. It exploded into razor sharp pieces. Zephyr silently pulled himself up, shook off the glass and wiped his bleeding face with the back of a clenched black fist. He uttered a long, deep, primal growl and dashed at Frederik. With no time to react, Frederik took the full force of the assassin's shoulder to his stomach. Heavily winded, Frederik still managed to lock his arms around his attacker's neck. Freeing one of his enormous arms, Zephyr rained down several devastating blows to Frederik's head, each one causing a large and brutal gash that spewed silver-black blood.

From the mezzanine, Alex could only watch as the desperate scene unfolded below him. Frederik seemed to be taking Zephyr's fury in his stride; a maniacal grin spread across his withered and bloodied face. It was then that something caught Alex's eye.

Konrad was looking up at him, trying to attract his attention and beckoning him to come down the stairs towards him. Without thinking, Alex dashed down the remains of the stairs, jumping over the piles of broken glass. Before he knew it he was standing in front of Konrad. Ignoring the epic battle behind him, his granddad placed his hands firmly on Alex's shoulders and stared intently into his grandson's eyes.

"Alex, look at me. Look at me and listen," he said quietly, his voice sounding clear, even over the raging storm.

He looked intently at Konrad, and saw, for the first time, a yellow light flickering in the depths of his eyes.

"Alex. I didn't kill your mother, you know that now," Alex nodded slowly and Konrad continued. "I am sorry if I have misled you in any way. There will come a time when I can make this up to you. Do you understand?"

In all honesty, Alex couldn't say that he did but he nodded anyway.

"Good. Then remember this. Above all, trust Henry. And trust this." Konrad patted Alex's chest, just over his heart. "Neither will lead you astray. Will you remember that?"

Alex didn't know why, but a feeling of impending disaster seemed to swell within him as he looked into his granddad's mournful eyes.

"Alex! Will you remember that?" Said Konrad forcefully and the yellow fire danced brighter in his eyes.

"Yes! Yes, I'll remember!" Said Alex quickly.

His words were returned with a smile. "Good. Then I shall see you again, Alexander. I shall see you again soon."

Konrad turned to face the ongoing fight that was steadily destroying his office. From nowhere, gentle, powerful music began to play. As much as he tried, Alex couldn't identify where it was coming from. It seemed somehow to be coming from inside him; from inside his own head, as if he were imagining the song but listening to a perfect recording of it at the same time.

Wherever it was coming from it had blocked out all other sound and now the scene before him had been given its own perfectly orchestrated soundtrack. It was slow and unusual, like a funereal waltz. As Konrad moved towards the combatants he too was moving slowly, stealthily, in time with the music.

Konrad can hear it too then. Alex watched as his granddad advanced slowly on the battling pair, as if he were waiting for the perfect time to strike. Such was the ferocity of the ongoing battle, mixed with thundering weather and constant flashes of lightning that neither Zephyr nor Frederik seemed to notice this imminent new contender.

The music continued to play in Alex's head, growing in volume and majesty with every passing second and he felt himself stand up, almost against his will. Konrad, who had slowly raised his hands above his head, was holding something; something short and silver. It could have been a knife, but at that distance Alex couldn't be sure. It suddenly burst into flame with a blinding yellow fire. Alex looked on in wondrous awe.

Frederik and Zephyr were still grappling with each other but Alex could tell that the battle had taken its toll. Both fighters were breathing heavily and their movements were sluggish. Neither were paying attention to Konrad who had manoeuvred himself directly behind Frederik.

His granddad now held the flaming torch above his head and finally made his move. Alex didn't see the strike, merely the look of shock and fear on Frederik's face. As Konrad stepped in towards him, the blazing flame disappeared from view.

A look of satisfaction was plain to see on his granddad's face. Alex saw Frederik's shock turn once more to fury and anger and he squirmed desperately against the tall white-haired man standing behind him.

Zephyr was standing silently watching his master, breathing heavily from his recent exertions and checking his numerous wounds. With a nod from Konrad, he advanced slowly towards them. Fear flashed once more in Frederik's black eyes. As Zephyr stooped and took hold of his enemy's thrashing feet, Frederik began to cry out. Together, Konrad and his assassin pulled the writhing madman towards the balcony's edge.

Despite his horror at the idea of anyone being thrown from the top of the tower, Alex couldn't tear his eyes away. He stared, awaiting the inevitable, but as the three figures reached the balcony's edge, Alex realised he'd been wrong.

In the driving rain, Konrad and Zephyr stood at the rail with Frederik still thrashing between them. Konrad turned his head towards Alex and gave him a small smile before all three men fell headlong into the black, thundering night.

In an instant the music that had been inside Alex's head faded to nothing.

Alex ran to the steel barrier, crashing into it in his haste. Looking over, he saw nothing but clear space between him and the well-lit grounds, some 800 feet below.

He collapsed onto the hard balcony floor, panting and wide eyed at everything he had just witnessed. He pressed his hands to the smooth stone slabs, desperate to feel something solid beneath him. The thought of falling such a distance turned his stomach.

His hand brushed against something on the hard stone. Something thin and cold. He instinctively grabbed it and felt a familiar pulse of electricity jolt through his body. He was holding his pen; the pen that he had used to write in his diary; the pen that Konrad had given him for Christmas all those years ago; the pen that Konrad had just used to kill Frederik.

He didn't know how long he sat there, the rain soaking him to the skin, but he slowly picked himself up and walked back into his granddad's study. Despite the carnage and devastation, it felt empty and quiet; peaceful almost. He walked to the lift, found the light switch on the wall and flicked it on.

The lights had already been dimmed, he assumed by his granddad, earlier that day. He wondered when, and what he might have been doing. Writing at his desk, perhaps. Or simply reading the newspaper on the sofa. As he stared around the wide open space, Alex heard a familiar low mechanical hum. The white lights above the door were moving rapidly from left to right and he stepped back quickly.

Before he had a chance to hide, the lift doors slid open, revealing the determined faces of Henry and Sara. Bryson stood behind them, looking solemn.

Henry and Sara both rushed at him and hugged him tightly. The smell of Sara's hair was like a drug to Alex. It warmed and comforted him in a single breath. Henry looked close to tears. His eyes were wide and red, darting around the room, alert to any foe that might come running at them. When no-one did, he pulled them both into a huge hug.

"I presume Mr. Steen has departed us?" Came Bryson's dry voice from over Alex's shoulder. Alex nodded.

"Well in that case," the butler continued, looking around the destroyed room, "I think it's perhaps time you were going. I'll sort out things here, don't you worry."

Alex felt himself being led slowly across the room by Sara who was smiling kindly at him. As they reached the lift doors, Bryson coughed in a very unsubtle manner.

"I expect I'll be seeing you shortly, Master Wolf. Good night."

Alex simply stared back at Bryson as he felt himself being guided gently into the small lift. Before he could reply, the doors had closed.

CHAPTER 46

A JOB TO DO

As soon as they had returned home, Henry had ordered Alex straight to bed. Despite the excitement of having Sara stopping in the next room to him, he'd gladly obliged. The second his head touched his beautifully soft pillow he was asleep.

The following day passed by in a blur, helped by Alex not waking up until the middle of the afternoon. It was, after all, the day before his mother's funeral. Although his first thought upon waking had been to run and find his granddad, he found that when it came to it, he just wanted to spend the day alone, quietly thinking about his mum.

His mum who had been murdered. The thought was almost too much to bear. Alex tried to push it from his mind, but the only other thought that would replace it was that at any minute there would be a knock on the door by a member of the police. He wasn't sure if there was a sentence for witnessing the deaths of your granddad, a half-human assassin and an 800 year old lunatic, but he could really do without it. Thankfully the knock never came.

The saddest day of Alex's life arrived. The service, in accordance with Wolf tradition, had been held very early in the morning and tears were shed by every soul in attendance. Alex's only comfort was to know that in her life his mum had been truly loved by many, many people.

After the service there were of course questions, particularly about how Rebekka had died. People had also been asking why Konrad Steen hadn't been at his own daughter-in-law's funeral. At these points, Henry would squeeze Alex's arm gently to stop him looking so panicked. Each time though, the conversation would drift on to other things and Alex could breathe again.

He spent most of that morning trying to support his dad. Both of them had spent an hour sitting quietly in a corner, remembering stories about Rebekka. Every so often Morten would break down and Alex, without words, would put his arm around him.

As the day wore on Alex became more and more frustrated. He just wanted time to talk to his granddad, to try and get some answers, but at every moment there seemed to be someone to talk to, or somewhere to be.

Thankfully, there was one person that brightened the whole day. Sara hardly ever left his side. They too spent a lot of time just sitting. Instead of reminiscing about Alex's mum they simply held hands, not even talking.

The day after the funeral, Alex awoke peacefully. For the first time in what seemed like an age, the sun was shining brightly through his windows. Climbing quickly out of bed, he pressed the button on the wall to open them. The huge panels of glass concertinaed together, opening up his bedroom to the outside world and the grounds of Wolf Manor.

He was about to take a shower when he saw a small piece of paper that must have been slid under his door during the night. Wondering if it was perhaps from Sara, he bounded across the room, picked it up and unfolded it quickly. It was a note, in Henry's handwriting.

Alex,
Time we had a chat. Come to meet me on the lake. I've got something for you.
Granddad.

Alex quickly got dressed and ran downstairs. Managing to avoid anyone on the way, he passed by the kitchen and grabbed a couple of apples from the fridge, which he ate noisily as he walked.

It wasn't long before he found himself standing by the tall glass cube, staring at the speedboat that was moored at the jetty. Wondering how his granddad had made the journey without it, he untied the mooring rope and jumped into the boat. Within seconds he was motoring out across the dazzling lake that shimmered gold and white in the morning sun.

He soon spotted the small indentation on the left that signified the entrance to his granddad's hidden house, but that wasn't all he'd spotted. Sitting on the jetty that extended from the house, with trousers rolled up, feet dangling into the water and a small makeshift fishing rod in hand was Henry Wolf. He grinned and waved as Alex drew closer.

"Getting the hang of that thing, are we?" Henry called out over the growling engine.

Alex did the best he could to gently steer the boat towards the mooring post before coming to a stop. He slowly disembarked from the swaying boat.

"Hmm, yeah, I *might* be starting to see why you like it so much," he said, smiling back at his granddad before joining him on the wooden jetty.

Keeping his feet well away from the water, Alex pulled his knees up to his chest and accepted a cold, fizzy drink that Henry seemed to have magically produced from somewhere. He took a long glug and wiped his mouth with his arm.

"So," began Henry in a soft tone. "How are you? Get through yesterday alright?"

Alex didn't reply, simply nodding slowly whilst trying not to look at his granddad for fear of welling up again.

"Good, good," said Henry and took a sip of his own drink, which smelt suspiciously like whisky and ginger beer.

They sat quietly for a few moments before Henry said more slowly, "So, it's been a strange couple of weeks, hasn't it? Bit of a different return from school than last year, eh?"

Alex laughed. "Yeah, you could say that."

His gaze returned the gentle ripples on the surface of the lake.

"Are you going to tell me what happened the other night, at Konrad's tower?" asked Henry quietly.

Alex looked down at the sunlit water. Sitting on the edge of the lake in the bright sunshine, next to his granddad, it all seemed so strange and distant. Slowly, he began to recount the events from the moment Aurora had taken him from his bedroom, right up until the point that Henry and Sara had come running into the room. All the time that Alex spoke, Henry appeared to be staring off into the distance but Alex knew that his granddad had been listening; his ears twitching every time he mentioned Frederik.

"So you think this Aurora woman took the book then?" Said Henry, pulling his pipe from his pocket and lodging it in his mouth.

"I guess so," replied Alex. "I don't know what she'd do with it though. I don't even know where she came from. She obviously knows who Zephyr is, so maybe she knows–knew–Konrad."

Alex thought some more.

"Hey, what if Konrad planned it so that Aurora took the book first, before Frederik got there?" He said quickly, the idea only just forming in his head.

"Hmm, it's possible," said Henry, not sounding entirely convinced. He was fishing in his waistcoat for a bag of tobacco. "Bit pointless now though, what with Konrad not being around anymore."

"Yeah… I suppose."

Henry filled his pipe, lit the end and began puffing away.

"And you say Konrad used your *pen* to kill Frederik?"

Alex looked to his granddad who had resumed his stare out into the water.

"Well it definitely looked that way yes," said Alex.

Rummaging in his own pocket, he pulled out the silver pen. Henry looked at it briefly and then to his grandson.

"Alex… Alex, I need to apologise."

"Apologise? Why?"

"Frederik. I trusted him… and I convinced you to trust him… and I was wrong. So wrong! If I'd have done things differently, maybe your mum would…"

His granddad's face mirrored the feelings Alex had been struggling with for the previous few days: Regret, pain, loss, grief. He swallowed hard; the lump in his throat had returned.

"It wasn't your fault," said Alex quietly. "Frederik was a headcase. A lunatic. I bought into his story as well, you know. It wasn't just you."

Henry just stared sadly into the lake.

"It's just a good job that Konrad was around to take him out for us, I guess? At least that's some payback for mum, isn't it?"

Henry nodded slowly.

"Shame though," continued Alex, almost to himself. "After all that, Konrad wasn't the bad guy at all. It would have been nice to get to know him better." Then Alex remembered something. "You know, Konrad did actually mention you the other night."

Henry looked at his grandson, suspiciously. "Why? What did he say?"

Alex looked back at his granddad.

"He said that above all, I'm to trust you. And to trust my heart."

Henry harrumphed dismissively, but Alex noticed the tiniest of smiles creep across his pursed lips.

Alex gave a small cough. "There was one thing I wanted to ask you actually," he said carefully.

"Go on, ask away!" Said Henry in reply, pulling out another match to relight his pipe.

"Well, I was wondering how much Grandma knew about all this?"

The lit match that Henry was holding stopped and hovered above the curling weed, but not near enough to light it. After a few seconds' thought, he dipped the flame into the pipe and fresh white smoke began to puff into the warm summer air.

"It's a question I've been pondering myself, and if you hadn't overheard those conversations I wouldn't have said she knew anything... but clearly that's not the case."

"But surely you must have spoken about it to her? Surely you must have said something?" Pressed Alex.

"You'd be surprised how little we speak, Alex." Came Henry's quiet response.

"In fact, we haven't really spoken properly in years. Of course, I was going to have it out with her this morning, after the funeral. But conveniently," another large puff of smoke billowed from Henry's mouth. "She's had to go away on that trip of hers with Lewis. Couldn't be rescheduled, apparently."

Alex scowled. He knew that his grandmother was involved but how much, he wasn't sure. He had heard her talking to Konrad twice; that much he knew. Now that it turned out Konrad had been on Alex's side all along though, did that mean that his grandma was as well?

All of the thoughts that Alex had been able to put aside during the funeral began to swirl in his head once more and his mind strayed, without thinking, to his diary; the one thing that had been of most use to him over the weeks when his head had become muddled in too many thoughts. Granted, if it hadn't been for the diary he probably wouldn't have needed to un-muddle his brain in the first place. Even so, he pondered with an unexpected feeling of disappointment that with Frederik gone, he wouldn't need to continue his writing.

If Frederik was no more, and it had been he who wanted to use the Black Fire Book for evil, then there was nothing to worry about. Frederik was gone and their ordeal was over.

It was then that a sudden thought popped into his head.

"Your note!" Said Alex, surprising Henry from his own thoughts. "The note you put under my door! It said you had something for me?"

"Oh! Oh cripes, yes!" Said Henry, scrambling to his feet. "Completely forgot about that."

"Well? What is it?" Alex called excitedly after his granddad, who had already disappeared into the house.

After a few moments, Henry came limping back, pipe bobbing up and down as he walked. "I wouldn't get too excited, young man, I just meant that I had some post for you. Arrived this morning. Thought you'd want to see."

Alex's shoulders slumped as Henry passed him a letter in a white envelope, another in a blue envelope and finally a thick, rectangular package wrapped in black paper.

"Well, open them then," said Henry, eyeing the packages.

Alex suspected what would be inside the white envelope. Slowly he ran his finger under the gummed flap and pulled out a single folded piece of paper. As expected, it was his exam results. He couldn't help but give a small chuckle at the 'A' grade he'd received in music. All the rest, unfortunately, were as expected. He passed the letter slowly to his grandfather who quickly muttered something about Alex's talents being in other areas.

Next, he opened the blue envelope. It seemed to be made of thick, expensive paper. Tearing it open, he pulled out the letter inside and unfolded it. It wasn't a long letter, but even after reading the first sentence, Alex's heart began to pound in his chest.

Dear Mr. Wolf,

We are writing to request that, as the sole beneficiary of Mr. K. M. Steen's will, you will be able to attend our offices on Tuesday, 12th August to sign documentation passing over full control of Steen International to yourself.

In relation to Mr. Steen's personal effects, as the will makes perfectly clear, we are pleased to inform you that the deeds to all of Mr. Steen's properties, including Steen Tower, have been signed over to you.

We would also like to confirm that the cash sum of £24,605,352,802.00 will be transferred into a bank account of your choosing once you provide us with the relevant details.

Finally, we include with this letter a package that was left with us by Mr. Steen with instructions that it should be delivered to you in the event of his death.

We very much look forward to meeting you in person.

Yours most sincerely,

Mr. W. Hitchley

Hands shaking, Alex slowly passed the piece of paper to Henry who was looking at his grandson with an expression of grave concern. Alex barely heard the coughing, spluttering cry of "Jackpot!" coming from his granddad as he ripped into the black paper package on his lap. He saw a single piece of paper on top of what looked like a block of burnt and charred wood.

Gently lifting the piece of paper, Alex held it closer to his face and read.

Alex,

If you are reading this, it is because I am no longer with you, and if I am no longer with you it means that I have left everything I own in your possession.

Explore, discover, enjoy, but above all, learn.

Learn the Origins of White Fire. Learn to channel your thoughts into great power. Learn to be the man we all need you to be.

This letter will have arrived with a book. This book is the book of sound; one of the original five that Henry and Frederik will have told you about. They have not been destroyed, as Frederik thinks. You must find or make the others yourself.

If Frederik has Black Fire, then you will need to start immediately for he has not gone. It will take more than a fall from my tower to destroy Frederik.

If you are not sure how to proceed then may I suggest you look to your pen.

I say again Alexander, trust Henry and trust your heart.

Yours, Konrad.

Ignoring the hundreds of questions Alex already had forming in his mind, he passed the letter to Henry before pulling out his pen and setting it on the jetty.

Slowly he put his hands on the burnt and charred block of wood that sat on his lap. He was unsurprised to feel a pulse of electricity travelling down his arms and into his hands, and see a yellow glow slowly envelop the wood. There was a small *click*. Along the right edge, he found the narrow crack that had opened up like a seam. He ran his fingers along it and slowly began to open the book.

As expected, every page was blank. Taking up his pen again, he removed the lid and lowered the silver nib to the page. There was a flash of yellow and immediately, delicate writing, drawings and verse flooded the pages. Even as he watched, the book grew in size and thickness and soft music began to hum gently from the open tome. Alex turned, open mouthed, to look at his granddad.

Henry, who had just finished reading Konrad's letter, looked back at Alex with an elated grin on his face.

"You know what this means don't you, boy." Henry said, grinning.

"No?" Said Alex.

"It means that we've got a lot of work to do."

FLIGHT

The black private jet was cruising comfortably, high above the Atlantic. After some initial turbulence, the pilot had finally announced that it was safe for the passengers to remove their seat belts.

Of the three on board, two had done so immediately. The youngest had moved quickly across the cabin to join the other.

"Do you know what the plan is when we land?" He said quietly, not wanting to wake the third, sleeping passenger.

"Yes, I do." Said the older woman; her voice calm, despite the feeling of great excitement that was coursing through her.

"And are you going to share it with me?" He said, a note of concern in his voice.

The older woman looked down to her lap and smiled. "Of course I am. I need *you* to understand it more than anyone."

Silence fell once more in the cabin. As Sofia Wolf sat quietly in her comfortable seat, she assured herself again that she had done the right thing; that she had picked the right one.

Rolling his eyes, Lewis returned to his seat and stared blankly out of the window. Sofia leaned forward to look at the sleeping passenger in the seat in front. Despite herself, she couldn't help feeling a small pang of guilt. But as she sat back in her chair and looked at the book in her lap, she at once became mesmerised by the dancing black flames burning brightly around its edges.

Rebekka Wolf slept soundly on.